VAMPIRE EMPIRE

BOOK TWO: THE RIFT WALKER

CLAY GRIFFITH & SUSAN GRIFFITH

VAMPIRE EMPIRE

BOOK TWO: THE RIFT WALKER

an imprint of Prometheus Books
Amherst, NY

Published 2011 by Pyr®, an imprint of Prometheus Books

Cover illustration © Chris McGrath
Cover design by Grace M. Conti-Zilsberger

Inquiries should be addressed to
Pyr
59 John Glenn Drive
Amherst, New York 14228–2119
VOICE: 716–691–0133
FAX: 716–691–0137
WWW.PYRSF.COM

15 14 13 12 11   5 4 3 2 1

Library of Congress Cataloging-in-Publication Data

Griffith, Clay.
    The rift walker / by Clay Griffith and Susan Griffth.
        p. cm. — (Vampire Empire ; bk. 2)
    ISBN 978–1–61614–523–1 (pbk.)
    ISBN 978–1–61614–524–8 (ebook)
    1. Vampires—Fiction. I. Griffith, Susan, 1963– II. Title.

PS3607.R5486R54 2011
813'.6—dc22

2011019050

Printed in the United States of America

ACKNOWLEDGMENTS

THIS BOOK IS dedicated with love to our mother, Melida, who is a constant example of determination, toughness, and grace. There are heroes in the real world too.

We also thank our wonderful readers and critics—Vivian, Lillian, June, Sean, and Ann.

And we laud the tireless crew at Pyr, including Lou Anders and Jill Maxick.

CHAPTER I

T HE VINEYARDS WERE dying. Overripe grapes lay rotting on the ground, fermenting in their own juices, leaking their sugars into the earth. Black flies hovered like thick veils on the sweating fruit while trellised vines looked down on the streets of Freiburg that were empty save for a woman being escorted toward the local inn, her face drenched in fear. The man beside her, holding her arm, was stone-faced, but fear also filled his eyes. He refused to look at the woman as she pulled back, trying to extricate her arm.

"Please," she cried. "There was some mistake. I'm not next."

"Yes, you are," was his harsh reply. "Your name was chosen by the committee. Think of it this way, what you do today may save the rest of us."

"We're all dead. You're just prolonging the inevitable!"

"Maybe. But better a few more days than none at all."

"A few days for you." She cast him a scathing glare full of spite and struggled harder, but could not escape. Another man and a woman came out of the tavern to help pull her along.

"Volker, you must stop this." A thin, aging man with reddish blond hair ran toward the group, desperate and angry, stepping purposefully in front of them.

"This is none of your concern, Matthias." Volker turned furiously on the older man, but Matthias held his ground.

"Then take me instead. Let her go."

"They don't want you," Volker sneered. "They want a woman."

With that they dragged her to the inn, closing the door and sealing them inside the building. The interior was dark and stank of stale ale, sweat, and something more pungent. Men and women slumped dejectedly in chairs. All were filthy and weak. On the floor lay four bodies.

The newly arrived woman recognized one of the bodies. "Johan!" She couldn't go to him as she was dragged toward the bar where three lean vampires sat waiting. She went limp and wept.

A trio of gaudily dressed vampires held an eccentric court. Their skin was akin to alabaster and nearly translucent in the dim light of the tavern. The nearest one, tall and poised, draped in a dark green velvet cape with tight riding breeches that disappeared into high, black, shiny boots, turned to regard the woman.

"Ahh, she's a ripe one."

Another vampire wearing only fine linen trousers sniffed the air and licked his lips. "Volker always brings us the finest choices. You've chosen well."

The man who had escorted the woman gave an exaggerated bow along with a shudder he could not suppress. He pushed her ahead to divert the piercing eyes of the triumvirate.

A third vampire slipped to his feet with eager intent. His fingers were laden with jeweled rings. With an effortless leap, he floated over the bar and landed in front of the woman. The vampire studied her before luxuriously sniffing the air around her, ending at her neck. Salty tears leaked from her eyes as she remained fixed on the bodies at her feet. She waited for the inevitable.

The door of the inn opened slowly, causing everyone to turn their heads and blink into the light. In the doorway stood a tall, lean figure dressed in a vintage rifleman tunic, grey cavalry breeches with red piping down the side, and high leather boots. His head was wrapped in a scarf, like a desert bandit, obscuring his face. Over his eyes he wore smoked glasses.

The three vampires crouched and hissed, followed by an audible gasp from the people in the room.

"The Greyfriar," someone whispered, as if saying the man's name would make him vanish like an apparition. Another said it almost like a prayer.

The newcomer took in the room, his gaze stopping on the vampires. The one closest to the woman stepped back to join his companions behind the bar.

The Greyfriar did not say a word as he slowly approached them. Walking past the woman, he stepped between her and the hissing vampires. It was not a sound of distaste or anger; instead, it was a language. These days, vampires used their old tongue only when surprised or when they didn't want to be understood by humans, preferring an eclectic mixture of human languages.

"He's alone," hissed the bare-chested one, rallying his companions.

"He's always alone," retorted the cloaked vampire. "It makes no difference. He kills us as though we are infants. We should flee."

"This town is ours!" the one wearing rings exclaimed. "We will defend it."

"But where are the others? They should have intercepted him." This from the hesitant one.

"How he got past the others is unimportant. There are three of us here."

Casually, the Greyfriar leaned his elbows upon the bar and remarked in perfect German. "When you are finished debating your options, you should know that you are already dead."

The three vampires shrank back another step. The fearful one looked about wildly for an escape route.

The swordsman added, "Your friends are all dead. I killed them as they gorged. They died far too easily, actually."

They attacked, flinging themselves into the air over the bar. Greyfriar stepped back and drew his sword. The pistol, already in his other hand, lifted and fired. The bare-chested vampire shifted at the last moment, obviously familiar with fighting armed humans. The bullet struck him in the shoulder and should have flung him back, but he altered his density at the last second and landed heavily in front of Greyfriar. Claws extended, he swiped as Greyfriar ducked and kicked the vampire aside. The masked man turned quickly, protecting himself from the attacks of the others. His rapier ripped into the onrushing vampires, connecting once, twice, again and again. The vampires darted out of range of the weapon's bite, their bodies streaming blood from the vicious wounds they did not feel. The skin of vampires, though flesh, was desensitized—making them incredibly hard to stop.

Greyfriar's pistol fired again, hitting one of the vampires in the heart. It staggered forward a few steps, reaching with its jeweled hands, before realizing it was dead. Then it dropped to the floor amid the human bodies.

The wounded one sprang back into the fight, and Greyfriar's sword swung up, aiming for the vampire's neck. It would have been a killing blow, but the creature veered again and the sword slashed its arm, which was nearly severed by the force. The vampire was sacrificing its limb to avoid more serious damage. It stood again and ran at the Greyfriar, its useful arm raised, displaying its deadly claws ready to disembowel.

The swordsman sidestepped the attack and then spun, driving the sword into the spinal column at the base of the neck, shoving the vampire downward. The body flopped to the ground, twitching uncontrollably.

The Greyfriar turned to the final vampire, the nervous one. The vampire held out its arms in supplication.

"Wait!" it shouted in German.

Greyfriar worked his blade free as he regarded the pile of dead humans on the floor, some only half-drained of their blood. "Do not expect pity from me."

The vampire's ice blue eyes filled with terror, as he inched toward the open door. When the Greyfriar did not advance on him, he bolted.

In a burst of speed no human eye could follow, Greyfriar rushed the fleeing vampire. One hand grabbed the collar of the velvet cape and threw the creature back into the room. The vampire didn't fall to the ground, however, but twisted in midair as its density changed, alighting on the far wall, hissing loudly.

Humans nearby scrambled out of the way, stampeding from the inn.

Soon the room was empty except for the combatants, the littered dead and dying, and the woman who still stood rooted to the floor, her eyes glued to the skirmish.

"Run," Greyfriar shouted at her.

The swordsman ducked under the first feral swipe of the creature's extended claws. The talons caught a corner of his head wrap and partially ripped it off his head, leaving his long black hair exposed. A quick hand held the lower portion over his chin and mouth.

Stepping back, Greyfriar slashed at the vampire, and the tip of his blade caught the muscle of the creature's abdomen. Blood spurted, but the thing didn't even flinch, only spun around and came again, giving no quarter to the swordsman. Greyfriar twisted to avoid the attack, but this time the vampire didn't turn back. The swordsman charged, but not fast enough, and the vampire grabbed the shell-shocked woman by the throat, its claws digging deep but not breaking skin. The creature pulled her between him and Greyfriar, stopping his advance.

"I will kill her!" the creature hissed in a mix of German and its own language.

"Then your life is forfeit."

"It will be regardless!"

"You have a choice."

The vampire hesitated a moment. "The Greyfriar never leaves any alive! You mean you would let me go?"

"No one has ever asked." The swordsman lowered his weapon as he repaired his torn scarf.

The vampire stood stunned. "All I have to do is ask and you would spare my life?" Ever so slightly his hand loosened from around the woman's throat, and she took a gasping breath.

"Your actions will dictate my response. Harm the female and I will kill you. Release her and we will discuss this further."

The eyes of the vampire darted wildly. Greyfriar's face, covered in cloth and smoked glass, offered no clue to his intent. The muscles in the vampire's jaw twitched, then hardened. He backed toward the door. "You lie."

Greyfriar's rapier rose again. "Don't be foolish. There is nowhere for you to go."

The vampire dragged the woman to the frame of the door, smelling freedom beyond. Blood dripped steadily to the floor from the slash in his belly. His nostrils flared and his fangs showed as his mouth yawned open. The hunger rose.

"Don't," ordered Greyfriar, recognizing the signs. He knew the wound was not severe enough to warrant hunger. It was instinct and fear driving the vampire; fear of not being at full strength to fight an unbeatable foe. Greyfriar lowered his sword again. "You have no need to feed. I will not harm you if you release the woman."

Steely, desperate eyes glinted. "It is your fault I am weakened. She dies because of you!" His teeth flashed.

With that, Greyfriar raised his pistol and shot the vampire through the jaw, inches from the woman's head. The creature flew backward and the woman crumpled to the ground, trembling. Greyfriar leapt over her to plunge his sword into the heart of the still-twitching creature. He yanked it out almost angrily.

He turned to the dazed woman and helped her to her feet. "I told you to run." Her dark eyes turned toward him. His irritation abated. The woman stood on shaking legs and he took a moment to comfort her. "You're safe now."

"My husband," she moaned, stepping toward the pile of bodies.

Greyfriar could smell which body had her scent on it. He was long dead. "I'm sorry. But you still live." It brought her little consolation.

"Not for long," she whispered angrily, caught up in her grief. "You'll soon leave us and we'll be left alone again to be ravaged by more of their kind. What good are you?" Despair laced her voice, but she was right.

"I cannot be everywhere. I am truly sorry."

Some of the braver villagers peered in, checking the outcome of the battle. Greyfriar waved them inside after making sure his mask was back in place.

The man named Volker approached Greyfriar and greeted him familiarly, clapping him on the back. "The Greyfriar has saved us!" he announced loudly. "Just in the nick of time. I'm glad my letter reached you."

Greyfriar's emotionless gaze fell upon him. The man stank of fear and lies. "I received no such letter. I know what's been going on here. You opted to sacrifice your own kind."

Volker hesitated, but then blurted out, "We had no choice. They would have just slaughtered us all without some sort of order, so we came up with a system."

"Which you controlled. Were you even in the game? Was your family?"

Volker pulled back, his shame plain. "I ran the lottery. Someone had to." The townspeople glared at him. The woman beside Greyfriar stepped up to Volker and slapped him hard across the mouth.

"It should be you lying there dead instead of Johan."

Volker sputtered and looked pleadingly around at the swordsman. "I only did what I thought was best for the town."

Greyfriar motioned to the older man with the ginger beard. He had witnessed this man's act of selflessness. "What's your name?"

"Matthias." The man was haggard but had an air of calm, with authority in his voice.

"Matthias, this town now answers to you until you come up with some new rule of your own. These people need your help and your compassion."

"Wait a minute." Volker shoved himself between them. "I'm the authority here!"

Greyfriar turned on him. "No longer." He addressed the crowd. "The punishment for his crime will be decided by you. Let justice be done here."

"You can't do that! I only did what I thought was best!" Volker pleaded, looking around for supporters. None stepped forward.

Matthias gathered a group of men to help move the bodies. The woman who had been spared followed her husband out in the morbid procession.

Greyfriar went outside to the cheering of the appreciative town. But the woman's words still echoed. For the first time in many years, he wondered the same thing. How effective could one man be? Stories and legends always made it sound plausible, but there were so many he couldn't save, so many towns where he arrived too late. Still, he would never stop. Long gone were his foolish dreams of dashing heroics. Now all that remained were nightmares of what might have happened if he had arrived too late to save one woman. Adele. Just the thought of her made his numb body ache.

People touched him, both lightly and some a tad harder, all gestures of gratitude, but he felt none of them. He walked among them, slowly cheered by their smiling faces. A small child walked alongside him, clasping his gloved hand, and tugging insistently. They followed him to the town's edge, their eyes gradually saddening with the knowledge that he was already leaving. He had seen it time and time again; every village was the same. Tomorrow they would be left alone to fend for themselves, and the fear and the uncertainty would return.

He hated to leave them; he hated to leave all of the towns, but he had to return to Edinburgh. It had already been far too long since he had stepped on his home soil. His own flock needed him, since they were just as much at risk as these towns on the occupied continent.

Matthias suddenly appeared in front of him. "We have no way to express our gratitude."

"It is not necessary."

"Of course it is," he insisted. "We would all be dead eventually. We have nothing to offer you but our thanks."

Greyfriar inclined his head graciously. This speech was not uncommon either. Many times they offered gifts. Food. Wine. Books. Cows. Most of it was useless to him. He spied a movement in Matthias's coat pocket, and up popped a small, white head. A cat, or more exactly a kitten. It was very small and bedraggled. Greyfriar reached to rub its head and it purred immediately.

Matthias grinned, extracting the tiny creature. "Perhaps we have something for you after all." Thick, gnarled fingers tousled the kitten's fur as it curled up in his large hands. "Her mother and siblings are gone. She is the last of her litter." He held out the kitten to Greyfriar.

The swordsman smiled, but shook his head. "I have a long journey ahead of me."

"And a companion would make it go faster. She is quite independent." He perched the kitten on the Greyfriar's shoulder and immediately the kitten dug in her claws and nestled against the soft scarf at his neck. The little boy beside him giggled.

Greyfriar regarded the lad. "Do you think I should keep her?" He tried to smile, though it was a gesture lost on the boy. Still, his cold, hidden features did not frighten. The child nodded vigorously. Greyfriar turned to Matthias. "Then I shall. Thank you."

Pleased, the older man reached out and clasped him on the opposite shoulder. "Such a small gesture in light of all that you have done for us. But our homes are always welcome to you."

Greyfriar turned to go, but the woman from the inn touched him lightly on the arm. He didn't notice her and walked on past, but Matthias saw it and stopped him.

"Brigida would say something to you, sir."

Greyfriar turned back.

The woman struggled to find her voice through her anguish and embarrassment. "I wanted to say thank you as well. I didn't mean what I said before. I was angry."

"You had the right. I will do what I can to make sure this does not happen again."

"I know you will. And I understand, you are only one man."

"I'm not even that," he replied quietly, and extracted himself from the crowd, heading for the wooded countryside. The kitten dozed next to his ear, its eyes narrowed to half slits. For the first time in a long while, he felt a bit closer to Adele. He rubbed the tiny cat's head, which lifted as the kitten meowed piteously. It pawed at the fringe of his ruined scarf, pulling it down from over his chin. Greyfriar grinned.

"Perhaps I should name you Adele."

—∿∿—

Edinburgh Castle perched on the top of a foreboding mountain of stone under a stormy sky. No lights blazed from its windows. It was silent and empty. The city below it, however, was warm and inviting in the darkness, where windows let soft light break through the gloom.

Inside the dark halls of the castle, a tall, thin figure walked toward an outer door. A multitude of cats followed after him and circled his legs, bare below his kilt. Baudoin scowled at his escorts. Somehow they always knew when their master would return, their senses just as attuned as his to the prince's arrival.

The heavy door creaked open to admit Gareth, the vampire prince of Edinburgh. Gone now was the soft, grey garb of the Greyfriar, replaced with a stark white shirt and black tuxedo coat with tails.

"Welcome home, my lord." Baudoin bowed, allowing his relief to show at the safe return of his sovereign. Edinburgh was a lonely place for vampires, as Gareth and he were the only two in residence in all of Scotland.

The mob of cats swirled nosily around the two figures, who had to speak louder over their cries of greeting.

"It's good to be home, my friend," answered Gareth, handing over his Greyfriar disguise and weaponry. "I'll be heading out before dawn. There is news of another group of clan outlaws setting up outside Ghent."

Baudoin scowled and wrinkled his nose at the stench of dried human blood on his master's body. Gareth applied it to himself when he was Greyfriar to disguise his scent from his own kind. It was a disgusting tactic, but it kept him safe. Baudoin had long since refrained from voicing complaints about his prince's foolish activities. They never held sway. In any case, Gareth would not be able to pursue more bandits for the time being. "Your excursions will have to wait. While you were gone, I received a messenger from your brother."

Gareth's face tightened. "Cesare? What does he want?"

"There is a clan gathering in London. Your presence is required."

Gareth narrowed his eyes. "Again? I've spent more time in London in the past few months than in the last one hundred years."

Baudoin gave a twisted smile. "How delightful that you and your brother are playmates again."

"Hardly. I just want to keep an eye on him and whatever he's planning. And I want to be near Father, now that's he's . . . failing. But I feel as if I've been neglecting my work as Greyfriar, not being as useful as I could."

The servant patted his master's arm gently. Then a flash of white on

Gareth's shoulder startled Baudoin. It was a tiny cat, and a pathetic creature at that. It yawned and stretched. The servant's eyes widened. "Really? Another one?"

"It was a gift."

"You didn't have to accept it."

The cats below caught the scent of the new arrival and stood up on their hind legs to get a sniff. The small kitten had already doubled in size from the journey to Scotland. Indecision tore at the kitten as it caught a glimpse of its new home. Its ears flicked forward and then flat again. It meowed and hunched closer to Gareth's neck.

"It does not want to be here," Baudoin responded, eyeing the feline.

"It is young and frightened." He reached a hand to stroke her reassuringly, smoothing down the fur that rose in its fright. "As with all things, one must go slowly. Life's not about rushing. There is much to enjoy if you take the time to find it and nurture it." Gareth knelt, bringing the kitten lower and allowing the other cats to investigate under his supervision. The kitten felt safer where she was, and she hissed.

Gareth laughed and stood, heading for the kitchen. "Perhaps Morgana can find you something delicious to eat, little one." The kitten sunk in her claws and settled down for the ride, as she had done all through her travels with the Greyfriar.

Baudoin raised an eyebrow after him and called out, "Will this infatuation with helpless creatures ever end?"

"No," came the immediate reply.

The servant sighed and followed his liege.

CHAPTER 2

THE EVENING AIR rang with the clash of steel, the sharp brutal clank of honed metal against metal, as sparks glimmered in the darkening sky. The stale stench of sweat permeated the press of bodies close around Adele, but her eyes were fixed on the figure ahead of her. The grey cape caught the barest breath of wind and swirled around the tall, lean swordsman as he spun under a swipe of his enemy's long broadsword.

Adele caught her breath as just for an instant his dark glasses turned toward her, perhaps seeking her out among the crowd. Her heartbeat raced against her breast. Then his attention again turned to the battle when his opponent snarled, revealing her long fangs. The vampire held a broadsword in one hand, but slashed out with the cruel claws of her other hand at the heroic man in grey. There was a unified gasp from the crowd as the claws shredded Greyfriar's cloak. The famed vampire hunter was unhurt, already leaping into the fray, his wind-forged rapier a blur, driving back the vampire. Adele could only surmise the vampire was Flay, though nowhere as beautiful and lusty as she remembered the fierce British war chief.

The vampire snarled, "Greyfriar, I have hunted you across Europe!

You who have battled my savage kind for so long from behind that accursed mask! I have murdered the princess Adele! And now I will put an end to your endless heroics!"

Adele leaned over to a middle-aged man with a stained coat who sat beside her. "So why is the vampire carrying a sword? They don't use tools."

"Shh," came his annoyed reply. "You're spoiling it!"

Adele craned her neck to see over the heads of the raucous crowd so she could get a clearer view of the two combatants fighting to the death.

The Greyfriar struck a heroic stance and pointed his rapier at Flay. He turned his head to the audience and shouted, his nasal voice carrying to all, "I will take everything from you as you took everything from me! Princess Adele was my life and my breath! Without her there is nothing left but vengeance! I will forever smite your kind from this earth. Never will you take over this beautiful land so long as I stand here to stop you."

"Greyfriar is very chatty," Adele commented to a woman on her other side.

The woman was cowled in a dark plum, raw silk burqa with antique and intricate geometric stitching, revealing only the darkest of eyes, almost a match to Adele's. Those eyes smiled warmly at Adele, inviting her to continue.

"Well, it just seems that he wouldn't have time for bantering while fighting to the death." Adele gestured to the two figures fighting on the wooden stage.

"This is true," the woman agreed with a rich Persian accent that Adele recognized immediately. After all, her own mother had been Persian.

"Greyfriar is a quiet man, on and off the field of battle."

"How about *you* be quiet!" growled the man on Adele's other side.

The Persian woman's dark eyes, accented with thick shadows of color and perfectly aligned black eyeliner, stayed on Adele a moment longer before slipping away to the show. "So this is not an accurate account of the princess's rescue by the Greyfriar?"

Adele was struck by a strange intelligence hiding in the woman's innocuous question, and she waved her hand, deflecting the relevance of it. "Oh, I couldn't say. It just seems silly for him to banter. I mean, he is fighting for his life."

The Persian seemed to study Adele's simple attire, a long dress devoid of lace or ornament, along with simple shoes, no jewelry, and a homespun cloak with a hood. Certainly nothing out of the ordinary for the audience in this working-class theater.

The woman asked, "Do you know something of warfare?"

"Well, I'm no Greyfriar." Adele laughed.

The Persian's head tilted quizzically at the young woman beside her. Then her eyes saddened. "None of us can be what we may wish."

Onstage, the middle-aged actress playing young Princess Adele moaned dramatically, indicating that she was still alive. She raised an arm slowly and draped it over the fainting couch where she sprawled. The audience gasped and several women clapped their hands. The Greyfriar half-turned to face the princess as he called her name.

"Now I will make you into one of my kind!" the vampire shouted as she took that opportune moment to strike, leaping onto Greyfriar and burying her fangs in his neck. The crowd shouted in alarm. The stage Adele cried out. Then a gunshot.

The vampire stiffened and staggered away from Greyfriar, clutching her heart. "Curse you, Greyfriar! I am undone!" She spun and swooned dead to the stage.

The Greyfriar posed again with a smoking revolver in his gloved hand. The hero pointed at the dead vampire, pronouncing, "Thus it shall ever be for your evil breed!"

The audience cheered wildly, but then the shouting turned to shushing as Greyfriar sprinted to his true love and cradled her helpless form.

"Be still, my darling. I have you now."

The actress clutched the arms of her savior with showy frailty, sobbing uncontrollably. "Thank you, Greyfriar. I was so frightened. Those monsters are horrible!"

The real Princess Adele watched the pathetic portrayal on the stage and wondered if she could have ever been like that. She sighed. Of course, the truth of the story was not depicted here, and if it were known, the whole of Alexandria and beyond would be in an uproar.

Greyfriar, the legend of the enslaved human world, who was now considered the true love of Princess Adele by the popular culture—drenched population of Alexandria, was a vampire.

It had been barely three months, although it seemed like a lifetime, since she had departed Alexandria as a young girl dispatched by the court to tour the free human city-states of the frontier in southern Europe. She had seen it as a girlish adventure before the reality of her impending wedding. But the adventure turned dark when vampires attacked her ship, and she was captured by a creature named Flay, the female war chief of Britain, the most powerful vampire clan in Europe.

Adele managed to escape, thanks to the miraculous intervention of the Greyfriar. Eventually she discovered the terrible truth about her savior. She came to realize Gareth was different than his bloody brethren; he was more Greyfriar than vampire. And they fell in love while in his city of Edinburgh.

"Never more shall they hurt you, my love. I will protect you." The actor playing Greyfriar then spoke the words that the real Gareth had never uttered. "And I will never leave you."

The language was stilted and silly, but an ache of regret overcame Adele, forcing her to look away from the brightly lit tableau. Her mind cast back to the last contact she had had with Greyfriar on the sinking airship. Faced with the chance to return home, Adele had wanted to stay with Gareth. It was Gareth, however, who had convinced her it simply wasn't possible. She had to return home and fulfill her duty, even as Gareth stayed in Britain to face his.

She had tried to push the painful memories away during the past months, but even if it had been possible to forget, Alexandria wouldn't let her. The Greyfriar was everywhere. Adele's adventures in the north had galvanized the citizens and spawned a small industry dedicated to feeding the common people's hunger for stories about them, real or imagined. That included her younger brother, Simon, who was mesmerized by the legend of Greyfriar. No one really knew what had happened in the north, but that didn't stop the publishers and playhouses from exploiting a good story. Countless books and plays had been rushed into print, leading to numerous productions chronicling the romantic escapades of Princess Adele and the Greyfriar, two daring, star-crossed lovers in their fight against vampires. Most of them ended with the princess and the masked hero embracing and embarking on a lifelong love. Few, if any, involved Adele's Intended, the American Senator Clark, in any meaningful way; his presence was a blight on a proper romantic story. They all had happier endings than the truth.

Every time Adele saw one of these shows or read one of the books, her melancholy returned with renewed vigor. Perhaps that was why she kept coming back. She didn't want to forget the pain. It was all she had left of that life, and of him.

The stage darkened over the two actors as they kissed and embraced, and the music rose to a heart-swelling crescendo. Adele didn't cry, although there were plenty of tears in the house. She merely sighed wistfully as ladies dabbed at their eyes, overcome by the romance. *If only they knew*, she thought. Then the image of plebian Alexandria screaming for the head of bloody Prince Gareth on a pike sobered Adele. The fantasy of the two lovers faded like promises on aged parchment. They could never be together. Gareth had been right about that.

"Did you enjoy the play?" the Persian woman asked.

"It had its moments." Adele glanced about to see the crowd dispersing through the double doors at the rear of the house. She was sad that the play was over, because that meant the evening was closer to ending. Soon she would once again return to her crowded yet lonely wing of Victoria Palace. Adele's time as a free commoner was all too fleeting. "What did you think of it?"

"Greyfriar is most mysterious. You never know what lies behind those smoked glasses and cowl. At times he is frightening."

Adele was surprised. That was not the usual drippy response one got when discussing the heroic Greyfriar. Immediately she leapt to his defense. "You shouldn't judge on looks alone. His deeds speak for his heart. That's surely enough, don't you think?"

"He *is* very dashing in his uniform. One couldn't help but fall in love with him." The Persian woman adjusted the lovely burqa shrouding her features. Her hands were covered with exquisite henna tattoos, as if her skin were a mere canvas to an artist's brush. They were as mesmerizing as the dark depths of her eyes. "I especially enjoyed the ending. Greyfriar is a man any woman, any princess, could worship."

Adele blushed a shade of crimson and joined in the woman's gentle laughter.

The woman said, "The vampires were very frightening, don't you think?"

"Oh yes. But they got a lot of it wrong. Vampires don't use swords. Their sense of touch is very poor. It's difficult for them to handle tools, unless they dedicate themselves to it, which they won't because they disdain human objects like weapons. And that part at the end about biting Greyfriar and turning him into a vampire. Nonsense. It doesn't work that way. I thought that foolishness about the undead was all settled by now. They're a separate species, a parasitic species. That's been proven by science. They create new vampires the same way we create new human beings." The Persian was nodding attentively, and Adele realized she was rambling far too much. She shrugged. "At least that's what I've read. But plays don't have to be accurate, do they? The truth isn't nearly as exciting as fantasies." She rose to her feet and tucked the playbill safely in a pocket. "We'd better go or we'll be locked in."

The two women were the last to leave the small theater, but the crowd was still thick in the street outside, discussing the finer points of the show. They glanced briefly at the poster on the theater wall: *The Greyfriar: Desire in the Dead North*. Adele tried not to laugh or retort to some of the comments she heard from the crowd.

"Now that's a man I'd be happy to serve under."

"I'm sure he's got royal blood somewhere."

"There's no way Princess Adele could kill a vampire. My word, she's a princess!"

"I wonder how much of that is true. Do you really think it was Greyfriar and not Senator Clark who won the day?"

"The princess *should* marry Greyfriar! Who cares if he wears a mask?"

The theater was in a working-class neighborhood of the Turkish Quarter, but the crowd still included a few affluent aristocrats in black tie or shimmering gowns, kaftans, saris, and thawbs, top hats, fezzes, or tiaras, walking sticks, monocles, and diamond bracelets. It was common to see such an eclectic crowd in Alexandria.

Alexandria was the capital of the great Equatorian Empire, which stretched from Mandalay to Cape Town. The city was a powerful magnet for all the people of the tropics. It was a glowing symbol of the revival of industrial human society after the vampire destruction of the north. Alexandrians, both cosmopolitan and common, took fierce pride in their rough juxtapositions of class and nationality. The city also served as a haven of sorts, protecting its citizens from harsh realities. Among the gardens, fountains, theaters, opera houses, gentlemen's clubs, restaurants, nightclubs, shopping districts, and busy avenues crowded with trams, hansom cabs, and steam cars, men and women taking their promenades might well forget that their world teetered on the brink of war.

As Adele and the Persian woman strolled along the curb, Adele wrapped her cloak tightly around her, drawing her face deeper into the shadow of its hood. The way the Persian woman stared at her made her uncomfortable. It wouldn't be inconceivable for her to be recognized, despite her common clothes. After all, she was the subject of countless photographs and portraits. The art of disguise was harder than it looked. She had to admire Gareth for keeping it up for so long, but she certainly didn't have his skill with masks and voice tricks. She envied his ability to slip away from his vampire clan at will and, with a simple disguise, achieve his wish to be counted as one of the struggling humans of the north.

Adele's companion said hopefully, "Perhaps I will see you at the opera in two months. The Macedon is staging *The Greyfriar*. It will be the jewel of their season."

"Perhaps," Adele answered vaguely.

"I will be sure to look for you."

And I will be sure to wear a completely different disguise, thought Adele, even though the idea of having a friend outside the palace was enticing. If only the consequences of being discovered were not so depressing. If her father, Emperor Constantine, or the prime minister, Lord Kelvin, found out she was roaming the city late at night, they'd have her clapped in irons. Worse than that, her Intended, Senator Clark, would have her dragged to the altar, chains and all, to extract her marriage vows.

Adele had spent the past few months successfully delaying her wedding to the senator for many reasons. First and foremost, she did not love him, not that it mattered; the marriage was for the good of the Empire. Still, she prayed that with time a miracle would occur and she wouldn't be forced to follow in her mother's footsteps and marry for politics rather than for love.

"It's a beautiful night; one can almost see stars," the Persian noted, her long, henna-painted fingers gripping her burqa as the wind buffeted it.

"At least the breeze is blowing the haze away from the city. Maybe it will rain."

"Yes, my pomegranate tree is looking quite sad."

Adele nodded distractedly. They rounded the corner of the theater and, in the shadows of the alley, a cloaked figure shifted, the breeze billowing out his cape.

Gareth! He had come for her!

The figure stepped toward Adele, the buttons on his military tunic glinting in the dim light from the street. His smoked glasses turned toward her, and he reached out to touch her arm. Adele stood transfixed.

"Is that you, my princess?" he whispered.

In that instant, her hopes shattered. This was not Gareth, only the actor from the theater, come to mix with the adoring herd, particularly the ladies. This man was shorter than Gareth's six-foot frame. His nose was squat and his face marred with smallpox scars. Not ugly, but not Gareth. His wiry hair was cropped too close to his head to be her Greyfriar.

Adele jerked her hand away from the imposter, a bit too harshly. He shrugged and instantly began the search of another princess for the evening.

The Persian woman regarded her curiously. "You are the first woman I've seen shy away from the touch of the famed Greyfriar."

"Well, he's no Greyfriar, and I'm past dwelling in fantasy."

"Then why do you come to see the plays? I have seen you here before."

Adele stiffened with alarm. She'd been noticed. How foolish to chat endlessly with this woman and parade her knowledge of vampires and Greyfriar like a smug child. She needed to get away from this strange woman who seemed far too curious. Even though Adele would've liked to linger and listen to the crowd's discussion, perhaps even follow them to their clubs or coffee shops, her evening's adventure must end.

"I hope you'll excuse me. I'm late for another appointment." Adele gave a polite wave and slipped into the crowd. The Persian woman slowed with silent acceptance and watched the young girl disappear.

Adele neared the promenade of the Eastern Harbor, listening to the waves washing the stone breakwater. She gazed eastward where she could just make out twin obelisks against the night sky. They were affectionately named Cleopatra's Needles, and she paused to stare at them. They were attributed to the ancient queen's desire to honor her doomed lover, Mark Antony.

Alexandria had known its share of tragic love stories, of which hers was just one more.

CHAPTER 3

THE WIND GREW stronger as Adele hurried away from the harbor. Her pace quickened, her booted feet nearly flying over the cobblestones as she headed north taking the long way home, her last bit of defiance.

With only a sliver of moon visible above the rooftops, the evening was a dark pitch broken only by flickering streetlights. Their chemical hiss was just audible over the rush of the wind. Her quickest route home was northeast, but it passed through a notably seedy part of the city.

An open-air tram hummed at a stop just ahead, spewing a cloud of yellow chemical fumes as it idled. Adele dashed for it, grabbing a rail just as it started moving. The smell of the tram's smoke grew thicker as it wound its way northeast through the old Turkish Quarter. Narrow streets crowded with stone buildings passed by slowly, giving Adele a close-up view of their heavy layer of soot coating the nooks and crannies. The white stone had a smudged appearance Adele knew was the stain of progress, but still it saddened her knowing the rails had cut through the ancient city. The tram deposited her at a grimy urban district and moved on. She began to walk the several blocks to the connecting north-ward tram line.

Adele hurried because the longer she was gone, the more chance she would be missed, not to mention that she wanted to get some sleep before the long, dull day began. Her attendants would rouse her for breakfast at an indecent hour and dress her appropriately for her duties. As much as she would love to daydream during the tedious meetings with her staff and doctors, or nod off during Mamoru's lessons and his endless questions about her time with the vampires, it simply wasn't done. Perhaps doing so, though, would indicate she was still not ready to be declared officially recovered from her ordeal. A great many events were scheduled to take place the moment she was declared to be in good health and sound spirit, the first being her wedding and the second being the start of the war against the vampires. She wasn't sure which she dreaded the most.

A shadow shifted to Adele's left. She steeled herself and glanced casually to the side. Then came a sound behind her. Two men were flanking her in the street. A woman alone in this part of the city was a boon to the likes of them.

Adele continued walking, keeping the one on her left in her peripheral vision as she kept an ear cocked for the man coming up from behind. She slowed her breathing and relaxed her clenching muscles, opening up her senses to the environment around her.

The stench of the men identified them as sailors. Their briny odor was even stronger than the air around them. Adele also smelled the telltale odor of chemicals before she saw a green glow from inside the tattered jacket of the man to the left. He was carrying a Fahrenheit blade, but it was a homemade switchblade version. It might as well have been a bomb. The chemical agents in the crude hilt used to heat the blade were so volatile that it was as likely to blow up in the man's hand as it was to deliver a searing blow to his target. Adele could see the chemicals glowing through the weapon's thinnest parts as they ate away at the inferior metal.

"Hey, girlie. Where you off to?"

Adele did not stop, her breathing deep and rhythmic despite the instinctive jump of her heart. She prepared herself, her hand already slowly rising to her waistband.

"Did you hear me? I'm talking to you."

"I'm heading home," was Adele's curt response as the man to her left maneuvered in front of her, blocking her path. A revolver was plainly visible in his belt. She sighed, unable to hide her annoyance. "At least I was."

The men laughed, closing around her while Adele sidestepped to put her back against a wall. Her face was shaded, but most likely these louts wouldn't recognize the princess of Equatoria regardless. Not that it mattered to her.

"You looking for some action, little girl?" The man brandished his Fahrenheit blade like a new toy. He kept pressing the switch, causing the hot blade to slip in and out.

A small smile curved her full lips, clearly visible to the men under her cowl as she lifted her head. It unnerved them, but only momentarily.

The second man laughed and leaned closer, his yellow teeth flashing as his hand reached for her. Adele grabbed his arm, slipping around his other side, preventing him from bringing the gun to bear directly against her. She spun against him, forcing his arm to the breaking point. Using a well-placed palm of her hand, she slapped him between the shoulder blades and sent him careening. His momentum caused the wrist that Adele held to twist agonizingly. He connected with the wall with an audible crack as his nose and forehead slammed painfully into the stone.

The sailor with the knife was trying to process the fact that a slender girl had just taken out his partner. He raised his knife as Adele drew her own Fahrenheit blade, a finely wrought khukri, and moved in a blur to slash him across the forearm. The man staggered back with a cry, but still held onto his weapon. Adele snapped out a rigid hand and connected with a pressure point on the man's shoulder and sprang away, twisting around and drawing her heavy cloak about her for protection. The homemade switchblade dropped from nerveless fingers and clattered to the ground, where it immediately exploded. The chemical spray hit Adele across the back, but the heavy weave of her cloak protected her.

The same could not be said of her attackers. They both screamed in agony.

Adele flung her smoldering cloak away and incapacitated both men with the pommel of her blade. Then she straightened and took in the battlefield. She wasn't even breathing hard.

"See?" she remarked to her now unconscious companions. "There was no banter."

Her victory was short as she heard the scrape of a sword from a scabbard. There was a third assailant! Without even turning, she ducked the slash of the blade, hearing it pass just inches over her head. Her right leg spun out as she tried to swipe him off balance, but he anticipated her move and leapt over it.

He was too far away to hit with her dagger, giving the advantage to the swordsman. There was only one other long-distance weapon in the fight, and she dove for the revolver lying on the dark cobblestones. She rolled to face her opponent, who raced toward her with sword raised.

Adele's first shot took him high in the chest, and he tumbled to the dirty street and lay still. She rose, the renewed adrenaline rush now causing her to pant slightly. The fight had hardly lasted a minute. She had dispatched all three of her attackers with no injury save to her cloak. Her training was definitely paying off.

She reached for the damaged garment, wondering how she was going to explain that to her maids. She decided not to and found a trash bin, listening to the sizzle as it was disintegrated with an acrid tang.

Adele was just turning around when a figure rushed her with an expression of utter rage on his face. One of the first two sailors had regained consciousness and was holding his partner's sword. His face streamed blood from various wounds on his temple, forehead, and nose.

A flash of steel and a swirl of dark blue blinded her as someone dressed in indigo sprang in front of her. The sailor's head rolled past Adele. She snapped into a defensive stance, but then her mouth fell agape.

Mamoru rose from his crouch, his samurai blade gleaming with dark red blood.

Adele gasped in alarm. "What are you doing here?"

"I could ask the same of you, Highness, and be more justified." The Japanese warrior ripped some cloth from the shirt of the decapitated man at his feet and wiped his short blade clean. Only then did he slide it back to its rightful place in its scabbard, content that it had been bloodied before returning home.

"Did you have to kill him like that?"

Mamoru looked stern. "What difference does it make? He is dead and you're not."

"Are you spying on me?" Adele accused him indignantly. "Can I have no peace from prying eyes?"

"You are my charge, Your Highness."

"I had no idea it extended beyond the classroom."

Mamoru bowed low. "May I beg to inquire what you are doing out so late, unescorted? And in this quarter of the city? It reeks of low life."

"They are called the poor. And what I do is my business."

"I beg to differ. You are the heir to the Empire."

Her shoulders lifted into a trivializing shrug. "What does that matter? No one here cares who I am. They are wrapped up in their own struggle to survive."

His hand gestured to the men lying around them. "These fellows were very much interested in you."

"Because I was a woman alone. And I was more than a match for them."

"Indeed?" Mamoru's eyebrow rose and glanced at the head near her feet.

Adele's exasperation fell away, though she assumed she would have been able to handle the situation herself. Still, only a fool refuses to accept help when needed. "I'm grateful that you arrived when you did."

Mamoru's head lowered with grace at her admission. "Now, Your Highness, we should return to the palace before anyone else notes your absence." He walked over to the groaning man who had held the makeshift Fahrenheit knife and made to draw his katana.

Adele grabbed his arm. "What are you doing?"

"He tried to kill the imperial heir."

"He didn't even know who I was!"

"We cannot allow him to live."

"Yes, we can. I order you to spare his life."

"That is unwise. If he recognized you or even overheard us . . ."

"So what? Ooh, the scandal." She mocked in a falsetto tone. "The princess appeared outside her harem. Heaven forbid she walk among her subjects."

"If you are going to play the populist, perhaps you shouldn't beat and kill the populace."

She cut him a scathing glance. "They attacked me and I had dealt with them. That does not warrant murdering a helpless man."

"Your father and future husband would think so."

"They would, but I don't. Many things will change around here when I am crowned."

"Of that, I am most sure."

"Leave that man alone," Adele said firmly.

"As you command, Your Highness."

"Let's just go home. I'm tired."

"I agree. Quickly. You cannot be found here." Mamoru smiled at her, but not with his eyes. His gaze was always that of a teacher, always observing his student and watching for signs of enlightenment.

"Should we contact the police?"

"No. There are bodies in the streets of this wretched district every morning. These few more won't attract great attention."

Adele turned briefly to look at the dead and wounded before striding purposefully away with her teacher. She rested a hand lightly on his arm. "Promise me, Mamoru, that you won't tell anyone what I was doing. Please."

Mamoru was silent for a bit as if contemplating the future, but then he nodded. "Of course. It shall be our secret. Your well-being is my utmost priority, nothing else."

"Whatever you do, don't tell Senator Clark. He still thinks I'm recovering from my ordeal. If he knows I'm well enough for this, he'll demand to hold our wedding. Not to mention what he'll say about the unseemliness of his future wife cavorting with sailors and commoners."

"And thugs," Mamoru added with a subtle smirk. Again her scowl turned his way, so he added more seriously, "I care little for politics and matters of state, Your Highness. I am a priest and a teacher. Thankfully, I have little chance for conversation with the senator. Even if he did find out, we could say this mad behavior is merely an example of your precarious mental state created by your treatment at the hands of the vampires."

"Aren't you a conniver?" Adele regarded her tutor. "And thank you, by the way. I am very grateful that you are concerned for my well-being."

"For as long as I shall live. You are the only thing that matters to me."

Adele nodded, smiling at the samurai. He returned her smile and removed his outer kimono and placed it around Adele's shoulders as much to cloak her from curious eyes as for protection against the wind. Adele burrowed deep into the sensuous warm silk, drawing it up around her neck, grateful for the small comfort.

—⁓—

The Persian woman from the theater stepped from the shadows of an alley, watching Mamoru depart with his young charge. Her eyes closed and her eyelids revealed the henna marks in the shape of eyes that endowed her with inner sight. She smiled, pleased with how things were unfolding. Mamoru's relationship with Princess Adele had been a bit strained since her return to Alexandria. They all worried that Mamoru had lost control over his protégé, jeopardizing the cabal's plans. Everything hinged on the princess, and on Mamoru's control over her.

The last wounded ruffian stirred at her feet. She dropped to her knees, soothingly whispering words of aching poetry.

> *"Your mistress bids you look upon my ardent flesh.*
> *And hear my call of worship. The flame of desire bears you to my cathedral.*
> *Kneel before me, whisper my name upon thy lips and all will be forgiven.*
> *Utter no more words, for I know thy heart."*

The man's unfocused gaze labored to stay on her face and lips as they moved. Unbidden tears leaked from his eyes as her words flowed over him. Her eyes slipped closed, and she saw he had drifted into her realm, whispering her name though he did not know her. With that she held his head in her henna hand and drew her knife across his throat. He made not a sound as he died.

CHAPTER

G ARETH WALKED THE crowded streets of Mayfair in London. With the clan lords in session, the city was packed with revelers. The air was pleasantly cool, so activity was high. Even given the absence of lights, he could see quite clearly in the moonlight. Vampires crowded the sky in black parliaments, while others strolled the boulevard, chatting and laughing like humans.

Respectful greetings from vampire passersby turned to scornful snickers behind Gareth's back when they recognized the failed prince. He didn't care; he had long since given up any desire for position or respect within the clan. He almost reveled in their disdain because it distanced him from his kind and made him feel closer to the humans.

There were humans moving about, trying not to stand out or attract attention. Some of them were bloodmen servants of the vampires. Others were craftsmen or farmers simply performing their duties to sustain the empire, toiling under their own rules, but always under the watchful power of the vampires.

However, even this furtive lot looked with derision on the other humans in town—the herds—soulless husks who typically stood in groups waiting to be culled by their owners. They were nothing more than blood afoot, and the city's parks and squares were bulging with these ragged masses.

A few humans actually hailed Prince Gareth, and at first he wondered if they recognized him. They openly greeted other vampires too as respectful underlings. Gareth then noted the jealous lunacy in their eyes.

Undead.

Here in London, clutches of these fanatics were practicing for the day when they could greet their brothers as equals. They believed in the legends of old and longed for the chance to become undead like their masters, believing that upon their death they would rise up as vampires. It was ludicrous, of course. Vampires were no more undead than were humans. However, Cesare brilliantly used their ignorance to his benefit. Gareth shook his head. Perhaps Cesare was doing more to unite vampires and humans than he was, in a terrifying way.

Gareth strolled past cadavers in all stages of decay, from fresh and bloated to awkward skeletons. London was full of the dead left to rot like garbage. Carrion birds couldn't be bothered to lift their well-fed bodies away from the piles of food, staring and cawing contemptuously as he stepped by.

Gareth paused in his stroll as the toes of his boots touched the body of a young woman. She was around Adele's age but looked so much older due to the life of fear and despair she had no doubt lived. She lay blood-soaked on the paving stones with her throat torn open. Her eyes were wide, and Gareth could smell she was still alive, but not for much longer. Her mouth parted as if to speak. The vampire who had fed off her was nowhere to be seen, but from the enormous amount of blood soaked into her clothes and pooling around her twitching body, her killer had just taken a small taste and left the dying girl gasping on the ground.

Typical.

"I'm sorry." Gareth knelt and killed her swiftly. He wished the vampire had been nearby, because he would've killed that wasteful cretin too.

———✳———

Gareth entered the cool stone cellars beneath Buckingham Palace where his father slept. He was dismayed to see King Dmitri on his bed, stinking and covered in dried blood. The old man seemed unaware of his miserable state, which frightened and infuriated Gareth all the more.

"Why is he so dirty?" Gareth snarled at the blank-faced attendant. "He's the king. Have him cleaned."

"We bathe him once a day, my lord. If we clean him now, he will be dirty again in an hour."

Gareth breathed sharply through his nose. His father's eyes fluttered at the sound of voices, and the bearded face turned slowly toward the visitor. The prince demanded of the attendant, "Has he eaten today? Has he been on his feet at all?"

"Of course, my lord. Prince Cesare is very attentive to His Majesty's needs."

The Scottish prince hissed with derision, trying to ignore the terrible smell in the room. "Yes, my brother is so solicitous. Get out. Leave us."

The attendant departed noiselessly as Gareth moved to his father's bedside. The king mumbled wetly as grey eyes struggled to focus on the tall figure standing over him. Gareth bobbed his head to match his father's gaze.

"Can you see me?" he asked. "Do you know who I am?"

"My brother?"

The nonsensical answer crushed Gareth, but he would not let his father know that. He braced himself for the despair that was to come, though his walls were never strong enough.

"No, I'm Gareth. Your son."

Dmitri reached out a clawed hand. "Have you seen the king today? I want to see him."

"You are the king," Gareth replied quietly. "Are you referring to your father?"

"Yes. I want to see my father. He said he was coming."

Gareth took the gnarled claw and squeezed it hard, his nails actually pressing against the aged flesh, hoping his father might see him for the son he was. Dmitri gave a brief smile. There was no point in repeating that the king's father had been dead for five hundred years.

Dmitri asked, "Have you eaten? We can find something, if you'd like."

"I'm fine. I've eaten. Have you?" Gareth suspected the frail old creature was starving despite the evidence of dried blood on his face and beard.

"Oh yes. We fed near Inverness this morning."

Gareth shook his head. The king hadn't set foot near Inverness in many decades. He dropped the hand and went to a table where a pitcher rested; it was full of slimy water. Perhaps the attendant wasn't lying and they made some pale attempt to wash the king every day. "Are you able to stand?"

"Oh, of course." Dmitri struggled to lift himself, flailing from side to side until he was in danger of falling off the bed and hurting himself.

"Stop! I'll help you!" Gareth snapped anxiously at the pathetic sight. He took his father's dead weight under the arms and eased him into a sitting position. The man was so light. He couldn't be so light.

The prince shouted for the attendant, and when the door cracked open, he snapped, "Bring a new mattress and bedclothes, and several more pitchers of water. And make it fast."

Gareth knelt beside his father, idly tapping the old man's knee. This was outrageous. The king could not be allowed to stay in such a condition. How dare Cesare leave their father down here wallowing in his own filth. It was unacceptable.

Dmitri seemed content to sit with no thought of moving farther. He touched Gareth's arm. "Good to see you, Carolus."

Gareth exhaled with annoyance. "I'm Gareth. Your son. Carolus was your brother."

"Ah. Where is Carolus?" Dmitri looked deeply concerned at the fact that his brother was suddenly not there.

He's dead too, Gareth thought, but he merely said, "I don't know. I haven't seen him today."

"You look like him. You have that same grimace from worrying too much. Are you sure you aren't him?"

"Yes, sir. I'm sure." Gareth laughed against his will.

Then the door opened and several humans entered laboring under a heavy mattress and piles of blankets. They were followed by others carrying numerous large pitchers sloshing with water.

Gareth asked his father, "Can you stand now?"

"Of course I can. What am I, a child?" And the king began to mime the act of standing, apparently without realizing he was still sitting.

Gareth stood, swallowing his bitterness, and pulled the old man to his feet. He held the wavering figure until the king gathered his balance. He backed away only when he assumed Dmitri would stay aloft. Gareth gestured to the disgusting bed and silently commanded it be removed and replaced. After it was done, he ordered all the servants from the room. Once the door was closed, he removed the stinking robe from his father's body.

Gareth nearly gasped to see the withered old thing before him. His father had been a giant, a titan, stronger than anyone, with arms like trees and legs like temple columns. This sagging husk, caked with filth, was unrecognizable as King Dmitri. Gareth hurled the robe across the room and collected his temper. He needed his father, not this shell.

He grabbed the man's gnarled hand and demonstrated what he wanted Dmitri to do. "Wash yourself." He lifted several pitchers and poured water over his father.

The drenched old man stood motionless as dirty water sloughed off him and pooled at his feet.

"Wash!" Gareth commanded again, hoping to cut through the old man's fog of the past and jar him to the present.

"I am," Dmitri replied, dripping but not moving.

Gareth angrily seized another pitcher and doused his father again. He threw it aside and began to run his fingers through matted hair, scraping old blood from the beard, wiping muck off the leathery frame. He then poured pitcher after pitcher over the old man, who spit water but otherwise stood complacent. Gareth was soon soaked and covered with filth as well, but his father was passably clean.

His father's vacant eyes locked onto the distant walls as if he saw beyond them, lost in his thoughts. Gareth's breath was ragged in his throat, his jaw clenched tight against the ache of his anguish. He draped a blanket around the naked Dmitri and wiped him dry. He threw the wet blanket aside and found a passably royal robe across the chamber, holding it open behind the king.

"Sir, your robe."

"Oh, thank you, Carolus." Dmitri slipped into the robe naturally and cinched it around his waist.

Gareth moved to face him, tight-lipped. "My name is Gareth. Do you remember me at all?"

The king nodded as he laid his arm across the prince's shoulder. "I have a son named Gareth."

"That's right."

"He is a good son. A bit bullheaded, perhaps. I taught him to think for himself, and he learned that very well." Dmitri narrowed his eyes in thought, actual deep thought. He worked his jaw side to side in contemplation. "But he didn't learn when to put the clan above himself. Sometimes you can be right, but you still have to give way to others. That can be a terrible undoing. I don't know if he ever grasped that." Then the king smiled generously. "But I've always been proud of him. Will you tell him so, if you see him today?"

Gareth stared deep into his father's gaze, seeking a hint of recognition, a flicker of the past, some shadow from their time together. Dmitri's eyes were honest, even charming, but they were deep chasms with no bottom. There was nothing in them to assuage Gareth.

The prince paused to find a steady voice. "I will."

Dmitri looked wistful. "I miss him. I miss seeing him."

"He misses you as well." Gareth looked at the floor as he adjusted the king's robe. His chest ached that his father had no idea how often Gareth visited him. He then guided his father back to the bed and helped him to lie down again. "I must go, Your Majesty. I hope to see you again soon."

"Good," Dmitri said. "You've been very kind."

Gareth cupped the back of the king's damp head. Then he silently turned to leave.

"Why don't you want to be my brother?" Dmitri asked.

Gareth smiled sadly. "I will be your brother if you wish it."

"Good. Everything is all right, then." Dmitri drifted off toward a satisfied sleep. "Good night, Carolus."

"Good night, Dmitri."

—◦◦◦—

"Gareth, can't you even pretend to care about your people?"

"I care, Cesare. More than you know." It took all of Gareth's reserve to maintain an air of disinterest when speaking to his despised brother. He was seething over their father's terrible condition, which Cesare supervised. He wondered how difficult it would be to assume the care for Dmitri, or even to remove him to Edinburgh. That would certainly be impossible. "I must say, I admire the new version of the events surrounding your capture of Princess Adele where you've somehow come out the victor."

"I am the victor." Cesare laughed loudly and slapped Gareth on the back. It was an act that surprised Gareth at first; his brother was never one for cheerful bonhomie. But this was, in fact, an act of superiority. The younger prince was so secure in his hold over the clan now, he could flaunt it with displays of filial affection that neither brother felt. As with all things between them, it was nothing but pretense. "I'm so powerful now, I even control history."

The two princes strode the musty corridors of Buckingham Palace, and Cesare moved through his domain with complete confidence. He was fine-boned but powerful, with close-cropped hair. He was prone to smug expressions and icy glares, and he enjoyed making dramatic gestures with his hands because he liked to watch them move. He tugged the cuffs of his formal coat and checked the cravat that had been carefully tied by a human slave. Cesare took pride in his appearance. Most vampires were festooned in garish combinations of colors and styles, even mixing clothes typical of male and female. They wore human clothes not because they needed to, since the cold didn't affect them, but because they liked to mock humans. Living as parasites scuttling in the dark for millennia had made vampires particularly showy conquerors.

"This is what you want anyway, Gareth." Cesare continued his bubbling chatter. "You don't want to be king after father dies. You want to play brooding benefactor to your herds in Scotland. I still don't know why you felt compelled to meddle when I captured the princess, but I forgive you. You've stayed quiet the last few months, and you sulked around London without bothering me." The younger prince attempted a sincere, "Thank you, Gareth."

The Scottish lord's sharply chiseled face remained down without apparent reaction, and Gareth wished again he had killed Cesare when he had the chance. His jaw was clenched tight against the urge. Unlike the blatantly sartorial Cesare, the elder prince was in his trademark simple black trousers and frock coat, highlighted by a bright white shirt. His arms were clasped behind his back. His dark hair was a little longer and wilder than normal.

Cesare continued, "It's best you steer clear of politics anyway, Gareth. Thanks to your ill-timed interference in the spring, the Equatorian princess escaped me. That loss means that the Equatorian-American alliance continues. For now. I hear reports of airships massing at bases in Gibraltar and across the sea in Cuba. Had you just stayed away, the princess would be dead now, as would the butcher Clark. The war would be over and I would have won. As it is, I have work to do. Fortunately, I have plans in place that will strike at the heart of Equatoria, and this time I will tear it out."

Gareth's stride almost broke, but he caught himself and continued walking beside his conniving brother. "What do you mean? What are you planning?" He looked up, staring hard at Cesare with dark intensity from inside his icy blue eyes. His brother's words frightened him. Cesare did not boast, at least not idly. The elder prince feared new schemes targeting Adele. Whether or not she was Equatoria's heart, she was certainly Gareth's.

The brothers reached a door where Cesare's bailiff, Stryon, waited patiently. As Cesare checked his suit, he said to Gareth, "Here we are. Listen to me, on the other side of this door are the keys to my new grand alliance to counter the humans. Three clan leaders from Europe and North America. King Ashkenazy of Budapest. King Draken of Munich. And the amazingly still-living Queen Fen of New York." Cesare paused to eye his companion with enormous self-satisfaction.

Gareth felt his breath quicken with surprise, but he struggled to maintain a steady stare. Three clan rulers here at Cesare's beck and call. It was an amazing feat given the increasingly fractious politics of the clans since the Great Killing. And it was startling proof of Cesare's political skill and growing power.

Cesare said in a confidential tone, "Now, King Ashkenazy and King Draken are completely with me on the war. Queen Fen has concerns, the vile hag. We can't wait, of course. If we wait, we die." He took his brother by the arm and whispered, "Gareth, if I need you to seduce that old crone, I'll give you a sign. Females seem to fancy you. Even my Flay would've turned against me for you, I think."

Gareth started with true surprise. It was shocking enough that Cesare was including him in his plans, even in a half-joking way. But Cesare's former war chief Flay had indeed offered to betray her master for Gareth before her death in Scotland. He couldn't tell if Cesare knew or suspected or was just making a jest.

Cesare shook his head in annoyance at the conference to come and said, "Follow my lead," by which he meant *don't cross me*, but it sounded more pleasant.

The chamberlain swung back the door, and the two princes entered the spacious chamber, once grand but now mildewed and faded, to find the three rulers waiting. Two males were finely attired in dress uniforms of old central European style, and an aged female wore a gown of shimmering silk.

"Your Majesties!" Cesare boomed. "Thank you for meeting with me. These matters shouldn't detain you long. Once we finish here, you can enjoy the prodigious hospitality of our clan."

The aged queen of New York shifted with a rustle of plentiful fabric. She turned her sallow, bloated face to Cesare. "We may not be so close as you imagine, young prince. I am not satisfied. Not at all."

Cesare reared back with pretended concern. "Indeed? I am saddened by that. Then we shall address all your issues, Queen Fen." He smiled. "Oh forgive me. I have the honor to present my brother, Gareth of Edinburgh."

Gareth bowed, noting the absence of the title *prince* in his introduction and the fact that his realm had been reduced from a nation to a city.

King Ashkenazy of Budapest was young, younger even than Cesare, and had recently displaced his father. With newfound power he had launched a series of stunning raids in the southern Balkans. Once thought a rival of Cesare's for leadership of any clan alliances, the two upstarts seemed to have formed a bond. Ashkenazy was tall and willowy thin, pale even for his species. His blond hair hung straight to the small of his back. He wore a relatively restrained uniform of navy blue, with highly polished shoes and a half cape thrown off one shoulder. He fidgeted nervously with the unpleasantness of a writhing eel.

Draken of Munich was heavier and more stable; in fact, he was virtually immobile. He had a florid, pleasant face with eyes full of perpetual distrust. He said little and meant less. Draken loved garish uniforms—today he wore scarlet trousers and a violet tunic festooned with gold braid on the shoulders and collar. His round chest and belly jangled with old decorations of valor nestled alongside strings of finger bones and human teeth. On his head he wore a helmet with a silvery peaked crest on which one of his human slaves had painted the image of a skull.

Queen Fen croaked again. "And where is my old friend, Dmitri? I should not like to come across the sea to treat with a boy."

Cesare nodded gravely and calmly, but Gareth noted with satisfaction that his brother was growing irritated.

"The king is unwell," Cesare replied with appropriate sadness. "His age is great, as you surely know. He is the oldest of the clan kings. Fortunately, I have been his right hand for years, so there is no distance from my ear to his. I am, for all intents and purposes, the king of Britain."

The three rulers turned their heads as one to Gareth for his reaction to a virtual coup d'etat by his younger brother. There was none. Gareth stood complacent and complicit.

The queen was in a fractious mood. "Nothing from you, Prince Gareth? You are the heir, are you not?"

"Indeed I am, Your Majesty."

"Do you leave all these matters to your brother?"

"Indeed I do, Your Majesty," Gareth said, with a grim visage. He thought of Adele, and any thought of distancing himself from his brother's counsel faded.

"Excellent," Cesare crowed and puffed with satisfaction. He clasped his hands behind his back and strolled across the room. "Now that we've settled that, shall we get down to it?"

"Very well." Fen tapped her cane on the marble floor with vigor. "It's none of my concern how you Brits run your affairs. Here it is, then.

While you European clans have sufficient combined power to meet the Equatorians, I am left against the Americans. Am I to face them alone, only to watch the rival clans in Chicago, Boston, and Montreal pick my weakened bones once the fighting is done? Those wretches itch to usurp my kingdom."

King Ashkenazy of Budapest shivered, and his head convulsed with a strange palsy. "Have you no friends at home?"

"I have my allies," Fen responded icily. "But perhaps you are unaware, boy, of the situation in North America. Our southward range is more limited. Our frontier is longer and more unsettled."

"Half your continent is unpopulated," the willowy Ashkenazy hissed.

The old crone scowled at the king. "We have organized human resistance as far north as Washington. I have had to slaughter Philadelphia twice! The heat is great far into the north. It is difficult for us to maintain complete control year round. Even in New York, the summers drive us north or nocturnal, far more than any of your kingdoms. If I have to fight the American army plus the rebels, as well as the other clans who hate me, I could lose all my territory. What are my guarantees? Will you send packs to serve me?"

A tense silence dragged until Gareth said, "If I may?"

Cesare froze in place with a question that was a warning. "You wish to speak?"

"I do." Gareth took a moment's pleasure at the consternation in Cesare's face. "Queen Fen's concerns are well taken. The situation in North America is different than in Europe. Or even in Asia. I would offer her this guarantee. She can, no doubt, defeat the invading American forces that are primarily aimed at retaking the major cities of the east coast of the old United States, which is largely her domain. Those Americans will be extended from their bases in Cuba and Mexico. But we have no doubt her packs can contain them until winter sets in when the Americans can be driven back to the tropics. Once we settle here with the Equatorians, we'll guarantee to provide Her Majesty packs to help secure her territories. And more, we will assist her to destroy the Boston clan and assume their properties."

The two European kings froze as Cesare slowly lowered his head, glaring at Gareth. Before any of them could speak, the aged queen snorted with laughter and stamped her cane on the floor with a crack and pointed it at Gareth.

"Done! Thank you, Prince Gareth. Finally some wisdom from the British clan." Fen gave Gareth a peculiar crinkle of her eyes. "Under those conditions, my clan and allies will go to war. Cesare, send a war chief to New York to consult. I will leave my son here for the same reason."

Ashkenazy and Draken deferred to Cesare for reaction. The young British prince took a breath and smiled warmly at his brother.

"The alliance is agreed, then. And no doubt once word reaches the provinces that you dread lords have combined forces, other clans will rush to join us. Perhaps, Queen Fen, the Boston clan will even join hands with you for the coming war."

"That would be fine," the queen snarled. "But I still want to destroy them afterwards."

"Quite. And so you shall." Cesare rubbed his clawed fingers together. "A new day has begun. We will see the most magnificent vampire force since the Great Killing and we will drive the humans back into their dark ages again."

CHAPTER

T HE RIVER WYE in Wales cut through an enchanted land of stone circles, many broken and tumbled to the ground. Once it was believed that dragons and wee folk lived beneath the ground. Those were myths. Vampires were not.

The Great Killing of 1870 had struck deep in Wales, as it had across all of the British Isles. Much of the population had been slaughtered. Humans across Europe fled to the tropics when they learned that the equatorial regions were free of vampires, and many Welsh joined the southward trek to escape the horror.

Those people left behind found life difficult, but not impossible. The vampires spent little time in Wales. They would raid for food and to shatter human attempts at consolidation of power, but the creatures didn't seem to care for the lovely green hillsides. Clan lordlings who did settle there frequently deserted their territories for other areas, which was why some of the villages of the Welsh heartland thrived in ways few others across Britain could.

The geomancer Selkirk knew why vampires preferred to avoid Wales. Skilled in knowledge of the Earth, its minerals and strata and, more importantly, its energies, he knew that the very earth of Wales gave off a taint that vampires abhorred. Vampires were visceral things, tied by their senses to the natural world. The interaction between vampires and the earth was not well understood, yet. It was the job of a geomancer, at least of Selkirk, to use his knowledge to study the earth's impact on vampires. That was why he had spent the last few years in Britain, which is what had allowed him to encounter the people of Trellech.

Selkirk smelled the cooking fires of the village and his stomach rumbled with anticipation. He took one last reading with his geolabe, a small brass instrument that resembled a marriage of a sextant with an astrolabe. Equipped with the proper stones, the geolabe was an essential tool for tracking the ley lines of the earth. The geomantic energies of those lines could repel vampires, and certain people could harness those energies to hide themselves from the creatures' extraordinary senses, although it required great knowledge and concentration. Selkirk had such knowledge.

The geomancer had almost lost the guilt he felt first coming to Trellech. Years ago in Alexandria, his teacher had told him, repeatedly and forcefully, to maintain his isolation while traveling in Britain. He was to stay hidden from both vampires and humans. Observe. Record. Report. Be dispassionate and scientific. The humans of the north were nothing more than the vampire's cattle. Engaging them only increased the chances of discovery by vampires, and death.

Selkirk had kept that stern counsel for more than a year after he arrived on the British shore near Plymouth. He traveled, recorded and mapped the lines. He compiled an admirable notebook of geographic and geomantic coordinates. Southern England. The Eastlands. Up toward York. Into Scotland. Down through the Lake District. It was slow, painstaking, achingly lonely work. He saw humans often, of course, but they rarely saw him. Sometimes they were nothing more than naked or ragged herds subsisting on roots and berries, just as he'd been told.

Other times, however, they were different. More often than not, they lived in villages and towns. They farmed, sometimes quite rudely, but still eking a living from the soil. They smiled and laughed. Fought. Played with children.

Selkirk also watched humans being killed by vampires. Twice, without warning, he saw the skies darken with floating shapes and peaceful villages were culled while he disappeared into the embrace of the lines. The creatures departed, leaving the dead behind along with the sure message that life was not certain nor peaceful. These humans in Britain subsisted every day under the threat of extinction.

Selkirk had assumed he would be unmoved by the violence. After all, it was no more than a farmer slaughtering a goat for a feast. The more he saw of these humans, however, the more he ached when witnessing their deaths. They were not animals; they were individuals.

Now, as Selkirk entered the bustling Welsh village of Trellech, he saw familiar faces. And he smiled, as if returning home. There were friendly waves and comfortable nods. He heard reedy music and beautiful voices singing. Festival time.

Selkirk had grown up alone on the streets of Alexandria. His mother worked various jobs to buy hashish. He had been sullen and withdrawn, a poor student with no friends, and destined for a short life in the alleys, or perhaps the army, if they'd have him.

Then one day, when he was about twelve years old, a kindly old man had stopped to speak. It was only years later he learned the old man's name was Sir Godfrey Randolph. Selkirk had seen the man before, wandering the alleys of Karmouz, not a proper neighborhood for such a man. But men of grace and position often came to Karmouz. Sometimes they came home with Selkirk's mother, stinking of wine or hash.

However, this man didn't want anything from the blond-haired boy except his name and the answers to a few odd questions, in exchange for several pennies. The old man held out his two closed hands. "Which hand holds a stone, my lad?"

Selkirk knew. He didn't guess. He knew. As if he could smell the stone through the man's fingers.

The old man shifted the stone behind his back and held out his hands once more. Selkirk knew again. He knew twenty times in a row. Then the old man handed the stone to Selkirk and asked the boy what he felt. He felt green and wet, and he could smell strange spice in the air.

The old man produced a folded map of the world and asked the boy where the stone came from. Selkirk laughed. How could he know that? But he pointed to an island labeled *Java*. The old man smiled. Keep the stone, he had said, and if Selkirk was kind enough to meet him tomorrow, there would be more pennies.

Selkirk waited there all day and through the night, afraid that other boys would come and take his spot and get his pennies. There were so many other boys who were stronger and smarter and more handsome. The old man might like them better if he saw them.

The next day, the old man came again, but accompanied by an Asian man in a linen suit whom he would later learn was named Mamoru. The friendly old man replicated the trick with the stone in his hand many times, and Selkirk was always right, including one time when the Asian man was actually holding the stone instead of it being held by the old man. Then came the map, and it was hardly unfolded before Selkirk pointed to Java again and said, "Green and wet."

The Asian man seemed disappointed, but the old man laughed and said, "This stone today, lad. Not yesterday. Today."

Selkirk's heart pounded. He had thought they just wanted him to repeat yesterday's tricks. He looked at the men hoping they would tell him. He just wanted to please these grand men and get their pennies and hope for the promise of more pennies.

The Asian man shook his head and tapped his stick on the ground. "No. He was impressive, but no. Keep an eye on him, but I don't want to take him."

"Brown," Selkirk blurted out. "Dry grass waving."

The old man smiled and held up the map. The boy had to stop himself from pointing at Java again. His hand moved slowly down and left. His dirty nail touched the word *Ulundi* in southern Africa.

The Asian man nodded and turned. "Bring him."

Selkirk never saw his mother again. That day, he left Alexandria for a school in Siwa, and then, after a year, he went off to Mamoru's school on Java in the South Seas, where he joined a wonderful new family of burgeoning geomancers and scholars of the occult. But then, just as he began to feel comfortable and needed, he was sent on an extended mission to far-off Britain, where the cold and the silence of his own head enveloped him.

Today, Trellech was crowded. People gathered and smiled and laughed. Quite a few were drunk. In one of the grassy squares, Selkirk clapped along with a group of men doing an intricate dance, hopping and clicking long sticks together almost in martial style. They were accompanied by fiddle and flute. He smelled meat grilling and noticed several lambs sizzling on spits.

A voice shouted his name. A man waved and came over. Richard Goronwy wore a long black waistcoat with a white collar that denoted his rank as religious leader. He greeted Selkirk with a broad grin and slapped a leathery hand on the geomancer's shoulder. "Welcome back, my boy! Welcome back!"

"Thank you, Reverend Goronwy. I'm glad I didn't miss the festival."

"You made it, Mr. Selkirk. It's still Whitsuntide. In fact, tomorrow I lead the service of prayer and thanksgiving at Tintern. You'll come, of course?" The Welshman's English was good, but his accent was thick with regional syrup.

"Yes, of course. I want to see it."

Reverend Goronwy was tall, with a neatly trimmed grey beard, and long white hair that spilled out from beneath a round black hat. He was a man of position in Trellech, a figure of religious and social authority. The locals called him "Vicar." He conducted religious services for the people of the area, but also took great interest in the occult knowledge of the earth, as Selkirk understood it. Their shared fascination had brought them together and made each man look forward to their next meeting, when they could share more information. Selkirk had learned a great deal of the provincial ideas about faith and spiritual power, and how those things could fight vampires. He hoped these ideas would surprise and delight Mamoru, Sir Godfrey, and the others in Alexandria.

Goronwy said, "You've grown thin on the road. Will you step into my home and eat?"

Selkirk pushed back his greying blond hair and scrubbed his beard. "Thank you. I must look frightful."

They reached a fine white house near the center of town, and Goronwy let them inside. With the sounds of Whitsuntide shut out by the door, the vicar instantly tossed his hat aside and pulled off his ecclesiastical collar.

Within moments, there was soup, bread, and beer on the table in front of Selkirk. The smell of it gave him a wonderful feeling of belonging. He relished it as he dove into the meal.

The vicar drummed his fingers impatiently on the geomancer's rucksack, watching his young friend eat. "Is it good?"

"Yes. Very." It had been weeks since he had eaten a decent meal in good company, or even spoken to anyone, and he was enormously comforted by his surroundings.

"Good." The older man pretended to notice the pack. "Where have you been these last months? Any new information?"

Selkirk said around a mouthful of bread, "I found a settlement called Hawkshaw that hasn't seen a vampire in living memory. I mapped a stone circle nearby. Not visible, but I found it easily enough. The energy from it was immense. Not far from the village's old church."

"So they're like us here in Trellech?"

"Yes. Not nearly so large, nor organized. But they have religious services, as you do. They claim it protects them from vampires. Plus they are sending pilgrims out, trying to spread that information to other communities. Very interesting."

"Yes. I should say so." The vicar tapped the traveler's rucksack. "Oh, I've arranged a supply of bluestone for our experiments."

Selkirk stopped eating and looked down at the table a trifle embarrassed. "I don't know if I'll have time, Reverend."

"Why? Well, no matter. We can do it when you come back next time, if you wish."

The geomancer took a deep breath of regret. "I have to leave Britain."

"What?"

"My commission is for two years. I hate to leave, but I must return to Equatoria to report my findings in detail. For the war."

Dejected, Goronwy shook his head slightly. "Don't leave. There's so much more we need to discuss."

"I'm sorry. I must. I may be back. But I don't know where I'll be sent next time."

"I wasn't expecting this." The old man sat back dolefully. "Well, you won't depart for a few days at least, will you? You need to rest."

"I'll stay a while. Perhaps we'll get in a few experiments before I go." Selkirk hated to disappoint his friend of these many months, but there was no way he could postpone his return home for long.

The Welshman smiled gratefully. "That would be grand." Selkirk yawned and Goronwy said, "Sleep now, lad. My son's old room upstairs is ready for you, as always."

The geomancer downed the last of the warm, foamy ale. "Thank you. I am tired. It's been a difficult trip. I'm grateful for all your kindness. You've made my time in Britain bearable."

Goronwy replied, "You're welcome. I daresay I've gained just as much from our time together." He laid his hand on Selkirk's rucksack.

—⁓—

Selkirk was shaken awake.

"Lad!" a voice called. "Rise up!"

Goronwy's whiskered face hazed into view. The old man shook him again.

"What's wrong?" Selkirk sat up with effort. "What time is it?" The window was still black with night.

"Stay quiet. We're leaving."

"Leaving? Where? What are you talking about?"

"Quickly now. Get dressed." The vicar pulled the geomancer up by the shoulder until Selkirk's bare feet touched the rough wooden floor.

"I don't understand. Are you in trouble?"

"I said get dressed!" The Welshman's voice was sharp, which was unusual.

Selkirk reached for his pants, not wanting to anger his friend. He saw Goronwy pick up the geolabe and study it.

Selkirk said, "Please don't. The settings are precise. I'll show it to you later."

"Quiet! Hurry, will you!"

The door opened, and two burly men pushed in with short broadswords in their hands. Goronwy regarded the two men and pointed at Selkirk's rucksack. "Take that. And there are many more papers downstairs that he left here before."

"No, I need them." The geomancer shook his head in confusion while eyeing the two raggedy men. "I'm taking everything back to Equatoria."

"You're not going to Equatoria, lad."

Selkirk hit on the wild idea that Goronwy was going to keep him here by force, out of some twisted sense of camaraderie. It was frightening, yet oddly comforting at the same time. With a calming voice, he said, "Reverend Goronwy, I can't stay in Trellech."

"You're not." The Welshman motioned to one of the men who grabbed Selkirk's arm roughly, while the other leveled his sword at the geomancer. Selkirk was hustled from Goronwy's home by a small squad of soldiers. The vicar himself followed, carrying Selkirk's possessions, including journals, maps, and papers filled with all the geomantic information gathered in Britain over the last two years. As they hurried along a dark path between cottages, Selkirk grew overwhelmed by a sense of outrage and began to struggle.

"Don't!" Goronwy snapped. "There's a ship full of bloodmen nearby. I shouldn't like to order them into town."

The geomancer grew passive again; no one should suffer on his account. "Where are you taking me?"

"My boy, you're going to London. To see the king."

The stench of urine, sweat, and offal hung in the air. Selkirk was chained to a wall inside a dank cell with nothing but long hours alone to consider his mistakes.

London. The vampire clan capital.

Selkirk had been in the great corpse of a city just a few months earlier, after receiving an emergency message via Mamoru's network of couriers. It was the only time he'd been contacted in all his time in Britain. Even deep in vampire Europe, word could still travel from the civilized south, although with great difficulty. Selkirk had penetrated London to locate Princess Adele, using the ley lines to go unseen by vampires. But even with that great skill, he was always a slip or an accident away from being discovered and killed.

Landing in London earlier today, through the wet air of early morning, he'd seen the towers of Westminster and the Bridge, so he knew he was south of the Thames River. But this part of the city was unknown to him.

The geomancer had been manhandled toward a hulk of a mansion, reddish grey brick covered with ivy and topped by a once-impressive dome. Two vast wings sprawled off a colonnaded portico with countless windows, some broken and most barred.

Goronwy had called it Bethlem. Or Bedlam. Before the Great Killing, it had been a madhouse. Now, the vicar claimed it was a research institute dedicated to understanding the spiritual and earthly arts. But a madhouse it remained.

Selkirk now found himself an inmate in that asylum. Cold air seeped through the stones, leaving him damp and freezing. He had lost track of the interminable, miserable time. Moans and screams echoed in the dust-filled building. A distant heavy door creaked open and admitted Goronwy, escorted by two bloodmen. The old man put an arm across his nose, grimacing at the stench.

"Ngh. I always forget the smell of science when I'm away."

The man smiled at Selkirk through the bars of the cell. Gone were his previous modest clothes of a vicar. Now he was draped in a long silk dressing gown and a soft cap with a tassel. He smelled of flowery soap. He carried a large book with obvious pride. The bloodmen unlocked Selkirk's cell and chains from the wall, leaving the manacles around his ankles. He was dragged before the man he had once called a friend.

They all climbed the stairs out of the dungeon. As they passed through a long empty corridor, a soldier approached. He was clean and straight, not hunched and cowed like most of the bloodmen Selkirk had seen. This officer was fully in command of his faculties. He didn't act hypnotized or dazed. He even had a smug grin as he looked Selkirk up and down.

Goronwy asked, "What do you want, General Montrose?"

"Message from the palace. Cesare wants you and the spy there. Now."

The vicar exhaled in disgust. "I've just arrived from Trellech. Surely I may eat."

The general snorted a laugh. "I'm only a messenger, Doctor. Do you wish me to tell the prince you'll attend him after you've had a leisurely meal?"

The Welshman watched the soldier without obvious emotion. "I'll thank you to keep a civil tongue in your head, General. I am the witchfinder-general, not one of your fanatical Undead. I should hate to mention to Prince Cesare that you have certain faculties that require close study here."

The bloodman officer shrank noticeably and lost some of his swagger.

With the upper hand retrieved, Goronwy resumed a professional respectfulness. "Please tell Prince Cesare, if you'd be so kind, that I will appear at the palace at my earliest opportunity."

"But he seemed—"

"At my earliest opportunity." The Welshman shifted the book, finished with the conversation.

General Montrose departed, leaving the vicar smiling. With a gentle shake of his fatherly head at Selkirk, he said, "I apologize for that unpleasant scene. General Montrose is rather full of himself. Typical of the Undead. They act like they drink blood."

"The Undead?"

"Just part of Cesare's genius. He took a myth and turned it into an army. The vampires feed from them, and then the Undead will do anything to die in their masters' service, so they can be resurrected."

"That's crazy," Selkirk snapped angrily. "This whole thing is crazy."

"Of course it is. No *educated* man believes vampires are undead humans. The Undead serve our lords because they're crazy. I do it because I'm a scholar."

Selkirk couldn't find words to reply to such insanity. He wondered briefly if he was dreaming, still asleep in Goronwy's cottage in Trellech. However, that was too simple to be true. They continued on to a large chamber lit with candles. Plates and glasses were set on a long wooden table as if it were a banquet hall in the heart of Alexandria and not hellish London. The bloodmen led Selkirk to a chair. Goronwy sat opposite him, then dove into the lavish meal with relish. Selkirk recognized

Goronwy's book with a start. It was al-Khuri's *On Concentrative Reflexes*. There were only two like it in the world, and they belonged to members of Mamoru's cabal. Selkirk trembled at the implications. The al-Khuri book was a singular text for geomancy, and its presence here in clan England was inexplicable.

"We're sitting on a circle here," the Welshman said, through a mouthful. "You sense it, no doubt. This place is on what you Alexandrian scholars call a rift. I don't think the power resonates a great deal, but the vampires still don't like coming here. What is your opinion?"

Selkirk stared around like a lost child. This couldn't be happening to him.

"You're confused, I know. It's all strange to you now, but you'll come around. We'll do great things together, you and I." The old man produced a long pipe and a battered tin of rancid tobacco. He offered a second well-chewed pipe to Selkirk, who merely closed his eyes in refusal. Goronwy put a flaring candle to the stuffed pipe and puffed clouds of vile smoke with the sigh of a contented squire. "Cesare is so keen for knowledge, I have carte blanche. Bethlem will become a renowned place of scholarship, lad. I will become the greatest man of the realm. With your help, of course."

Selkirk sought some bit of focus. "What does Cesare care about your spiritualism? Those practices are anathema to his kind."

Goronwy shrugged. "Cesare has vision. It was only a year ago that he sent his old war chief Flay to snatch me up in Wales. He'd heard of me, as a practitioner of religion. Of course I thought I was a dead man, but as it happened, he wanted to tap my expertise. He wanted to create an institute of spiritual advancement and chose me to direct it. I have the authority to seek out all other practitioners in the realm and bring them here for examination."

"Examination? Or extermination?"

Goronwy merely puffed his pipe.

"You're a traitor," Selkirk said.

"A traitor? To whom?"

"Humanity."

"Bah." The old man blew another cloud of smoke and crossed his slippered feet. "What do I care for some vague notion of humanity? I live in Britain."

Selkirk sat forward. "But you're hunting the enlightened and bringing them to Cesare for slaughter. They are the only salvation humanity has against the vampires. You're helping him destroy them!"

"No, no, no. You misunderstand. I merely do research. I uncover principles. Just as you do."

"You call yourself witchfinder-general."

"Ah. Just a bit of drama awarded by Cesare. That's a political office. My scholarly title is Doctor of Comparative Spirituality. Here in London, I prefer the title *doctor*. Among the herds, I use *reverend*. Town and gown, you know." Goronwy waved his hand with an impish grin. "You don't understand. You've been conditioned by the Equatorians to believe lies about the north. You'll see. With time, you'll see."

The sound of a commotion reached them. Voices shouted for Goronwy. The old vicar stood slowly, his pipe clamped in his teeth, annoyed at the interruption. When the office door swung open, General Montrose stormed in and moved to one side.

Prince Cesare entered.

Goronwy jerked with surprise. "My lord! I was just planning to depart for the palace."

"You miserable goat!" The vampire's face was like white marble with sharp edges. His blue eyes almost steamed. His taloned hand grabbed the witchfinder by the throat. "How dare you force me to set foot in this wretched place. Tell me why you should still be alive when I stop talking."

In Cesare's grip, Goronwy managed to croak, "So that I may present my latest colleague, Dr. Selkirk of Alexandria, a renowned and illustrious geomancer."

Cesare eyed the captive with sudden interest, shoving Goronwy back in his chair. The vampire could tell by the dejected southerner's appearance that he was no local bog priest. Selkirk, in turn, couldn't take his eyes off the fearsome, legendary vampire as he approached.

The prince said, "So, this is one of Constantine's spies. Is he important? Or a nobody?"

"Imminently important, my lord. He is the very one sent to London in the early spring searching for Princess Adele."

Selkirk's heart pounded, terrified now as Cesare growled, "You? You walked into London and helped the princess escape? You must be dear to the court of Alexandria. Excellent." The vampire turned back to Goronwy. "I want to know everything he knows. Everything!"

"Of course, Prince Cesare. We've had many useful conferences and seminars already. For instance, I can tell you of a village that hasn't seen a vampire in many years, which practices vigorous religious rites. It's called Hawkshaw."

Selkirk buried his face in his hands, trembling.

"Yes? Perhaps we can arrange for them to see a few vampires shortly." Cesare fussed with his coat in mild agitation. He was growing perturbed in the troubling air of Bethlem. "Break him, Witchfinder. Turn him into something I can use. And if you keep me waiting again, I'll choose another witchfinder from among the wretches in your cells. Do I make myself clear?"

"Yes, indeed, Sire."

Prince Cesare swept from the room. General Montrose grinned and followed at some distance.

Goronwy inspected his cold pipe without great concern. "You see? Cesare values me greatly. And he'll come to value you as well. I'm very excited about our future collaboration."

"Collaboration!" Selkirk cried. "What are you talking about? You just spew words like *colleague* and *institute* as if they had meaning. You pretend to be some sort of scholar instead of what you are, which is a slave. Don't you understand where you are?"

"On the contrary. I think it's you who doesn't understand where he is. But you soon shall."

CHAPTER 6

I T WAS A long, hot coach ride to Giza. Adele saw snatches of green
fields and palms rolling past, surrounded by the turgid waters of the
Nile delta crowded with barges pumping smoke into the air as they
churned through canals. The riverbanks were crowded with warehouses,
factories, and homes born of Alexandria's southern sprawl. She chatted
amiably with Mamoru, who sat across from her in the spacious steam
carriage, about numerous topics—geology, botany, mineralogy—but
they never touched on politics or the wedding, much to Adele's relief.

They passed the narrow green boundary between southern greater
Alexandria and northern greater Cairo. Steam-driven cargo carriers
moved up the Nile. Trains whipped past, trailing smoke and cinders.
Camel caravans wandered in and out of the morass, fearlessly driven by
Bedouin merchants. The traffic crushed the carriage to a crawl, and
Adele found herself staring at the sharp bulk of the Great Pyramid as it
appeared through the haze. Mamoru seemed inordinately impatient,
craning his head out the window, clucking his tongue at the driver's
inability to penetrate the phalanx of traffic.

"Relax," Adele said to him. "Giza isn't going anywhere. If you'd
wanted speed, we should've made this an official visit and cleared the
roads."

The teacher tried to look calm. "No, no. There's no great hurry. We don't want to attract undue attention. But I don't want to be late. My colleague is expecting us."

"Sir Godfrey Randolph? Surely it can't be such an emergency for him to confer with me on vampire issues?"

"No, but he's eager to speak with you. Your reports on the north have circulated throughout the Imperial Academy."

"Really?" Adele leaned forward with excitement. "I was wondering. I hadn't heard much since I wrote them."

"They've been read by serious scholars. Sir Godfrey is very interested."

Adele wondered at how best to approach her next observation. "Sir Godfrey has a reputation as . . . an odd duck."

Mamoru didn't remove his gaze from the distance. "How so?"

"Well, he's a gifted surgeon. Wealthy. Respected. Then he became a vampirist and an occultist. Wrote several books, didn't he?"

Mamoru nodded.

Adele thought back to the book she'd seen in Greyfriar's possession months ago in France. It was Sir Godfrey's *Treatise on Homo Nosferatii*—a massive folio of plates depicting anatomized vampires. She had been eager to secure a copy upon her return so she could compare the anatomy of vampires to humans, and she found them quite similar in most ways, reassuringly so. She had wanted to meet Sir Godfrey since her return and tell him how his book was in the possession of the great Greyfriar, but she had decided to remain evasive on the swordsman whenever possible. The less said about her time with Greyfriar, the better. Lies had a way of unraveling.

She said, "I know he's your colleague, but surely you've heard the stories of his decline in favor. They say his home is full of stuffed vampires posed in terrifying tableaux."

Mamoru glanced at her with an indulgent smile.

"Does he have them?" Adele blurted.

"Not that I've seen. But I haven't been in every room."

"Surely you've heard these things also. Everyone says he's something of a crackpot."

"That's what they say about me too," Mamoru replied, and then he thought, *And about you as well.* "Sir Godfrey is a genius. He is the finest surgeon in Egypt. A man of vision."

Adele sat back, not wanting to offend. "Of course. You know how stories get started."

"I do. We're here." Mamoru seized his walking stick and said, "Your veil, Highness."

Adele wore a traditional robe with a headscarf, which she draped across her lower face. It seemed odd, but no doubt Sir Godfrey desired discretion. The carriage rocked to a stop and sat humming as if impatient while the driver opened the door. Mamoru was quickly out and handing Adele down the kick step. He led her on his arm across the sidewalk, now cast in late-afternoon shadow, and up the steps to a townhouse stoop. He had barely reached to knock when the door swung open and a butler bowed them inside. From the way he looked at her, Adele could tell he knew her identity, but he didn't speak as he collected Mamoru's hat and stick.

"Welcome! Welcome!" came a booming, jovial voice. A large, rotund, red-faced grandfather surged down the hall at them. He paused on the tile foyer and bowed deeply before Adele. "Your Highness, I am honored."

Adele removed her scarf and bid him rise. "Thank you for your invitation, Sir Godfrey. I'm delighted the Imperial Academy has taken an interest in my papers."

The bewhiskered doctor raised his eyebrows, eyeing Mamoru briefly. "Oh, indeed we have. You are now Equatoria's leading vampirist, Your Highness."

"After yourself, of course."

"You've surpassed me by a long shot. I've written a few books on the topic, but I've never traveled north of Alexandria, except for a brief jaunt to Cyprus on vacation. Have you ever been to Cyprus? It's quite lovely. I can recommend a nice restaurant, if it's still in business. I was there over twenty years ago."

Adele laughed as they entered a beautiful library with floor-to-ceiling bookshelves. Tables were covered with books and oddities, large crystals, busts, unidentifiable pieces of creatures, Egyptian washabti, and

Chinese porcelain. There was a sumptuous buffet laid along one wall, with several servants standing by. A string quartet in a shadowy corner began to play Mozart.

Mamoru asked, "Would you care for a bite to eat, Highness? Or would you rather get down to business, and then relax later?"

Sensing her mentor's anxiety, Adele said, "If the food will keep, I'd prefer to get to it, gentlemen."

"Excellent." Mamoru turned to Sir Godfrey. "Shall we repair to the operating theater?"

Operating theater, Adele thought with unnerved excitement. An anatomy lesson, perhaps? How gothic. And what to think of a man with an operating theater in his own home?

Sir Godfrey took a deep breath and extended his arm. Leaving the soft strings behind, they went through a door and down a staircase. With each creaking wooden step, Adele felt a gruesome chill. She pictured the taxidermied scenes she might see below with glass-eyed vampires frozen in permanent, terrible melodramas. Another door led to an open room, this one with high ceilings and hissing gas jet flames in sconces that provided light. Two chairs stood against the wall. Adele felt hot, but there was something strange about the heat. Her heart began to flutter and she flexed her hands.

Mamoru said, "Are you unwell, Highness?"

"No." Adele shook her head and breathed out heavily. The warmth piled up inside her. It was reminiscent of Canterbury. She smiled at the comforting throb in her chest. "It's the . . . the heat. I'm fine."

Mamoru and Sir Godfrey exchanged glances, and the teacher nodded to his old colleague before the surgeon moved to the middle of the room where there was a long table covered with a sheet. Without fanfare, he reached out and yanked the sheet away to reveal a vampire strapped to the table. The creature gnashed his teeth at Sir Godfrey, who immediately stepped back.

Adele reached for the hilt of her Fahrenheit dagger beneath her robe. Mamoru stepped in front of her.

"No, Highness. The creature is quite secure."

Adele stared at the growling vampire and felt the cold of London stiffen her joints. She could smell the stink of the Thames River lapping over piles of bodies and saw the fresh wash of blood spreading across the floors of Buckingham Palace. She heard the screams of the people of Reiz as Flay's packs descended on them in the dark.

Then a calming warmth spread through her again, forcing the darkness aside. She took a deep breath, inhaling the saltiness of the desert around them. Her feet were firmly planted on the floor, with the sensation that they were almost sinking into sand. Her heartbeat slowed.

The two men stared at Adele. She nodded for the program to continue and asked, "Where did this thing come from?"

"Oh, we occasionally run across them," Sir Godfrey began casually. "Blown off course. Lost. Weak. I believe this particular chap came from a friend in Constantinople."

Adele added, "Fortunately, he does look weak. And the heat is making him sluggish. Otherwise, I'm not sure your bindings would hold him." She studied the wide-eyed beast. It was naked, but it wasn't one of the ferals that *civilized* vampires used as trackers and killers, those fearsome beasts called hunters. The creature's helplessness was pathetic, but Adele had seen too much vampire brutality to feel a great deal of sympathy. The thing hissed, and Adele understood it on some level. She had the uncanny ability to decipher vampires' incomprehensible language, through no special study of her own, a fact she had told Mamoru, but no other, upon her return from the north.

Her teacher asked, "Can you understand what it's saying?"

"He's angry." Adele stated the obvious. Perhaps that was the reason for this impromptu visit—a test of her language skills.

"Is that all?"

"Technically, no. He's threatening to kill Sir Godfrey; in fact, to kill all of us. He's being quite rude and explicit."

"Remarkable," Sir Godfrey exclaimed. "I've made a detailed study of their language myself, wrote a dictionary, yet I've only ascertained a few words here and there."

Mamoru nodded with pride at his student. "Yes, I've studied it for over a decade as well. Yet it appears we're only novices, Sir Godfrey. You can't speak their language, can you, Adele?"

"I've never tried. I can't emulate the hissing. I don't know if any human could."

"Amazing, simply amazing." Sir Godfrey shook his head. He put a hand on the vampire's chest and leaned on it casually as the creature snapped the air, his jaw clacking loudly while spittle flew. "Your Highness, I believe you have a Fahrenheit blade on your person. May I borrow it to perform an experiment?"

She pulled the weapon from her robe. "This blade is a dangerous thing. Are you familiar with them?"

"I am, Highness. I have experimented with Fahrenheit scalpels. But I have none here."

Adele presented the weapon to the surgeon and then retreated across the room at his urging. Sir Godfrey slowly slid the khukri from its ceremonial scabbard, revealing the glowing blade.

He whistled. "It's beautiful."

"Thank you. It was my mother's." Adele stood next to Mamoru, watching her precious dagger in the hands of a stranger. Her teacher handed her several crystals. "What are these?"

"Talismans. Similar to the pendant I gave you before your trip to the north. Hold them in your hands for protection."

The stones felt hot and heavy.

"I say, what's the creature going on about now?" Sir Godfrey was waving the searing dagger a few inches from the snarling vampire's face, resting his other hand on the edge of the table.

"Nothing new," Adele replied. "He still wants to kill you. And then us. And then everyone else he can find."

Sir Godfrey chuckled until the band holding the vampire's chest and arms suddenly released. A long clawed arm snapped up and slammed into the man's head. The old surgeon dropped suddenly behind the table as the vampire sat up and shredded the bonds that held his legs. The naked vampire rose on the operating table with a screech of triumph, calling out how he would now slaughter everyone. The vampire's cold eyes found the old man on the ground.

"Good God!" Mamoru shouted. "Stop him!"

"Over here!" Adele shouted to bring the creature's attention on her.

The vampire's head snapped around, and his blue stare locked on her. The creature immediately lunged, so Adele reacted. Something in her mind snapped, and his muscles twitched slowly, like a moving stereoscope show. Each instant of the creature's attack was another click, another lantern slide. The thing leapt from the table in what should have been a flash of catlike speed, but he seemed slowed, as if swimming through paste. The vampire's face grew long with shock.

Adele felt the crystals burning her hand. Waves of shimmering air and smokelike tendrils rose around her from the earth. Something rumbled under the pale green tiles, straining to burst up into the room. Her hands lifted, the air around them boiling with swelling vapors. Pulses of heat circled her, spiraling into her and then out in waves.

The vampire screamed, even while it came forward, with an agony that his kind rarely felt. His skin began to bubble and heat; boils rose and popped. The creature tumbled through the air, slamming into Adele and carrying both of them to the floor. The vampire twitched in the palsy of death and fell still.

Mamoru instantly dragged the scorched vampire away from Adele. Her eyelids fluttered, her eyes darting beneath as if caught in the throes of dream sleep. He pressed a hand against her forehead. She was warm, but not feverish. He pried the crystals from her clenched fists and pocketed the steaming stones.

Sir Godfrey joined him quickly. "How is she?"

"Bring cool water."

"I've never seen anything like it." Sir Godfrey went to a sideboard where sat a pitcher and a cloth, eyeing the dead vampire as he stepped around its blistered corpse. He signaled into the mirror on the wall, letting the two women on the other side know that the princess was well.

"There's never *been* anything like it." Mamoru took the pitcher and draped a cool cloth on Adele's forehead. "That's the point."

"Lucky for me, I'd say. Was my performance convincing? Did I fall to the floor like a helpless old man in danger? I rather felt like a helpless old man when that monster looked at me."

"I told you that you'd be safe. So close to the rift under the Great Pyramid, the crystals acted as a catalyst. Plus, given her natural response to a person in danger, she simply acted. She couldn't have stopped if she'd wished it. From the stories she told me about her experiences in the north, I suspected I could bring this out of her."

There was a click, and a panel opened in the wall. Two women started out. Nzingu, the tall Zulu in a white satin gown, stared with intensity at the dead vampire. And Sanah, the Persian cloaked in a black burqa, looked at the supine figure of her former theater companion with concern. Mamoru shook his head for them to stay hidden in case Adele was more aware than she appeared. He wasn't ready for her to meet the entire cabal yet.

Sir Godfrey shoved the vampire's body with his well-shined shoe. "Seems completely dead! Still, I should decapitate him to be sure. I'll anatomize him to ascertain the physiological damage. Then I'll add him to the collection." There was a gleam of anticipation in his gaze.

Ignoring him, Mamoru wet the cloth on Adele's forehead again and hummed a soothing tune he remembered his wife singing to their baby.

—∿—

Adele saw dark plaster and a wooden ceiling swim into view, and she wondered where she was. A few flicks of her eyes showed a crimson brocade fabric next to her head, and a room full of books. Her fingers played over a soft blanket at her waist. She saw Mamoru start up from an armchair at her feet. His concerned gaze swept over her.

"Highness, you're awake." He took her wrist and fumbled for a pulse as she sat up on the plush sofa in the dimly lit library. "You should remain still until Sir Godfrey can examine you."

"I'm fine." Then a memory washed over Adele and she gasped. She saw a vampire tearing free from its bindings and leaping for the poor white-haired surgeon. "Sir Godfrey! Oh God! How is he?"

"He's perfectly well," the teacher said as he stared deeply into her left eye, then her right. "Thanks to you. How do you feel?"

The princess exhaled with relief and then realized she felt remarkably fine. "I'm actually very well, if a bit tired." She looked at her hands. They looked incredibly normal. Just the delicate fingers of a young woman. But it seemed as if there should be something special about them.

Mamoru sat back and observed her with crossed arms.

She asked, "What did I do? It's hard to remember."

"I don't know. I need to learn more myself."

"Did you see me? I remember fire and smoke around me."

Mamoru stared deeply at her. "No. I saw nothing around you."

"What is it?" Adele asked. "What is happening to me?"

"Be patient, Highness. You must be patient."

"But you have to help me. I told you about my experiences in the north. Now this."

Mamoru took her hand gently and said without hesitation, "I ask you to trust me. This cannot be rushed. We are treading in new fields. I must study these events. Soon, I will come to you with information. But to tell you something wrong would be worse than telling you nothing. Please, a little more time and I will have answers for you."

Adele nodded, but she was deep in thought, trying to recall more details of the night. It was hazy, but she certainly remembered reaching out to the vampire and calling a fire that swept over the creature. She remembered a somewhat similar powerful physical and emotional epiphany she had experienced in Canterbury. But more, she recalled Edinburgh and how she had burned Gareth with a power she didn't understand. And then she had burned Flay, sending the creature to her death over the side of Prince Cesare's wretched airship with a cross looped around her neck, a cross charged with some strange power that Adele could command. But now she had destroyed a vampire with only her hands. No, not even her hands; she hadn't come near the creature.

The door across the library opened and Sir Godfrey entered. He wore a heavy leather apron stained with old blood and flecked with fresh bits of something foul. He was smiling, unharmed, and whistling cheerfully.

"Ah!" he exclaimed at seeing Adele sitting. "Highness, I am gratified to see you up. How do you feel?"

"A trifle warm, but never better, Doctor. How are you?"

"Splendid. I must thank you for saving my life."

Adele smiled at the old gentleman. "I wish I could tell you I knew how I did it."

Sir Godfrey crossed the floor and started to take her wrist. Mamoru rose and indicated his gruesome apron. "Oh my. Terribly sorry. Hardly appropriate attire. I lose myself when anatomizing." He slipped it off and tossed it out in the hallway.

Adele raised her eyebrows and was grateful she wasn't his maid.

Sir Godfrey returned to the princess. "Marvelous. No fever. Pulse is steady and remarkably low. You are in excellent condition. Highness, won't you please eat something, if you're so inclined?" He stepped to the sumptuous buffet, now devoid of servants.

Adele joined him. She began to fill a plate, surprised she had an appetite after all the excitement.

Sir Godfrey reached into his coat, handing her the Fahrenheit dagger. "I return this to you none the worse for wear."

Mamoru stood to one side, watching the princess intently for signs of weakness or anything unusual. They took their seats at the grand table. "Sir Godfrey, what can you tell us about the creature?"

The old surgeon cut into a dripping pink rack of meat. "Quite dead, old boy. And more besides, virtually cooked through. Unlike my lamb here. Internal organs charred beyond repair."

Adele looked instantly at Mamoru with surprise, but he smiled serenely, deflecting her renewed questions. He didn't have answers, his eyes told her. Yet.

He said, "If you feel up to traveling, Highness, we should return to Alexandria."

"I feel perfectly fine." She finished eating a stuffed grape leaf. Even her weariness had been fleeting. She now felt energized.

"Good. We'll be back very late and you have a full schedule tomorrow, so make sure you stay in and go to sleep at a reasonable hour."

The princess exhaled in dismay. "After this sort of event, I have to attend meetings and receptions? How ordinary."

"That is one thing that you are not," Sir Godfrey said.

"Quite so." Mamoru raised a cautionary hand. "Needless to say, what occurred in this house stays among we three."

Adele said, "Do you think I'm channeling some power from the crystals?"

Her teacher raised his eyebrows in warning. "I told you, Highness. It will take time. In the interim, you must live your life as before, difficult as it may be given your natural enthusiasms. Time alone will unfold your future."

"Well, I suppose time is what I have." Adele stood and pushed her mother's dagger into the belt under her robe.

CHAPTER 7

THE GRAND DAMES of the Phoenix Society had broken into post-lunch clutches inside the splendor of the Delhi Room in Victoria Palace in Alexandria. Gowns rustled. Diamonds and rubies sparkled. Champagne tipped. Heads with fantastic feathered hats and fine embroidered scarves tilted with discreet laughter. Hushed, droll voices droned as conversation topics competed between discussions of failed dinner parties and horrific country weekends on the Red Sea, with eyes darting to ensure the targets of the excoriations weren't within earshot.

Princess Adele remained in her seat on the dais between two matronly monoliths of society. Servants cleared dishes with the residue of a remarkably mediocre meal as she pretended to study sketches of the Monument to Our Beloved War Dead. The planned bronze cenotaph was gigantic, gaudy, and inelegant. It was also quite forward-thinking, as the coming war had not yet begun. It strove to overawe the viewer's emotions with sheer mass and melodrama, presenting heroic Equatorian men firing rifles, cradling wounded comrades, saying good-bye to sweethearts, and, in one tableau, several men holding a struggling vampire while another soldier impaled the creature with his bayonet. Adele toyed with the idea of making sure the vampire resembled Cesare.

Lady Tahir, the chairwoman of the Phoenix Society, cleared her throat. "Do you approve of our design, Your Highness?"

"Hm?" Adele was shaken from her memories of the events in Giza the night before. "Oh yes. It's . . . monumental."

"Yes, we agree," cooed Mrs. General Alfred Cornwell (ret.). "My husband, General Alfred Cornwell, retired, personally vetted the soldiers' appearances."

"They are very military."

"Your Highness"—Lady Tahir indicated the monument tableau with the soldier and his sweetheart—"in this scene, which I suggested to the sculptor—"

"Who is?"

"None other than Tomas Chaudry, the man who reimagined the façades at Petra."

"Oh, him," Adele said flatly. "Yes, those remarkable old ruins were long overdue for a sprucing up."

"Exactly! Anyway, as I was saying, I suggested this touching scene of a proper Equatorian lady bidding adieu to her beloved husband as he departs for the vampire front."

"Stirring," Adele lied.

"Thank you, Your Highness." Lady Tahir chuckled with great self-satisfaction. "You may be even more pleased when you note that the soldier's visage is based on your own betrothed, Senator Clark."

"What!" Adele jerked the sketch closer and, with a shock, saw the resemblance. She remembered not to scowl and grunt, and instead smiled politely. "I see. Well, it is pleasing to imagine him going off to war."

"We thought," said Mrs. General Alfred Cornwell (ret.), with jealous emphasis on the *we*, "it an appropriate honor to Senator Clark as our gallant ally and soon-to-be prince regent."

Across the room, the Phoenix Society began to churn from some disturbance. The two chairwomen at the dais lifted their heads to study the alarming activity. The buzz of female voices was undercut by a deep male sound that came closer and closer as a figure moved through the throng.

Only when the words, "Ladies, if you will make a lane, please!" penetrated the air did Adele rise to her feet with a sickening stomach.

Senator Clark appeared from among the dowagers like an explorer cutting his way through an overgrown couture jungle. Hat in hand, he was smiling generously as he nodded at each kind word and gently grasped each gloved hand that was extended his way. But his eyes were hot with impatience.

"This is most irregular," Lady Tahir murmured. "He was not invited."

Adele knew sadly that the likelihood of these matrons throwing him out was slim. When his eyes locked on her, she felt angry, for the first time, that proper protocol wasn't being observed and wasn't serving as her protector.

The senator finally reached the long white-clothed table where Adele stood. He bowed properly, sweeping his hat to the floor before him.

"Your Highness," he said. "How delightful to see you."

"Senator," she intoned. "This is an unexpected . . . well, it's unexpected."

"Yes, indeed. That's how I operate. Strike fast when they least expect it." He nodded to Lady Tahir and Mrs. General Alfred Cornwell (ret.). "Ladies."

Adele held up the monument sketch. "Alas, I am quite occupied. You should see my secretary for an appointment."

Clark's smile twitched. "I'm a bit fatigued fighting through the skirmish lines of your staff. It was hard enough just finding out you were here. I was hoping we might have a stroll and a few words."

Adele sat purposefully. "You may have a few words."

"Not here. I'd appreciate a moment in private." His smile twitched harder and he glanced at the matrons again. "If you ladies don't mind."

"Oh no," Lady Tahir bubbled girlishly. "Not at all, Senator Clark."

Adele glanced coldly at her, then took a deep breath. "Very well, Senator."

"Call me Miles."

"Why would I call you that?"

"It's my name."

"Really? I didn't realize you had a first name, only a title." Adele rose slowly and started down the table. Stepping off the dais, she headed for a side door and heard a murmur of excitement as she pushed through into the kitchen. By then, it was too late to turn back, and she didn't care anyway.

The serving staff was relaxing, smoking cigarettes and chatting. Most of the men had removed their tuxedo jackets, while some of the women sported bare feet instead of shoes under their long skirts. They all froze in shock at the appearance of Princess Adele and, on her heel, the uniformed Senator Clark. Stubbing out their smokes, they stood at attention.

"Sorry to interrupt," Adele said to the wide-eyed staff. "Please, stay. This won't take long." She gave Senator Clark an impatient gaze, her arms crossed over her breasts.

He laughed uncomfortably. "I felt it was time you and I had a chat, face-to-face. It is our wedding, after all."

She stared silently.

"It's just that we need to make a decision. You do understand the stakes, don't you? How close are you to being recovered?"

"Thank you for caring."

Clark narrowed his eyes. "Let's stop pussy-footing around, Adele. You're fine. You're traipsing around at official lunches and garden parties and such. Hell, it won't take any more time or effort to get to the altar and say *I do*."

"Don't curse at me. And what the hell do you know about how I'm feeling?"

"You can only play this game for so long. Look, I'm sure it was bad up there—"

"The worst part was when you shot me."

He rolled his eyes. "We are way behind schedule. We are losing the summer. Do you have any idea what will happen if we commit troops to North America and Europe in the fall and winter? We lose all our advantage. This delay is going to cost lives."

From a purely strategic level, Adele knew he was right. Her stiff shoulders dropped a bit; she hated his tone, but heard his logic. She didn't want to put the men of her army, or her American allies for that matter, at greater risk. If this wedding was inevitable, perhaps it was time to end the stall and set a date.

Clark seemed to sense her crumbling façade, so he continued, "You've got huge fleets gathered at Gibraltar and Aden, and we've got ours at Havana and Vera Cruz. They're waiting for the word to head north and start operations. We've got to have a target date. There's no point sending airships in harm's way to strike the food source without ground troops ready to follow up and seize territory. And we can't coordinate it all until the alliance is finalized."

Adele nodded. "I know. I understand what you're—" She paused. "What did you say? Strike the food source?"

"That's phase one."

"What do you mean by 'food source'?"

He looked at her with confusion. "You know what their food source is. You more than anyone."

Adele felt a chill. "You mean humans? You're going to attack the humans in the north?"

"Attack them? No, that implies they're an enemy. I'd say we're going to slaughter them. Like cattle. It's a common strategy in war throughout history; deprive your enemy of food. Burn their crops. Drive off their herds. It's an elegant solution, if I do say so myself. We'll gas and firebomb the human population centers, driving the vampires out in search of food. We then occupy, fortify, and defend. As we march northward, this constant pressure will create competition for food among the vampires and destabilize the clans. Then we just pick them apart." Senator Clark smiled, waiting for his fiancée to praise his military genius.

"No." Blood drained from Adele, and she had to steady herself. "No. You can't do that. They're people."

"They're animals. So what we need to do is set the date for the wedding and then—"

"I said no! Does my father know about this?"

Clark appeared more irritated, no doubt because he had to coddle an emotional girl. "Of course he knows about the war plans." He checked his pocket watch. "In fact, this chatter is making me late for a planning session with the emperor. So I can tell your father we're in agreement?"

Adele reached out and seized the front of his blue tunic, causing the senator to rear back in shock. "You can tell my father that I wouldn't marry you now, even if you weren't a murderous, filthy reptile! You might be too stupid to understand, but I know he believes what I've said about the northern humans."

Clark angrily slapped her hand away. "Everybody knows what you said about those creatures in the north. We all saw your papers and reports. But it doesn't matter, because everybody also knows that you're a histrionic lunatic. Your opinion means nothing."

Adele glared at him. She couldn't feel her fingers or feet, and her face flushed with rage. She stood breathing hard for several long minutes. Clark went from vicious to slightly worried, watching her for signs of a nervous breakdown.

Finally she looked him in the eye. "We'll see. We'll see how my opinion matters."

Adele slammed out though the door and surged past the Phoenix ladies, whose heavily powdered faces were frozen in shock after overhearing much of the unpleasant exchange between their future loving rulers.

—◦◦◦—

Word spread rapidly through the palace that something had happened. Princess Adele left her staff behind at the Delhi Room in the east wing. Messages flew through pneumatic tubes clanking into in-baskets across Victoria Palace. Retainers and footmen raced through corridors to intercept the princess as if she were a ship torn loose from her moorings and endangering all other ships in the harbor.

The princess crossed the central atrium of the palace and turned up the wide stairs to the upper floors. Heads turned to watch. Then Senator Clark passed too, with a face like a thundercloud. He took the stairs three at a time.

Adele saw the great door of her father's council chamber at the far end of the hall. A group of soldiers standing outside suddenly came to attention at the sight of the princess. Some twenty yards from the door, Adele's secretary sprinted from a side corridor, looking both ways and expelling her breath with enormous relief at intercepting the princess.

"Your Highness," the secretary said pleasantly, but out of breath, "may I help you?"

Adele surged past without a glance. She marched to the soldiers—imperial marines—who blocked the door.

"Step aside, please."

A marine, Persian by the look of him, responded, "I fear I cannot. Entrance is forbidden by His Majesty Emperor Constantine."

"I am his daughter."

"Yes, Your Highness." The marine commander's eyes shot over her head to the approaching secretary and Senator Clark, seeking guidance or support.

"What is wrong with you?" Clark snarled as he neared. "Stop it, Adele. You're only making a fool of yourself."

She whirled. "I won't let you kill thousands, hundreds of thousands of innocent people! The vampires call you a butcher, and that's exactly what you are."

Adele's secretary stood with her hand at her mouth. The crowd behind her was aghast.

Clark laughed and stepped past Adele. Flashing a quick salute to the marine commander, he reached for the ornate door handle and pushed it open. He turned to give Adele a nasty grin. "If you'll excuse me, the emperor is expecting me. Good luck with your agenda."

As the American stepped inside, Adele caught a glimpse of her father and Lord Kelvin before the door shut with an echoing click.

She said to the marine commander, "Will you please send word to my father to tell him that I'm out here?"

"I am not allowed to interrupt His Majesty. But if you command it, I will do so."

Adele had to make her voice heard. She was dismayed that all her reports about the state of the north had been ignored. She couldn't allow her nation to be party to a barbaric strategy. Equatorians couldn't participate in slaughtering the northern humans as if they were merely trampling a field of barley. The thought of Equatorian airships firebombing Edinburgh and killing all the people who had been so good to her made her sick. The thought that Senator Clark had ready access to the emperor while she, his only daughter, was held up in the corridor like some low-level office-seeker infuriated her.

"Highness?"

Adele snapped around with a ready retort, but she saw Colonel Mehmet Anhalt, the commander of her household troops, the White Guard. He stood calmly before the crowd.

The colonel moved quickly to her side, announcing, "I have been searching for you. I need your attention in a matter of grave importance. Can you please accompany me?"

"What matter?"

He replied in a quiet, but assured voice. It was unlikely that anyone else could hear him. "Highness, you must withdraw. You can do no good here. You will accomplish nothing by embarrassing His Majesty or endangering these marines. They are bound not to allow you to enter, but if they dare lay hands on you, their careers are through."

"My father has to hear what I have to say. He is planning a great tragedy."

"He has heard you. I know this to be a fact. I beg you to hear me. This is a disaster for you if you push any further."

Anhalt was sincere, yet firm. His warm, dark eyes burrowed into her with an intensity that belied his calm voice and woke her to reason.

It took everything she had to master her fury. Only Colonel Anhalt could have delivered this message to her. She finally nodded with formality. "Very well." The words tore through her.

The colonel said, "Thank you, Your Highness." He saluted the marine. "Captain Eskandari, please give the emperor Her Highness's regrets, but she has been called away."

"Yes sir."

Anhalt extended an arm away from the council chamber. "If you please, Highness. Thank you for your help."

As Adele took Anhalt's arm, the crowd parted for her, the colonel, and her secretary. Despite his kind bluff, no one was fooled. They watched Princess Adele withdraw, defeated, from the field. Yet, for many, there was also a new respect for the girl's intensity and passion. She had stood up to the American who seemed to want to run the Empire.

CHAPTER 8

"My wedding date has come and gone, much to the detriment of the war effort, not to mention my personal inconvenience and embarrassment!" The council chamber could hardly contain Senator Clark's foul temper. Only the presence of the emperor kept him civil. "I want a new wedding date set. I want it written down and agreed to. And it needs to happen now or we lose any hope of a weather advantage up north. All this dillydallying jeopardizes the war—if you want to win, that is. I'll not be held back by a hesitant bride!"

Lord Kelvin, the prime minister, replied, "I understand your eagerness, Senator. But after the ordeal suffered by Her Imperial Highness Princess Adele—"

"Good God yes!" Clark snarled. "I know all about the horrific ordeal suffered by the fragile princess. After all, I was the one who rescued her from Edinburgh. But by God! Enough is e-damn-nough! Any more dithering from the court will endanger the alliance. I have a war to start!" He regarded the emperor, who was sitting quietly, absorbing the various arguments. "My apologies, Your Majesty, but you need to know where we all stand. Reports are coming in from Panama that there have been attacks in Philadelphia and Charleston. The New York clan is stealing the march on us. We should be in Paris by now. We should be in Washington and St. Louis. If we wait much later we will bog down in southern France and in the Ohio Valley this winter."

As Clark grew hotter, Kelvin iced over and his words became slow. "His Imperial Majesty Emperor Constantine the Second is well aware of the views of all sides, sir. You surely appreciate that he is balancing the needs of state with family."

Clark's eyes narrowed and he stared directly at the prime minister. "There are no needs of family compared to those of state."

The prime minister didn't move. "His Imperial Majesty Emperor Const—"

"For crying out loud!" the senator bellowed. "Maybe if you didn't have to spout a ten-mile title every time you opened your mouth, I'd be your emperor by now!"

"My *emperor?*" Kelvin actually started, then laughed, perhaps for the third time in his adult life. "You will not be endowed with the title of emperor. You will, of course, be prince regent to Her Imperial Majesty Empress Adele the First."

Clark stared at the reedy bureaucrat, flexing his hands into fists, clearly working through the long-term implications of murdering the Equatorian prime minister, but then he turned his attention back to the emperor, the man whose opinion was the sole one that mattered.

Emperor Constantine sighed loudly and shifted in his chair. Despite his crisp and elegant uniform, he seemed fatigued. Lord Kelvin remained motionless at the emperor's right. The polished table reflected the gaslight and the four men around it.

Laurence Randolph, Lord Aden, crossed his arms thoughtfully. "Perhaps it would be best to wait until next year."

"By all means!" Clark scowled savagely and refused to face the Equatorian lord. "They know we're coming. Let's give them another year to fortify."

"Fortify?" Aden mocked. "Come now, Senator. Vampires don't fortify. They don't even use tools, according to all the reports I've read."

With a cold glare, the American turned to him. "I didn't know you had purchased the Imperial War College, Lord Aden. I don't have time to lecture you on vampire warfare, but I'm telling you that giving the clans another year is a mistake of apocalyptic proportions. I've bloodied them. They obviously are not sitting idle hoping it will all blow over. Aside from shoring up their own defenses, they'll have a year to destroy the port facilities in New Orleans, Savannah, and Marseilles that we need to move our seaborne heavy equipment and massive troop deployments into North America and Europe. Without those ports, we'll have to drop men into vampire territory with limited artillery, and that's a recipe for disaster. Even better, maybe there will be a nice cold snap so the vampire packs can sail down to Gibraltar or Havana, or even here in Alexandria."

Lord Aden prepared to speak again, but Clark leapt to his feet and slammed his fist on the table with a crack that echoed throughout the chamber. "No, dammit! We have no choice. War! Now!"

The emperor pursed his lips and looked down. His once-vigorous face looked aged, aided by his thinning hair and greying sideburns, and his left eye drooped from an old war wound.

The American pressed on. "Your daughter, sir, is standing in the way. The decision we face is not about a marriage or a young girl's emotional state. It's about the future of our people. I will win this war for you, and there is only one choice to be made."

"What would you have, Senator?" Constantine murmured, and held up a silencing hand when Lord Kelvin stirred.

Clark said, "Schedule the wedding, Majesty. Now. It must happen within the week. We must start the offensive or a lot of boys will die who shouldn't have."

Kelvin spoke quickly before the emperor could quiet him with another gesture. "That simply cannot happen, Your Majesty. The planning is so far behind, we—"

"Stop," Emperor Constantine whispered. "The senator is correct. Adele must conform."

Lord Aden stood. "Sire, if I may."

"No," said the emperor decisively. "Stay quiet, if you please, Lord Aden." He settled his dark-rimmed eyes on the bearded American. "Two weeks, Senator? Is that a satisfactory time to you?"

Clark nodded. "Yes, Your Majesty. That'll do."

Constantine lifted a finger at the prime minister. "See to it. I want a wedding in two weeks without fail."

"As you will, Majesty."

"Good. Senator, tomorrow we will begin to finalize the war plans so dispatches can be sent to America in due course."

Clark saluted with one hand while resting the other on the hilt of his Fahrenheit saber.

Lord Kelvin dutifully collected his papers. "I will have Her Imperial Highness Princess Adele's household informed of the schedule."

"No." Emperor Constantine rose slowly. "I will tell her, personally. Good day, gentlemen."

Kelvin and Aden bowed to the departing emperor. When the teak door clicked shut, Kelvin straightened to see Senator Clark's grinning face.

The American clapped a sturdy hand on Kelvin's narrow shoulders. "Book the hall, Mr. Prime Minister. I'll see you at the reception." Clark's boisterous laughter echoed as he strode away.

The two Equatorian gentlemen watched after their esteemed guest, embarrassed by his behavior and sad that either of them had to witness such a barbaric performance. They paused a long moment in case he should stomp back in and make further pronouncements, but thankfully there was only the sound of fading footfalls.

Lord Aden cleared his throat. "Well, he's a hot one."

"Yes. Bit too." The prime minister adjusted his fez an iota.

"We tried our best." Lord Aden shrugged. "No doubt the theater productions have riled him. It must be difficult to take second place to that heroic Greyfriar."

"Yes, but instead of driving him away, it seems to have made him more eager to possess the princess and beat the Greyfriar out of her."

Lord Aden rubbed his sharp jawline and took out his gold cigarette case, removing a hand-rolled Turkish cigarette. Kelvin politely declined. Aden lit the cigarette and blew aromatic smoke away from his friend. "What shall you do? How do you stop the wedding? How do you keep that American buffoon off the throne?"

"I cannot stop the wedding now. But I must insure against the insanity of Clark becoming emperor. That way, if something unfortunate should happen to Adele, Prince Simon would succeed to the throne. I fear he may be our best hope now. True Equatoria must be preserved." Kelvin muttered as if he didn't know anyone else was in the room. "This war is such a terrible mistake. But I accept the burden of guiding the Empire past these dire times."

—∽∾∽—

"Come en garde in fifth position, please."

"Just attack. I'm not in the mood for drills."

Mamoru lifted his fencing mask and looked askance at Princess Adele, who stood five yards in front of him. They both wore traditional white fencing togs, but that was where the traditional fencing ended in this session. Adele stood fully open, with her foil pointed at the mat.

Mamoru was in classic stance. "Would you prefer a different weapon? Sabers? Épée? Or would you prefer kendo practice?"

"I would prefer you simply attack."

"You are content with your grasp of fundamentals, then?"

"Yes." But still Mamoru remained in his stance, so Adele charged. Mamoru dropped his mask and parried. He backpedaled as the princess lunged. She was fast, incredibly fast. But she had become predictable. Mamoru dueled a few swift exchanges until he knew her upcoming maneuver, and sure enough, Adele raised her arm to strike down on him. He easily slipped his blade along hers, deflecting her point and delivering a touch to her midsection. For good measure, the samurai drew back an inch, locked up her blade, and twisted. The foil flew from Adele's gloved right hand, somersaulted across the practice room, and clanged to the floor.

Adele held her arms out at her sides in exasperation. "That was uncalled-for. You had the touch already."

The Japanese man pulled off his mask angrily. "If you'd rather not fence, I understand. But if you want me to teach you, then learn!"

"What does this foolishness matter?" The princess yanked the mask from her head. Her anger still burned hot from Clark's brutal words about culling innocents. She knew it was her anger fueling her sharp tone, but she couldn't stop it. "I need to know real fighting, not gentleman's play."

"If that last bout had been real, you'd be defenseless and dead."

"I need to know what I can do to vampires. We should be practicing that."

"I have already explained it will take time. To rush now is foolishness, and could invite dangerous consequences. I will not risk your life."

The young woman retrieved her foil, made a couple of angry swipes in the air, and replaced her headgear. "Again."

"Come en garde in five."

The princess stood in front of him, open stanced and waiting.

"This is not an alley in the Turkish Quarter!" Mamoru snapped.

"Nor a town home in Giza," she pointed out. "I'm ready. Come again!"

Mamoru slid his mask over his face and came en garde. After a few seconds of blurring action, Adele was on the ground with the point of his foil against her back.

She rolled over and jumped to her feet. "Again."

This time she was disarmed and the samurai crashed the bell of his sword against her mask, knocking her to her knees. She rose.

"Again."

He stood motionless until she lunged. His blade barely flicked, parrying her point a few inches from his head, and he drove home, exploding against her shoulder until his foil bowed nearly in half. Adele jolted back and dropped hard to the mat.

Mamoru came en garde in five with leisurely deliberateness. "Again?"

The princess sat up slowly, rubbing her shoulder. "How can this help? Vampires don't fence. They don't follow rules."

"You're not a vampire. Your world has rules. You must master the fundamentals first. Know the basics from top to bottom. Then, when your world becomes confused, you have a foundation to return to. Once you learn to come en garde in five, you can improvise as you wish, but you can always come back to it when you need it."

Adele dropped her mask to the ground and scrubbed through her curly auburn hair. "I'm running out of time. The war is here!" Her anger dissipated suddenly as she saw his face harden. She wasn't angry with Mamoru, just herself and her inability to be effective, in any sense. "I'm sorry, Mamoru."

"There is much to do, I grant you, Your Highness." He reached down and brought her to her feet. "I am here to help you."

"I know. Thank you. You're the only one who is helping. I shouldn't be taking my frustration out on you."

He handed her a towel. "You have much on your mind. You are just beginning to discover your true nature, and you're impatient. Understandably."

The door across the chamber flew open, and Adele's maid, Zarina, raced in. "Oh! Highness! There you are!"

"What is it?"

Mamoru noted how quickly her tone of voice changed from a frustrated young woman to one who possessed the firm steel of command.

The maid curtsied while nearly hyperventilating. "Your father. The emperor. He's looking for you. His Majesty came to your chambers. He asked me where you were. He talked to me!"

Adele smiled gently and took the poor girl's hand. "And what did you tell him?"

"I told him . . . His Majesty . . . the emperor . . . I wasn't sure but I thought you had fencing practice with Master Mamoru. Then I ran to tell you."

"He's coming? He must've heard I tried to see him." Adele pondered whether this was a visit of consultation or, more likely, of anger. Surely her father wouldn't come personally just to berate her for being impulsive. That's what Lord Kelvin was for. "Did he seem upset?"

"Upset? No." Zarina paused in confusion, as if the idea of the emperor having human emotions was inconceivable. She gasped. "Why? Could he be upset? Should I not have come?"

"No, no. You did fine. Thank you."

"Ah, there you are, Adele."

All three turned to see Emperor Constantine enter. Mamoru and the maid dropped to one knee. Adele rarely saw her father except at state occasions, so it was jarring for her to watch him striding across the practice mat in his splendid uniform. He seemed terribly out of place.

The emperor inclined his head to Mamoru. "I would speak with Ade—with my daughter."

The samurai bowed deeply. He saluted Adele with his foil, replaced the sword and mask in the wall rack, and walked from the room as the maid genuflected out, never turning her back on the royal pair.

Even before the door closed, the emperor gave a wan smile and reached for Adele's sword. "How was practice today?"

"Not as well as I'd hoped."

Constantine nodded without meeting his daughter's eyes. "Hmm. Yes. Mamoru is the finest swordsman I've ever seen. Western. Asian. Any style."

Adele massaged her aching shoulder. "Certainly the best I've seen today."

"Yes. Quite." Constantine laughed.

Adele smiled with relief at her father's laughter. It was something she hadn't heard in years, and it was surprisingly boyish. He didn't seem to be on the mission of an executioner. Then there was a long silence as the emperor pretended to be fascinated by the foil's heft and balance. Adele waited patiently, then nervously.

Finally she said, "Your Majesty, is there something you'd like to tell me?"

"There's much, Adele." He handed the sword back to her. "You know the delay of your wedding cannot go on forever."

"Yes sir." She braced herself.

"Two weeks."

"Two weeks until the wedding?"

"Yes. Senator Clark makes a persuasive case. The campaign season wanes when we can make ground on the vampires. We dare not delay any longer."

Adele's mind buzzed with arguments. She could make a persuasive case also. She wanted to refuse. Instead she merely said, "I understand."

Constantine tightened his mouth. "I realize you aren't pleased with this, but I know in time you may learn to tolerate Senator Clark, perhaps even love him."

Adele snorted with derision. "Neither of those are possible. He wants a wallflower, a doll to play with as he sees fit. I refuse to accommodate him on those terms."

Constantine remained austere, but not angry. "He has interests of state on his mind. It will keep him very busy."

"And you think I don't? Equatoria means everything to me, and I'll have to watch that obnoxious martinet run it. He cares only for the war, or rather how Equatoria can benefit America's war aims against the vampires."

"Perhaps. But the war must come first, and Senator Clark is the best man for that job."

Adele did not miss his emphasis on gender. Ire bristled within her. "He intends to slaughter the humans in occupied Europe, on the pretext of eliminating the vampires' food supply!"

"Yes, I know."

"You know?" Adele's face reddened and her fists tightened. "Those humans are not animals! Some of them saved my life. They gave me shelter even though it meant their own deaths. They are eking out a living under horrible conditions! They deserve to be liberated! Not murdered because it's convenient for us."

"Adele, you do not understand the complications of war. Sacrifices must be made. That is the nature of war. It is for this reason that Equatoria needs a firm man at the helm."

"You mean a butcher! And you're going to allow him to slaughter innocents in our name!"

"Enough!" Constantine held up a stern hand, his expression rigid, no longer a father, but an emperor. "My decision stands. In time you will understand."

"At least tell me *you* care about the people of the north?" Adele's voice fell to a harsh whisper.

"I read your reports, and naturally I do feel for them, if what you documented was accurate."

"If?" She spat out the word.

"Our objective is to create a future for all those who will be born free people once we are victorious. I foresee no practical way to save the vampire herds without jeopardizing the whole war. As it is, we are late to start and the advantage may swing to the vampires. Drastic measures are called for."

Adele's throat constricted painfully. Her father seemed to be implicating her in the culling of Europe because of her delaying tactics. "They're not herds. They're people."

"Semantics. The war strategy is sound. We can't concern ourselves with minor issues."

"Minor? Clark will run Equatoria into the ground in order to win this war, and he's making decisions that will soil our reputation! Don't you see that? This is wrong, Father. I can't be a party to such a massacre."

"You won't. Any blood will be on my hands, not yours. You need not worry about these things. Instead, you will maintain your daily schedule."

"Which is nothing but frivolity and useless parties."

"Your mother was content enough."

"You think so, do you?" Adele snapped.

The emperor reared back, but then faltered in his anger, as if his daughter spoke some truth. His mouth drew into a grim line. "If you believe so strongly that there is another way, then sway Clark to another tactic. Trust me, a woman has ways of wresting control even if she never steps foot in a war council."

Adele's cheeks flamed red at the indecent proposal her own father was dictating. "Is that how Mother . . . ?" But she couldn't finish her thought.

"She had her duties, and you will have yours."

"Am I to have no say at all in affairs of state?"

"I am emperor and I dictate policy. And Senator Clark will be named commander in chief of allied forces."

"Father, you can't do this. Please. You can't be this man."

There was a long pause as the emperor's regretful gaze held her. "I'm sorry, Adele. Every decent man wants to ensure his daughter is safe and happy. I can do neither." He lifted a hand as if to touch her, but saw her eyes flashing full of anger. He exhaled and dropped his hand to his side, the mantle of emperor settling upon him once more. "The wedding will move forward. You may have free rein over it. Plan it how you will. But in two weeks you will be married and the war will commence. God help us all."

He turned and strode from the room, leaving Adele trembling with fury in his wake. The princess stood alone, pondering nothing. She couldn't think of what to do next. The world swirled around the room.

Adele slowly placed her feet in position, raised her foil, and came en garde in five.

CHAPTER 9

"THE DATE IS set."

Sir Godfrey Randolph wasn't listening. He was too busy studying his colossal bookshelves. His head swiveled left and right, up and down. Mamoru glanced around the leather club chair, expecting some response to the announcement of the social event of the century. Sir Godfrey posed in a smoking jacket in the flickering gaslight, seemingly perplexed by his own books.

"Did you hear me?" the samurai priest asked. "I said the date for Princess Adele's wedding is set."

"Hm? Yes. That's nice."

Mamoru's irritation did not quite make it to his words. "Is there a problem, Sir Godfrey?"

"I'm missing a book."

Mamoru pursed his lips as solicitously as he could. A misplaced book was hardly momentous enough to overshadow his news. However, Sir Godfrey's library was a significant resource—the finest collection of arcane ephemera and spiritualist writings known to exist. It wouldn't do to mismanage it. The former priest from Java brushed nonexistent lint from his gabardine trousers. "It will turn up."

The butler appeared at the door. "Your other guests, effendi."

"Thank you, Majid."

Two women came into the library. Nzingu the Zulu sorcerer wore a fashionable gown of light magenta with a bustle and high collar. Sanah the Persian was swathed in black from head to toe with only her hennaed hands and her onyx-black eyes showing.

"Ladies!" Sir Godfrey kissed their hands with a charming flourish, as though they had come a great distance instead of just the rooms upstairs where they were staying.

Mamoru bowed to the women.

The Zulu woman vigorously drew off her lace gloves, already tired of her ensemble. "Mamoru, is the news from Alexandria what we expected?"

"No doubt," Mamoru said. "Princess Adele's wedding date is set for a fortnight hence."

"Really?" Sir Godfrey exclaimed in surprise. "Two weeks, you say? So soon? Are preparations in place?"

The Japanese man smiled slightly at his comrade's shock. "Many of the more elaborate plans are going by the boards in the interest of alacrity. Foreign dignitaries may not be present in such enormous coveys as the court would have liked. And perhaps there won't be quite so many garish public festivals or displays as originally planned."

"But the Great Clark has spoken," Nzingu said snidely.

"Indeed yes," Mamoru responded. "The calendar drives."

The Zulu stalked the rich carpet with a predator's tread that seemed barely contained by her shimmering silk gown. "So we have a wedding. A wedding night. And then a war. What becomes of the husband at that point? Does he join the troops at the front? Or does he stay here to create both tactics and an heir?"

Sir Godfrey cleared his throat with discomfort while Mamoru's expression clearly exposed his dislike of such rude talk about Princess Adele.

"My point is, Mamoru, how much time will you have with the princess after the ceremony?" Nzingu rolled her eyes at the men's prudish attitude and took up a glass filled with Lebanese wine. She was always a bit of an outsider in the cabal, but tonight she seemed perturbed with everyone. She took a deep breath and looked at Mamoru. "The date grows late, don't you agree?"

"I do. I do not know Senator Clark's agenda, but from what I gather, he intends an ambitious schedule of coordinating the war from here and America. So I predict he will be away frequently. Which is what we hoped, and expected. I think we were all favorably impressed with the princess's actions the other night."

Nzingu downed her wine in a single gulp. "Yes, she blasted a single vampire to death. That's still a far cry from her ultimate goal."

"Yes, it is." Mamoru sighed with frustration at his colleague's argumentativeness. "The princess is receptive to training; in fact, she's straining at the bit. The announcement of the wedding has also left her shaken and looking for something on which to focus her mind. As we all struggle to compile our geomancer reports and begin to craft a map of dragon spines and rifts, I will redouble my efforts to shape the princess."

The Zulu said, "My geomancers have all reported in. I should have the African map compiled within the week."

"Very commendable," the Japanese priest replied dryly.

Sanah added, "I convened most of my geomancers in Qom. I have two in China from whom I have no word. But I expect they will succeed. They are excellent scholars and explorers. However, I fear I will be a bit longer than Nzingu in sorting through my notes."

Sir Godfrey looked up from an inspection of a pile of books in a dark corner. "I have received reports from the American geomancers. Well, most of them. But I've never lost one yet. Unlike my books." He laughed. "The results are voluminous, but I should be able to manage a capital schema at the end of it."

Mamoru saw the three members of his cabal looking at him, expecting a report on his network. He preferred to keep his own counsel on that issue, but he couldn't refuse now. "The European cadre has delivered their readings. Save one."

"Selkirk?" Sanah asked.

"Yes. I haven't made contact with him. But he is not overdue as yet. There are many factors that could account for it—weather, difficulty crossing the Channel."

Sir Godfrey raised a glass of red wine jauntily. "Should we send that Greyfriar fellow to retrieve him?"

"We don't need to retrieve him," Mamoru responded seriously. "I feel certain."

—◦◦◦—

"I have not yet had the opportunity to offer congratulations on your coming nuptials, Your Highness," Mamoru said.

Adele glanced at her teacher with an acerbic squint.

"Or should I instead," he added, "offer condolences?"

It was a warm night, but the Mediterranean breeze made it pleasant. Alexandria was a late-night city; it prided itself on its bustling cafés and bright clubs. It was close to midnight, yet carriages and hansoms—both horse-drawn and powered, spewing yellow smoke—sped along the Rue de France. Taxis waited everywhere for fares needing conveyance to their next night spot.

Adele was again covered in a long robe and veil, well hidden from curious eyes. Many affluent diners in sidewalk cafés and prominent strollers making the nightly promenade would have known the princess on sight. Very few knew Mamoru, dressed in his best black suit and pearl-grey homburg. His walking stick ticked along the pavement, keeping pace with his grey-spatted shoes. He was undeniably handsome, Adele noted, almost regal. He maneuvered the avenues with comfort.

"This is a surprising turn," she said while staring into glittering shop windows at jewelry displays as if this were a normal stroll. Couples passed with much hat tipping and fan fluttering. Their blank polite faces caused Adele to abandon her fear of discovery, even though some of the faces were known to her. Lord So-and-So. Lady Somebody. I-Can't-Quite-Recall Pasha.

"I felt we had issues to discuss that were best done away from the prying ears of the court. And I assumed you have no problem slipping away from the palace for an evening."

"An evening? I could happily slip away for a lifetime."

Mamoru reached into his waistcoat and drew out a thin gold chain.

As he held it up, Adele saw a crystal pendant, a talisman, like the one he had given her before her ill-fated trip to France. The one she had lost to the vampires.

"I would like you to have this," he said.

"Oh, thank you." Adele took it eagerly and felt her hand tingle. She studied its sharp bluish edges. "I feel it. And I taste it. Ice."

The samurai smiled. "Excellent. That crystal is from far to the Arctic north. You are experiencing its nature. As do the best geomancers."

Rather than peppering Mamoru with questions, Adele stayed quiet, inviting him to fill the silence.

He continued, "All humans are geomancers, to some very limited extent. We live on the earth. But most cannot access that knowledge, except perhaps through corollary activities such as prayer or meditation. Vampires have this same connection to the earth, but on an infinitely more sensitive level." Mamoru enfolded her hand that held the crystal with his own. "Geomancy gives us knowledge and weapons to affect vampires. It serves as a focus to assault their heightened senses. Those few with the skills still require tools to manipulate that knowledge. Botany. Crystallography and mineralogy. Chemistry and prayer. These are all paths to awareness and control. Geomancy is not some ancient method of divination. We do not throw sand in the air and study how it falls for a key to the future. We seek to understand and codify the rules that will make these disparate practices into a unified and predictable science. There are a number of us who can already wield this knowledge and power definitely."

Adele asked, "Like your man Selkirk whom I met in London? Won't you tell me about him?"

Mamoru tipped his hat brim to a passing couple. "Selkirk is one of my geomancers. I have a collection of these specialists around the world."

"He could make himself invisible to vampires."

"Yes. A few are such extraordinary adepts, they don't just feel the power of the Earth, they manipulate it. Like saints or mystics of old. Selkirk is the best I've seen. He can use the spines to shield himself from vampire senses."

"Spines? The dragon spines? You mean ley lines?"

"What the old British culture called ley lines are known by many names. In the East, we called them dragon spines. It is the web of the earth. They are proof of the power of creation. My geomancers are mapping the spines and particularly the locations where spines intersect. These intersections are called rifts, and they are places of extraordinary power and sensitivity. Many of these rifts are marked with stone circles from ancient times when our ancestors were more attuned to the earth's power and used it against the great evil of the vampires, or whatever name they called it in their particular locations. Spirits. Ghosts. Djinns. Monsters. All spring from vampires."

"So Selkirk can only hide from vampires on a ley line or a rift?"

"Yes." Mamoru chuckled. "His geomancy is prodigious, but compared to yours, it's nothing. You will walk the rifts like no one else on Earth."

"I will?" Adele stared at her teacher. He was hypnotic. His eyes were clear; his voice was steady. She put a hand to her damp forehead.

"You have nothing to fear," he said softly. "Your education will proceed at your pace."

Excitement surged in her chest. With so much in her life out of her control—both the wedding and Gareth—she craved a path she could follow on her own. She wanted to build something of her own making. This was the knowledge she wanted. This was a key to everything in the world. She didn't know how, but she knew it was so.

Mamoru continued, "This is a secret. Between us. We cannot bear for it to become known. Tell no one. Not your brother. Not your maid. Not your cat. The court would not smile on this education."

"Of course."

Mamoru gave a tight bow. "Your mother would be very proud."

"My mother?" Adele's voice caught.

"I taught her too. She was a most excellent student. A gifted geomancer."

She asked, "And my father?"

"Alas, no. He is of the steel-and-steam school, a consummate technocrat. A magnificent man to be sure, but his vision does not extend to what he considers to be occult knowledge. I have some of your mother's papers and notes. I'll bring them to you."

"Why didn't you tell me any of this before?"

"You weren't ready. Or so I thought. But I am convinced there is nothing for which you are not ready. Now, what do you know of the Soma?" Mamoru asked as he again touched his hat brim with soft grey gloves to a passing dowager.

Adele was preoccupied by thoughts of her mother treading, in some way, the same path she was on. She barely heard his question. "Soma? That's what they used to call Karnak Square. Where Alexander the Great was supposedly buried. So my mother had great skill in geomancy?"

"She did, yes. But that is not the topic for tonight. If you will give me your attention for now, I will tell you about your mother's studies in the future. Now, the Soma. Yes, Alexander was buried here, although his body may have been taken elsewhere later. Or it may still remain under our feet somewhere."

Adele got the glint of adventure in her eyes. "Are we going to look for him?"

"No."

"Oh."

"Here." Mamoru stopped at a corner.

Adele said, "So Alexander was buried here? Hmm. Now his neighbors are a bank, a hotel, town homes, and shops. Likely not what he had in mind for eternity."

"What do you feel?"

She shrugged. "What do you mean?"

Then, beneath the assault of horses and hoarse voices, the clatter of wheels and wheezing of motors, and the strangling stench of humans and chemicals, she did feel something. Warmth opened inside her and filled her with calm. The noise faded, and confusion seemed unimportant.

Mamoru could see the change come over her. "You sense it so quickly. There is a rift here. Come. Let's move somewhere more conducive to conversation."

He led the way into the sumptuous lobby of the massive Hotel Saladin, where bellmen bowed deeply. Patrons sat in clutches, smoking cigarettes or pipes, sharing a cocktail, laughing or deep in conversation. Gas chandeliers glimmered overhead. Adele could still sense the heat emanating from the rift, but it was just a warm glow, distant yet comforting. Mamoru angled to a dark, wooden door set into an alcove surrounded by luxurious palms. He slid between the foliage and opened the door.

The princess stared wide-eyed after her silent teacher. She lifted the hem of her robe and followed. "Is this your secret geomancer society?"

"No. Could you please not say 'secret geomancer society' out loud?"

Adele was awash in the stench of burning hashish. She instantly covered her nose.

Mamoru turned back. "Ah yes. I would recommend you not breathe too deeply. Unless you have a predilection for hashish I am not aware of."

"Funny." Then Adele asked from behind her hand, "What is this place?"

"It's a hash den, of course. Please step in."

She entered to find the most well-appointed hashish parlor she'd ever seen. Not that she'd seen one, but she'd read about the vile coves of sin in a few of the penny dreadfuls. This place could have been a fine coffeehouse on the Rue Rosette or the ultrafashionable Rue Sherif Pasha. Overhead fans turning slowly were reflected in the dark, lush wooden walls studded with brass fixtures. Comfortable divans nestled in private alcoves along with full-curtained opium beds. A small Turkish band droned from the corner. It was quite crowded; obviously, it was a very popular hash den.

Adele almost pointed and instead exclaimed in a hushed voice, "Is that Lord Gillingham from Treasury?"

Mamoru arched his eyebrows. "Yes. I believe it is."

"That's not Lady Gillingham with him."

"Definitely not."

Startled by a familiar face glimpsed through the hashish haze, Adele backed behind a large leafy palm. "You criticize me for walking the back streets, but you bring me here? There are people I know. What if I'm recognized?"

Mamoru turned calmly. "No one even noticed you until you leapt into this shrub." He moved close to her. "This is simply a hashish parlor favored by certain men of the city. It is quite safe."

"Mamoru, do you take hashish?"

"Don't be silly."

"Good evening, Mamoru pasha." A white-robed man in a tarboosh bowed to the Japanese visitor. "Good to see you again. Your usual room is ready."

"Thank you, Khalifi." He turned back to Adele. "Are you capable of crossing the room without breaking into an impromptu scene from a drawing-room comedy?"

Scowling at her mentor, Adele stepped away from the plant, her hand at her waist where her Fahrenheit dagger lay beneath her robe.

Mamoru regarded her blandly. "This is a gentleman's club. It is doubtful you'll have reason to stab anyone."

"I'm not sure what to expect anymore."

They crossed the parquet floor. Adele kept her head down and her shoulders hunched. Few paid her any attention, although there were occasional eyes tracking the nattily attired Easterner and his veiled companion. Mamoru pushed back a sliding panel and ushered Adele into a spacious private room. Large pillows surrounded a low, brass table in the center of the room. Several plush divans lined the walls, which sported beautiful tapestries.

The waiter asked, "Your usual, Mamoru pasha?"

Adele tensed in surprise as Mamoru told him yes and correctly ordered green tea for her. When the waiter withdrew, she barked, "You have a usual?"

"Yes. Turkish coffee."

"Oh."

"I assure you, Highness, I am not an opium eater. I use this room because it is private; everyone minds their own affairs." Mamoru paused as the waiter brought a tray of drinks and sweets, then left dutifully. "What do you feel?"

Adele took a deep breath and concentrated. She thought she felt something but wasn't sure. Her heart sank. Something was wrong. She felt nothing. The warmth was gone, crowded out by growing confusion.

"You're trying too hard now," Mamoru said. "Stop thinking about it and listen to me. And sit down, please. Using the furniture won't make you an addict."

She settled with a sarcastic tilt of her head onto a couch with her tea.

Mamoru paced. "All nature can be described by science, although we may not possess the knowledge to codify it. What we do not yet grasp or accept is often described by rules called superstition or magic or religion. These rules are vaguely comprehended, like some aspects of chemistry or physics. However, if properly understood and applied, these occult rules describe a science as reproducible as any chemical process."

Adele interrupted. "But at Sir Godfrey's I wasn't doing anything consciously. I wasn't exercising any knowledge."

"Do you know individuals who are natural athletes or musicians or mathematicians? Or have extraordinary memories? While others, try as they might, simply never excel?"

Adele shrugged in assent.

He continued, "While all humans have shared abilities, there is a wide range of variation within humanity."

"Like speed in horses?"

"Yes. We understand the nature of breeding animals for particular traits. Humans are animals. All aspects of our nature are created by our composition; we simply don't understand fully the mechanisms of those traits. You have brown eyes. Your children will likely have brown eyes. Why? We don't know—some pieces of information that migrate from you to your offspring."

"Why do we—?"

Mamoru waved his hand. "I've gone too far afield already. I am not a biologist. I am a geomancer, so let me confine my comments to that discipline. Throughout time, many people have sought to make sense of their place on Earth with concepts typically known as magic or faith. Modern geomancy has gone far beyond that to create a sophisticated system of knowledge. It is not yet an accepted system. It is not yet complete, as is chemistry, for example. We cannot yet answer all the questions our science raises, which is the great test of a science. But that will change with you."

Adele looked at him with surprise.

He said, "It's true. You are the transcendent figure in the geomantic sciences. You will allow us to codify the science, first by experience, and then by interpreting that experience into human terms. Geomancy will usher in a new age for humanity. We will advance more in the next century than we have in all previous history."

Adele slowly raised her hand like a confused student.

Mamoru pointed at her. "Yes?"

"I am going to do all that?" Her disbelief showed in the slow rise of her eyebrows.

Mamoru sat next to her with a comforting sigh. "Not you alone. I will be with you every step. Teaching you, and, I suspect, learning from you. And there are many others around the world ready for the revolution of ideas. Ready for you."

He leapt to his feet again. "I can't tell you how eager I am to be under way. I have bided my time for so long. I knew you were the right student, but the court controlled you. Lord Kelvin and his technocrats are not friendly toward explanations of the world that do not involve combustion or pig iron."

Adele's elation was tempered by a little trepidation at being part of some vast secret scheme. But she had seen the force of this power and knew it could be a key to help destroy Cesare and protect her people, and all humans.

She asked, "How do we proceed?"

"What do you feel?"

A searing excitement passed through her. It had come on as she watched Mamoru spring in front of her like a boy. It was more than that, however; she had again invited some omnipresent energy to filter through her. She could stretch out her hands, but there was no limit to her reach, across the city, or wherever she wanted.

"Yes," Mamoru said quietly. He reached into his coat pocket and removed a white crystal several inches long and placed it in her hand, jarring her awareness back to the room.

Adele felt heaviness in her hand and a drag on her arm as she moved it through the air. She tilted the crystal, and it was as though her hand had plunged into a stiff flow of warm water. Through her motions, the current shifted in one direction or another. Every time she moved the crystal, she felt physical reactions all around her. She was inside some great river of energy, but was altering its course with her movements.

"I don't understand. What is the crystal doing?" she asked.

"It is a focus for your natural talent. It's a lever and you are the fulcrum. You are moving the earth."

"What?"

Mamoru chuckled. "Since you are near a rift, the earth's energy is close and thick. You feel it. The crystal allows you to engage it, although I'm surprised you can touch it and still talk to me. Such a feat normally requires total concentration from even the most adept of geomancers, but you wield it like it's a simple act."

"Am I hurting anything?" Adele continued to twist the stone, enraptured by the sensation of pushing herself through some unknowable flood.

"No. The power is so vast it barely notices you. Yet."

"Is this how Selkirk does his magic?"

"It isn't magic. But yes."

"So would vampires see me now?"

"Yes. You are simply dipping into the sea. You are not directing the waves."

"Will I learn to control it on command?"

"Soon enough. The crystal, please."

Adele gave a few more twists, exulting in the sensations under her skin. Then with a disappointed huff, she passed the stone to her teacher.

Mamoru shouted and drew back his arm. He grasped his hand in pain. The crystal hit the floor with a splatter. Silvery drops splashed and a tiny sliver of stone lay in a small pool.

Mamoru forgot his scorched hand as he stared at the liquefied crystal.

She saw the incredulity etched on Mamoru's face. She had never seen him truly surprised and found it disturbing.

"I'm sorry," she said. "I ruined it."

"No, Highness." He exhaled and sat down heavily. A slow smile drew his lips up. "Not at all. It's just a bit unnerving to finally see one's dreams made flesh."

CHAPTER 10

CESARE'S INVITATION HAD been vague. "An event" the messenger had said. The leaders of the new Grand Coalition would all be present—Draken, Ashkenazy, Fen, and of course, Prince Cesare as master of ceremonies. The event was being held north of London, well north, at a pointless town named Hawkshaw. Gareth had never been there, although as Greyfriar he'd heard it mentioned by humans in Britain as a place relatively free of vampire threat.

Gareth suspected that his brother preferred he not make an appearance because Cesare's interlocutor had appeared with the message at the doors of Gareth's London abode mere hours before the event was to begin. However, he felt compelled to rush northward in case Cesare was testing the strength of their new fraternal bond. And it was yet another opportunity for Gareth to find out all he could about his brother's scheme.

Gareth drifted over the rolling green northwest countryside, noting the fields were rustling with new crops. But it wasn't long before he sensed something else beneath the temperature of the air. Uneasiness flared as his skin crawled. He knew the sensation well, for he felt it every Sunday in Edinburgh when mass was held by his flock in the massive St. Giles Cathedral. Gareth's curiosity and apprehension flared as a figure rose from a wooded copse below and approached. It was Cesare's bailiff.

"Prince Gareth," Stryon said flatly with his teeth clenched against discomfort, "how good of you to come. Won't you join the party below?"

Gareth didn't reply, but merely followed the lanky servant toward the ground. The scents of numerous vampires filled his nostrils, including one that jarred an old memory, an old and unpleasant memory. They descended through the leafy canopy into the cool, shaded forest where vampires turned to gaze at Gareth with surprise and disdain. The clan lords stood in agitated clumps, whispering at the new arrival, but wary of showing open distaste for the king's son.

"Gareth!" Prince Cesare separated himself from a crowd and approached with a smile of satisfaction. He clasped his elder brother by the shoulder. "Delightful to see you."

"Thank you for the invitation. I was glad I could make it."

Cesare pulled his brother toward a group that included the foreign rulers, as well as a very familiar female. "You remember our great allies, King Draken, King Ashkenazy, and Queen Fen."

Gareth bowed.

"And, of course, you know Lady Hallow. She is my right hand."

Gareth stiffened, but held his emotions in check as Hallow's luminous face stared at him openly. Her familiar and dreadful scent cut through him. He silently cursed his brother for bringing her back to court.

"I do know her." Gareth kissed the female's long, pale fingers while glaring into her blue eyes. "Though it has been years since we've spoken."

"Prince Gareth." Lady Hallow smiled with what appeared to be warmth. She was tall, quite half a foot above Cesare, and slender. Her frame was elegant and smooth like ivory. Her face was distant yet inquisitive; she seemed interested in everything yet unaffected by any of it. She exuded a demure sweetness that made her seem unthreatening.

Gareth knew better. "It's surprising to see you in Britain again." He kept his responses cordial and monotone.

Hallow nodded politely. "I go where my lord needs me."

Cesare said, "Lady Hallow's skillful diplomacy had much to do with the coalition we see today."

"Yes," the corpulent King Draken snorted agreement and touched the incandescent Hallow on the arm. "If I hadn't had so many queens already, she'd be my sixth."

The lady bubbled with polite laughter. "Your Majesty does me great honor."

Gareth knew Hallow would just as soon gut the disgusting bulk from Munich. However, the bloody deed would have been done already if Cesare's previous right hand, Flay, had been the subject of Draken's lechery instead of the politic and well-bred Hallow.

"What is that stench?" King Ashkenazy interrupted with a bitter face. His writhing was more pronounced now due to his discomfort. "I noticed it before, but it seems to be growing stronger. I do not like it."

"That is our entertainment for the evening," Cesare replied. "Just beyond this forest is a town called Hawkshaw where, I am informed, the humans have not encountered a vampire for a generation or more. You will all recall that stench from before the Great Killing? It's the abhorrent smell of free humans doing as they please."

Queen Fen snarled at Cesare as she sidled next to Gareth. "So you dragged us out here to clean out your rebels, Cesare?"

"They aren't rebels, Majesty." Cesare's kept a plastered smile on his face. "They are merely unaware. I thought we might all enjoy a hunt this evening. My gift to you: a human town to slaughter."

Gareth's stomach turned and his hatred for Cesare spiked. He could smell the town as well, and it reminded him of Adele. It wasn't the smell of "free humans" per se; it was the scent of their power. Gareth was inured to the odor, as well as the uncomfortable tension and warmth that wafted through the air. He was, however, disturbed by the thought that perhaps he had avoided this area as Greyfriar because of the discomfort it may have caused his vampire self. The people of Hawkshaw were just the type he should have contacted. Soon they would all be dead and there was nothing he could do about it.

Queen Fen huffed dismissively as she brushed against Gareth. "I haven't lived this long and worked as hard as I have just to go back to the old days. If we wanted to hunt our meals, why did we bother to destroy the humans in the first place? You poseurs go and pretend you're still living in the wild, if you wish. I have no need for such fantasies, thank you." Painfully, she lowered herself to the mossy ground.

"As you will." Prince Cesare soldiered on, unwilling to let the cranky old crone derail his party. "I'll have something sent over to you. For the rest, sharpen your claws. The moon is up." The young prince rose into the boughs and the rest of the party followed, laughing with vicious anticipation.

Gareth struggled to think of something he could do to prevent the coming destruction. His nearest Greyfriar stash containing his weapons and costume was many miles away; by the time he got there and returned, the deed would be done. He couldn't fight all these vampires. He couldn't warn Hawkshaw; death was on them already. He knew that thousands of humans were threatened with death every day across the north, and that Greyfriar saved only the smallest percentage of them. That realization still didn't dull the pain of watching it happen.

"Are you not participating in the party?" Lady Hallow's voice broke into Gareth's dire thoughts.

He realized he was scowling in revulsion, so he resumed his blank regal face. "I will. Shouldn't you be at Cesare's side? You did arrange this event for him, didn't you?"

She raised an eyebrow at the edge in his voice. "No, my lord. This event was all Prince Cesare's idea. He learned of this place and their miserable activities. And so he decided to deal with them and amuse his guests at the same time. Quite intelligent."

"It's wasteful. Typical."

Hallow remarked, "You are your father's son in some ways, aren't you?"

"Thank you," was Gareth's clipped reply, unsure if she meant it as a compliment.

"King Dmitri always preached against waste; I remember it so well."

"Did you learn anything from him?"

"While he hated waste, he didn't believe in coddling humans. They're food. You know, Gareth, I hardly recognize you as the same war chief who killed a regiment of human soldiers on the moors outside Fort Augustus. Do you remember that night?"

He stared coldly. That night was long ago, and it was the last time he had touched her with anything resembling affection. He looked away. "I must go. I'd hate for Cesare to slip in blood with no one near to lift him to his feet."

Hallow murmured sarcastically, "I don't recall you ever having concerns for your brother's welfare. Why are you suddenly so solicitous to Cesare?"

"Times change." Gareth shook his head, impatient with her sparring. "It used to be we all lived in tombs and holes in the ground. We've come far as a people."

"They say you treat your Scottish herds well, that they volunteer their blood out of love for you. Is that so?"

He exhaled through his nose. "Do you have a point?"

"I'm just curious. It's been decades since I laid eyes on you. We were close once."

"Once," he snapped quickly.

"Who changed? You or I?"

"Both. Now we both love Cesare."

Hallow asked with an undertone of sincerity, "What happened to you, Gareth? You could have been king, a great king. Now Cesare is carrying all the clans before him, and you merely step aside."

"I don't want to be king. Look what it did to my father."

Disappointment washed over her features. "What will happen to you when Cesare succeeds King Dmitri?"

Gareth shrugged with cavalier disregard.

"I think you know the answer, Gareth," Hallow continued. "He'll kill you."

"Has he confided it to you?"

"No, of course not. He never tells me any more than I need to know for my mission. But he'll have to kill you. You're the heir."

"Am I?" Gareth smirked coldly. "Perhaps you haven't heard, but I'm eccentric and weak. Practically impotent. I'm no threat to anyone."

Hallow stepped close to him. "Cesare does not underestimate you. He may demean you in public, but he hates you. And he fears you."

"Thank you for the warning, Lady Hallow. Surely he'll keep me as fodder for his war." He wasn't sure what new cruel game she was playing, but he wanted no part of it.

"Cesare doesn't intend to fight a war. If the war with the humans begins, he believes he has lost. He knows the fight will be in our territory. Therefore, he intends to stop the war before it begins."

"He tried that, and failed." Gareth lifted into the air to head for the village to do what he could, but Hallow's next statement brought him back to the ground.

"He has gathered knowledge that no vampire has dared touch. Knowledge from humans who know about religion and the magic of the earth. Gareth, you make the mistake of underestimating him because you hate him, but Cesare is remarkable. He is plotting strategies that no other clan leader has ever conceived. He has brought in humans with specialized knowledge that he values and given them certain freedoms in return for information."

"Impossible."

Hallow rolled her eyes. "Stop being shocked. It's so. Believe me."

"Why? Why would any human cooperate with vampires?"

"Because," Queen Fen croaked from her spot on the damp ground, "there are humans who are more interested in their personal welfare and comfort than the good of their own kind. Imagine that. Cesare has humans in his thrall even in the south."

Gareth and Hallow glanced at the crone, having forgotten she was even there. The old queen struggled to her knees and then, with the aid of her cane, rose unsteadily to her feet. Fen waddled forward and tapped Gareth on the shoulder. "If your brother wasn't so personally unctuous, he'd be a great leader. And you, you let him do as he pleases. What in hell became of Dmitri's offspring? Now Dmitri was a wonder to behold."

Hallow lowered her face to cover a wan smile.

Then from the distant darkness came the sound of screaming, and the hissing and feral cries of vampires. Gareth sprang into the air and streaked toward Hawkshaw as the smell of fresh blood and fear filled his nose. His brethren flitted through the starry sky, dropping into the narrow lanes of the town. Figures raced wildly through the shadows, seeking escape, but there were far too many vampires. The great clan lords and their chief retainers unleashed their pent-up savagery, killing with joy, not feeding, merely killing.

Even Gareth felt hints of the old power welling up in him unbidden. The scene below him was reminiscent of so many from the Great Killing; there was a piece of him that glowed at the sounds and smells. To Gareth's relief, the stronger senses in him were terror and disgust as he clutched onto a tile roof over Hawkshaw. Figures settled on either side of him, and he turned to see Cesare and Lady Hallow perching beside him, also watching the scene below.

The hunting was sloppy. Many of these nobles hadn't attacked true prey in more than a century. Add to that the abhorrent power resonating in the town and vampire blows were ill-timed and weak, leaving humans sprawled on the ground, screaming in pain, crawling for safety. With shuddering laughter, the vampires would race after another poor target to savage and leave lame in the dirt.

"Look at this," Cesare muttered ruefully. "Disgusting."

Gareth exchanged a look with Hallow, who seemed as surprised by the younger prince's outburst as he was.

Cesare looked at Gareth with a rare open expression of confidence. "I've never been so ashamed of my people. It reminds me of the first time you tried to kill."

"You're ashamed?" Gareth said hesitantly, ignoring the insult. "But you planned this slaughter."

"I know. I wish I wasn't here to see it. Look at them. It's as if they have forgotten everything. The greatest of our nobles. Slow. Pathetic. In the old days, this town would have been dead by now."

Gareth sighed with disappointment; how foolish to even suspect Cesare was capable of some level of self-criticism. But Cesare was right, again.

Two humans below actually repelled an attack, making another vampire rear back in surprise, but not for long. The vampire pushed through its mild shock and backhanded one of its prey as the other ran. The vampire staggered after him, although it didn't appear as if he would catch the human.

Gareth could only hope the human would escape. He pointed out the obvious to his brother. "We are soft. War with the humans is a terrible mistake."

"I agree. The humans are lean and hungry. Just look at Senator Clark. I took his mate and he attacked me." Cesare smiled. "Like a vampire."

On the street, portly King Draken fell on an elderly man, raking with his claws once, twice, three times. The man continued to pound the king's chest and scream curses.

Cesare rolled his eyes. "Look at that spectacle. That sack of guts can't even kill an old man."

Gareth pressed. "How do you intend to prevent the war from occurring? How will you strike at Equatoria's heart?"

Cesare didn't answer, muttering angrily, absorbed with the surrounding carnage.

"Cesare. I should like to come into your inner circle."

Now the young prince raised an eyebrow and glanced at his brother.

Gareth continued, "Of course, I have no intentions on the throne, as you know. I will make that declaration to the clan, if you wish. But I would like to participate more in clan affairs. I feel as if I let our father down, and I want to make amends." The taste of bitterness welled in his mouth, but he maintained an earnest and supplicant stare.

Before Cesare could respond, Gareth saw a young boy on the street. The lad was alone and crying, wandering aimlessly among the dead and wounded. Then the prince's attention was caught by the sight of thin King Ashkenazy, airborne, but rolling into position to strike the boy from above. Gareth launched himself down the slope of the roof and slammed into the street like a stone, landing jarringly in a cloud of dust. He laid a hand on the bawling child's shoulder just before the Hungarian king dropped hard beside him with an imperious glare.

Gareth kept his grip on the panicked boy, but smiled pleasantly at the king. "Ah, Your Majesty, I had no idea you were—"

"That is my kill," Ashkenazy snapped.

"Who? Oh this? I had no notion you were interested when I laid hands on him first."

"Surrender it."

Gareth's smile vanished. "I will not."

The young king went wide-eyed with disbelief. "I don't think I heard you correctly."

Cesare settled beside them, followed by Lady Hallow. The young prince was all solicitous host, asking cheerfully, "What seems to be the problem?"

"Your brother," Ashkenazy said, "stole my kill."

Gareth pulled the struggling and screaming boy closer.

Cesare swiveled to Gareth. "Surely there are others you could take. His Majesty has a fancy for this one."

"I've taken rather a fancy to him myself," Gareth replied.

His brother glared coldly. "The king desires it."

Gareth was silent. The sounds of terror had diminished around them, replaced by the forlorn moans of the injured and dying, and the laughter of the nobles. With none left to attack, the vampires had begun to gather around the main square, attracted by Cesare, Ashkenazy, and Gareth, none of whom looked very happy. The growing audience whispered to one another about the unfolding tableau.

"Gareth," Cesare intoned quietly, "yield to His Majesty."

"I will not. This is my kill by right."

The younger prince reached out suddenly and took the child's arm. Gareth snarled and, in the blink of an eye, seized his brother's wrist and nearly flung Cesare to the ground. The collected mob froze in alarm and anticipation. Lady Hallow audibly gasped and eyed Gareth with surprise.

Cesare rose to his full height and straightened his jacket, trying to gather control of himself. His features twitched. "One last time. Yield the boy."

Gareth clearly enunciated, "No."

King Ashkenazy waved a twitching hand in the air. "Never mind, Prince Cesare. This isn't worth further discussion. Let your brother have his magnificent kill. Likely it's the first one he's managed in many a year." The king laughed, but he stared at Gareth with a mix of fury and confusion. "I don't want Prince Gareth's deplorable behavior to color your delightful diversion."

Relieved by the king's generosity, Cesare bowed to his young ally, then paused briefly to whisper to his brother, "Get out of my sight, Gareth. Stay in your museum. Go back to Edinburgh. Do whatever you choose. But don't let me lay eyes on your face again until I call for you."

Cesare resumed his grand persona and led Ashkenazy back toward a crowd of nobles as if the matter had been a mere trifle. As the group began to drift away, many of them gave Gareth disdainful glances over their shoulders.

Gareth knelt in front of the child, who stood with quivering lips and blank eyes. "Shh. Stop crying now. There's nothing I can do to help your people, but you are safe, I assure you."

Lady Hallow stepped closer. "What's wrong with you, Prince Gareth?"

"Why do you tarry?" Gareth snarled over his shoulder. "Your prince is departing."

She stared down at him with her face full of confusion and anger. "If the boy is your kill, why don't you kill him? If you're going to create a scene over it, then kill him and feed."

"Why don't you be quiet?"

"You've earned the ire of King Ashkenazy. And completely alienated yourself from Cesare. For this thing?"

"The child seems a fair trade." Gareth turned and walked from the village on foot with the boy by the hand. Hallow jerked as if slapped, watching him go, shaking her head. She then raced to catch up to Cesare.

From the shadows, Queen Fen smiled, quietly enjoying the entire show.

—✺—

Gareth stared at the giant stone trunk and head of Ramses the Great looming above him in the British Museum. He was grateful to be indoors away from the death and decay outside. At least inside he could reminisce in solitude. In his mind, he could see Adele reading the hieroglyphics to him. She had been a prisoner in the hands of mortal enemies, yet she maintained her dignity and humanity.

Now the vast museum felt empty. The artifacts that had once crowded him seemed like flat background scenery. Without Adele to teach and tease, his home in London was dead. He drew no pleasure from it.

Gareth heard a pounding sound from the distance. As he wandered toward the reverberations they stopped, then resumed more forcefully. The prince reached the rotunda before he realized the sound came from the imposing front door. Gareth grasped a brass handle and pulled the door open.

There stood Queen Fen with cane raised to beat the door further. When she saw Gareth, her immediate reaction was sour displeasure.

"Prince Gareth," she croaked, "if you're going to close your doors, can't you at least have a trained chamberlain standing by to open them to visitors?"

"My chamberlain is in Edinburgh, standing by my doors there," he remarked dryly. "I'm surprised to see you here. I sent a request to meet with you, but I expected to attend you at your convenience."

The queen huffed and started to enter, surprised that Gareth didn't instantly move back. With disdainful shock, she asked, "Well, may I enter?"

"Of course, Your Majesty." Gareth stared out beyond her into the thin light of dawn to see who might have followed the queen, but there was no one. He noted how the crone leaned on her cane as she shuffled inside. A vampire using a cane, and not even realizing how odd it was, given that their species never used any sort of tool. In the old days, the feeble Fen would have been killed long ago, but in this era of gracious living, she thrived beyond her time. As did his own demented father, he thought sadly. Gareth shut the door after the queen's noisy gown. She stared at him with complete disinterest in the magnificent surroundings.

She attempted a smile, creating a fearful gash in her leathery face. "I felt it would be more useful to meet here, far from your brother's toadies. I wanted to say how impressed I was with you at the meeting. And in that beastly little village. It's easy now to see who got Dmitri's intelligence, and his backbone."

"Thank you."

"And his looks," she added with a terrifying lilt in her voice.

"Oh?" The prince suddenly pretended to hear a noise in the distance —anything to avoid looking at the queen. Her intent was becoming obvious, much to Gareth's discomfort.

The rustling of her silks drew near. "You know, young Gareth, I knew your father quite well . . . in my youth."

"Oh?" He felt a claw on his forearm.

"Yes. He was a magnificent specimen. As are you."

"Oh?"

"I do not waste time with words when I see what I want."

"That's a pity."

"I would like to feel Dmitri's touch again, but he is old and infirm and, I suspect, quite disgusting. You are not."

Gareth forced himself to look down into the dewy eyes of the old queen, swallowing his anger. "I am a poor substitute for my great father, Your Majesty. Now Cesare—"

"Cesare!" she hacked. "Don't mention that little jackal! Pompous little upstart! He needs to be killed. Why don't you kill him?"

Gareth almost grinned, but kept a dutiful demeanor. "He is most able. Far more suited than I. He is a master of political intercourse."

"No doubt." The queen stroked Gareth's chest lightly with a palm like sandpaper. "He is pure politics and no conviction. He makes deals with humans. Shameful!"

"I agree." Gareth tried to avoid her gaze. "Do you know what sort of deals he is making?"

Fen arched her caterpillarlike eyebrows playfully. "Perhaps we can discuss it . . . after."

"Your Majesty, I need to know anything that could call Cesare's loyalty into question." Gareth drew closer and narrowed his eyes at her dramatically as he slowly extended his claws from long fingers. "In case I have to kill him."

The queen shuddered with dredged-up excitement. She breathed out through her nose with a long wheeze meant to be sensuous.

"It seems," she began with a husky voice, "that your brother has witchfinders scouring the herds looking for those who know magic."

"What good could that possibly be to him?"

"Cesare believes he may be able to find some weakness in their magic." She laughed. "Imagine that."

"Does he have such knowledge? Is that how he plans to strike at Equatoria?"

Queen Fen cleared her throat. "But come, my prince, all this talk of human slaves is becoming tiresome. Won't you offer me something? Where's that boy you took from that little eel of a king?"

"He's gone." Gareth left it at that. She could well think he had killed the child when, in fact, the child was on his way to Edinburgh. Gareth still had enough power to have a single human taken safely to Edinburgh by couriers. They knew their lives would be over should any harm come to the boy.

"Oh. Well, we can eat afterward." She twirled her fingers in her brittle hair, causing clumps to pull out of her scalp. She giggled playfully as she tossed the locks at him.

Gareth caught the hair instinctively and tried not to look horrified at the wads of wirelike locks in his palm. The queen gazed expectantly at him, so he pushed the hair into his pocket.

"Thank you," he said. "I'll certainly treasure it. Now, I wonder if you might tell me something of Cesare's plans in Equatoria?"

"I'd rather tell you of my plans for the next several hours."

"Um. Yes, I'm eager to hear them, Your Majesty. Please, business before pleasure. I must know what Cesare is planning. Only then can I concentrate on . . . other things."

"If we must." Queen Fen smiled like a long-dead coquette. "Your brother seems sadly fixated on that little girl from Equatoria and her murderous mate."

"Adele?" Gareth blurted quickly. "Princess Adele?"

"Who can remember the little creature's name. She's the one whose union with the American war chief will signal the beginning of the war from the south."

"What are Cesare's intentions toward her?"

"What do you think? He's going to kill her."

"When?" Gareth began to squeeze the queen's arms in brutal concentration, much to her misguided excitement.

"Prince Gareth," Queen Fen purred and pretended to struggle. "You are hurting me."

"I said *when?*" he shouted.

The old female now looked askance at him. "Don't take that tone with me, young prince."

"When does Cesare intend to strike? Tell me!"

Queen Fen's slight blush paled to her normal cold marble. Her eyes sank with disappointment at the crumbling façade of a man before her, typical of all males in her eyes. "Apparently the humans perform some ceremony before they mate. It will take place in only a few days. Cesare has forces in place to kill both the girl and the butcher Clark during that ceremony. Your brother has extensive contacts among the humans of the south. It seems that humans will betray their own kind for mere objects."

Gareth froze in horrified contemplation.

Fen stared at him in curiosity. "What is the girl to you? Are you and Cesare both hypnotized by her?"

He was so lost in thought, he no longer heard her.

"Hmph." Fen rolled her eyes and dropped her gnarled fingers from Gareth's shoulders. She brushed her skirt and recovered her cold distance. "I see now you are nothing like Dmitri. It's no wonder you don't have any women or children. Who would put up with you?"

Gareth said with a distant voice, "I'm sorry, Your Majesty. Perhaps another time."

Queen Fen whirled to go. "Pfft. I leave for New York tomorrow. Where men won't waste my rare passion with chitchat. I should've expected as much from a man who opens his own doors."

"I'll give my father your best." Gareth shut the door behind her, then ran to prepare his departure from London.

CHAPTER

"**I**T'S SO BEAUTIFUL," Major Stoddard repeated for the
tenth time.

Colonel Anhalt smiled. It was gratifying to see the Sahara's impact
on the American. The desert's power was at its most exquisite at night,
with its unseen horizon and an endless dome of brilliant stars overhead.
Even the meandering caravan, several miles of men and camels and
horses ferrying great slabs of salt southward, was dwarfed by the surroundings. The sounds of talking and laughing and braying were swallowed up by the unbounded winds.

There were few places where Anhalt felt happier. The desert made
men feel small because all they had to keep them upright was their inner
nature. Men of no character feared the desert, but in reality what they
feared was the emptiness the desert brought to them. A man could survive a mistake in life—Anhalt was proof of that—but the desert, like
the world at large, did not forgive failures of character. Anhalt knew that
the day he was afraid of the desert was the day he had betrayed himself.
And he would—and deserved to—die.

"One day," Stoddard said, struggling to settle on the rocking camel
as his hand sought the small of his aching back, "I'll show you the Grand

Canyon in the old Arizona Territory. I flew over it once. You've never seen the like."

"I'd enjoy that." Anhalt swayed easily with the camel's gait. He had ridden these beasts so many times he found the odd pounding steps relaxing. "I thought you would appreciate a few days away from Alexandria, traveling with a caravan, before the wedding."

"Thank you. After the wedding, we'll all be busy, I suspect. I doubt the senator will give me much leave time." Stoddard noticed Colonel Anhalt give a short, cynical huff. Senator Clark was certainly not the colonel's favorite person, since the embarrassing public shaming Anhalt had received in Marseilles. To Anhalt's credit, he never tried to make excuses; he understood his fault in the debacle that led to Princess Adele's capture by vampires. Stoddard had spent enough time around Anhalt in the last few months since returning from Edinburgh to cultivate a great respect for him. Anhalt was a consummate soldier with steely loyalty for his charge, Princess Adele. Even in the face of Clark's emasculating rant, Anhalt had borne up like a man of character, acted with respect toward a superior officer and the intended husband of his princess. However, there was something tragic in Anhalt, as if his life was merely a series of events leading to some great sacrifice. He was a purpose, not a man.

Stoddard said, "Colonel, if I may, I'd like to tell you how much respect I have for you, sir. All of the American Rangers feel the same."

Anhalt's head turned slowly, and his hands flexed with confusion. "Thank you, Major."

"And I'd like to tell you about Senator Clark," the American pressed on. "Certainly, he can be brusque and difficult. But there is another side to Senator Clark that few see. His men would follow him anywhere. Myself included."

"Clearly. Your raid on Edinburgh is already legendary. As well it should be."

"It all comes from his willpower. I've never known a man as brave as he, sometimes to the point of foolhardiness. But he's not a normal man. He sports an aura of invincibility. He is so sure of his victory that we all believe it."

"I assumed as much. He is a . . . forceful personality."

"I will tell you the truth, sir, and this is something I believe as surely as I believe the sun will rise tomorrow. If there is one man who can defeat the vampires, it's Senator Clark. He will make it happen. In our lifetime, we will be in Washington and New York, and you will be in Paris and London. But not without him. This war will fail without Senator Clark."

Anhalt considered his companion's words. He knew Stoddard well enough to know this wasn't the meanderings of an acolyte. The major truly believed that the senator had some special place in the world. Anhalt could understand it, but found it difficult to credit.

Before he could formulate a reply, up the plodding caravan, no more than twenty lengths ahead, a dark shape rushed at a Tuareg walking beside a laden camel. A terrified scream erupted, and a wash of dark matter flew from the man. The long corridor of panicked camels plunged and veered while the Tuareg struggled to hold them. They shouted in their Arabic-Hausa pidgin and pulled guns and swords.

"Ambush!" shouted Anhalt, yanking his Fahrenheit blade from the scabbard as he slapped the hindquarters of his beast, startling the camel into a lope. He clicked the shroud gas filter onto his goggles, and the camels and men appeared as red shapes. Sure enough though, Anhalt saw the dim blue form of a vampire. The shout of the doomed caravaner seemed to hang in the desert air for long seconds as the crouching thing dragged his victim into the darkness of the desert.

Anhalt charged at the retreating blue shape, saber held high, the weapon casting a green hue in the colorless pitch. The creature dropped the lifeless Tuareg and, in a blur, rushed under the belly of Anhalt's camel just as the blade swept down. The animal grunted and plunged to its knees, Anhalt leaping before it crashed into the sand. His saber spun in a wide arc as he jumped, catching the vampire as it flew toward him. Holding its chest, the thing staggered and then scrambled toward a hole in the sandy ground.

A rifle cracked and the vampire stumbled to the dirt. The weapon fired twice more, each bullet finding its target before the vampire slid away into the dark pit in the earth.

Stoddard appeared with his rifle trained on the hole, while Anhalt ran to the blue-robed Tuareg lying nearby. But even in the desert night, it was not difficult to perceive the man was already dead. Anhalt hoisted the man over his shoulders and rose to his feet. He waited until Stoddard awkwardly brought his camel alongside.

"Are you all right?" the American asked.

"Yes. The same cannot be said for this man, however." Anhalt jerked on the tasseled bridle of Stoddard's camel, forcing it down onto its knees. "Kush! Kush!" The agitated camel, its eyes wild, groaned and threatened to spit. Anhalt slapped its fatty mouth and turned away. He heaved the dead man over the saddle behind Stoddard. He refused to let vampire vermin feed on the poor soul despite his inability to save him. He stripped his saddle off his dead mount, then swung up behind Stoddard.

"Hut! Hut!" The camel lurched to its feet and, without coaxing, veered back toward the column. The caravan leaders stood, robes billowing in the wind, debating with the captain of the Dyula mercenary guards, many of whom wore quilted armor and sported rifles or massive swords and axes on their backs

As the soldiers rode up, two men gently retrieved the body of their fallen brother while Anhalt dismounted. Stoddard shifted in his saddle with a creak of leather and a tinkle of bells.

"A vampire," Anhalt told the group.

"We call them djinns, Monsieur Colonel," replied Askiya, the captain of the Dyula. "And where there is one, there will be others."

Anhalt knew the creatures existed nearly everywhere, even here in the Sahara Desert, although their numbers were quite small. Unique terrains created unique vampire types. These desert vampires appeared only at night; the day was far too hot. They spent the sunny hours buried deep under the sand or nestled in underground pools and caves. They lived along caravan routes or near oases to be close to food. Typically vampires who eked out their meager lives in the tropics were frail, desperate things that hunted with caution. They were nothing like the bold, vicious northern vampires who had wrecked industrial civilization.

Anhalt scanned with his goggles, but saw no sign of their presence. "Askiya, I see no others. Are you sure?"

The Dyula commander touched his nose. He could smell them. He was sure.

Stoddard checked his pocket watch, whose face glowed from the drops of chemical in its frame. "We've got about five hours until sunrise. We could just wait until the heat of the day."

Askiya looked up, his dark face framed by a white headscarf. "No, Merikani. They won't wait now. They know we're here and they'll come. If we try to go around, they'll chase us. We have to fight. Here."

"So what's your plan?" Anhalt inquired.

"We flush them out like rats. And we kill them." The Dyula reached beneath his white robe to finger small fetishes attached to his quilted jerkin. "Do you pray, Equateur?"

"Not as a habit," Anhalt replied.

"It helps against the djinns, as do our arrowheads made from the sacred stones."

All the Dyulas began to chant in low murmurs as they deployed with practiced precision. Ten men unslung long-barreled breech-loading rifles and formed a skirmish line ahead of the camels. Another group began to string short bows and check quivers of feathered arrows. They took each arrow, murmured a prayer over it, and placed it in their quivers. Yet a third group pulled pistols and war axes, and prepared to assault the vampire warrens.

Anhalt asked, "Where would you like us, Askiya?"

"Hah!" The Dyula commander pointed back at the scores of camels that the Tuaregs were pulling down onto their stomachs to create a living fort in the lonely desert. "You and Merikani stay there. You are both guests of the caravaners. Plus, I don't want an Equatorian colonel's blood on my hands. I want to work this route again."

"We've known each other for years," the Gurkha replied stolidly. "I repeat, where do we go?"

Askiya grinned and swung his axe with a whisper of night air. He glanced at Stoddard. "You fight djinns, Merikani?"

"Many times." Stoddard unslung his rifle and checked it.

Anhalt said, "He is the right hand of Merikani Clark."

Several of the Dyula turned their heads to look intently at the American for the first time. There was some relieved laughter and friendly smiles, and their worry suddenly turned to confidence and expectation. Stoddard didn't speak, but he felt a sense of pride that his commander's name carried such weight, even out here. He hoped to live up to their expectations.

A loud jangling of bells filled the air, and the soldiers turned to see several Dyula leading horses. Arabians. Stoddard gasped at the beauty of the animals with their muscles twitching, their heads up and eyes bright. Blacks. Greys. He slid from the camel awkwardly without waiting for the beast to lower itself to his knees.

"These animals are magnificent."

Askiya laughed at Stoddard's awe. "You ride, Merikani?"

"I do." The American stared at the horses as the archers mounted. A Dyula handed him the reins of a dappled grey stallion. "I trained with cavalry."

Askiya outlined the plan. He believed he knew where the vampires were hidden; he had seen this type of landscape many times. Rocky out-croppings straddled the caravan route where the creatures liked to shelter. The footmen, with Askiya in command, would move in, hoping to lure the vampires into the open. Failing that, they would find the creatures' pits and dig them out. Then the mounted archers would charge down to support the fight. Any creatures that tried to float away or attack the caravan would be picked off by the long guns.

That was the plan, at least. With vampires, there were countless things that could go wrong. The humans had no idea how many of the creatures were hidden in the rocks. They had no idea how hungry and desperate the things were. Plus, it was cold and dark, the two elements where vampires thrived.

Askiya gave a sharp whistle and his units moved out. Stoddard saluted Anhalt as he wheeled his mount and cantered off with the horsemen. The Gurkha fell in with the praying Dyula footmen trotting down the trail toward the rock formations. He drew his Fahrenheit saber and wished he knew a prayer to say, but he had never learned one.

Fifty yards from the rock face, Askiya halted to study the terrain. He conferred with several of his men with much pointing and gesturing. Then he returned to Anhalt's side.

"I see five holes that would suit them, Monsieur Colonel."

"So only five vampires?"

"No. Five holes. Could be many inside the holes. And there could be more dwellings besides the five. I've never seen more than twenty in a nest like this. But who can say this time?" The Dyula eyed the Fahrenheit blade with a grunt of approval. "Nice sword. Don't die, Monsieur, okay?"

"I'll do my best."

Whispering prayers, the Dyula footmen moved into the nest. Axe-men went straight for the holes that were surrounded by sand piles. One man took up a position by each hole as the other warriors waited nearby with weapons in hand. When Askiya snapped his fingers, the men plunged axes into the narrow pits. They jabbed deep into the ground, twisting the long-handled cleavers with great effort.

One man shouted and started to pull back on his axe when he was yanked to the ground, and his head and shoulders sank into the soft sand. Dyula fighters raced to his side and seized his waist, dragging him out in a rush of sand, a ghostly white figure clutching his head. Multiple axes crashed onto the vampire, slicing flesh and breaking bones. The creature hissed and fought even as it was being dismembered.

Anhalt heard noise at his feet. Pale arms reached from the sandy ground. He struck the vampire a deep blow into the shoulder with his glowing saber, cutting through the breastbone and into the rib cage, leaving scorched flesh behind thanks to the chemical burn of the Fahrenheit blade. He fired his revolver into the thing's gnashing teeth, and several deadly Dyula axes sliced past him to shatter the creature into bloody bits.

The warriors turned in slow circles, waiting for more djinn. The men who were probing the pits with their axes continued to dig. Minutes passed with no response. Weapons went to shoulders and prayers ceased. Only Askiya continued his low chant, searching the ground with unsure eyes. This was wrong. There couldn't be only two.

In the distance, Major Stoddard slapped the neck of his stallion. A cold wind ruffled the horse's mane. He scanned the sky for telltale blue shadows passing in front of the stars.

"Keep your eyes down, Merikani," instructed one of his companions astride a jet-black steed. "Djinns come from the ground."

Stoddard's gaze dropped. He heard a scream and a pistol shot in the night. All the horsemen tightened their fingers on the reins, waiting for the general eruption of battle—their cue to charge into the fray some three hundred yards away. Then there was quiet. Some of the riders murmured to each other with relieved laughter. An easy fight this time.

Then Stoddard saw numerous blue figures rising from the ground, the sand pouring off them. They weren't inside the rock nest at all, but in the open desert. And they were preparing to take Askiya's men unaware.

Stoddard drew his saber in a metallic song. "Follow me! Charge!"

The other horsemen were surprised by the Merikani, but kicked their mounts into a gallop. Soon, they too could see the enemy in the open desert, silhouetted against the dark desert skyline. Nearly twenty djinns crouched there, some already rushing for the footmen, others turning toward the onrushing cavalry. The Dyula shouted loud prayers and sent up silent arrows. The shafts tore into bodies, wrenching screams of pain from typically stoic vampires. Stoddard slammed his mount into several vampires and began slashing with his sword.

The horsemen galloped through the mob of djinns, turning in their saddles to keep up a murderous rate of fire even as they passed. Arrows punched the slim creatures and spun them in circles, knocking them to the sandy ground. When they rose, another arrow would knock them over again. A few of the things managed to rise into the air.

Stoddard wheeled his mount with his knees, slashing and firing at the ghouls around him. He felt pressure on his right thigh and saw a vampire pincushioned with arrows clinging to his leg. Stoddard shot the creature in the snarling face. Then a body slammed against him and he lost one of his stirrups. His horse reared and the American cartwheeled hard to the ground.

Stoddard scrambled to his feet, swinging his saber. He heard the pop of a gunshot and something tumbled past him. A figure appeared, holding a glowing beam of red. Anhalt. They stood back-to-back, watching the vampires circle. Askiya leapt toward them, swinging his battle-ax through the trunk of a djinn and coming to rest on one knee.

Askiya ran the palm of his hand along the blade of his axe, leaving a bloody gash. He placed the hand to his mouth for a few seconds, then sprayed bloody spittle high into the air. The creatures all turned to face them, swaying and snapping. The three humans raised their weapons for the assault.

In the desert beyond the snarling mob, Anhalt saw the rest of the foot soldiers trotting slowing toward them. "Your fellows seem to be taking their time."

Askiya said, "They don't want to be here for this."

"For what?"

Stoddard shouted, "For this!"

The three men felt the ground shudder, and suddenly they were helpless among a thundering charge. They felt the rush and power of horses pounding past, hooves exploding sand into the air. All the ghouls disappeared under the dark wave of horseflesh.

When the torrent of beasts passed, Askiya yelled a war cry and sprang to dispatch the crumpled vampires struggling to rise. With axes flashing, the footmen raced to the fray. Anhalt checked above, but saw the archers were already raking the few vampires who were floating away. Stoddard slashed and shot, kicking battered vampires to the ground and executing them.

Finally, when the battle was done, Askiya's men gathered, crushed, and hacked djinns. While many of the creatures were still alive, they were too damaged to fight. The Dyulas dismembered every ghoul until they were irretrievably dead.

It seemed an easy enough fight until Anhalt counted. Seventeen vampires dead and perhaps three escaped. Eleven humans were dead, and out of forty Dyula mercenaries equipped with weapons and horses, many were wounded. Seeing again the danger of vampires, even these nearly feral types, reminded Anhalt how difficult this coming war would be. So many men would be lost.

Anhalt found Stoddard back at the caravan, applying a field dressing to his leg. "Well done, Major. Most impressive horsemanship."

Stoddard smiled sheepishly. "Right up to the point I was dismounted. By all rights, I should be dead."

"But you're not. How's the leg?"

"Not bad. Few scratches." He slapped his thigh with a wince. "These Dyula fellows had pretty good success with prayer and magic arrows. You think we should look into that sort of thing?"

Anhalt handed his canteen to the American and chuckled without much humor. "If prayer helps a soldier fight, I'm for it. Magic arrows I have less confidence in. I'll still put my faith in repeating rifles and incendiaries when I can get them." He caught the canteen as it was tossed back, then took a drink. "You'll have a painful ride to the next oasis. I'd like to let you recover for a bit, but we do need to get back to Alexandria to confer with our respective commands."

"I've had worse." Stoddard stood with a wince. "You know, after the wedding, we'll practically be in-laws."

The Gurkha laughed loudly. "You'll be a fine addition to the family. Come, I'll get you cola nut to chew. It'll deaden the pain. And I've something a bit stronger than water to drink."

Anhalt put an arm under Stoddard's shoulder, and together they hobbled under the starlight.

CHAPTER 12

ADELE'S WEDDING DAY dawned clear and cool.

She studied herself in a long mirror. Her wedding gown was made of the most luxurious white satin and silk. The beading was a mix of pearls and opals, diagonal bands filled with close floral ornamentation. Every few strands there lay a black pearl like a soft shadow. Her bodice was set with pale precious gemstones, and Persian silk of the barest rose laced her waist, accenting her trim figure. Her veil was so thin she could barely see the weave even as it was draped over her face. Long strands of silver chains curved around her head, each peak attached to a large diamond in her tiara.

Adele wondered what Gareth would think of the gown. He had never seen her in anything but well-used travel clothes or northern homespun. He would be shocked by this vision. She smiled at the thought of the amazed look on his face.

As she ran her hand down the gown, it felt strange. Opulent and beautiful, but not a part of her. Adele had always imagined she'd be wed in her mother's wedding gown, but she had also imagined herself marrying someone she actually loved. To wear her mother's dress for Senator Clark would leave a bitter taste in her mouth, and she had adamantly refused. She'd be damned if she'd soil the memory of her mother.

The princess's chambers were crowded with people and the sound of pneumatic messages flying about the palace. Handmaidens bustled around her, attending to details that she cared little about. It was only when her chief maid, Zarina, tried to remove Pet for fear of getting cat hair on the gown that Adele responded, showing her displeasure. Zarina complied reluctantly. Adele stroked the sleek cat's fur as he reposed on her dresser. If it meant making Clark displeased with her, she'd roll in cat hair right before the ceremony.

Zarina's eyes brimmed with happy tears as she looked at Adele in the mirror. "You look so beautiful, Your Highness. Senator Clark will be so very pleased."

"I am not really interested in pleasing the man," Adele remarked blandly.

Zarina's expression fell. She had been with Adele since infancy, and in her eyes, as well as in the eyes of all Alexandria, *her* princess was about to be married. Naturally, the maid was excited and happy. Adele didn't want to dampen the woman's spirits.

Reaching around, despite the sharp bite of the stays on the tight corset, Adele laid a gentle hand on Zarina's arm. "My father will be very proud of all your hard work. Your diligence to my elegance is to be commended. I feel very beautiful and regal today."

Zarina smiled warmly, brimming tears falling in gratitude.

Simon sat on the floor nearby, reading a dime novel called *Greyfriar Wins the Day*. Pet wandered to the boy, trying to attract his attention by pawing the pages. Simon glanced up at his sister. "You're always regal, Adele. Not that stupid Senator Clark cares."

"Simon, hush. You must promise to be civil to the senator today." Still, Adele was warmed by her brother's words.

"Why should I be civil? Because you're marrying him?"

"Mostly. Also because I ask it of you."

He shrugged and turned his attention back to his book and the cat.

Dangling from the mirror was her amulet, the one Mamoru had given her. She had intended to wear it during the ceremony, but had changed her mind when Simon appeared at her door, escaping from his own wedding preparations. Now she lifted the necklace from its place.

"Simon, I have a favor to ask you."

He looked up eagerly. "Sure! You need me to start a commotion during the wedding ceremony?"

"No!" she exclaimed through a bright grin. "I need you to keep something for me. Guard it with your life."

Now he was curious. "What is it?"

She showed him the amulet and his eyes widened. "It's a special stone."

"What do you mean?" Simon's eyes studied it as she placed it into his open palm.

"Mamoru gave it to me. It comes from a far-off place. A land of ice and snow. Will you safeguard it for me?"

"Of course!" He slipped it over his head and its long chain slipped inside the collar of his suit.

"Your Highness, stand still please."

Drawing in a sigh, Adele's gaze lingered a moment on her brother while countless hands pressed against her, pulling her body this way and that. She gave in to the ministrations, letting her mind wander to happier days. Simon's small, thin novella lay on the floor. She leaned down and retrieved it, and her fingers brushed over the cover, tracing the illustration of the tall man in grey. She wondered if news of her wedding day had reached him in Edinburgh, or wherever he might be. Even separated, their pain must be the same.

A quiet knock at the door made her stiffen.

It was time.

"Enter," she commanded, handing the dime novel back to Simon.

Colonel Anhalt stood in the doorway, resplendent in his finest dress uniform, the heavy wool neat and brightly colored red and white. Six members of her White Guard stood at attention behind him, waiting to escort her to the magnificent Suez Hall.

"Your Highness." Anhalt bowed deeply, his eyes on the floor.

Adele tucked the playbill from *Desire in the Dead North*, which she'd brought with her, into the sleeve of her dress. She would carry it with her as she was wed. Perhaps Gareth's strength would see her through this ordeal.

Turning, she faced her royal guard. "I'm ready." Servants darted in to rearrange the long train so the princess would not be encumbered by it.

Anhalt straightened and stood transfixed by the magnificent sight of his charge, so very much a mature woman in place of the young girl he had known. He had no recourse but to drop to one knee before her. The rest of the room followed his lead. "You are a reflection of your mother. I am honored, Your Highness."

In a cacophony of silk, Adele stepped up to Anhalt, laying a hand on his epauletted shoulder, urging him to stand. Her cheeks flushed, feeling silly and inadequate of such reverence. Compared to many in the court, Anhalt's respect was genuine, and it moved her always. "Colonel, rise, please. It is merely the dress that has mesmerized you so. If it were up to me, I'd be wed in my traveling clothes. I suppose the world is waiting for me now."

"When you are ready, Your Highness. Not before."

The word "never" almost crossed her lips, but she refrained. It would do no good to reiterate her feelings on the matter. She had shouted it to the heavens to no avail. There was no stopping the wedding now.

Adele twisted back to her brother. "Simon. Leave the cat and go. You have to enter with the family. You're the Prince of Bengal, after all."

The boy extracted the sacred medal proclaiming his royal title from the claws of the cat and started out with a huff. Adele stopped him, brushed the dust off his crimson silk jacket, and kissed him on top of his head.

He said, "So the next time I see you, you'll be married?"

"Apparently."

Simon jammed his turban on his head. "Sorry."

"Me too. Off you go. Find your secretary and get in the right place."

Colonel Anhalt saluted the lad. As Simon passed, the White Guard parted with a clash of swords and rifles, much to the boy's delight.

Zarina fussed with the drape of Adele's train as another servant applied henna to her lips. Despite the heaviness of her regalia, Adele stood straight, her long neck giving her some added height. Every bride wanted to look this magnificent. Of course most brides would want to look so for their husbands to be. All but Adele.

Turning away from her own haunted eyes, she nodded to Colonel Anhalt. "Let's get this done."

Anhalt spun on his heel to precede her to the waiting escort. Zarina arranged Adele's long train again before grabbing the massive bouquet from the table.

It was a long march through the palace to the Suez Hall, and each step closer made Adele's stomach knot. The guards marched stiffly around her, their swords held tightly before their faces. Her newly re-formed White Guard stood with her no matter the peril, she thought with a trace of amusement. Her lips quirked a bit and she drew in a deep breath, at least as much as possible given the tightness of the corset encasing her ribs. A bead of sweat trickled down her neck. She just wanted the day over, as well as the night.

More furrows marred her brow at the thought of being alone in a room with Clark. Her mouth drew into a harsh line, sweeping aside the humor of just a moment before. Despite what Clark believed, he would not make the decisions in the bedroom or anywhere else. That was fact. She had faced and defeated more horrific things than him.

Her nerves settled and she kept pace, Anhalt before her, her guards at her sides. Zarina and a convoy of servants trailed behind. Adele briefly touched the pamphlet tucked in her sleeve.

Anhalt abruptly halted before wooden double doors that rose almost three lengths above them. Four men stood on either side, including one of Lord Kelvin's nameless protocol officers. He consulted his leather-bound schedule. "Your Highness, you and your escort will wait here until we hear the music begin. Then we will receive the signal to enter."

Adele rolled her shoulders and snapped an arm back toward her handmaiden with her palm open. Zarina ran forward and placed the bouquet in her hand. The princess brought the bundle of flowers forward against her breast as Zarina resumed adjusting the gown and veil.

Adele narrowed her eyes and jerked her powdered chin at the door. "Let's go. Now."

The protocol officer replied, "Forgive me, Your Highness. We wait until the signal."

Colonel Anhalt stepped forward and seized both brass handles. As the bureaucrat reached out to him, one of the White Guardsmen pulled the weedy little man aside, a bit roughly. The Gurkha officer tugged, and the doors budged with a mighty creak. The guardsmen lent a hand

and the great doors swung back. Anhalt and his soldiers moved to the side, leaving Adele framed in the vast entryway with her head lifted defiantly.

Thousands of lilies festooned every corner of the Suez Hall. Despite the couple's rush to the altar, the chamber was still filled with thousands of guests in their finest. All eyes fell on Adele in a massive roar of turning bodies. Eyes widened and heads swiveled, searching for cues.

At the end of the white corridor, Senator Clark and Lord Kelvin stood with mouths agape. The two men exchanged hurried comments. Clark was heated, but Kelvin merely shrugged. Major Stoddard, who stood at Clark's side, lowered his head to hide his laughter. The prime minister, who was officiating over the ceremony, glanced to his right, and in a flurry of brass and wood, the orchestra brought instruments to bear. The conductor raised his baton, and the old "Wedding March" commenced with barely noticeable flaws.

Adele had wanted a wedding with a Persian flavor, but Senator Clark and the European-descended powers in court, led by Lord Kelvin, pushed for a northern-style ceremony. The reason, they argued, was that this marriage was the key to the liberation of the north. She had her doubts about their rationalizations, but she didn't care enough to fight.

Adele surveyed the hall with cold eyes. Perhaps a manic, bridal cart-wheel down the aisle would remind the assemblage that she was a mentally deranged, tragic figure being bayoneted into marriage. She noticed Mamoru off to the side standing near the table where she and Clark would soon sign their wedding certificate. Today he wore his most elegant red and black kamishimo. He nodded with an expression of gentle awe, reminding her of her own appearance and the importance of the day.

Then her father stepped into view, his old eyes sweeping over her. For a moment, Adele could almost see them glisten. What was it that Anhalt had implied: a spitting image of her mother? Adele's expression softened, her hand reaching out to her father. He grasped it a little too quickly and guided her arm to interlock with his own.

The music swelled and echoed in the chamber as the entire room rose as one. The flickering gaslight shimmered in the air as it reflected off a hundred crystal chandeliers like fireflies dancing across the water.

As she and her father started the long walk down the aisle, Adele turned her attention to the man waiting at the far end of the aisle. The bridegroom was in his navy blue dress uniform, brass buttons afire in the light and his saber dangling from his hip. The reflections sparkling off Senator Clark's multitude of medals made him sparkle. It amused Adele and she smiled.

Her father noted her attention. "You are too good for him."

Adele turned to him. "Yes, I know."

"As your mother was too good for me."

Adele gripped him tighter, and the two supported each other under the canopy of raised sabers courtesy of Clark's American Rangers lining the aisle. Lord Kelvin's mortified eyes were wide as a bug's as he noticed the two imperials talking during the processional. *Good*, Adele thought, and her smile widened. Clark interpreted that her joy was meant for him and came briskly forward to claim his bride, but His Majesty, Constantine, stepped between the groom and his daughter. Gnarled hands reached for the delicate silk veil, taking his time lifting the material away from her face. His fingers slid ever so lightly across her cheek in a rare show of public affection. He took Adele's hand, squeezing so hard her eyes widened. Only then did he turn to Senator Clark. He took Clark's gloved hand and placed her hand in his.

"I give you my only daughter in hopes that the Equatorian Empire and the American Republic can unite to make our people strong enough to withstand all blows." His booming voice brought chills to Adele's skin.

Clark grinned, but surprisingly followed protocol, bowing deeply. "Thank you, Your Majesty. I will treasure Her Highness, Adele, and our united nations till my dying day, and defend them both with my final breath."

Constantine stared at Clark and then, after a long moment of silence, stepped back. The warmth of his large hand covering Adele's own fell away, and she took her bouquet in both hands to avoid Clark's grasp.

This is it, Adele thought. The smile on her lips faded. Her eyes were hard and regal as she moved to Clark's side, a bride of duty and nothing more. Her gaze drifted to Lord Kelvin as he began to drone through the opening remarks, but the splendor of the window behind him drew Adele's attention as the lowering sun shone through and an open sky beckoned. The beautifully colored panes of glass were prison bars this day. Her eyes closed as she summoned thoughts of happier days, playing with the cats in Edinburgh Castle, Gareth's attempt at writing, the meal the townsfolk had prepared for her.

Kelvin said her name for some reason, and her attention came back to the present. She tried to listen to the words and repeat them, but they meant little to her.

"I, Adele, take you, Miles, to be my husband to have and to hold from this day forward, for better or for worse, for richer, for poorer, in sickness and in health, from this day forward until death do us part."

Clark put his hand out, and Stoddard stepped up smartly and placed a ring in Clark's hand. The wedding ring was an ornate masterpiece rimmed with jewels. There were American-mined chrysoberyl, their gold and honey tones mingling with the sherry-red topaz set on either side. Two oval citrines sat beyond that. It was a bold wedding band, not typical for Equatoria, diamonds being rarer in the Americas. Clark had also chosen not to include emeralds in the design, not because they'd clash, but more likely because Equatoria was famed for her gigantic emeralds.

Senator Clark took Adele's hand with much ceremony for the benefit of the crowd, and slipped the ring on her finger. It was heavy enough to feel like shackles. He grinned as he rushed through the vows, and his mouth opened to utter his declaration of "I thee wed," but a sudden crash of glass brought screams and shouts from the crowd.

A shower of colored fragments from the beautiful windows rained down just behind Lord Kelvin. The tinkling of a thousand painted shards filled the air even over the exclamations of the disrupted wedding party. Everyone came to their feet, moving backward or forward depending on whether or not they were armed.

Adele ducked her head but then was up quickly, facing the window and whatever threat had dared to interrupt. To her annoyance, Clark attempted to push her out of the way, but she sidestepped his gallantry and moved toward her White Guard, who were already running up the aisle with Mamoru just behind them.

A flutter of a long grey cloak around a tall, slim figure rose from a crouch amid the shattered glass.

"The Greyfriar!" someone shouted.

CHAPTER

THE ROOM ERUPTED with gasps, shouts, and applause. Adele stood transfixed with astonishment and cried Greyfriar's name with elation. Smoky glass-covered eyes snapped toward her voice. Without hesitation, she bounded around the stunned figure of Lord Kelvin, as best she could in her bulky wedding dress.

"What are you doing here?" she shouted breathlessly as Greyfriar reached out to her.

"Come with me! You're in danger!"

Senator Clark ran toward his bride, rage smeared across his features. All his planning and hard labor were being taken from him by an upstart's ridiculous showmanship and utter audacity. Greyfriar swung Adele behind him and drew his sword as he faced the infuriated American.

"I'll have your head on a pike for this!" Clark ground out through his clenched teeth.

Drawing his saber, he charged, his sword swinging. Greyfriar countered his mad thrust, deflecting the blade away from Adele and himself.

"Don't kill him!" Adele shouted, though to the gathering crowd it wasn't clear whom she was talking about.

Blades rang as the rivals fenced past the empty throne. Greyfriar either didn't see or wasn't concerned with the six White Guard rushing toward him, Colonel Anhalt in the lead. A twist of Greyfriar's wrist and a flourish of his powerful arm sent Clark's saber flying from his hand. He kicked the disarmed senator in the chest, shoving him back into the oncoming soldiers. Anhalt was the only one who managed to sidestep the pileup.

Clark shouted, "Kill him! Kill him!"

Greyfriar angled back toward the smashed window, guiding Adele with him. The crowd was surging forward now, half in outrage and half with wild excitement, consumed by the spectacle before them. A long rope hung from the broken panes. Greyfriar tossed his rapier to Adele, who caught it expertly. He seized her, then the rope, and began to scale the wall. He was aided by his vampiric flight, though done so subtly, no one could tell. He carried her quickly up thirty feet to the sill of the smashed window. The train on Adele's gown hung to the floor below.

She turned back to gaze over the chaotic Suez Hall, searching for her father. Her brother Simon was clearly visible standing on a chair, waving his turban and cheering. Then she saw Anhalt hefting an ornamental dagger. She held out a desperate hand as if that would be enough to stop his fatal throw.

The dagger flew through the air toward Greyfriar's head, but miraculously it missed, thunking with reverberating force into the window frame inches from his cheek. Greyfriar tuned back to address the new threat, but Adele clutched him around the neck.

"He missed on purpose," she whispered hurriedly.

"I doubt that."

"Trust me, he doesn't miss."

With a perfectly controlled slash of his blade, Greyfriar cut the gown's long train and it fluttered over the throne in a heap of satin and silk while Adele kicked off her high-heeled shoes. The couple moved onto a narrow ledge outside. From this dizzying perspective, Adele saw a huge crowd gathered around the palace. Shouts of Greyfriar's name echoed up from the square below. She also saw soldiers attempting to get through the thronged mass.

Adele's veil caught hard and her head jerked back painfully. "Wait!" She tore the tiara from her head and tossed it, veil and all, to the crowd below, who converged on the grand souvenir. The ensuing tumult slowed the guard's advance. Adele tried to manage her unwieldy dress as best she could for the moment, but it kept snagging on stone and iron fixtures as Greyfriar helped her to a more spacious ledge.

"We have to hurry," he told her, searching around them.

"Wait!" Adele grabbed his arm. "What are you doing? What am I doing?"

"You are in danger."

She laughed. "Danger how? From a boring life maybe, but . . ."

"Cesare planned to kill you during the wedding."

Adele rubbed her forehead in disbelief. "That's why you came? Wouldn't a warning have sufficed? You couldn't have sent another cat with a hidden message?"

"No time. I had to come myself."

"I do have an entire army to protect me."

"You had an army in France too, and you ended up in Cesare's power." Greyfriar took her by the shoulder with a grip of sincere intensity, as if convincing a disbelieving child of some difficult fact. "I came because I had to. A message would not serve."

"I can't just run away."

"I trust your life with no one but me." Greyfriar's voice was burdened with desperation. "Please, Adele. This place is dangerous for you."

"But . . ."

"Do you want to marry Senator Clark?"

"No," Adele said quietly as a flutter of excitement born of a free horizon rose up inside of her. Then her face grew more determined. "No, I don't. All right, then, let's go." She looked around the windswept ledge. "I hope you have transportation waiting for us."

"Transportation?"

"Don't you have an escape plan?" Adele cursed before laughing desperately. "We need to work on your forward planning."

"My plan was to get you before you were killed. I came all the way from England. I barely reached Alexandria in time."

With Greyfriar's balance and strength, they gained the rooftop of the Victoria Palace and, to their great relief, found it empty. They could see the Mediterranean crowded with ships just below them, as well as the Nile delta and Lake Mareotis sparkling in the descending sun.

"We need to get out of the city." Adele grabbed Greyfriar's hand, pointing south. "That way."

"North is faster."

"Like when you dragged me to Edinburgh to escape from London? Just trust me!"

An iron door crashed open and troopers poured out onto the roof. They quickly spotted the couple. Greyfriar and Adele ran to the parapet. With his arm around her waist, he pulled her close and jumped. Adele's breath left her as they flew through the air in a barely controlled drop to another rooftop almost thirty yards away. The guards rushed to the edge, but none dared make the jump. They lifted their rifles, but no shots followed.

Adele and Greyfriar ran for the next roof in the palace complex. He again grabbed Adele's waist and jumped down to a lower level. Changing direction multiple times, they ran from peak to peak until they reached the high outer-palace walls. They paused and looked down to a dark corner of the city below. He pulled her tight against him once more. She exhaled against his neck and wrapped around him as he jumped, never tiring of the free-fall sensation when in his arms.

In seconds, they were outside of the Victoria Palace grounds, but few citizens were allowed in this part of the city so close to the palace, which was why Adele had led them here. She tugged Greyfriar into an alley, staying hidden as much as possible from eyes that might still be on the high palace spires, watching for them and signaling to the soldiers on foot.

"Give me your cloak." He tugged off his cape and wrapped it around her shoulders. She drew the cloak tight about her. "At least I won't be as obvious."

The imperial quarter fell away as they ran into the Turkish Quarter, which Adele knew well. People were at their windows, caught up in their own daily routines. A few glanced down at the odd couple. Some pointed. Adele was sure they were a sight. Her in the remnants of a white wedding dress wrapped in a long grey cloak, running alongside a soldier wrapped like a Tuareg with smoked glasses, armed to the teeth.

Adele led the way as they curved around the Western Harbor. She kept to backstreets near the water, where laborers continued to ply their trades no matter the holiday. It would be impossible to remain undetected for long. They had to leave Alexandria quickly. Orders were no doubt already flying to lock down the city. Roads would be closed. Rail and air would be suspended.

Shrill whistles sounded, and Greyfriar tucked Adele into a dark alcove where they pressed close against each other as a squad of police raced past. Greyfriar's attention stayed on the street for another minute until he was content immediate danger had passed. Turning back to Adele, he watched her as she ripped out another layer of satin petticoat from under the massive skirt and tossed it aside.

She glanced up and caught his bemused smile. "Oh, believe me, I have more."

He fingered a delicate curl of her hair. "You look exquisite."

He lifted his smoked glasses, and their gazes finally met in a moment of calm, his pale blue eyes boring into her dark ones. Adele's hand pulled down the thick cloth wrapped around his mouth and chin until it revealed his lips. In the dark alcove filled with frail, drifting cobwebs and dust-covered timber, they kissed, passionately, desperately making up for the months of separation.

When they pulled apart, he wiped her lip where his sharp teeth had nicked her. He wanted to lick the blood from his thumb, to taste her once more. The hunger welled up in him like a lion's roar, and it took all his willpower to refrain. He smoothed her hair, trailing his fingers through her curls.

In a strained voice, he said, "We need to go."

She leaned into him. "I know." Licking her bleeding lip, she straightened. "I suppose I will have to learn how to kiss a vampire properly. You're dangerous."

His breath was quick as he gazed at her. She was here beside him, willingly and without regret, full of life, full of blood. She looked beautiful.

"Why is it always danger and dire situations with you?" she asked.

"Nature of the beast, perhaps." His smile showed a glint of his sharp teeth. Then he replaced his glasses and lifted his scarf to become Greyfriar once more.

She had missed his dry humor.

Together they slipped from the security of the dark cul-de-sac and onto the street. The way seemed clear and they darted out, only to run straight into Colonel Anhalt with a contingent of the White Guard. The officer's face was like stone, his dark eyes locked not on the princess but on the tall figure of Greyfriar. Adele stood wide-legged in front of the swordsman, protecting him in case her personal guards tried to act. Adele didn't know what to say to her loyal guardian. She was almost ashamed. Her breath was trapped painfully in her chest as she tried to think of a way out of the situation that did no harm to any of them.

Colonel Anhalt said, "Your Highness, the court is frantic with concern for your well-being."

"Colonel, I know this may seem a bit odd, but—"

"A bit odd? You departed your wedding through a broken window with a masked man. Odd, at the least."

"The Greyfriar heard about an imminent attack at the ceremony. My life was apparently in danger."

Now it was Anhalt's turn to be startled, but then he regarded the stoic swordsman. "Allow me to escort you both back to the palace. We'll make sense of everything there."

"No," Adele said firmly. "I'm not going back. Not yet. I've come to a decision. We're on the verge of war. I cannot help my subjects both here and in the north by becoming a royal flower and allowing Clark to run roughshod over Equatoria. Provisions must be made. Greyfriar has provided me with an opportunity."

"It isn't safe for you to be with this man, Highness. There are shoot-to-kill orders for your companion. The police and the army are mobilizing."

"Shoot to kill!" Adele snarled. "Senator Clark's orders, no doubt."

"Yes," the colonel replied. "What are your plans?"

"We're going south." Adele felt Greyfriar seize her with alarm, fearful that she should trust this man too much, but she shook her head to dismiss his concerns. "We must leave the Empire. After that, I'm not sure yet. I thought I could have influence on the war effort due to my time up north. I'm the only person in court who has actually seen vampire territory. And yet, they ignore and dismiss me as a lunatic. I won't be a party to genocide. They will agree to my terms, or I won't return. I'm holding my wedding hostage."

Anhalt tightened his mouth, his face a mask of pride. "Command me, Highness."

Adele fought back the overwhelming sense of joy and love for this man who had always stood by her side. "You shouldn't be involved, Colonel. It could mean your career."

"Or my life. Please don't waste time. I can lead the search away from you. I'll have them combing every ship between here and Cyprus, and every railroad carriage steaming east or west. You must get out of the Home Counties. Can you manage the river as far south as the First Cataract?"

Adele glanced quickly at Greyfriar. She certainly didn't want to go that far south, although she couldn't tell Anhalt it was because Greyfriar was really a vampire. Taking him deep into the Sahara was a death sentence.

"We can," Greyfriar replied quickly.

"Are you sure?" Adele asked him. "Shouldn't we just get over the imperial border? South out of Alexandria, but then swing north?"

Greyfriar whispered, "It will be fine. Trust me."

With a fearful breath, Adele said to Anhalt, "Yes. We can make the First Cataract."

"Good. Go to Abu Simbel. All things considered, you should reach it in a week or a week and a half. I will handle matters here, then be there to meet you. I will bring provisions and arrange transport for you. If that is what you wish."

She impulsively hugged him, pressing herself against the hard brass buttons of his uniform. Words of gratitude were not enough to convey all she felt.

Hesitant at first, but then more boldly, his arms wrapped around her. "It is my honor, my princess. Go now. We will make sure your way is clear." Anhalt regarded the tall swordsman. "Watch out for her. My dagger won't miss a second time."

Greyfriar gave a single nod. "I'll protect her with my life."

It satisfied the Gurkha, who turned and headed out into the bustling street, his company falling into step behind him.

Adele stood for a few seconds caught up in the amazement of what had just occurred. It was Greyfriar's voice that broke her reverie.

"That, I take it, was your Colonel Anhalt."

She spun back to him, grinning widely. "Yes, that most certainly was."

"I would not want to disappoint such a man."

"You won't." She grabbed his arm. "Come on."

They ran into the southern districts of Alexandria. The whistles and marching feet of troops faded into the distance, no doubt compliments of Colonel Anhalt's misdirection. They avoided hansom cabs, and the chemical carts preparing to light the evening lanterns. They reached the canals, which meant that Lake Mareotis was close by. Already she could see smaller cottages dotting the edges of the inland waterway, the sails of feluccas forming a procession beyond them. To the south towered great smokestacks belching black dust into the air.

The couple crossed the nearest bridge crowded with foot traffic and closed on the lake. Adele ran for the wharf. She knew exactly where she was heading. Greyfriar chased after her, his eyes watching the suspicious fishermen. There was a tearing sound as the dress snagged on a protruding nail. Adele did not stop, just grateful that more of the heavy dress fell away. She wondered if the soldiers would be able to follow the discarded petticoats like breadcrumbs.

Adele approached a bearded old man sitting on an overturned pail, mending a weathered sail. He looked up at her approach, smiling.

"Salaam, Miss. You're looking quite lovely this evening. That's a fine dress, though I fear you may get it dirty if you're not careful."

Adele grinned back at him. To her relief, she spied a boat along his dock that would suit their needs perfectly. It had a small engine as well as sails, and a hold for protection from the sun.

He nodded toward a felucca bobbing gently as he rose on crooked legs. "Do you want to take her out for a romantic sail?"

"Actually I'm interested in buying that small dahabiya over there. It's yours, right?"

"Taken a liking to that one, eh? No wonder. She's a fine boat. Seen her share of storms and fair waters alike. I can fix her up for you. Should be ready in a few days."

"As is." Adele slipped off her gem-encrusted wedding band and pressed it into his twisted hand. "Today. Right now."

"But I . . ." The old man trailed off into stunned silence as he gazed down at the riches in his hand. "*Fata barruk Allah.* I don't know that I can sell this."

"Pry the gemstones out and sell them piecemeal. The ring itself is unique, and if it's recognized, it will attract attention from the authorities. But, trust me, you can buy five boats for what that ring is worth. I'm buying the boat and your silence."

He glanced up at her and her mysterious, armed companion and scrutinized them both. For a moment Adele was afraid she would have to steal the boat. Not many women would be wearing a butchered wedding gown and have a ring worth enough to feed his family for years. The sailor merely grinned beneath his white beard. The waterfront was not a place for too many questions into people's backgrounds.

"If you insist, miss. She's all yours. There's food in her pantry and tins of chemical mix for the engine."

"Would you throw in some fishing poles and an extra sail? And do you have any extra clothes?"

He laughed and nodded at three poles lying on the deck and hefted the sail he had been working on. "It's as good as I can do, but it should hold in a stiff breeze." Then he stepped into a shanty nearby and came back with a small bundle of clothes. "They belonged to my son, but they should fit you, ma'am. I've nothing for the gentleman."

Adele thanked him and readied to cast off while Greyfriar retrieved the poles and brought the material aboard before cautiously settling into the boat as Adele hoisted the sail with a wild laugh. In moments, they were under way toward the Nile and freedom.

CHAPTER 14

FOR A LARGER vessel, the dahabiya handled sharply, and soon Adele had the bow aimed up the delta for the main trunk of the River Nile. There was a great deal of traffic on the water, which actually helped calm her anxiety. It wouldn't be long before the search widened beyond the Ras el-Tin district and Alexandria proper to draw in the River Guards. Among the countless boats, however, they would be hard to find.

Adele was thinking how best to camouflage themselves. The wedding dress would obviously be the first thing to go as soon as they were out of the heavy river traffic and she could dispose of it surreptitiously. For now she kept it hidden under the folds of Greyfriar's cloak.

Greyfriar emerged from belowdecks, where he had stowed the spare canvas. His head wrap was gone, revealing his shaggy dark hair. He still wore his military garb and gloves, but his weapons were out of sight. He brushed persistent drops of water from his cheeks.

The weather was fair, and the two large lateen sails billowed full and fat with the wind's breath. The hull skimmed over the surface, the bow rising and falling in a rhythmic sunburst cloud of spray. But their speed was slow compared to those going the opposite way with the current as it raced for the sea. Adele knew how to capture every scrap of the wind for now. Soon, they would lose the northerly sea breezes and rely more on the motor to fight their way upriver.

Adele was happy. Like a ship, she was always best under full press. There was a light in Adele's eyes; her auburn hair danced in the wind like an ominous crown set upon her temples. The remnants of her wedding dress fought from under his cloak and flew with the wind like a flag.

She smiled at Gareth. She couldn't help it. How long had she hoped for this moment? She hadn't thought it possible. Only hours ago she had been willing to give up her freedom, and now suddenly the world was once more open to her, with Gareth at her side.

Immediately her heart quickened. Standing by the rail, he was as tall and straight as she remembered. He looked the same as he had in Europe, though his hair was a bit longer and more unkempt. There were lines around his mouth, deep with strain. It had only been a few months, after all, but the length of time spent apart was immeasurable. Silhouetted against the setting sun, his chiseled features were shadowed, but his azure eyes shone bright and hungry. She saw his nostrils flare as he took in her scent. Her breath caught, wondering what message her adrenaline-soaked thoughts were sending. But she knew. Because it was mirrored in his face. Their gazes locked on each other.

Gareth crossed the span in two large strides and gathered her up so swiftly in his embrace that Adele's breath rushed out. Their lips sought each other desperately. His fingers found her tresses, entwining and pulling, but she didn't care. Her own hands were exploring his hair, soft and shaggy. Where most vampires handled humans so roughly they left bruises due to their dulled sense of contact, Gareth's touch was gentle, caressing. He understood pressure and always worried about what he could do to a human's frail body.

She fell against him and it was like leaning against a stone. He was immovable.

"I've missed you," he whispered in her ear.

She let out a soft sob, hugging him tighter than she had ever dared hold anything. Her throat was so tight with emotion she couldn't speak. She didn't need to. His lips found hers again. Shivers rushed over her skin that had nothing to do with the nip in the air. Her breath sounded loud and throaty. This was a scene she had seen played out on stage or in her dreams and, for a moment, she wasn't sure she was awake.

He took her cheeks in his large hands and stared intently in her eyes. Whatever breath was left in Adele's lungs vanished. The chill of his palms cooled her heated skin, traveling a quicksilver path to her core.

"Don't leave me again," she pleaded.

"Never. Whatever the cost."

"I didn't dare hope to see you." He drew her tight as they stood on the stern of the boat.

"I tried to stop thinking about you," he admitted.

"Did it work?

"Not that I recall."

He didn't pull away, only held her, as if just that simple act was enough. Such love was something that had been long missing in her life. They stayed that way for a long while, just holding one another.

Adele pulled away with a worried look. "If Cesare is planning some attack, shouldn't I go back? Is my family in danger?"

"Not so far as I could tell. He wants you. And Senator Clark. You are the two who drive the war machine. Killing your brother or father only fuels human determination and hatred. He wants to break the alliance, and stop the war. He is more likely to wait for you to return than to stage an attack against lesser targets. You are safest away from Alexandria."

She relaxed, relieved by Gareth's words. Then she noticed him staring out over the dark waters as the river traffic increased, eyeing each ship as they passed, each set of eyes that moved over them, expecting pointed fingers and shouts of discovery.

"We're safe," Adele assured him. "We're one of thousands now. The river will hide us."

He glanced down at her, his expression dour. "I have no doubt. I couldn't be in safer hands."

A gust of wind threatened to ruffle Adele's dress, and she fumbled to keep his cloak covering the stark white of her gown. "However, it would do well to get rid of this thing. I'll go change."

She indicated for Gareth to mind the tiller, then paused, contemplating something. She threw one leg up on the rail and tossed the silk away from her thigh, revealing the Fahrenheit khukri strapped there.

Gareth's brow furrowed. "Were you expecting danger as well?"

"A girl needs to be prepared for anything on her wedding day." Adele drew the blade and handed it carefully to him. She turned her back. "Do you think you can cut me free? I'll never get the thing off."

"Hold still." With a quick slice of her blade the torturous ties flew from her midsection.

"That's a relief. Thank you." Unhindered, Adele drew in a deep breath for the first time since she'd squeezed into the gown. She held the sinking bodice of the dress tight against her breasts and gathered the fluttering skirt as Gareth stared openly at her. She pointed firmly ahead of them. "Just keep her prow following that ship dead ahead. I'll be right back."

Scrambling down the short steps she came into the hold. It was sparse, but Adele could see where the old man had been storing bottles of date palm wine. A few bottles, both empty and full, rolled with the sway of the ship. She picked one up and studied the bottle. Not a bad brand. She stored them more securely. In the hold, there was an old tarp in addition to their extra sail as well as some old buckets, a light emergency anchor, and coils of cable.

She inspected the boyish clothes, simple but serviceable. Then she realized, wiggling her toes on the rough deck, that she had no shoes. She slid out of the wedding gown and changed from glamorous princess to water rat with a laugh.

Adele came back on deck. Gareth raised an eyebrow, but said nothing. She had the wedding dress wrapped in a blanket and tied tight with twine. A moment later she had the spare anchor tied to the bundle and was dragging it to the rail. Gareth got up to help her, and together they dropped the wedding gown overboard. She stared after it to make sure it found its way to the bottom of the river. Gareth mistook the concentration for emotion.

"Regrets?" he asked.

"None. I hope some lucky she-crocodile enjoys it." Adele held her arms outstretched for inspection. "How do I look?"

"Strong. Determined."

"No. I meant my disguise." She smirked.

"You look like an urchin."

"Perfect." Adele settled against him as if they were taking a holiday. The western sky was blossoming into the shade of a lotus flower with the last burst of the sun. Its colorful tapestry stretched across their heads. "How are things in Edinburgh?"

"Much the same as they've been for a hundred years or more."

"No, I mean how are the people? How is Morgana?"

"Oh. She's well. She speaks of you often. Your time there was very special to her. To everyone."

"She has no idea what it meant to me. I miss her, and everyone. But Morgana particularly was so sweet and helpful when I first arrived and I thought everything I believed in was a lie." Adele sighed with memories. The friendship with the serving girl had been her salvation in those earliest dark nights in cold Scotland.

Gareth didn't speak. He well remembered the moment on Castle Hill when he revealed the true identity of Greyfriar to Adele. Feeling betrayed, she had run him through with his own sword. Her limitless trust and affection had turned to hatred, which cut him more keenly than any physical wound. That was the reason why the eventual but gradual return of her affection had washed over him like a flood and altered his life forever.

Adele asked, "What about the cats?"

"They're fine."

"Thank you for Pet, by the way. It was the most amazing gift I've ever received. I can't believe you moved him from Edinburgh to Alexandria."

"The Greyfriar has a long reach when necessary." Gareth reached out his hand dramatically and then smiled at his foolishness. "I'm glad he made it to you."

"Oh yes. My brother, Simon, loves him. Partly because he came from the mysterious Greyfriar." Adele listened to the ruffle of wind in sails and the gentle lapping of water. "How is my good friend Baudoin? Is he still with you?"

"Of course. Baudoin has always been with me. And he always will be."

"He doesn't much care for me, does he? I think he was unhappy with your dalliance with a human."

"Nonsense," Gareth replied flatly. "He adores you."

"You're a worse liar than I am." She playfully patted him on the cheek. "So what did he say when you told him you were coming to Alexandria to rescue me from my wedding?"

"Nothing. I didn't tell him."

Adele laughed.

"I am the prince," Gareth retorted stiffly. "I don't need Baudoin's approval to come and go as I please."

She laughed even louder. "Oh, no doubt. Just like I don't crave the support of Colonel Anhalt and Mamoru in everything I do."

Gareth breathed out in acceptance. "I suppose you're right. Baudoin means more to me than anyone, except you. I would do anything for him. Except give up the Greyfriar and you." He shifted his weight, scanning around the boat for any undue attention to them. "Adele, when we encountered your Colonel Anhalt in Alexandria, you mentioned being a party to genocide. What did you mean?"

Adele felt a little sick at the question, but there was no way to break it gently. "In the coming war, the Equatorian and American armies, under the command of Senator Clark, intend to slaughter the humans in the north."

Gareth reared back, his teeth flashing. "For what purpose?"

"To remove your food supply and diminish your ability to resist. Clark's mad." Her face fell. "And my father as well it seems. He agreed to this insanity."

"That strikes me as the type of strategy Cesare might have birthed." Bitterness laced Gareth's every word. "Can humanity be as horrific as my own kind?"

"Believe me, I'm ashamed to be human at the moment. I had hoped to stop it, but no one would listen to me. No one cared. I don't deserve to be empress if I can't even sway my own father. I have failed my people."

Gareth straightened, rising to his full, imposing height. "That you care for your people—and even for the humans of the north, who are no direct charge to you—does you credit, Adele. It is for that reason alone you deserve to be empress. Rich, poor, slave, or free—you care about them all. Apparently it is something both your father and my brother have forgotten."

"But we are both outcasts now. So what can either of us do?"

Gareth took her chin and tipped her face up at him. "As you told your Anhalt, you will make them see reason. True leaders, even displaced ones, can effect changes. You will alter the future of your people. Although, personally, I would prefer you do so without marrying that blowhard."

Adele blinked. The wind and Gareth's words were blowing away her worries. Her hand covered his. "We'll find a way to do it together."

"As it should be," he told her. "How long a journey do we have?"

"Abu Simbel is at least a week upriver. Maybe longer. We'll have to live like vagabonds and river folks. We can stop in Cairo for provisions for the long haul up the Nile. I kept a few of the gems from the dress to buy what we need. We'll be fine."

Gareth's gaze lifted to the spectacle of fading color above them. "It will be a warmer day tomorrow. I may have to hide belowdecks when the heat becomes too much. I won't be of much use to you."

She drew in a breath, suddenly unsure of her decisions.

Gareth leaned forward to kiss her. He couldn't feel her lips against his, but once more the tang of delicate spice and rich sweetness washed over his tongue and lingered there at the back of his throat. He heard her heart fluttering wildly in her chest. The musky scent of passion blended with the sweet perfume of an inexperienced woman was a tantalizing mix. He held her lightly and his heightened senses absorbed her, feeling her spent adrenaline and growing weakness.

Someone shouted across the way at the young lovers. A bemused river captain cruising his own boat waved at them.

Adele laughed with embarrassment and sat back. "I guess we should be watching where we're going. And keeping an eye out for pursuit."

Gareth relinquished the tiller. "When did you last eat?"

"A little this morning. Not much. The thought of marrying Senator Clark made me nauseated. What about you?"

"I can go for a time without feeding."

"How long?"

"Don't worry. We have always survived on infrequent feedings."

"Really? When I was in London, it seemed like your people fed constantly."

"They do now, but they don't have to. Since the Great Killing, we've become fat and debauched."

"Well, you don't need to be an ascetic for no reason," she said firmly. "You can feed on me."

"Yes. But I won't dare weaken or hurt you irreparably."

"What about animals?"

Gareth shook his head. "Their blood is not suitable. It is nothing more than water to me."

"So without human blood, you will die?"

"Let's not be overly melodramatic."

"But it's true, isn't it?"

"Well, yes."

"How can we manage this?" Adele lamented wearily. "There are no willing humans save me to help you."

"Don't worry. I'll make do." He didn't elaborate further, but assumed the implications were clear enough. He would feed on unwilling humans if necessary.

—⁓—

They sailed through the night utilizing Gareth's exceptional nocturnal vision to navigate. The night air held a chill that he relished, and he finally breathed easier as his internal temperature dropped back to comfortable levels.

Adele held a small gemstone that she had torn from her wedding gown. She concentrated with her eyes shut.

"What are you doing?" Gareth asked.

"It's a geomancy exercise Mamoru taught me. I'm tasting iron." She took a deep drink from their freshwater supply, rinsing the taste from her mouth. Yawning, she slipped the stone back into her pocket, then nestled deep in Gareth's embrace, drawing his cloak closer around her. "I'll try the others later. Hopefully they come from tastier surroundings."

"I'm sure," Gareth remarked, amused.

Despite her determination to stay awake, she finally succumbed to the weariness of the day's events and her eyes closed. Gareth watched her sleep, observing how the resolute face of a future empress melted away as her muscles relaxed and allowed the young girl to once more emerge. Where Adele had shown strength of character and perseverance during her time in Europe, the months back in Alexandria had wrought another change in her. She stood straighter; her decisions came sure and fast. Uncertainty was gone. Adele's confidence in herself was intoxicating. His fingers brushed at a wayward curl that chose to rest over her eyes. Her breath deepened at his touch, but she did not wake.

Gareth knew that he and Adele were in a desperate situation. Romantic it may sound, but he doubted their relationship, whatever it was, could ever work. She was human and he wasn't. It was as simple as that. Still, the pain of being apart was apparently too great for both of them. They deserved to try. This undertaking was immense and could prove to be terrible folly, especially for him traipsing around in a desert, but he felt no dread. He was at peace now. Regardless of what his future held, he knew that it would always be at Adele's side. He simply would have to be even more like a man, and less like a monster.

Hours later, the first rays of light were spreading out over the horizon to Gareth's left. He could feel the change in the air and the temperature rising. His chest immediately tightened as he attempted a deep breath. He could only hope that the sun would not gain too much strength since there was much to do once they reached Cairo. Word of Adele's flight was certain to have reached there and, no doubt, soldiers and police would be swarming the streets. Though Gareth knew Adele could look after herself, the thought of not being able to help her ate at him.

The banks of the Nile River grew more crowded as the green shores gave way to tan stone and bricks, and then grey steel and iron. The occasional shepherd or villager became mobs of people hurrying on foot leading camels and oxen, and finally carriages and trams. The river itself seemed suddenly clogged with boats and barges, tugs and feluccas. On every side were whistles and horns and shouting men. The sky turned yellow with the haze of humanity.

Then, beyond the jumbled buildings crowding the river to the west, Gareth caught sight of the Great Pyramids. Even from this distance and shimmering through the filthy air, the pyramids towered like something that belonged in another world. Their sheer mass was astounding. Gareth had read that kings were buried inside them. All that effort for just a tomb. How great those kings must have been.

Adele roused at the noise of the river traffic. Her gaze found his and she smiled. "Good morning."

"Good morning."

Her arms stretched out as her back arched, easing muscles stiff from the unfamiliar position. "Have you been awake all night?"

"Of course." He quickly straightened the tiller again, narrowly avoiding a small boat with a wide-eyed man at the helm.

"You should have woken me. I could've helped."

Gareth said nothing but continued to watch her with crystal-blue eyes. Bemused, his head bobbed to his left and Adele turned.

"Oh Cairo! We're here!" She rose and made her way forward, intently watching the traffic passing close by the dahabiya. Then she turned to the other bank. "The pyramids! Can you see them?"

"They are hard to miss." He regarded the fading giants again. "Human ingenuity is amazing. I'd give anything to take wing and fly over the structures."

"Maybe someday. Let's keep flying to a minimum, shall we? Unless you take me with you."

They passed under a massive steel bridge, and the steady hoofbeats of hundreds of brougham carriages and wagons thrummed overhead. The waters off the docks of Bulaq were choked with steamers and cargo ships. Tiny vessels, some smaller than their own, darted daringly between the behemoths competing for the river road. Swarms of people crowded the immense wharf.

A River Guard patrol boat drifted past and Adele stiffened. Gazing upward she saw airships hovering high above the city. She checked her veil, fashioned from cloth she had ripped from the hem of her wedding gown, and came back to Gareth, taking the tiller, which, given their proximity to towering vessels, he gratefully relinquished. She steered toward a crowded wharf, purposefully keeping a barge between their dahabiya and the patrol.

"Is it safe?" Gareth asked.

"As safe as it's going to be. We have to take the chance. We need supplies. There's less of a chance my jewels will raise an uproar here than in a small town."

"Surely your father will come to the same conclusion."

"Maybe, but hopefully they are still looking elsewhere if Colonel Anhalt came through. And besides, Cairo is a very big city. It would be impossible to scour every inch for only two people. We'll keep to the crowds, and just get in and out with what we need. We should be fine." Adele braided her hair while Gareth removed his military tunic and stood in a white linen shirt. She eyed him enviously. "That's the good thing about you having a secret identity already. No one knows who Greyfriar truly is, and you can easily pass for a human as long as you keep your gloves on and don't smile too much." Adele laughed weakly at her strained wit.

"I'll get my weapons."

"No. People don't carry weapons in the streets here. We're very civilized." She put an arm around his waist. "Just stay near me, and let me do the talking. Unless you speak Arabic, of course."

"I don't. But likely by the end of the day, I will. I learn your languages quickly. It's a facility my kind has."

Her smile faded as her head tilted up at the strengthening sun. "Speaking of your kind, are you going to be able to take this heat?"

"For several hours at least. If we keep to the shade and stay indoors when possible, I should be fine. But let's stop wasting the coolness of the morning."

Adele was in agreement. The boat glided to the wharf, and she waved to a dockhand to catch the bowline Gareth tossed.

Now they were committed.

CHAPTER  15

AS THE TWO entered the city, Gareth was amazed to see even more people than in Alexandria. They jostled one another at every turn, paying little heed in their rush. Never had he seen so many humans at once. Cesare would literally be drooling at the vast numbers. Such herds as these were only to be imagined by the northern clans.

Thankfully, Adele knew where she was heading, so Gareth let her take the lead. There was so much activity, he couldn't decide what to stare at first. Beautiful medieval buildings rose several stories above the crowded streets. Glass windows shone in the sun's rays despite the industrial filth on the stone walls. Modern buildings towered over those. As they neared a busy intersection, the rumble of metal wheels on tracks combined with the hiss and cloying heat of steam announced the passing of a trolley.

"Where are we going?" Gareth asked.

"We'll head for the common bazaars and look for a pawn shop. We should find what we want in the old Suk es-Saigh, the gold market."

Adele tried to watch where she was stepping to avoid broken glass or animal waste, but occasionally she'd fail and step in something un-pleasant but at least not dangerous. Only a low curse would cross her lips as she hopped for a moment on one foot, but for the most part she was agile enough to dart over the worst of the urban obstacles. A water-bearer stalked past in his flowing burnoose and heavy load and chuckled at her.

Adele scowled in his direction. "I'd like to see him walk barefoot through the city."

The deeper into the old neighborhoods they went, the more Cairo churned like a barely contained madhouse. Mobs of children played happily in various nooks and corners near little shops with ragged awnings and fly nets drawn across the doors. A goose vendor drove his sizable flock before him, guiding them unerringly with a palm branch among the trolley cars, steam wagons, bicycles, and pedestrians.

Soon Adele and Gareth passed into the frantic bazaar district. Vendors shouted at them, reaching for them, plucking at their arms, fighting for their attention. Yards of brightly colored material stretched between the buildings, offering poor shade from the glare of the sun. Nonetheless, Gareth was thankful. Already the temperature was extreme, making him sluggish and distracted.

"Here!" Adele called out, and pulled Gareth into a shop. A number of people waited for attention, but luckily, in this case, Gareth was a strikingly noticeable man.

"What do you need, sir?" the merchant asked in Arabic, eyeing Gareth's vintage clothes curiously.

Adele stepped in front to indicate she was the customer, and said in English so Gareth could follow, "I'm interested in selling this." She carefully drew out one jewel. A diamond. Through her touch, she felt the heat of the sun and tasted the dry soil she knew was the great diamond reef of Cape Province.

The dealer's eyes immediately widened, and he eagerly reached out, more than a little dubious that it was real. The gem was quickly brought up to his loupe for further study. The man knew better than to coo over such a gem. Instead he *tsk*ed at the merchandise in his hand.

"It is very subpar," the merchant muttered. "Regretfully, there are many imperfections."

"There are none. Trust me, I know."

"Well, they are small," he graciously conceded. "But visible to the trained eye of a professional. I can only offer you a meager price. It is only just."

"If she says there are no flaws then it is so," Gareth intoned, stepping forward.

With alarm in his eyes, the dealer gave ground. Gareth was a menacing figure even when not dressed as Greyfriar.

"I came to your shop," Adele lied, "because I was told you were honest. I did not expect to be robbed."

"Robbed? I am aghast. Aghast! Please allow me to make an offer." The merchant smiled tightly at her. "After all, I would not have you scuffing your poor bare feet on the marble floors of some fashionable jeweler in Heliopolis." Clearly he knew a woman such as Adele appeared to be would not risk parading such a fine diamond to mainstream dealers and invite the interest of the Cairo metropolitan police.

"Very well," she replied. "We both know it is flawless. So I do not expect to be made of a fool of."

"No doubt, mon petite." The merchant beamed his good fortune as he once more scrutinized the diamond. His tongue darting out to wet his lips was the only indication he was contemplating his next decision. "Two hundred pounds."

Adele raised an eyebrow and finally allowed her scowl to appear. She reached for the gem. "You insult me and my family."

The merchant pulled it closer to his chest. "Eight hundred pounds!"

Adele threw up her hands. "I should call the police."

Gareth held out his hand. The merchant gazed longingly at the stone, but gave it to the man.

"One thousand pounds." Adele folded her arms sternly across her chest. She was still greatly undervaluing the diamond, but they needed the money, and quickly. Plus, she still had more gems.

"One thousand?" The merchant wiped his brow. "Would you have me remove my son from the university where he is studying to be a doctor so that I may pay you for this one rock?"

Adele whirled on her heel.

"Done!" The merchant shouted loudly, making everyone in the

shop glance their way to Adele's dismay. He ran toward the back room. "A moment!"

Grinning at Gareth, Adele began to browse the rest of the store. Her eyes spied a welcome piece of wardrobe. "I'll take these boots also," she shouted.

"Of course," the merchant called back through the partially open door. "Take whatever you want." He paused. "I will give you the same discount I give my parents."

Adele whispered to Gareth, "That stone could buy this storefront a hundred times over. I wouldn't be surprised if the shop closes permanently and the merchant retires to a villa on the sea."

She procured an extra pair of smoked glasses for Gareth as well as a new wardrobe for both of them, several canteens, and by sheer luck, a heat-reflective blanket that she quickly snatched up. Gareth added a few lanterns to the growing pile as she slipped on the soft leather boots. They were nearly a perfect fit, well worn so the leather was supple, but with a great deal of mileage still left on them. Gareth watched her as she sighed in sheer pleasure.

"Never underestimate a pair of good boots," Adele told him wistfully.

His voice dropped to a whisper. "Is that man trustworthy? He could be calling for the police in the back."

"I don't think we need worry about that." Adele glanced around the room, relieved that most of the customers had gone back to what they were doing rather than watch them. "Hopefully he will be content about his good fortune and not brag or question where it came from. Or at least we can be gone from Cairo before he does."

Finally the merchant came out, never so happy to hand over so much cash on one purchase. He didn't blink at the pile of supplies they had gathered, nor at the fact that she refused to pay for them. The exchange went smoothly, and soon Gareth and Adele left with their arms full.

As Gareth stepped out in the sunlight, he was rocked back on his heels. The sheer weight of the heat hit him like a wall. He could feel the difference between Mediterranean-based Alexandria and desert-bound Cairo. The stone buildings seemed to capture the heat and radiate it out.

"Are you all right?" Adele's worried gaze was on him.

"I can manage."

"We'll stick to the shade as much as possible."

The traffic was still shoulder-to-shoulder in the narrow lanes. Voices filled the air as everyday conversation competed with merchant advertising. Hands shoved objects in front of them, pleading for a sale. They proceeded to another vendor to stock up on cooking utensils, blankets, and a variety of goods. Soon they had more than they could carry.

Rescue came in the form of a small urchin on the corner of the street holding the lead rope of a drowsy donkey. The boy's clothes were rumpled, but his eyes were bright, studying all the passersby like potential customers. Most ignored him. Adele stepped in front of him. His small, dark head bobbed warily. She held up two coins, and immediately his suspicion faded.

"Do you need help, lovely miss? Clearly you are too cultured to walk to your destination. Please ride my donkey in style." He gestured grandly to the small, bored donkey that wasn't as excited as the boy by the prospect of work.

"Actually," Adele said. "I need you to transport my goods to the harbor."

"He lives to carry your wares! He is very strong. Do not judge him by his small size or lazy attitude."

Adele patted the dozing donkey on his head. "For these two coins take all that," she pointed to the sizable pile under a shaded alcove where Gareth stood, "to Bulaq. Slip Fifteen near the end of the Blue Wharf. Stay and guard it until we return later today and you will get five more just like these."

Eyes wide, the boy nodded eagerly and reached for the money, but Adele held it back.

"However, pray nothing is missing from our wares. My friend over there is a vampire, and I will order him to chase you down and eat you."

The boy's mouth gaped open as he stared at Gareth in his dark glasses and dour mien, but then he scoffed. "You are very funny, Miss. Don't worry. You won't regret hiring me. Your supplies will be under my protection!" He tapped his chest firmly with his right hand.

"I tip very well for hard work and loyalty," Adele promised him with a glint in her eye.

The urchin bowed low. "I am Nasir at your service."

Adele dropped the two coins into his outstretched hand. "I'm glad to make your acquaintance, Nasir. I am Pareesa." Her mother's name was common enough and made a comforting alias.

The boy dragged his reluctant business partner toward the pile of goods. He eyed her tall companion warily as Gareth stood protectively over the merchandise. The two males stood staring each other down until Adele motioned Gareth to follow her. He frowned, glancing down at the boy sternly before stepping up next to Adele.

"Are you sure he can be trusted?" he asked as they headed north along the avenue.

"Sure? No. But the promise of more money is a great motivator. And all the professional porters probably follow the news, and will wonder about us." She veered toward the shaded part of the busy street.

"What more do we need here? The more we linger the greater our chance of being discovered."

"I agree. But we still need food . . . or at least I do. The produce is at the northern market. It's not far. If you want, I can take care of that. You return to the boat and make sure Nasir doesn't rob us blind."

"I won't leave your side."

"Even if you're miserable?"

"A discomfort at present, nothing more. And I feel better with you in my sight."

"All right. We'll finish up as quickly as we can."

Adele tried desperately to keep to the shade, but they had to dart across open streets where the sun beat down mercilessly. While she moved as quickly as she could, Gareth actually slowed as if he were wading though something physical rather than just warm air. She ran back and grabbed his arm, hurrying to the other side of the oven-baked pavement.

"You're scaring me, Gareth."

"I don't mean to. I'm not in pain, Adele. Don't worry. I'm just tired. It takes great effort to move in this heat." He straightened from his hunched position, regarding her reassuringly, but there were beads of sweat on his brow, and lines of distress furrowed his face. "See, I'm fine."

"Stay here. I won't be long."

He nodded, slumping against the stones of a building.

The smell of spices and cooking oil wafted into the air, though the heat only let it rise so far, so instead it settled over the customers. Adele browsed quickly through the produce stalls, each laden with fruits, vegetables, spices, and various meats, dried, smoked, and filleted. She chose items that wouldn't perish quickly, mostly dried or smoked. One vendor had baskets for sale, so she purchased one to more easily carry her load.

Then she spotted a magazine rack filled to the brim with penny dreadfuls and potboilers, many of them featuring herself and Greyfriar. With a grin, she bought one and stuffed it in the basket.

Barely fifteen minutes had passed when she ran back to Gareth. He was where she had left him, but he was surrounded by merchants and hawkers, all shouting at him for attention. He stood stone still. Adele waded into the crowd, screaming at them to leave him alone, he had no money, he was sick. She shoved several men away. Some laughed, some cursed, but they continued barking their silks, cottons, jewelry, shoes, and cameras.

Gareth just stood there, his gaze locked on some distant point.

"Gareth," Adele called to him, fear bubbling up in her throat. She dropped her basket and grabbed his arm.

There was no response and his breath was shallow.

Panic gripped her. "Gareth!" She shook him.

Finally, he blinked, his eyelids lowering slowly and then back up.

"Gareth, can you hear me?

His gaze lowered until he found her. He drew in a deep breath. "I'm sorry. I was . . . ," but his voice trailed off as if he couldn't remember.

"Can you make it back to the boat?" She was ready to abandon everything and carry him if necessary. The din of the merchants disappeared into the background as they realized there was no sale to be made here.

He shook his head as his breathing became more regular. A quivering hand wiped at his face. He looked drained, but he patted her hand that still gripped him. "I was just conserving my strength." His eyes were narrow slits behind the shades, as if the sunlight were still blazing into them.

"Let's just go. Leave all this and let's get back to the boat."

Gareth grew more awake and took in the parcels scattered at his feet. "Nonsense. You went to all the effort. It'd be foolish to leave everything behind now." He bent to pick them up, but she pulled him back up almost angrily.

"I don't care."

"I do. It means survival for you." He grabbed the basket and, to Adele's shock, he struggled with it.

"Gareth," she whispered, frightened to see him weakened.

"Lead the way back to the boat. I just need to lie down for a bit."

He refused to relinquish his hold on their provisions, so Adele grabbed the other end of the basket. "We'll do it together." To her relief, he didn't argue, but that only worried her more.

Up ahead on the thoroughfare stood a squad of uniformed policemen, showing pamphlets and photographs. They were stopping everyone passing by. Adele jerked to a halt.

Gareth stopped beside her, breathing heavily. "What is it?"

"Road block." She altered their direction, aiming for a dark alley. Unfortunately one of the sharp-eyed policemen saw her hesitation and purposeful avoidance. He elbowed another officer and came after them. A curse slipped through Adele's lips.

"I can't outrun them," hissed Gareth.

"I know." She stopped and shoved the basket behind some crates strewn in the alley. "Can you fly?"

"I can't carry you. Not now."

"Just float up and hide. When they go past, come back down. Simple."

He hesitated. "They'll find you."

"Just go." She darted for a dark alcove, rewrapping her scarf into a new shape and stripping her cloak off to lie on the ground. She watched Gareth drag himself up the wall until he alighted on the roof. The sun beat mercilessly on his shoulders and he hunched over like a dark gargoyle, watching her.

The policemen rounded the corner with weapons clattering. Adele sat back into the doorway, bent over and appearing to be no more than a street urchin herself. The officers glanced at her and ran on. Adele sighed with relief, thinking she was in the clear. Then one slowed since the empty alley gave them no clue as to where their prey had gone.

"Miss?"

Adele looked up hesitantly, her head wrap held tight to her face, her eyes downcast with contrition.

"Did you see a couple run past here?" the policeman asked.

She nodded and pointed.

"Thank you." The officer turned to go.

Adele could not believe her good fortune. But the other policeman's feet still stood before her.

"Show me your face, miss."

Her heartbeat raced. There was no doubt they would recognize her. A photo of Princess Adele was in his hand staring back at her. She realized she would have to fight her way out of this. She couldn't leave Gareth here in this heat. Her hand shifted to grip a nearby brick. The man's partner was coming back.

She looked up at her target and steeled herself. A dark shadow dropped on top of the approaching policeman. Gareth landed heavily on him, and the man collapsed without a sound. The partner turned toward the new threat, and Adele stood up and swung with all her might. The brick clipped him on his helmet, but with enough force to stagger him. Adele followed through with a sharp jab to his chin, and the man fell next to his partner.

Gareth was on one knee, trying to rise. She grabbed him and helped him stand.

"I don't have much time." He was shaking and pale.

She swiftly kissed him and then pulled him down the alley.

"Wait, your basket." He grabbed it.

"Forget the basket!"

"No."

Together they slipped out of the alley, heading away from the police. Adele spied an empty carriage and whistled shrilly for the driver's attention. Within moments, they were inside the slightly cooler interior of the cab with the basket at their feet.

Gareth sighed as he sagged against the cool leather. Adele squeezed his hand, directed the driver to Bulaq, and then proceeded to yank down all the shades on the cab, plunging the interior into darkness. Gareth's blue eyes opened to regard his princess and found her face full of worry.

"Stop that," he ordered. "If anyone has a right to be vexed it should be me. I'm hardly any help to you. Nothing more than a burden."

Adele let out a little sigh, attempting a small smile that her anxiety could barely tolerate. "It will be fine. We'll make it."

"I fear that little boy could best me at the moment. Add the donkey, and I would surely fall. It's not something I find comforting."

"I'll protect you," she teased. "That nasty donkey won't hurt you."

He scowled at her, but then a weak smile creased his lips. "You're not funny."

She pressed her cheek to his. "Liar. You find me hilarious."

The trip to the harbor was soon over, and as the carriage halted, Gareth had to gather his remaining strength. He hissed slightly as he stepped back into the sun, his skin feeling as if it was shriveling up to parchment.

Nasir was waiting at the correct berth, guarding their wares with a stout stick in hand. Adele thought it was more likely he used it on the donkey, but it wouldn't surprise her if he whacked a beggar or two who strayed too close. The boy brightened immediately upon seeing his employers approach.

"Lady Pareesa! No one has touched your belongings! I have seen to that. I held off three burly sailors who wanted to steal from you. And numerous desperate vagabonds!"

Adele gestured to the boat. "If you could help us load the supplies on board, I will double your compensation."

"And by compensation, you mean cash?" he verified.

The princess laughed at his shrewdness. "I do."

"Done!"

Adele helped Gareth carry the basket onto the deck. He was so unsteady she was afraid he'd pitch over the side, but soon she had him down in the dark hold.

"That's a relief," he said tiredly.

"Stay down here."

He closed his eyes.

The princess returned to the wharf where Nasir waited patiently. She handed him his payment. It was much more than was agreed upon, and he beamed his good fortune.

"You more than earned it," she assured him. "Both of you." She glanced at the sleepy donkey.

"Ha!" exclaimed Nasir. "I did most of the work while he just sat there and brayed at the sailors. Lazy animal. I should trade him for a camel."

Adele knelt beside the little donkey. "Does he have a name?"

"He doesn't have one. I just call him Knothead when I yell at him."

Her hand brushed down the long face of the donkey, who opened bleary eyes at her before sighing and leaning into her touch. "Every animal deserves a name. Knothead. Most likely you named him for this small bump on his forehead." She rubbed the little bump set high under his forelock. "I've been told that such a knot was once the horn of a unicorn."

"Really?" Nasir's eyes grew round. His hand reached out to touch the small bump on his donkey's head. Then it dropped away quickly. "Aw, that's just from when he ran into a door." But his argument was weak and his tone soft.

"Perhaps, but it might be wiser to believe otherwise. Just in case." Adele winked. "Farewell, Nasir. It was a pleasure doing business with you."

The young urchin bowed low to her. "If ever you are in Cairo again, be sure to find me."

"I will." Adele yanked free the knot restraining the boat and shoved its bow away from the dock before leaping lightly onto the deck. She waved good-bye.

Nasir stood resting one hand gently on the withers of his partner as he raised his other hand in farewell to his best customers. "Good luck, Lady Pareesa! To you and your vampire friend!"

Thankfully, no one on the dock reacted to the child's bizarre remark.

Soon the wharves slipped out of sight between the large ships and barges, and Adele slipped the dahabiya into the river traffic. The heavy airship coverage thinned with time, and she didn't feel safe until they were at least an hour outside the city. As the sun dropped below the distant horizon, Gareth struggled topside.

"Are you hungry?" Adele asked.

"No. I won't need to feed today."

"How long can you last?"

"Quite a while. But you can't. Eat."

Adele put together a simple meal for herself, eating self-consciously in front of him. As the stars brightened and the air cooled, they lounged on deck. She reached over and squeezed his hand, hoping to bring him comfort.

He observed her with a weary smile. "The heat was more intense than I imagined today. You took command of the situation admirably."

Adele snorted with mock derision. "Would you mind writing a letter of recommendation to the court? They seem to think I'm only suited for teas and christening ships."

"Why would they think that? You survived Cesare. You are obviously more capable than anyone else."

"Well, several reasons. First, I'm a woman. Second, I'm half Persian."

Gareth shook his head in confusion. "Why should that matter?"

"It shouldn't, but that's what *some* in Commons believe, that bunch of stuffy old men with giant mustaches. You see, the days of the vampire conquest are like epic myths to many of the old families, who like to pretend they're purely descended from the northern exiles. They prefer to ignore the fact that the Empire is built on Arabs, Africans, Indians, and Persians as well as Europeans. It's sad. But that's not the primary reason why the grandees look on me with disfavor. They're much more prejudiced against me as a woman than as a Persian."

"They're fools. Females possess a unique perspective on ruling. They often temper their force with compassion and understanding. Often, avoiding a battle is greater than winning it. Males find that difficult. You have the balance of a fine sword. You can strike, but you can also parry. I see you as a magnificent ruler."

Adele blushed at his praise. "Are you just saying that because you love me?"

"Yes," he said firmly.

Adele grinned widely. "So do vampires have many queens? Or is your society strictly ruled by men? I could have seen Flay as a frighteningly capable queen."

"Flay could never have been queen. She had no ancestry. But we have many queens. The New York clan, for instance, has a queen. Fen." Gareth suppressed a shudder. "I might add, she is fond of me."

"Is she now?" Adele leaned forward. "Do tell."

"She is ancient and brittle. An old paramour of my father."

Adele's smile turned into a grimace. "Okay, that's disturbing. How old is she?"

"As old as rocks. But the point is she's smart and calculating. She's held off rival clans for centuries, not to mention the Americans for over a hundred years. The fact that she's a female has no impact on her skills. Nor on yours."

"Thank you. I think that if given the chance I will do a good job ruling Equatoria."

"Yes," he said succinctly.

"Someday," she sighed wistfully. "Until then, we are just simple river folk."

"How delightful."

Adele set a bright lantern on the prow of the boat. "I'll take first watch."

"Please sit with me for a while. Days from now, I may be so incapacitated from the heat I won't be able to enjoy your company."

"Of course." Adele complied. "Here, rest your head in my lap."

Curious, he lay back against her and found peace from his weary day. They talked of all the things they had experienced in the months apart. Adele showed him the dime novel with its garish and bawdy cover art. *The Princess and the Swordsman.*

Gareth studied it with great interest. "What is this?"

"It's a story. About you and me. They're very popular. And there are also plays. That's where people pretend to be others on stage, for an audience." She showed him the playbill for *Desire in the Dead North.*

"People pretend to be us?"

"Yes."

"Are they good at it?"

"They're all right. I've seen a few dramas starring us. Some were better than others."

He opened *The Princess and the Swordsman* and saw a black-and-white drawing of a man in a flowing long robe with a head wrap similar to Greyfriar's, carrying a broad-bladed scimitar. Cowering behind the dashing adventurer was a frightened young woman dressed for a harem. Under the picture was the legend: *The Greyfriar stands ready to defend the helpless Princess Adele.*

"That looks nothing like either of us. And why are you cowering? That's not like you."

Adele shrugged. "It's just for entertainment. Accuracy isn't the point. Here, this is my favorite drawing." She flipped to another picture of a man with a cape and a sword, his arm around the waist of a beautiful woman. The two were on the verge of a kiss. In the air around them were hairy, clawed beasts with wings. Adele read the caption in a melodramatic voice, "*She was betrothed. He was a hero. But they found forbidden love in the crypts of Scotland.*" She laughed. "But at least all the stories have happy endings."

"Are we always together?"

"Every time."

"Good." With that knowledge, Gareth relaxed, and he fell asleep.

CHAPTER 16

COLONEL ANHALT CLOSED the drawer of his desk and locked it. He turned off the gas light on the wall and glanced around the small office he maintained but rarely occupied—perhaps for the last time. As he reached for the door, it flew inward and the shadowy space was filled by a small figure in a Bedouin robe. For a moment, Anhalt thought a street urchin had found his way into the palace.

"Colonel!" Prince Simon exclaimed. "Have you heard anything?"

"I have not, Your Highness." Anhalt stepped into the corridor, pressing the boy out, and closed the door behind him.

"Then where are you going?" Simon indicated a fat valise in the colonel's hand.

"I am going to investigate a report of Her Highness in Damascus. But it is likely false, as usual."

"Can I go?"

"*May* I go." Anhalt immediately assumed the corrective role of Adele in her absence. "No, you may not."

"Why? It's boring here. Everyone's all upset over Adele. Senator Clark walks around like he owns the place."

The colonel started down the hall with an arm looped over the boy's shoulders. "I understand, but you must remain. Until your sister returns, you are the heir."

"That's stupid!" Simon shouted. "She's the real heir, but she's the one always out having adventures all the time. And I'm stuck here in boring Alexandria!"

"It does seem silly, doesn't it? But your sister is a unique individual. And if you leave, who will care for the cat?"

"I'll bring him."

"Cats don't travel well."

"This one does. He came all the way from the north."

Anhalt chuckled. "True. But even so."

"And I didn't get to meet the Greyfriar," Simon grumbled. "He was here and I didn't even talk to him."

"He was busy. Perhaps he'll be back."

"If he does, Senator Clark will shoot him." The boy brightened. "Or maybe Greyfriar will shoot Clark!"

"No one will shoot anyone."

"Please let me come with you. Please!"

"Nothing would give me greater pleasure, Prince Simon. But where I'm going, you can't follow."

"Damascus? I've been there."

Colonel Anhalt halted before the prince. "There are times when we all must do what we'd prefer not to. You have been called on to do such things more than most your age. But you are a prince, and it is your lot in life. I have been very proud of you. No matter what happens, please don't forget that."

Simon regarded Anhalt with a curiously adult gaze. "You are coming back, aren't you?"

The Gurkha paused. He reached up and touched the Imperial Service Medal he wore on the chest of his red tunic, the only decoration he displayed despite earning many. He saluted the boy.

"It has been an honor to serve you, Your Highness."

Anhalt spun swiftly and strode away.

The candles that lit the interior of the Djibouti tavern were guttering and stank of cheapness. The entire room reeked of sweat, beer, hashish, and repressed fear and anger. Hushed conversations buzzed along with the flies.

When Anhalt entered, bleary eyes turned on him. Then some swung away, but others continued to stare at the stranger. Despite the nondescript khakis, this man was clearly not a regular. He was firm and straight, not bent with secrets. His eyes were not red with alcohol or hatred. The curiosity was palpable as the stranger crossed to the bar. His hands rested on his holstered revolver and the hilt of his sword, but he was likely the most lightly armed person here. That included the bartender, who regarded him without moving.

Anhalt said, "I'm looking for someone."

"Don't know him."

"I am not with the authorities."

The bartender grinned at the unintended joke. "Oh, you're not, are you?"

Several men at the bar turned to the newcomer, annoyed at being interrupted from their quiet quest for cirrhosis. One of them growled, "There's no one here. Be on your way before we get annoyed."

Anhalt ignored the man and continued, "I'm looking for Captain Aswan Hariri. I am a friend of his."

"If you're a friend, then you'd know where he was—if he existed, which he don't, so far as I know."

Anhalt felt sweat dribbling down his neck. The air was stifling. "I was told Captain Hariri frequented this establishment."

The bartender rubbed his dark Somali face. "I'll give you some free advice, mate. Leave now. And don't come back."

A man laughed as he lay in the corner working the overhead fan by pulling a string attached to his big toe. Dust sparkled in the sun shafts penetrating the broken window shutters. Chairs across the room scraped as more men took interest in the scene. There were murmurs of "imperial" and "police." As they found more bravery in numbers, figures moved toward Anhalt with open sneers and hands in pockets or on belts where weapons rested.

"Attention, gentlemen." The colonel inched away from the bar in case he needed more room to maneuver. "This is a simple transaction. I am looking for my friend. If I find him, I will go away. No one needs to die."

Several men snickered and made comments about exactly who would die today. Then a thin European seated at the bar came at Anhalt with what he must have felt was a cunning move, swiping with a dagger.

Anhalt easily slipped the strike, kicking the man in the chest and knocking him off his stool while drawing his Fahrenheit saber. The glowing green sword held the room in amazement for a few seconds, since such finely wrought examples were still rare in such sordid environs.

Another blade came at Anhalt and he struck the man's arm, raising a scream of pain from the attacker. Now the colonel's revolver was out too. A large brute lunged and he sidestepped, bringing the pistol butt down on the back of the man's head. A glimpse of a threat from behind brought the saber in an arc so it ripped through a man's shoulder with fire.

Anhalt vaulted onto a table, scattering liquor bottles and beer pints. He kicked a large hookah at a man who caught the glass and water full in the face. At the first sign of a pistol in the mob, he fired and dropped the gunman.

The door was blocked by a crowd, some of whom were rushing out, but others stood and waited, smiling and hoping for a chance at loot when the foolish intruder was eventually brought down.

"Kill him!" came a shout. "Damned imperial! Kill him, boys!"

Anhalt slashed again and again, driving the mob back, leaving streaks of green chemical in the air. He fired at another man who reached for his leg. The bullet impacted the table, spraying shards of wood. Then the man's hand separated from his arm. Anhalt watched curiously as the disembodied hand slid off his boot to the tabletop.

A man jumped onto the table with him, and he saw behind the trailing turban the dark face of Aswan Hariri. "Follow me, my friend. I'll cut a way out!"

Instantly, Hariri leapt from the table, swinging a broad scimitar and firing point-blank into the crowd. The drunks fell back, shouting and screaming, flailing to be out of harm's way. Anhalt followed, striking around him with the saber, firing only when a threatening blade or gun came too close. Hariri kicked a man through the door and they surged out into the bright African sun. The two men spun in the dusty street and fired around the tavern's door frame to drive their pursuers back inside.

"Run!" Hariri shouted.

Anhalt followed the flowing robes of his friend, slipping between tan brick buildings, hurdling low fences, cutting through open doorways of homes. He occasionally turned to fire back at dogged pursuers, who became fewer and fewer with every twist and turn through the chaotic town.

Finally, Hariri stopped, with chest heaving, to scan the empty street behind them. He kept his pistol extended, waiting, as many faces stared out from behind doors and windows.

Anhalt said, "We're attracting attention with weapons in the street."

"This is Djibouti, not Alexandria. Count yourself lucky children aren't returning fire." Hariri then took off at a trot. "Come. I've a safe place not far from here."

Apparently, *not far* meant fifteen minutes running through the searing heat. Finally, Hariri led them through a nondescript archway into a courtyard with a cooling fountain. They passed into a dim room looking out on the blue harbor crowded with dhows and steamships, while the achingly blue sky was full of airships.

Hariri pulled off his gun belt and sword, stretching with relief. He was tall and dark and thin. He wore a slight beard that curled off his chin. His deep brown eyes were quiet and haunted, no matter the smile beaming from his lips. He tossed a heavy water skin to the colonel.

Anhalt downed the water greedily and wiped his mouth. "Thank you." But he didn't mean for the drink.

"You're welcome. To say that I'm surprised to see you is an understatement. Someone found me on the street telling me that a policeman was asking for me by name. I had to see for myself who would be so bold or desperate. Or stupid." Hariri laughed and dropped onto a pile of cushions. "And behold, it was you in the process of being killed."

"I did not realize I stood out so. Apparently polite enquiries are frowned upon in that place."

Hariri nodded with a sly eyebrow. "I'll never be able to drink there again. Ah well, their ale was like bath water."

Anhalt sheathed his sword and sat on a bench along one wall. "I'm glad to have found you, in any case."

"It has been years, my friend. Was it Zanzibar when we last fought together?"

"Yes."

"I'm surprised you can afford to be seen with one such as I."

"What passed between you and the Imperial Air Command isn't my concern."

"Of course. I hear you have done well. Commander of the princess's guard?"

"That is correct."

"The lady Adele is quite the handful, so I've heard." Hariri laughed, but when he saw Anhalt's grim reaction, he became serious. "I'm sorry. Can I assume she is the reason for your visit to my humble home?"

"You can. I need your help, Aswan. I need a trustworthy captain and crew who can handle a brig in the face of difficulties. Without questions."

Hariri sighed. "I can always find men who have no curiosity. But, forgive me, they will require payment."

"I have money," Anhalt said. "And if we succeed, there will be great rewards. If we fail—" He shrugged.

"It is not for me I ask." Hariri sat forward earnestly. "I would serve you for no reason other than that you are Colonel Mehmet Anhalt, commander of the White Guard."

The colonel finished reloading his pistol. He sat back and crossed his legs. "I am no longer commander of the White Guard. As of yesterday, I am a traitor and deserter."

"Well, who among us is perfect?" Hariri pursed his lips with concern. "Is this turn of events something you have done for your lost princess?"

"It is."

"If I may, my friend, you were always the most loyal Equatorian I ever knew. Why do you risk everything for her?"

"I promised her mother."

CHAPTER  17

As the week passed sailing up the Nile, Gareth was forced to retreat to the hold of the boat. The air was livid with heat that sapped his vigor and his wits daily, leaving him panting and weak. When he was able, he read from the book that Adele had bought. During the worst baking midday heat, he used the blanket from the market in Cairo. It was an invention used primarily by the army; its chemical coating gave off cooling vapors, but it only lasted so long and this one was already fading.

When Gareth opened his eyes, he saw the wooden beams of the ship's hold above him. His shirt was open and damp, a wet rag pressed on his forehead. He tried to rise but only managed to make it to one elbow, cursing the weakness that seeped through his frame. He couldn't remember ever feeling so helpless and sick. He fell back, breathing roughly, sweat dotting his skin, the back of his dry throat convulsing as his nausea flared. He lay motionless, trying to think of what needed to be done, but his brain was consumed with fatigue. Footsteps sounded on the ladder, and Adele came down with a bucket dripping with water.

She knelt beside him. "You're awake! I've been frantic." Her cold hands touched his fevered face and offered a respite. She sank the cloth in the water and then pressed it against his skin.

"How long?" he muttered.

"Almost a full day. It's evening now. I've put to shore."

"It's still hot," he panted.

"I know. It was blazing today. It will cool off soon."

He nodded, willing himself to stay awake. Despair ate at him. He had hoped to leave the boat to try to find food. He must feed soon or he would be unable to move. And then he would die and Adele would be alone.

"There's a town ahead," Adele said. "It's not very big, but I'm sure we can find you someplace better than this stifling hold."

"It's too dangerous. We were lucky in Cairo, only a hairbreadth from discovery."

"I'm willing to take the risk!"

"I'm not. I won't be of any help to you if we're discovered. There are airships everywhere. And we've seen the river patrols every night. It's only luck that has prevented us from being boarded. And I'm certain I've seen a boat following us."

"You're exhausted. I haven't seen anyone following us. Every boat on the river looks alike to you." Still, Adele knew that Gareth was extraordinarily observant. If they were being trailed, pulling ashore for the night could be disastrous. Better to continue through the night.

She would have to stay awake. Gareth was too weak to sail. His skin was sallow and his eyes glassy, as if he were running a fever. His cheeks were peppered with a raw rash from the heat. Even the water of the Nile was slowly becoming ineffectual at keeping him cool. It terrified her.

"I'm not going to die from the heat," he assured her. "It won't be much longer."

"It's been three days since you last fed from me, and I'm fully recovered." Adele rolled up her sleeve on the arm that was unmarked by his teeth. At his hesitation, her hand stroked his cheek, gazing into his light eyes. "You worry too much about me. But can't you see that I'm fine with this? I'm offering and I gladly give it. I'm frightened of losing you. You can't even stand. Please. For me." She kissed him. It was a gentle caress to him, though she pressed her lips hard against his.

"You can never lose me," he said softly as she pulled slowly away. He felt her hand against the back of his searing neck.

"Then show me." She again offered her wrist to him, her olive skin even darker in the filtered moonlight while he appeared a pale wraith. His exhale shook with longing as he lifted her arm and quickly sank his fangs just deep enough to catch the shallowest of veins. Adele stiffened for a moment and then relaxed as she grew accustomed to the rhythm of the feeding.

Gareth lay on the deck losing himself to the intensity of her life-giving blood. The spice of her anxiety for him spoke clearly, as did her robust devotion. He could feel his awareness becoming sharper, his body stronger. The blood sang with power and filled him with sensations both bad and good. As it seeped through him, his own blood caught the awareness of what she was in body and spirit, and the dreadful strength of which she was capable. No human's blood had ever told such a story of marvelous life and complete death.

Gareth listened carefully to Adele's pounding heart. It didn't take long for it to start laboring. She was exhausted too. The feedings, combined with working in the unforgiving heat, were draining her. Afraid he would hurt her, he let go and sank back. He needed more blood, but he refused to place her in harm's way. The fitful feeding would have to be enough.

"Thank you." His eyes closed as the call of misery-free oblivion beckoned and he willingly gave in to lethargic slumber, conserving what strength her blood provided. He would rise when the desert air had released its taxing heat and allowed the land to cool once more.

Adele watched him slip away from her into what she hoped was just sleep. She tied a quick bandage over the small wound on her wrist. Usually, Gareth was the one to do that for her, always thinking of her first. The fact that he was barely aware enough to feed, much less worry about her, was frightening. She soaked the rag again before placing it on his forehead, hoping it still offered him some relief.

There was still much to do tonight. Adele was almost too tired to eat, but she knew she had to keep up her strength if she was to continue her vigil. Wearily she shoved herself to her knees, but not before she kissed his damp forehead.

As days passed, Adele became even more worried for Gareth. There were times he lay as if dead down in the hold, motionless, his chest barely rising and falling. It was difficult to rouse him. She now knew how those legends had started about vampires lying dead in tombs until the fall of night, when they rose from the grave. His pale skin was much too warm and positively brittle, and his cheekbones more prominent.

However, at long last, the huge statues of Abu Simbel rose on the west bank with the sun glaring behind them. They were deep in the south now. The air patrols had thinned in the last few days, and the River Guard were much less apparent. The maw of the temple's entrance promised a dark interior. It would be stale, but cooler than the boat. Gareth desperately needed a chance to rest and regain his strength.

Adele was shaking with relief that help was so close as she veered the dahabiya for shore. Thanks to the old Aswan Dam, the water of the Nile almost lapped the very face of the huge temple. She didn't see any sign of occupation, and her heart sank. Colonel Anhalt wasn't here waiting, as he had promised. Disastrous scenarios ran through her head—perhaps the colonel had been discovered aiding her escape and had been arrested; or he had failed to convince his men to accompany him; or he had failed to arrange transport; or the worst possibility, that he had decided not to help her, that he could not abandon his oath to king and country.

She took a deep breath to calm useless fears. One step at a time. She would get Gareth into the temple first. Then, they would wait. She had to assume Colonel Anhalt would come. If he didn't arrive in a few days, she would form another plan. He had chosen Abu Simbel because it was an excellent place to hide. Up until a decade ago, it had been an extensive military compound, but when that base was moved to Wadi Halfa, it left the temple precinct isolated.

Adele didn't dare bring Gareth out in the heat until she knew this place was unoccupied by anyone, or anything. If the temple was cool enough to succor Gareth, it could very well be cool enough for other vampires. She knew the creatures lurked everywhere. She hastily anchored the boat, shoved her Fahrenheit dagger and one of Gareth's pistols into her belt, grabbed a lantern, and went ashore. She dipped her head in gratitude as she approached the four colossal seated figures towering a hundred feet over her. She could only hope that their old friend from the British Museum, Ramses, looked down kindly on them. She passed between the immense thrones, while far above, the Watchers of the Dawn, a row of stone baboons, raised their hands to the sun. They worshipped the rising sun, as it was believed that they had a hand in helping the sun god Ra defeat the darkness of night.

After a cursory exploration, Adele was satisfied the rooms were free of unwanted visitors, and so she returned to the boat. The sun had set finally, and just now the first bright stars began to appear in the pink sky. She slipped belowdecks and knelt beside Gareth, pressing her hand on his chest as much to rouse him as to once again reassure herself that he was still breathing.

"Gareth," she called softly.

His breath deepened as if trying to wake. It took another minute before she could get him to open his eyes to look at her.

"It's dark," he muttered. It wasn't a question, but a whisper of relief. His body trembled and his skin burned.

"We've reached Abu Simbel. It's nice and cool. You'll like it. It's a ruin."

Gareth managed to sit up dizzily as Adele tried to get a shoulder under him. Together they stumbled up to the deck. The heat was still oppressive enough to make Gareth shudder and pull back.

"It's not far," she urged him. "It will be better once we get inside."

His head nodded as he slumped against her. Gareth let her guide him to the side of the boat. He collapsed to the deck, but managed to swing his long legs over the side. Adele jumped into the calf-deep water and helped him over. He didn't even notice the water as he sank to his knees before Adele grabbed him. Struggling up the sandy bank took energy, but soon they reached the temple. The moment they staggered inside, he immediately noticed the difference. He drew in a great lungful of the slightly cooler air and sagged against a column.

"It's even cooler farther in," Adele urged him.

That was all he needed to hear. Gareth stumbled after her, keeping a hand on her shoulder at all times to steady himself. They shuffled down a long, sand-dusted passageway, and Adele could tell he was getting stronger. She sighed gratefully.

She turned to the left, toward one of the wings out of the path of the sun, which would shine all the way to the back during a sunrise. They went as far back as they could, and Gareth sank to the floor with his hands pressed against the hard earth as if he could siphon cold up from the very ground. His loud gasps of relief were a welcome sound to Adele. She knelt beside him, holding him tight.

"Thank you," he gasped out weakly. "This is good."

"I'll be right back. I'm going to bring in some supplies." She rose, but he gripped her hand tightly for a second. She leaned over him, her lips brushing against his hair. He slowly released her hand.

Adele retrieved her lantern, and a half hour later they had what they needed. She left the small stove in the main chamber near the door to vent the smoke, and because there was no reason to heat up Gareth's room any more than necessary. Finished with the small chores, she hurried back to him. To her surprise, he was standing near a far wall. His body was not plagued by the weakness of before. She couldn't help but marvel as he began to revert to the man she knew. As soon as she stepped inside, he turned toward her and reached out. She gladly went into his arms.

"Thank God," she whispered.

"How cool is it outside?" Gareth took deep breaths just because he could. With it came the scent of Adele, robust and earthy. He hoped, if the night was cool enough, to go out to feed. With any luck, he could happen upon another wanderer or farmer.

"We have another couple of hours till the heat dissipates. I'm afraid you're stuck here with me for a bit."

Adele continued to talk to him, but it was hard to hear over the rush of her blood coursing just inches away. He was stronger now and it was hard to deny his drive to feed. Still, he had to try. It was only a few more hours. He turned away abruptly, stalking to the far wall to distance himself from the temptation.

"Gareth?"

"I want to walk around a bit. Stretch my legs." Again he lied. The sensations flooding him were surreal and frantic, and he worried that he didn't have the strength to keep away from Adele. A wave of repulsion pushed the hunger down. He pressed against the wall, letting the chill in the stones distract him.

"You have to eat," Adele said bluntly as she pulled up her sleeve, revealing numerous bite marks on her forearm.

"No!" He snarled as the hunger rushed back at the mere words. At her wide-eyed expression, he relented. "It's too soon for you. I can wait."

She crossed her arms. "I'm willing to take the risk."

He shook his head mutely as he paced the wall, trying to keep distance between them. Her sheer willingness fanned his hunger to monumental levels. There was a red haze before his eyes.

"What can I do?" she asked him quietly.

His laugh was desperate and haunted. Then his pacing abruptly ceased, his blue eyes boring into her. "I need to be alone."

Anxiety immediately flared in her face at the thought of leaving him in such a state.

"It's for the best, Adele. You are a walking reminder of what I long for." He could see that she understood.

"I'll be nearby. Call if you need me."

The moment she left, Gareth sagged to the ground, his legs buckling beneath him. Every limb shook with the restraint it took to calm himself. The hunger began to subside to normal levels that he could control. He was used to fits and starts in his meals, but never like this. Not to mention the oppressive heat. It was all he could do to keep sane. He had no idea what would happen to him if this deprivation continued. He might just react on instinct and attack Adele, or perhaps he would be too weak to do that.

Miserable, Gareth huddled alone in the dark, waiting for the heat to fade.

CHAPTER 18

ADELE ATTEMPTED TO stay busy by making her evening meal, knowing that Gareth was starving just below her. Her heart broke as she stared at her food and sat back with her hunger forgotten. He had paced like a wild animal. His behavior frightened her in ways it never had before. She couldn't believe he'd hurt her, but his desperation was a cruel thing to watch.

The hopeless situation was coming down to either watching Gareth slowly die or encouraging him to feed, on someone. There was finally a desert chill in the air. In a fluid motion she rose to her feet and padded back into the temple. Gareth was already standing in the shadows of the doorway. For a split second, his sudden appearance jarred her. He looked dreadful, his features sunken to dark hollows.

"It's okay," she said softly.

His head swiveled toward her sharply.

"You have to feed," she continued. "If you won't do it with me, then you need to find someone. Go while you still can. I know you won't harm them."

Gareth looked away, his head lowered.

She hesitated. "I . . . I know you don't need my permission, but I just wanted you to know I'll be here when you get back."

Gareth silently slipped past her, aiming for the door. As he passed, he reached out and touched her hand, his long fingers brushing against hers, feather-light, a caress. Her chest caught in a swell of emotion. Suddenly she was frightened for him. An irrational desire to go with him swept over her, but she refrained. Instead, her fingers curled around his, clinging to him for just an instant before releasing her hold.

With that they separated, Gareth to the embrace of the desert night and Adele to the dark chambers of the temple.

———

A scrape of feet on stone woke Adele. She sat up abruptly, her blanket falling to her lap. It took only a second to turn up the flickering lantern beside her. Her sleep had been fitful with dreams of Gareth in trouble, but he was coming back now.

She hoped he had been successful, no longer caring about the monstrous implications of that wish. She only wanted to see him stride in full of life and vigor, the man she remembered.

The footfalls ceased suddenly, which was odd, but perhaps Gareth's attention had been grabbed by the many monuments and he'd paused to study them. He had been trapped in the hold of the boat for days, and he wouldn't be in a hurry to come underground again. Then the footsteps continued, but they had a strange echo to them. She rose to her feet, coming forward to meet Gareth, when four men entered the room.

Three were Bedouin in light robes and burnooses while the fourth was European with a stained linen suit. All four were heavily bearded and leathery from the sun. Their eyes swept the room, and they expressed their good fortune by grinning menacingly at the woman they found alone.

"We followed you a long way from Cairo, mon petite Equateur," the northerner said in a French accent, likely from Marseilles. He pointed a pistol at Adele and nodded at her gun belt on the floor. "Please don't move toward your guns or I will have to shoot you. And I truly don't wish to do so."

Adele slowly inched away from the pistol belt and toward her pack, where her Fahrenheit dagger lay hidden. Gareth had been right; someone had followed them. Foolishly, she had disregarded his comment. Now, she kept her hands in front of her, keeping the men's attention on her upper body until she nudged the rucksack with her toe. Adele made calculations as to how she might reach her dagger and strike the men without getting killed.

The Frenchman said, "We want the jewels you have. No doubt they are stolen from some rich family. You're going to give us what we want. Such a pretty little girl to hide such expensive gems."

Adele's odds lessened as the thugs spread out, making it harder to deal with them in tight quarters. Then, in the trembling shadows behind them, stirred another figure.

Gareth.

The sunken hollows of his eyes were fixed on the men. She could see from his hunched stance that he had not fed. His stare at the intruders was one of undeniable need. He was dark and terrifying, a creature of nightmares.

Adele glanced at the men who stalked toward her with cruel grins. A sense of dread for them slipped over her just before she used her foot to tip over the lantern and plunge the room into pitch darkness.

Chaos broke out. Flashes of pistol fire lit up the room. Someone rushed her and shoved her to the floor. Screams echoed horribly around the walls soon after. Even the burly man pressing her down paused, suddenly unsure what was happening around him. Adele slammed an elbow into his face with a resounding crack, and the weight shifted off just enough to allow her to grab the heavy lantern next to her. She swung it, and the howl of pain pleased her as the man slumped to the side. She pulled her dagger and swiped out. It failed to connect. Her eyes struggled to see past the eerie glow of the Fahrenheit blade.

With legs bent and arms outstretched, she paused, straining to see shapes in the gloom, listening for everyone's location, but there were only moans and sobbing. Someone was crying hysterically.

Another shouted, "What the hell was that?"

"Heaven help us!"

Something shifted beside her and she spun, her knife darting out, this time connecting. A scream of pain followed. A meaty hand grabbed her other arm and pulled her close. A man's foul breath washed over her face. She struck again, aiming for a more vital area now. The blade cut and bounced off bone but settled in silently. With a strangled gasp, the man slumped against her.

Adele shoved him away and rocked back on her heels. Now there was only a lone, muffled sobbing in the silence. Her hands fumbled for the lantern in the dust nearby. Trembling fingers turned the knob, and the gaslight bathed her corner of the room.

Three men lay dead. Blood was everywhere. The sobbing stopped. An icy chill enveloped her as she saw Gareth in the filtered light. He was hunched over one of the robbers with his fangs plunged deeply into the man's neck. His white shirt was soaked red. The figure in his arms was motionless except for an occasional twitch of his loose limbs. Gareth stared up at her over his meal with a crimson face. When their eyes locked, he turned away and dragged the man into the dark out of her sight.

Adele's breath came out in gasps. The smell of blood filled her nostrils. She turned and vomited.

The attack had been feral, a slaughter. Adele's brain kept repeating that he had had no choice. If Gareth had not been here, she would have been killed. She knew that. Still, her hand turned off the light and the carnage faded from her sight.

It was several minutes later when she heard Gareth approach. He gently touched her on the arm.

"Come."

She obeyed, permitting him to help her to stand on shaky legs. There was more strength in him now than there was in her. It was shock, she knew. It would pass. He steered her unerringly in the darkness toward the temple entrance, where the faintest of light was just seeping over the horizon. The air outside was fresh and clean and devoid of death.

"Go to the boat," he said. "I'll clean up."

Adele nodded, wanting to say something to him, but unable to think of anything suitable. Instead, instinct took over and she walked to the boat. A bottle of palm wine from the hold washed away the taste of bile in her throat. She took a deeper draft to steady her nerves.

Eventually she heard Gareth by the river's edge. He was on one knee, washing his torso, now bare of the blood-drenched shirt. The human blood from him stained the Nile red like the old Biblical tale.

There was just enough light to see that Gareth was truly recovered. The pallor that had hung over him was lifted. That sight brought Adele back to center somewhat. His gaze strayed to her as he approached the boat.

"Are you all right?" he asked.

She nodded and found her voice. "I'm fine."

"Adele, I'm sorry for reminding you of what I am, but they would have killed you. I could taste it in them. They would have killed you and worse."

Adele fought a chill at his words, and then asked, "What do you mean you could taste it?"

Gareth continued to stare into the distance beyond her. "When we drink the blood of humans, we get a strong sense of them. Not memories, but emotions. We can sense their nature. Fear. Anger. Sorrow."

"My God," she breathed. "I never imagined . . ."

"I could taste Cairo in them. They had followed us."

"The merchant where I sold the diamond?"

"Likely. But I know their intentions toward you." His tone was near snarling. "For that alone they deserved death."

His violence had been in her defense, and not just from his insatiable hunger. Knowing that eased Adele's fears, but then she realized another disturbing fact. She asked, "You've had my blood." He shifted away from her at the comment, but she continued, "What did you taste in me?"

There was a long silence covered by the whistle of the desert wind and the lapping sound of the Nile. Gareth finally turned his head slowly and looked her in the eye.

"Power," he said quietly before turning back toward the temple. "I'm almost done inside."

As he walked away from her, Adele took guilty pleasure in the fact that he was once again the man she knew, despite the heavy price.

Adele wondered again about Colonel Anhalt as she methodically checked the small motor on the boat in the predawn glow. The colonel knew to meet them here in this temple, but she could only stare at the gigantic façade with a shudder now. Gareth had removed the slaughtered corpses and buried them in the desert, but the place conjured horrifying memories of him she'd rather not have.

Thankfully there was another place of refuge no more than a hundred yards distant. They could wait there for Anhalt. However, they couldn't abandon the temple without leaving a message about where they had gone. Adele hopped off the boat and made her way toward the huge, uncaring pharaohs. From her earlier campfire, she took a sturdy piece of burnt wood that would serve her perfectly for what she had in mind.

Gareth appeared from the interior, carrying a bundle of their belongings. He paused and silently regarded her, unsure of her reaction toward him.

She held up the bit of charred wood. "I think we should move. But we need to leave Anhalt a message."

"Where will we go?"

"The Temple of Hathor is just north of here."

"Will we give ourselves away by leaving him a message to follow?"

"I'll use code. Anhalt will recognize it."

"Hieroglyphics?"

Her lips quirked upward slightly. "I doubt he knows how to read those. But something pictorial will work. The colonel is rather clever."

Gareth nodded and departed northward with their possessions. He passed near Adele, but still left ample room between them. Adele wanted to reach out and touch him and tell him she was not afraid or repelled by him. The animal in him was gone like a sudden rage. He was Prince Gareth once again. Her shock had passed, but she still couldn't find the right words to assure him.

She found a smooth surface on the temple entrance and attempted to draw a cow of some sort, a representation of the goddess Hathor. It wasn't the best-looking cow, but it would do. At least it was better than Simon's stick-figure bovines.

Now she needed to let Anhalt know who had drawn it. The new

symbol had to represent her in a way that was unmistakable, but without informing all others as well. It had to be something shared only between them. She and Anhalt shared a love of the desert, but she couldn't think of a way to draw it so it would be obvious to him. Anything to do with her royal station was out of the question.

Then she had it.

Pet!

The thought elicited a laugh. Often Adele had caught the sturdy Gurkha playing with her small cat, amused by his playful antics. Few in the palace were enamored with the feline save Simon, Anhalt, and herself. Hopefully she could draw Pet's likeness well enough. She was not an artist by any measure. Still she tried.

Sadly it came out very unlike her little companion. Frustrated, she started smudging.

"What are you trying to do?" came a quiet voice behind her. Thankfully she didn't jump out of her skin.

She wiped an itch at her nose and gestured with the stick. "I was trying to draw a cat."

"That looks like a cow."

"Not that. That." She pointed at the smudgy catlike thing.

Gareth's head tilted to the side. "Is he supposed to be sitting or standing?"

"Ha, ha. Very funny." A pause. "Sleeping," she admitted in defeat. "It's supposed to be Pet."

"The cat I sent you? Well, his lines are all wrong and his eyes are too far apart."

Exasperated, Adele shoved the charcoal stick in his hands. "Here, you try it."

He stared at the implement in puzzlement. "I cannot draw."

"Oh please! You draw all the time. Those archaic letters you draw are art."

He quirked an eyebrow at her. "I believe you said that was copying, if I remember correctly."

"Yes, well, it still shows you have the skill. Much more so than I do."

"I don't have him here to look at."

"Close your eyes and picture him. Remember him with me playing by the fire in your castle. Then start drawing."

Gareth regarded her dubiously and closed his eyes. After a few moments he opened them and set the charcoal to the stone. Soon, a detailed sketch of Adele's cat began to emerge. Even though it was a rough charcoal, Adele could immediately see Pet come to life on the ancient stone.

"That's amazing," she said. "And very annoying."

Gareth looked at her only to see her smiling. "Ah, you are joking." He relaxed, lifting the charcoal once more. "Perhaps I should make it look like you drew it. I can give it stubby legs and unidentifiable features. No one would be the wiser."

"Don't you dare."

———✻———

It was past midday, and Gareth had retreated to the darkest recesses of Hathor's temple. Even with fresh blood coursing through his system, the temperature had an immediate impact on him. He had wordlessly taken the weak cooling blanket and departed for the darkest area.

Adele kept vigil near the entry, out of sight, but with an open view of the sparkling river and clear sky. There was no way of knowing what means of transportation Colonel Anhalt would arrange. She hoped for an airship since it would be difficult to continue sailing up the Nile with the cataracts growing in frequency.

Adele's stomach remained in knots as she waited with both anticipation and dread for any sign of Anhalt. She had no choice but to lie to her commander about Greyfriar and hope for the best. With any luck, no one would discover what he was. So it was little wonder that when the great shadow of an airship fell across the sands, Adele did not jump with joy, but instead walked toward the dark interior where Gareth hid and announced, "They're here. There's an airship."

"That's good. The air is cooler aloft." Gareth nodded, his eyes already covered with the dark glasses. "You are sure it's them?"

"What do you mean?"

"Isn't it possible that we have been discovered? Perhaps it's Senator Clark with an armed escort to bring you back." He picked up the head wrap and began to cover his face, becoming the Greyfriar once more.

Adele's lips pursed, not wanting to think that this trek could have been for nothing. She strode back to the temple entrance and went out into the blistering glare. She made her way to a rocky overlook where she could watch the four colossi of Ramses at Abu Simbel without being observed. She knew that whoever had just flown in would go to the major temple first. As she hugged the ground, her breath creaked out dry, blowing little clouds of dust.

After a few moments, Adele heard the sound of approaching soldiers—boots, jangling metal, voices. They certainly weren't being stealthy, or perhaps she had simply grown used to Gareth's shadowy style and all humans sounded like tramping cattle to her now. Ten figures emerged from around the base of the temple façade, trudging with difficulty through the loose sand. They were not her White Guard. There were no red tunics and black trousers. On the other hand, they weren't dressed like Senator Clark's American Rangers either. The uniforms were unknown to her, and she knew every unit of the imperial armed forces. These men wore nondescript uniforms of plain khaki tunics and trousers, gaiters, and desert boots, with cloth-covered peaked pith helmets and simple leather belts and ammo sashes. They carried bolt-action rifles that appeared to be standard-issue Mausers. Adele stared hard through the glare, wishing for a spyglass.

The soldiers paused outside the temple. A few gazed up at the magnificent monument, but most swigged from canteens. Two turned toward Adele's cliff. She dropped her face to the dirt and lay still. She waited for the shout of discovery, but it didn't come. Slowly, she rose and looked down at the men again. One soldier spotted the anchored dahabiya. He shouted, and several of his comrades jogged forward.

The princess cursed. Without that boat, there was no way out except on foot, and Gareth certainly could not get far. She could surrender herself to prevent the soldiers discovering Gareth, but that would solve nothing long-term. She conjured the image of poor Gareth lying comatose and panting in the temple, slowly starving to death like an abandoned dog.

The soldiers all responded to a sound and turned toward from where they'd come. They all stood or straightened, lifting their rifles smartly. A group of three men appeared around the foot of Ramses.

Colonel Anhalt was in the lead.

CHAPTER 19

LORD KELVIN HAD an unaccustomed look of real emotion on his hatchet face. He didn't want to speak, but he was compelled by duty. For moral support, he ran his fingers over the minutes of the Home Affairs Committee he had just chaired in the House of Commons in central Alexandria.

Emperor Constantine stared at him with the same directionless anger and dismay he'd shown since the wedding disaster the week before. The emperor lived every minute now unsure whether he was furious or broken-hearted.

Kelvin said, "Your Majesty, the overwhelming sense in Commons is that Princess Adele should be removed from the line of succession."

The emperor began to shake his head slowly.

The prime minister continued, "The negative reaction to her behavior is palpable. Commons is quite distraught. No confidence remains in her. I'm sorry to tell you this, Your Majesty, but our way seems clear. His Imperial Highness, Prince Simon, should be made emperor presumptive."

"What do I care what Commons thinks?"

Kelvin hid the alarm he felt. "We must, Majesty. The Empire is in crisis. The heir has fled with a common masked rogue, and her whereabouts are unknown. Her disposition is obviously called into question. It pains me to say it, but she is unfit to rule by any definition. Strong action is required to restore public confidence in the crown."

"What of Senator Clark?"

Kelvin raised his eyebrows in slight confusion. "What of him?"

"He intends to search for Adele and bring her back. He's done it before. Commons would surely accept Adele with the senator at her side."

"Despite the senator's unquestioned experience in bringing the princess back to Alexandria, Senator Clark is not Equatorian. Majesty, the people demand Prince Simon. Princess Adele is no longer feasible."

"No. That's impossible. We have a treaty with America."

"There is no princess. There can be no marriage. Therefore, the treaty is moot, through no fault of your own."

"What about the war?"

Kelvin took a deep breath of apparent regret. "Commons is prepared to recommend we postpone any offensive in the north. We dare not put our armed forces in harm's way until we have set the Empire on a solid constitutional path. The very real potential for internal rupture must be faced, Your Majesty."

The emperor rose and paced before a vast sweep of windows. In his white uniform, he was a pale shadow against the colorful spray of flowering shrubs in the private gardens outside. A warm summer breeze swirled sweet scents through the Privy Council chamber now bathed in the red light of the sinking sun.

"I could suspend Commons," the emperor said.

"Majesty." The prime minister actually shivered and placed his hands flat on the table with an audible thump to steady himself. "That is a precedent you dare not set. I can't count the evils such action would create. Many of the provinces would resist."

Constantine looked out the window with his back to Lord Kelvin, and his silence disturbed the prime minister. The thought of the emperor declaring personal rule and disbanding Commons could mean the end of an empire that Kelvin had labored to build and preserve.

The prime minister knew that Emperor Constantine had to forget

Adele and turn to his son, Simon, who could be molded into an excellent ruler, given time. Constantine simply couldn't accept that he had lost his daughter, and that the Empire had already abandoned her. But Adele had always been an unrelieved irritation; she was unfocused and undisciplined, and exposed to ideals not in accordance with proper society, thanks in part to her mentor, Mamoru, whom Constantine refused to dismiss. Something to do with Adele's mother, the former empress, who had personally requested Mamoru come from the Japanese Empire in the East Indies to teach her daughter. Then the empress had extracted a promise from Constantine to retain the teacher no matter what. It wasn't enough that Mamoru was a religious fanatic and a dangerous subversive, he also had some personal intelligence network that the emperor refused to seize and control. At least with Adele gone there was no reason for Mamoru to continue skulking about Alexandria. However, that was a moot point if the emperor tried to force his misguided will on the government.

Lord Kelvin cleared his throat and prepared to launch into a thoughtful, measured lecture on the delicate balance of crown and Commons, and of metropole and provinces in imperial politics when Constantine said, "Summon the General Staff. I want Army Chief of Staff Singhal, First Air Lord Kilwas, and Admiral of the Blue Petrov here this evening. And I want the Tewfiq Barracks on standby in case of action."

"If I may," Kelvin began slowly with a quavering voice, "perhaps I should place a motion before Commons in general session to vote on the issue of Princess Adele's succession. A favorable vote or even a deadlock will allow you to—"

"There will be no vote on my daughter, Mr. Prime Minister." The emperor's face recalled the hard features of the man who had campaigned to break the Zulu Kingdom back when Kelvin was a young adjutant on Constantine's staff. "I won't stand for her to suffer the humiliation of a public rebuke. Call the General Staff. I want troops in place should I need to close parliament."

"Your Majesty, I implore you—"

"Do as I say! Or step down!"

The prime minister felt as close to tears as he had in his life. He stood up with visage unmoved and departed to make ready to destroy his government. All because of the regret of an old man and the lunacy of a young girl.

—∿—

Lord Kelvin couldn't suppress the apprehension he felt as he strode the halls of the palace. He had discussed many possible coming events with his friend, Lord Aden, and this was one that neither had believed likely but couldn't dismiss completely. If Constantine closed parliament and ruled by force, the role of the prime minister would diminish and likely the power of Senator Clark would elevate. However, if all units of the military didn't support the emperor's seizure of power, Equatoria would be thrown into chaos and perhaps internecine bloodshed. The Cape or Kashmir might declare independence, as they had threatened for years. The crazed Legionnaires in OutreMer would move to seize Saharan resources. He could foresee no positive outcome to Emperor Constantine's clumsy actions.

This act was as potentially destructive as the northern war, perhaps even worse. Lord Kelvin had done his best to delay the campaign against the vampires. In his mind, the war could only result in a stalemate that would weaken the glorious Empire, as well as place an American, whom Kelvin couldn't control, close to the throne. He finally had given up and accepted that the wedding would occur, but he had taken solace that the emperor would continue to rule, hopefully for years, which would give Kelvin time to restructure his plans.

And then the wedding hadn't happened. The lunatic princess disappeared into the night with a masked vigilante. How fortunate. Kelvin had seen events shift his way and he had foolishly relaxed, knowing he had only Constantine to manage for the present, and a future to look forward to with the pliable Simon as the ruler. However, Kelvin had underestimated Constantine's emotional distress. Was the entire imperial family deranged? Now Kelvin had to save the Empire from the emperor.

There was nothing Lord Kelvin would not do to protect Equatoria.

The prime minister reached the front portico of the palace and asked the footman to summon his personal carriage. He then instructed the driver to take him to an address that was barely half a mile away. After the very short trip, he signaled the carriage to a halt.

"Shall I wait, sir?"

"No. I'll find another way home, thank you."

The carriage rumbled off, leaving Lord Kelvin standing in the street, draped in the long shadows of evening. He slipped into the darkness between buildings. Searing light from the Pharos One air tower swept over his head every minute as he made his way through untended gardens in the empty spaces between old structures that had yet to be reclaimed or demolished. He swatted wild shrubbery aside and cursed at thorns that clutched his pant legs. His polished shoes caked with soil as he trekked farther from the pavement. Between the gnarled trunks of scrub brush he found his objective—a hidden doorway that appeared to untrained eyes as nothing more than tumbled stones.

Lord Kelvin ducked low and heard his coat rip as he squeezed into the cleft between rocks. With effort, he pushed through, and while his eyes fought the darkness, he tapped his toe and found the edge of a step. Carefully carved limestone stairs took him down into blackness. At the bottom, he entered a vaulted area and coughed from a stench that filled the air. Covering his mouth with a silk monogrammed handkerchief, he inched forward, but he tripped over a large sack and fell onto the stone floor. He cursed and kicked at the bundle, dislodging arms and legs from the mass.

Human bodies. Several of them.

Kelvin cried out and scrambled away from the cadavers. He bumped into another object and turned to see luminous eyes staring down at him. Sharp fingers touched his shoulder.

"No! No!" Kelvin screamed and scrambled to his feet as more shapes shuffled around him. "I have business here!"

Kelvin backed against a flaking wall and screamed out, "Flay! I'm here to see Flay! Where is she?"

A tall figure appeared across the chamber, growled, and sent all the shadowy things sinking closer to the floor. The newcomer, visible in the fresh moonlight drifting down from cracks above, was a female wearing the white robes of a Bedouin that barely concealed her naked form beneath.

"Kelvin," the female snarled in English. "Why are you here? What if you were followed?"

"I wasn't followed, Flay." The prime minister adopted an authoritative voice, which he didn't feel. He found himself staring at the vampire despite her terrible nature. She was physically striking, long-limbed and powerful, with smooth, pale skin and oil-black hair draping her shoulders. Her cruel face, only partially visible in the shadows, was almost beautiful. His gaze fell on her hips and thighs, and he looked hurriedly away, shocked and embarrassed by her nearly naked state.

She sneered at his prudish demeanor. "What do you want?"

"I've come to unleash you."

———

The time had come for Flay to return to life.

She had existed for the past months—it might have well been years —in a fetid necropolis beneath Alexandria. The city was pockmarked with undiscovered subterranean catacombs, and now they were full to bursting with vampires. The heat was crushing, and Flay's packs were even more fractious because they were drawn from allied clans from Britain, Hungary, and Bavaria. They were close to starvation, eating only the few rationed humans they could steal without notice. Now, they undulated with nervous energy, sensing that full-fledged feedings were upon them.

Flay knew this mission for what it was—her last chance, a forlorn hope. Cesare had blamed her for the loss of Princess Adele in Scotland. The war chief of the greatest clan was manhandled by a human girl and then thrown to her *death* from an airship. The shame still stung even though Flay knew there was something enormously peculiar about Adele; the girl wielded power in a way that hadn't been seen in centuries.

Flay had been lucky to survive the fall and luckier still that Cesare hadn't simply executed her in a rush to cover his failure by rewriting history. Instead, Cesare had sent her to Alexandria. He had made it clear to wait for the signal from his human ally, Lord Kelvin. The signal was supposed to come on the princess's wedding day, but that day came and went without word from Cesare's toady.

Flay wondered why the attack was going forward now without the prize kill present in Alexandria. She knew that Princess Adele was gone from the city, spirited away by the damnable Greyfriar. Even though this Greyfriar was a mere human, Flay longed to kill him more than anyone else alive, except perhaps Prince Gareth, who had rejected her.

Before he slipped away to hide himself, Kelvin had told her that plans had changed. The targets were Emperor Constantine and Senator Clark. The heads of the Equatorian military were useful secondary targets. As important as the assassinations were to Flay, her true object was sowing terror among the Equatorian citizens. They should be made to believe they were starting a war they could not hope to win, or even survive.

Flay's intention was to make this night so apocalyptic the Equatorians would count their calendars forward from it.

She climbed the rough steps to the warm night air, followed by the light footfalls of her pack. The weight of the day's heat still pressed down on her. Plus, the air was noxious. It was full of sweat from people, and rife with cloying undercurrents from chemicals poured into the air by the human industries. She couldn't wait to return to the freshness of England.

Flay smiled. The wind was strong, which was good. Her packs could fly fast and strike hard. The temperature was relatively mild, so there was no danger of heat failure, at least in the next couple of hours.

She leapt into the air and gave a cry too shrill for humans to hear, but it carried across the city. Inside the catacombs and ancient cistern systems, the screech was heard and passed on. Rocks were shoved aside and dirt shifted as shapes scrabbled from holes in the ground. Those people who were about at the late hour doubted what they saw. Arms and legs pushed free of the soil, or figures emerged from inside rock faces or scrub. Witnesses saw ferocious eyes lock on them, and in a blur they were dead.

Flay floated above Victoria Palace and drew in a deep breath. She had planned for this night with the same thoroughness that had allowed her to successfully marshal the depopulation of Ireland in the Great Killing. That island had properties that made it a likely haven for resistance; it was full of stone circles and reeked of power from the earth. Cesare had ordered her to brave its painful shores and slaughter everything that moved, which she had done. In this city, she sensed none of that power, or at least none that was active. There was nothing to hinder her rampage.

From testing the air, she knew where to find the emperor. Senator Clark, the American butcher, was farther away, but detectable. She even caught the scent of Prince Simon. Her objectives loomed before her and her mood lightened. Her lust for slaughter rose as she laughed and dropped heavily toward a huge palace window.

Glass shattered. Flags and tapestries fluttered in the rush of bodies as Flay and over thirty vampires poured into the grand chamber where four old men in uniform sat around a table with startled eyes. Hands reached for weapons on instinct and nearly cleared holsters and scabbards before three of the old men dropped dead.

The chief of staff of the army.

The first air lord.

The admiral of the Blue.

All gone in the first rush of claws.

Emperor Constantine was not so easy to kill. He kicked back his chair as he tore free a Fahrenheit saber. Putting his back against a gilt wall, he shouted angrily and the blade became a blur of green and crimson. Creatures surged and fell back, clawing, ripping his uniform. The saber connected, cutting a bloody swathe, and several of the monsters scurried back, screeching. He grabbed a chair and heaved it ineffectually, shouting in rage at the circling vampires.

Flay reveled in the despair that flickered briefly in Constantine's gaze as his eyes darted to his dead officers, old friends from many battles, their spilling blood red on the pristine floor. She snapped a command, and her blood-slicked creatures moved away from the old soldier who stood red-faced and bleeding, his chest heaving.

Flay said in English, "Emperor Constantine, I pronounce the death sentence of Prince Cesare upon you as an enemy of the British clan."

He squeezed the hilt of the saber with an age-spotted hand. "Come, my dear, and carry out your sentence, then."

Flay moved with a grace and speed honed to perfection. In a blink, the sword fell with a loud clatter to the marble floor and Constantine dropped to his knees for the first time in his life.

"I had hoped for more." The vampire constricted a clawed hand around the old man's throat. "You are not the warrior your daughter is."

"No," the emperor gasped and looked her cold in the eye. "And neither are you."

With a spray of blood, Flay ended the reign of Constantine II.

CHAPTER 20

"THE REPORTS TO the palace," Mamoru said quickly, "have the princess in Suez, Damascus, and Cyprus. Among others."

Sir Godfrey regarded his friend. "Any validity to the reports, old boy?" He reclined on a low settee, smoking a hookah and dressed in a fine worsted wool suit and leather shoes with spats. He held the long tube to his lips, seemingly lost in the moment. Sanah sat next to him on voluminous pillows with her gaze clear. Nzingu stood strangely calm in the corner under cheap paintings of blood horses, prize cattle, and voluptuous harem girls.

Mamoru paced. He no longer even pretended to retain his normal façade of serenity. His face was drawn and pale, and he exuded a tragic energy. "There are stories from all across the Empire of Adele in her wedding dress and Greyfriar in his cloak dashing pell-mell through the night. All romantic nonsense. There have been no sensible leads to her whereabouts."

Sanah asked hesitantly, "You have heard nothing from her, then?"

"No." Mamoru stopped pacing and rubbed his bristly hair. "No."

Nzingu said, "Where would this Greyfriar take her?"

"I don't know. I don't know enough about him to predict. Adele would hardly speak of him, despite my best efforts. Of course, I must assume they've left the Empire, but he doesn't seem to have a single base of operations in Europe. He's everywhere."

"She'll contact you in time, surely," Sir Godfrey said with a drowsy smile. "Or contact someone. The emperor, perhaps? She wouldn't just run off with some chap and turn her back on her responsibilities, would she?"

All four of them stayed quiet.

The old gentleman blew smoke into the air and continued idly, "Well then, do you think it was planned? Did she stage the whole event?"

"No," Nzingu replied firmly. "If she had wanted to run off with him, they would have run off quietly. Why put her man in danger? No, that disaster was a man's idea. Or a boy's. Shattered windows. Sword fights. Escapes. I fear that Greyfriar has read too many cheap romances." She smiled.

"Perhaps," Sanah added. "But this city has never seen anything like it, and its daring has swept through the heart of the people."

Sir Godfrey nodded in agreement. "Certainly. But my colleagues in Commons want the princess removed from succession so Simon can be handed the mantle. Being a folk hero doesn't translate into being a proper empress."

Mamoru sipped a small cup of dark Turkish coffee. "That may work to our advantage ultimately. If she is passed over in favor of her brother, then there is nothing to distract her from training. And the marriage would be a moot point as well. Senator Clark would have no interest in marrying some cast-off dowager, so he would be out of the picture. If Adele does not become empress, it would certainly not be catastrophic for us."

"If we can find her," Nzingu muttered.

"Just so."

Sanah asked, "What shall we do with the Greyfriar?"

Mamoru stared into space for a moment. "He will either cooperate with our goals or he will be eliminated."

Sir Godfrey stirred uncomfortably. "Dear me. So harsh? He seems a very useful fellow to have around."

"If he proves so, I welcome him. But I distrust anyone we don't control. This event only demonstrates his disruptive nature. We are too late in this game, and the stakes are too enormous, to allow some duelist to endanger our plans."

The Persian woman gestured with her hennaed hands. "I caution you, Mamoru. The girl's feelings for this man are deep."

"I well know that, Sanah," the Japanese man snapped. "But we are dealing with the fate of the world. Immature infatuation must be put aside."

The other three members of the cabal exchanged worried glances. Nzingu was about to speak when several loud crashes from outside interrupted her. She went to the door, and her sharply drawn breath caused the others to turn in her direction.

The main floor of the hashish house was in chaos. Men and women scattered with shouts of fear and alarm, running into tables, scrambling for a back way out. At the front door was a vampire, red-faced and clutching a writhing man. Three other people lay dead at its feet.

Nzingu shouted in her native tongue and reached for the cinched waist of her elegant gown. Both hands came away from the embroidery with six-foot wires. She leapt over a collapsed table while whipping the silvery lines over her head with a high-pitched whine. The vampire saw her and started to move. The thin whips cut the creature across the face, slicing to the bone. Nzingu spun and dropped while claws raked the air above her and she lashed the thing again, her limbs whirling a macabre dance. The vampire staggered, but came again at the woman, whose movements were hampered by her clumsy dress.

Mamoru appeared with a small, flashing blade and planted it deep in the vampire's chest. It screeched and turned its palsied hands to the hilt.

"Get down!" Nzingu rose and drew her arms back almost in slow motion. Mamoru dropped flat to the wooden floor. Both razor whips gracefully encircled the woman before they slung forward and wrapped around the vampire's throat. A snap of her elbows sent the creature's head somersaulting.

Both Mamoru and Nzingu heard distant screams. They ran into the chaotic lobby of the Hotel Saladin and to the ornate entryway only to see a multitude of figures floating in the air above the dark cityscape of Alexandria.

"My God," Nzingu breathed. "My God. How is this possible?"

Sir Godfrey and Sanah attempted to help the wounded or comfort the shocked in the decimated room. Sir Godfrey knelt beside a man choking on blood and did what he could to assist him.

"Sir Godfrey!" Mamoru tossed a small bag of crystals to Sanah. "You and Sanah go to Rue Karam, to the rift at the Gate of the Moon near the old Franciscan school. Do what you can from there. Nzingu and I will go to the palace."

The old man looked up. "This fellow needs a doctor, Mamoru, or he will die."

The samurai yanked his blade from the vampire. "Leave him or thousands will die!"

Sanah laid a gentle hand on Sir Godfrey's shoulder and gave him the strength to rise from the injured man. Taking his place, she bent close and whispered to the dying man, who immediately stilled at her words, his eyes focusing strangely on the Persian beauty before him. In seconds, his life fled silently from his body. Then Sanah followed her colleagues into the horror of the street. Godfrey stood there, taking in the carnage erupting over the city. She said, "We must go. There is too much at stake to pause for even one life."

"Then what's the point?" he muttered. "What's the point?"

—ɷ—

Mamoru and Nzingu ran without speaking, but their gazes were riveted upward. The sky over the Imperial Quarter was thick with hundreds of vampires floating in the stiff wind, diving in horrifying flocks. Gunfire was audible from around the city. The two pretended they didn't see vampires striking people dead in the street as they ran on. The samurai gripped his small blade tightly.

The grand avenues were chaos. Theaters, restaurants, and clubs were scenes of panic and inhumanity. Masses streamed in different directions seeking to flee attacks, but then grew confused by encountering another terrified crowd from the opposite direction. Men and women sought refuge inside shops or warehouses. Moments of civilization punctuated the horror as some paused to help those who had fallen or who were in danger of being trampled. Carriages and steam cars struggled through the wild mobs, or were abandoned.

Mamoru tugged on the taffeta sleeve of his companion and jerked his head toward a narrow door in what appeared to be a long-abandoned building. He quickly pressed several carved lions in succession and the door clicked open. The two started down a stuffy corridor lit by dim chemical bulbs. They ran for several minutes, turning so often that Nzingu was soon lost. Then they emerged into the night air with a great complex of buildings looming before them. Nzingu realized they were inside the walls of Victoria Palace, surrounded by shouting and weapons fire and a sky dark with *Homo nosferatii* above them.

"Stay close to me," Mamoru commanded without breaking stride. "Our talismans will keep us only so safe in such a frenzy."

Nzingu fingered her crystal pendant as they crossed manicured grass between marble sculptures and fountains. They leapt over a few bodies and raced up the wide sweep of stairs into the main entry of the palace. Soldiers ran around them in all directions, attempting to combat the unthinkable.

Inside, they passed a formal ballroom hastily converted to a surgery. Wounded lay on tables and on the floor. Doctors and attendants hovered, and a few rough operations were taking place under the sparkling light of chandeliers. The smell of blood and gore was all the more revolting for the ornate setting.

Mamoru paused to unbuckle a saber belt from a moaning soldier. "Find a weapon."

"I have these." Nzingu held up the razor whips which she now had looped in each hand.

"Dr. Kemal!" the samurai called out. "Where is the emperor?"

"I don't know." A man wearing a blood-soaked tuxedo didn't pause from sewing up a gash in a soldier. "I haven't heard anything about the family. I only know they are not here."

Mamoru and Nzingu continued up another marble flight. Gunshots erupted nearby, then quieted. The carpet runners in the hallway were stained with blood. They nearly slammed into two figures at an intersection of corridors. Mamoru brandished the saber, and it clanged against glowing steel.

"Wait!" a voice shouted.

Senator Clark stood with his Fahrenheit blade pressed to the samurai's saber and with pistol pointed at Mamoru. Major Stoddard gripped his commander's gun arm, and the American leader stepped back. His uniform was spotless, but Stoddard's was torn and bloody.

Clark squinted and growled, "Schoolteacher! What are you doing here?"

Mamoru asked, "Where is the emperor? Is he safe?"

"He's dead. We're going for Prince Simon."

Mamoru steadied himself from the shock. His mind raced with implications from the loss of his great patron in court. Still, there was no time to worry about that with fresh blood still running through the palace and vampires gliding freely around the city.

The two Americans started running again, so Mamoru and Nzingu followed. After a wordless minute of pounding feet and jangling steel, they entered an airy atrium with a small tiled fountain and lush green potted plants. All the doors stood wide open, but for one. The four gathered at the closed door.

Clark tried the handle and pushed, but it refused to give. He pounded with his fist. "Prince Simon! If you're in there, open up! It's Senator Clark!"

"Smart boy." Mamoru gave an approving and hopeful nod. This was the servants' quarters with no windows. He called out, "Your Highness, open the door, if you please. We must get you to safety."

"I'm already safe!" came the defiant reply from inside. "Where's Colonel Anhalt?"

Clark slammed against the door again. "Open up, boy! We've lost the top floor and we have to take you below!"

They heard the sound of objects being moved away from the inside of the door, which then swung back. Prince Simon stood barefooted in a linen robe and pants. He seemed composed enough, given the circumstances.

Mamoru heard a soft wind behind him and turned. Several figures detached from the shadows of the cupola above the atrium and hurtled down like cannonballs. The samurai shoved the boy back into the room. "Brace it!"

The four humans took the vampires' charge with their backs planted against the wall. The creatures lunged with claws and teeth, ripping and shredding, but they were driven back with steel. Those monsters that grabbed the two occultists hissed in pain and recoiled. Mamoru moved with a speed that rivaled the vampires. His sword was a constant blur, his face a mask of concentration. Mamoru knew that as fast as the vampires seemed, it was the heat that hampered them, giving the humans a fighting chance.

Mamoru and Nzingu were machines of violence, striking and slashing. The Zulu's whips sang a horrific dirge as they sliced the air about her. Clark and Stoddard exchanged quick glances of surprise and admiration as the samurai and Zulu actually took ground from the vampires and relieved the pressure from the two Americans and their exhausted arms and empty revolvers.

A shattering screech tore through the air, and the vampires suddenly drew back. Clark lowered his sword arm but noticed Mamoru stood firm, so raised it again. Her whips coiled momentarily, Nzingu drew closer to the Japanese swordsman. Stoddard leaned against the wall, fighting for breath.

"What is this?" Nzingu asked.

Mamoru didn't reply. His eyes flicked over the bloody, exhausted mob in front of them. The vampires were badly wounded, and a few were actually dead. He didn't want to admit it, but his sword arm was numb and bleeding. This respite from the fighting was actually hurting him; he could feel his muscles stiffening and his adrenaline slowing. Without help, this standoff would be over soon. And they would lose.

A tall female appeared in the atrium with her figure caressed by a white robe. Petite spots of red dotted it in odd, random patterns. She studied the four humans before smiling directly at Senator Clark. "Prince Cesare sends greetings."

Clark tried to cover his exhausted wheezing with a vicious snarl. "You tell that stinking animal that I'll see him in Britain soon enough."

He paused as recognition dawned on him. "Wait. I know you. You were at the Tower of London. You killed some of my men."

She laughed. "I know you too, Butcher. I am Flay. I defeated you in London. And again in Edinburgh. Now I've taken your emperor here in his own homeland. And you did nothing."

Clark stepped forward. "Let's just finish it here and now."

Mamoru planted a hard arm against the American's immaculate blue tunic. "Stop, you fool! She's baiting you."

Flay regarded Mamoru curiously. "You smell odd. Princess Adele had the same smell. As do you." She glanced at Nzingu. The stench brought back memories of the excruciating agony she felt when Adele placed the cross on her. Her hand went to the spot on her chest where the object had burned her permanently. Here was Senator Clark eager to be killed by her hand, but she hadn't anticipated that Clark would be protected by those with abilities similar to the princess. She took a deep angry breath, steeling herself to attack despite the fear and the weakness coursing through her. Then she heard something distant: the sound of many soldiers running with metal weapons ringing. The smell of guns. Many guns. Flay had fewer than ten soldiers around her. Most of her foreign pack were spread around the city, or had already fled north after sowing havoc. She didn't have the power or the strength to match the number of men she heard coming. She hissed to her ailing troops.

"My work here is done," Flay said to the humans. "Your king is dead. Your war chiefs are dead. Your city is broken. I no longer need to live among you." She pointed at Clark. "Come to us in the north, if you dare. We are waiting for you." The vampires all lifted off the ground and drifted out through the shattered glass of the atrium roof.

Nzingu raced to the window and watched the vampires depart, mere black spots against a lightening sky. To her relief, they did not vanish back into the city, but veered north. "They're leaving."

Clark turned angrily on Mamoru. "You shouldn't have stopped me! I could've killed her!"

"Be quiet. She would have slaughtered you."

A large squad of Persian marines appeared with rifles at the ready. Clark recognized Captain Eskandari from the glorious attack on Bordeaux as the marines expertly fanned out to search the rooms off the rotunda.

Captain Eskandari saluted Senator Clark. "Sir, where is Prince Simon?"

Clark slapped the closed door with his hand. "In here. Safe and sound. Get him out of there and take him somewhere better fortified."

"Well done, sir. The vampires appear to be abandoning the palace precinct."

"I've driven them off," the American replied.

The Persian officer replied, "There have been attacks all over the city. The House of Commons has been struck. The Tewfiq Barracks was hit. The airport. The telegraph exchange. We're only just getting reports, but there are many casualties. Many."

"That's fine, Captain." Clark sheathed his Fahrenheit blade and indicated Nzingu. She had fallen to one knee, dripping blood. "Get this woman here to the surgeon. Then find whoever is in charge of the Imperial Air Force now and let's get some ships aloft in case more attacks are coming. Come on, we need to get on top of this disaster. Then we can see about getting me sworn in as emperor before this empire goes completely to hell."

Captain Eskandari watched the Americans stride across the broken glass, their boots crunching with every step as they went out of the ruined atrium. He turned to Mamoru. "Is he the next emperor?"

The schoolmaster shrugged, kneeling beside Nzingu. "If Lord Kelvin is still alive, he should know."

CHAPTER 21

ADELE HEARD THE distant water of the Nile as she neared the entrance of the Temple of Hathor. Colonel Anhalt stood nearby studying a map book, silhouetted against the deep orange sky. "Colonel?"

"Your Highness." Anhalt snapped to attention.

"As you were. I've been thinking about our options."

"Is one of them returning to Alexandria?"

Adele took a deep breath. "Not yet, I fear. As I told you, I won't return until my demands are met. So I need a safe haven from which to negotiate with my father, and to send him word that I'm fine." She joined Anhalt in a study of the map of the vast Nile region. "Our best hope is Katanga to the south."

"King Msiri's country?"

"All other surrounding territories are either imperial provinces, or client states that might have reason to curry favor by shipping me back. Msiri is entirely independent. I've met him several times and like him. And I trust him. Plus, in terms of pure politics, if Msiri thinks he can ingratiate himself with the future empress, temporarily displaced or not, it would be to his benefit to help us."

"He is reputed to be a rather . . . unconventional royal."

"He is." Adele smiled. "Like I am."

Anhalt nodded approvingly at her analysis. "Then I agree. I suggest we move west for a hundred miles to remove ourselves from the Nile air corridor, and then strike southward across the Sudd."

Adele could see worry in her commander's face. Surely he wanted to believe she would return home eventually, and that he hadn't turned his back on his nation forever. She wasn't so sure, however. Right now, that possibility seemed bleak.

Anhalt said, "I recommend that we leave tonight. It has been nearly two weeks since you disappeared, and panic will be setting in. The net is tightening. Every ship and airship out of Alexandria and Suez is searched. Patrols are increasing out of Aswan, Port Sudan, Aden, and Khartoum. The Nile and the Red Sea are becoming an armed camp. We'll be lucky to escape."

"I agree."

"Shall I arrange a litter for Greyfriar, given his illness?"

"No!" she exclaimed. "He wouldn't have it. The medicine you provided is working well. I'll get him." Adele didn't mention that she had stuffed the tablets into her baggage; they were pointless for Gareth.

Adele swept past the dim paintings on the monumental walls. In a quiet alcove, she found Gareth crouched in the corner under a silvery blanket, reading the penny dreadful. At his feet was a khaki helmet. Adele stooped and picked it up.

"You're supposed to wear this," she whispered to keep her voice from echoing through the ancient halls. "It will keep you cool. Our army has operated in the desert and jungles long enough to come up with a useful cooling kit."

"It's too heavy."

Adele rolled her eyes and placed the peaked helmet on his head. "It will keep your brains from boiling. And it looks damn good. Every woman likes a soldier."

Almost immediately, Gareth felt clear-headed as the chilled air pushed away the weight of the heat. He stood without weak knees and gave Adele raised eyebrows of acceptance.

Adele remarked, "See? If your people could make those, you could conquer the whole world."

"So long as it's fashionable," he said, eliciting a smirk from the princess. He briefly wondered if perhaps Cesare had thought the same thing and that's why his brother was aligning with humans, something so unlike him. Fortunately, the cooling mechanisms only lasted a short time. Vampires would have to import them by the boatload in order for them to be viable. "I assume we're moving on?"

"Yes. Listen, we're bound south across the desert and toward the tropical forests of the equator. However, northeastern Katanga is relatively high country, so maybe it will be a bit more suitable to you."

He sighed. "Stop worrying. I did survive the Nile, after all."

"Barely." Adele took a worried breath and extended her hand. He took it, and together they went to the main entrance. The sun had set, leaving them in darkness until the stars began to wink on. They left their brief home and hiked down past Abu Simbel and beyond into the desert. More guardsmen appeared over a rise and saluted Colonel Anhalt and Adele, then watched in a mix of awe and suspicion as Greyfriar passed them with cloak flowing.

The party climbed the sandy rise, and there waiting on the other side was an airship staked to temporary anchors. A few men worked the shrouds and yards in the ghostly yellow chemical lights. The boat was relatively small, a brig with four square-rigged masts, two extending horizontally from either side of the dirigible.

Anhalt said, "Your Highness, this is HMS *Gordon*, a fine relic rescued from the breaking yard in Suez. She is not the newest model off the line, but she'll hold together to Katanga, or so I'm assured by the reputable and now wealthier yardmaster. But as she is now absent from the imperial registers, and is a refugee with the rest of us, you may name her as you will."

"Remarkable," Adele replied. "Well done, Colonel. She'll do admirably. I believe I will call her *Edinburgh*."

Greyfriar moved his shoulder to touch hers. "Excellent."

The fugitives went aboard their new vessel.

—ᘐᘖᘗ—

"Do you feel that?" Adele sat up in her simple bed abruptly, alone in her spartan cabin on the airship. Her voice was not raised beyond that of a normal speaking tone.

Not to her surprise, the door to her cabin flew open and Greyfriar appeared, his senses, as always, attuned to her. "What's wrong?"

Something had awakened Adele. Something strong flowed through her, and she planted her bare feet firmly on the rough wooden deck and stood, but felt almost as if the scorching sand of the desert were beneath her. There was a wonderful, wild flutter in her chest.

A worried Greyfriar approached with his hand outstretched. "Are you unwell?" He touched her bare arm, but drew back from the searing heat of her skin.

Adele caught his eye, still immersed in the sensations flooding her. "You can feel it, can't you?"

"It's you. You're burning."

"Sorry." She tried to focus her attention on the ripples of energy moving through her body as Mamoru had taught. The air grew very hot, and her breath rushed out dizzily. She felt the sun and wind. Sand pricked her face. The smell of smoke and chemical soot wafted over her with a slight hint of lemons. Like Alexandria? Then she felt the air freshen and it was wet. The taste of salt on her tongue and her skin went brinish. Then sun again and hints of olives and the flapping of wind in sails.

Adele was breathing hard—panting, in fact. Her nightclothes were soaked with sweat. Her knees gave way and Gareth rushed to her.

"Don't!" she warned as he grabbed her.

He grimaced in pain, but swept her up and carried her to the bed. Once she was sitting, she swatted his hands away.

Adele asked, "What happened to me?"

He knelt in front of her. "You began to shake. And your breath was too fast. Your scent changed drastically."

She gingerly pinched the edge of his leather gloves and tugged them off. His skin was pink and blistered. "You shouldn't have touched me."

"That will heal. Something is happening to you." His blue eyes studied her, and his nostrils flared as he took in her fluctuating aroma.

She began to stand again, but Gareth said, "Just be still."

"No. I have to check something." Adele staggered from the bed and grasped the walls to stay upright.

The air was blissfully cool as she came up from the companionway to a sky that was cobalt and star specked. The crew was startled by the unexpected arrival of the unkempt princess and her grim guardian on the quarterdeck. They stared at Adele in her nightgown until Greyfriar draped his cloak around her.

"Captain," Adele called as she padded to the rail. "Where are we?"

"What do you mean, Highness?" Captain Hariri appeared. The master of *Edinburgh* was a tall, dark figure in a flowing brown robe.

"What's down there?" She peered over at the invisible black earth thousands of feet below. Greyfriar was at her side, keeping a hand near her.

"The Sahara Desert, ma'am." The captain shrugged at the questioning glance of the helmsman, both wondering about the princess's mental state.

The princess scowled. "Are we over Nabta Playa?"

The helmsman consulted the charts and nodded. "Yes, ma'am. Nabta Playa. Or thereabouts."

"I knew it!" Adele pounded her hands on the rail and laughed. "I felt it!"

"What are you talking about?"

She lowered her voice. "Nabta Playa is an ancient stone circle. Built over a rift. Like the ones in Britain, but even older. Built when the Sahara was green, probably built to help fight vampires. I felt it when we passed over. It grabbed me and took me, for some reason. I could smell and hear the earth. Maybe like you do."

Greyfriar felt her warmth. He recalled the first tasting of her blood and how he'd touched the truth of her nature, which was the destruction of his kind. He sensed the same thing now even without tasting her blood. It coursed through her like a molten core at the heart of the sun, and he briefly wondered if he fed from her now whether it would burn him from the inside out. Not that he would care.

The day was dawning with the threat of storm clouds as a massive curtain of grey came rolling in from the west. Amid the creaking yards and thundering wind, Colonel Anhalt found his mind drifting to the matter of treason again. His uniform now in his baggage, he had abandoned most of his command for their own good, allowing only the most trustworthy of the White Guard to follow him on this insane mission to help his princess. Adele mattered more than Equatoria. To him, she was Equatoria. He had defied the orders of his emperor for her. His duty had been to return the princess to her government and secure the Greyfriar for prosecution. Now he was a traitor.

"Colonel, I don't believe I've seen you sleep since this voyage began."

Anhalt turned to see the familiar face of Captain Hariri, darkened by the shadows of the early sun in the east. The captain handed him a cup of steaming coffee. He sipped gratefully.

"Thank you, Captain. I've never slept well aboard ship."

"I recall." Hariri smiled with his eyes. "During the Siege of Zanzibar you stayed awake for a week."

"That was unmitigated fear."

"Doubtful. Is everything to your liking?"

"Yes. The coffee is delicious."

Hariri laughed. "Well, that's not what I meant, but I'm glad. The ship. The crew. Are they performing to your satisfaction?"

"Yes, Captain. Your people are excellent, particularly given how short-handed you are for this brig. And I appreciate you giving up the stern cabin for the princess."

"Of course. She is a princess." Hariri continued in a voice barely audible over the wind. "I know it disturbs you to deal with such people as I. A pirate. And the crew members are hardly Imperial Air Academy." He glanced at the red flag snapping over his head. It was the banner of the South Arabian Company, quite illegal since *Edinburgh* was not a vessel of that grand old trading firm.

Anhalt stared hard at the captain. "You are the finest airman I've ever seen, Aswan. I would put Her Highness's safety in no one else's hands."

"Thank you, Colonel. We will serve you"—Hariri touched his heart, lips, and head—"until the end."

Anhalt clapped a grateful hand on the captain's shoulder. "I can certainly use you during this trying time."

"I should tell you that I heard in Djibouti that all manner of men and ships are about, searching for your princess. The Equatorians put out the call, and every vessel flying is traveling under letters of marque hoping to lay hands on her and make their fortune from the court."

"I have no doubt you can avoid them all."

Hariri chuckled. "But of course. Now, may I ask you a question?"

"Certainly."

"Tell me about this Greyfriar fellow. What do you make of him? He's the talk of the ship. We've heard the stories, but you've seen him in action, yes?"

Anhalt shook his head. "I've seen little enough action from him, aside from *rescuing* Princess Adele from her otherwise orderly wedding. He's an enigma to me. I too have heard amazing stories, primarily from Princess Adele. From all accounts, he's quite the wonder worker." Anhalt left unsaid that although he would never believe Adele was the type to succumb to the mythmaking that surrounded the swordsman, some of her tales of adventures in France and Britain belied reason. He needed more evidence that this mystery man deserved such adoration. Anhalt couldn't stop the hateful ache in his chest created by the dread that he was watching the world's greatest empire dragged down by a romantic fake.

"You should get some rest, Colonel," came a soft voice.

Anhalt turned with a start to see Princess Adele standing close, buffeted by the wind, with Greyfriar as her ever-present reflection. The colonel looked at the deck, embarrassed by his thoughts.

Captain Hariri took Anhalt's empty coffee cup and retreated.

"I will, Highness" the colonel replied sheepishly to Adele. "I was taking one last turn about deck. Double-checking supplies."

"Is Katanga within our safe reach?" She pulled her cloak tight to ward off the cold.

"I believe so. In another three or four days we should reach Bunia, Msiri's northern capital. As long as the winds hold and the weather doesn't turn too dear, and the ship stays together, we should have food and water for the trip."

The activity around them abruptly heightened. Men clambered into the tops. Adele wondered if it was just a change of morning watch, but somehow this felt different. The intensity was very high. Storm clouds rumbled beneath them, though she had thought they were out of the thunderheads' reach. She and Colonel Anhalt both turned to the quarterdeck, where Captain Hariri now stood at the rail with a spyglass to his eye.

Anhalt pulled out his own glass as Adele tapped Greyfriar, who was already scanning the sky with his preternatural vision. He saw two ships in the distance with gunports along the hulls to demonstrate they weren't merchant vessels. Their sails were full.

"They're flying Equatorian flags," Anhalt announced. "A forty-eight and a twenty-four. Hmm. The frigate isn't Imperial Navy. She's a privateer."

"Have they seen us?" Adele asked.

Before he could answer, Captain Hariri leaned over the rail from the quarterdeck with a stern visage. "They have and are in hot pursuit."

"How could they know I'm on board?"

"Likely they don't, but I imagine their orders are to intercept any ship that appears suspicious, at the captain's discretion. We are not on a common flight path, and we are a brig of war flying a merchant flag. So we are, therefore, suspicious."

"Can we outrun them, Captain?

"Let us hope so, Your Highness. We are crowding on all sail she will bear."

White canvas soon cracked from every yardarm. The minutes of frantic activity passed slowly. Adele moved to pace the quarterdeck, watching the imperial pursuers astern, trying to pretend they weren't growing larger in the sky. But they were. After an hour of the chase, it was clear they were gaining on *Edinburgh*.

There was a distant boom, and Adele saw smoke belch from the bow of the Equatorian cruiser.

"Are they firing on us?" she asked in alarm.

"A warning shot," Hariri responded. "They are politely requesting us to heave to. Soon they will shoot for our yards—our sails—if they have the gunners for it."

"What are our chances in a fight?"

"Slim. We are outgunned by a great margin. And I note the cruiser is armed with the newest azimuth guns, one-hundred-ten pounders with perfect balance. They can sweep the skies high and low. Lovely things."

"And our guns?"

Hariri smirked. "We'll count ourselves lucky if they don't explode when we fire them."

Colonel Anhalt said, "Highness, the danger is that those ships will fire on us, not knowing you are on board. You are in grave peril."

"What would you have me do, Colonel? Surrender myself?"

"It would be safer. It will prevent you being injured, or worse."

Captain Hariri nodded in agreement.

"And what of you, Colonel? Or Captain Hariri? Or Greyfriar? If I allow *Edinburgh* to fall under our pursuers' guns so that I may surrender myself, I will have no control over what becomes of everyone else. You said yourself that you are a deserter, as are your men, so you would fall under a court-martial. And let's face it, Captain Hariri would be viewed as a pirate. And Greyfriar kidnapped the imperial heir. Do you think I could convince my father or Senator Clark to go easy on him?" *To say nothing of the fact that he is a vampire*, Adele thought. "No, gentlemen, as far as I'm concerned, none of us is welcome in Equatoria. We shall live or die together."

The pirate captain was about to speak when the sound of another distant *whoomp* froze the quarterdeck in anticipation. After several seconds, a topsail on the port side ripped and several yardarms cracked into splinters.

Hariri slapped his forehead in amazement. "Nice shot! Bad for us." He turned to Adele. "We're coming into effective range. We can't stand under their guns. But I have an idea."

She raised an eyebrow. "I won't like it, I'm sure. But do it."

Hariri laughed. "Very well. You might wish to hold onto something sturdy."

Adele seized the rail, while Greyfriar locked one arm around her and clasped a sturdy cable. As orders were shouted around the ship, the captain signaled to the binnacle. The air filled with the terrible roar of chemicals venting from the dirigible. The deck of *Edinburgh* dropped from beneath their feet. Adele felt air between her soles and the wood for a few seconds, but Greyfriar held her tight with steel-corded muscle. The ship plummeted as if the cables connecting the hull to the zeppelin had been cut. The wind tore through the sails, canvas ripping and yards bending with pressure.

They were crashing! Adele panicked. Anxious memories of plummeting to the earth on *Ptolemy* crowded her thoughts.

Suddenly they were surrounded by whiteness. Mist. Clouds. The air was wet, and the sky around them crackled with bursts of phosphor. A jagged trail of light struck a mast and traveled to the hull of the ship. Above their heads, the metal cage enclosing the dirigible sparkled with fairy fire.

Over the bellowing wind, Adele heard Greyfriar laughing. His cloak swirled about both of them and he stared upward. He seemed perfectly at home in the chaos. His utter lack of fear was both disturbing and calming.

Then *Edinburgh* dropped below the clouds. Rain and marbles of ice pelted the ship. Greyfriar pulled Adele back against him and wrapped his fluttering cape about her. Lightning slashed above them. The air below was grayish green and had a strange rolling texture. Then Adele realized she was looking at the tops of trees. A vast carpet of forest, unbroken for miles around.

Over the drumming rain and wind came the roar of buoyant pumps refilling the dirigible. But the ship still dropped. The rain seemed to push it down toward the featureless green. Sails flapped loose, torn and tattered. Men shouted. Adele pulled up wildly on the rail as if that would help keep the ship aloft.

Edinburgh shuddered with a great scraping and rustling, and many crewmen were knocked off their feet. It was only Greyfriar's strong embrace that prevented Adele from falling, but still they knocked into the rail and back again. Incredibly, lush green foliage reared up above the rail. She gasped. It was as if the trees had seized the ship and were dragging it down to consume it. They waited for the sound of the hull being crushed by the remorseless forest.

Then the treetops fell back, snapping branches and dropping a carpet of leaves across the deck. The ship rose awkwardly back into the driving rain. They were flying free again.

"Are you hurt?" Greyfriar asked, finally releasing his steadfast hold.

Adele exhaled. "I'm fine now, but . . . two airship crashes in one year is enough to last me."

Captain Hariri called out to his crew, sending them to inspect the damage. Men climbed along the yards, trying to manhandle rebellious sails in the tropical deluge. Others dove below to check the hull for breaches.

The captain crossed to Adele, accepting a passing backslap from Anhalt with a grin. "Now, that was an evasive maneuver."

"Well done, Captain—" Adele suddenly froze midword as a bulk dropped into sight less than a mile astern. It was the privateer.

Hariri turned because of the princess's widening eyes. "No! That's impossible!"

And a mile farther back, an even larger shaped lowered into view, trailing clouds. The Equatorian cruiser. But its massive dirigible was a ball of green fire, a victim of the storm. It appeared as a bright glow in the slate rain before the fire was swallowed up by the forest, and the great ship was gone.

"My God," Adele breathed. "All those men."

Hariri was already at the binnacle shouting orders over the thunder. *Edinburgh* lurched forward, crippled and foundering. The battered privateer frigate swung its bow to bring its flank to bear.

Greyfriar grabbed Adele again and bore her to the deck before the distant broadside roared. Rails splintered, sails ripped, and masts shattered. The dirigible cage bent and cracked. Men screamed, torn by heavy shrapnel. The little brig's guns returned fire, sending smoke rising up and over the deck.

Hariri leapt to the ship's waist and shouted back to Colonel Anhalt, "I'm serving out weapons. We've no chance of escape. Prepare your men for hand-to-hand combat!"

"Go below, Your Highness," Anhalt commanded Adele, and then he yelled to his men to fix bayonets.

Greyfriar grabbed Adele's arm and pulled her to the companionway. She fought back against his iron hand as he dragged her below.

"What are you doing?" she cried angrily. "I'm going to repel boarders with my men!"

Greyfriar thrust the princess inside her stern cabin and shut the door behind them. He ripped the scarf from his face, and unbuckled his gun belt and swords. "There won't be any boarders to repel, if I can help it."

"What are you thinking? You're *not* thinking. You can't go out unmasked. What if you're seen?"

He flung his cloak away and unbuttoned his tunic, revealing a plain white shirt. Then he pulled off his gloves and flexed the claws from his fingertips. He went to the stern gallery as another wave of shells crashed into the ship, shaking the deck, sending dust and debris over their heads. He threw open the large window and turned back to a stunned Adele with cold blue eyes. Wind and rain poured over him.

"They won't have you today. I'll be back when their ship is crippled or there isn't a man left alive who will harm you." He leapt into the storm, leaving Adele holding his hooded cloak.

—⁓—

Gareth dropped away from the stern. No one should be able see a single figure in the sky washed near black with rain. The wind was strong, almost too strong. He rode the updrafts toward the privateer airship, which vomited another wave of red cannon fire. *Edinburgh* shuddered. More masts snapped, and the dirigible cage shattered. The privateer turned its bow to close on the crippled brig.

In the strong wind, it was complicated for Gareth to reach the frigate. The sensation from the air that helped him navigate was almost overwhelming in his head. He didn't feel the wind so much as smell and taste it, sensing his way through the updrafts and avoiding the deadly wind shear. He could sense his location in relation to the ground far below and used that to focus his approach to the privateer.

The frigate had three masts extending from both sides of the dirigible. Gareth swept past the starboard side and caught hold of a topsail with his claws. He began to shred the canvas, letting the wind find the tears and rip them further; then he tore lines loose and sent sails flapping wildly.

Topmen moved unwillingly into the rain-soaked yards to attempt to repair the damage. They hadn't seen the lone figure slipping from one mast to the next. The privateer lost headway and slipped to starboard as damaged sails lost their bite.

Gareth vaulted from the foremast to the dirigible cage. He quickly crawled over the vast egg-shaped metal mesh to where he could spy the port side masts. Men were already aloft, trying to furl sails to balance the ship and let it gain way again.

Gareth launched himself at the masts again, shredding and tearing. He appeared only as a blur in the eyes of the privateersmen, who could barely credit what they thought they saw: a man slipping across the yards like a shadow in the lightning.

With damage done, he fell from the masts and angled for the ship's hull. He landed hard on the wooden side and clung there for a second. To his left, above him, he saw cannon muzzles waiting. He crawled sternward and up toward the quarterdeck.

Gareth rose to the rail and saw several men gathered around the binnacle. He had watched actions on *Edinburgh* enough to know that it was the standard airship control post. The brass pneumatic tubes and speaking tubes all ended there for communications to the tops and chemical deck. Airships had no wheel, as a rudder served no purpose. Navigation was a delicate feat of management, like a conductor with an orchestra spread in different parts of a vast concert hall.

He crawled over the rail slowly, marking his targets—four men at the binnacle who were shouting and gesturing to the tops. Another stood forward with a spyglass trained on *Edinburgh*, which was slowly gaining distance on the privateer.

Gareth struck. One man turned in time to look surprised before he died. Blood sprayed the brass pneumo tubes. The three others only had time to grunt in shock before claws raked them, opening their throats, flaying cheekbones clean of flesh. They smashed against hard metal, dropping to the deck. The man with the spyglass whirled and died too.

The sound of struggle brought several men up the portside ladder to the edge of the quarterdeck. They saw a tall, pale figure kneeling with a blood-smeared face over their captain. He looked up with fierce blue eyes and came for them. Some fled, blocking others who wanted to fight. Men raced up the starboard companionway to the quarterdeck. They brandished cutlasses, axes, and pistols.

Gareth rushed the mob. Bullets flew as he clawed guns from hands. Blades sliced the air. He blocked a cutlass deep in his forearm and had to smile at the shocked face of the sword's wielder. Vampires were not something these men fought often. He took an axe by the handle and threw it away.

The crewmen seemed to move in slow motion. Gareth could sense their every action and block or dodge or strike to stop them. The captain's blood warmed him. He felt strong and fit. He took no great pleasure in hurting or killing these men, but he knew every one he stopped, and every minute he kept this ship foundering, gave Adele a better chance to escape. The privateer had attacked *Edinburgh*; Gareth felt no compunction to spare them.

The ship rolled, and men sprawled with shouts of alarm. Gareth merely lightened and rose into the air. The deck tilted as the storm seized the ship and twisted it. With no orders coming, the topmen had no way to coordinate the sail load. The wind was spinning the directionless ship, threatening to flip it over. Men slid along the deck and tumbled over the side. Some toppled from the yards, falling into the endless air. The crack of masts could be heard even over the wind and screams of panicked men.

Gareth saw *Edinburgh* vanishing into the storm. The privateer would take hours to recover, if she ever did. He drifted away from the lost ship and followed Adele's vessel.

With time, Gareth crawled into the stern window of Adele's cabin. He found her sitting and waiting, her hands wringing his cloak.

She stood up abruptly, her eyes taking in the blood. "Are you injured?" She moved toward him, covering his drenched form with the cloak.

He held up his arm with the bloody gash, inspecting it curiously. "Not really."

"Running off like that with no help, you could've been killed." But her fingers gingerly brushed his wounded arm.

"If I hadn't gone, you could have been killed. I had no choice. There was little danger."

Adele shook her head in admiration, despite the desperate worry. He wasn't boasting. It was simply a fact. He was trained to be in the thick of battle. Clearly, he didn't believe he could be defeated. It was frustrating for her, but he was so sincere and without artifice that she couldn't be angry.

There was a knock at the door. Gareth drew up his hood before moving into a dark corner. Adele called out to enter.

Colonel Anhalt leaned in, noting the open stern window and the shadowy Greyfriar with brief curiosity. "Highness, the weather is breaking and there is no sign of the privateer. Luck was with us today."

Adele smiled. "Yes, it certainly was. Thank you, Colonel."

"That lake below us is Luta Nzige." Anhalt pointed over the rail at a vast silvery sheet set amid a landscape of vibrant greens and reds. The air was wet, and the high clouds that surrounded the limping *Edinburgh* were again turning grey and sparking with lightning. "Some of our charts call it Lake Albert. And south of the lake are the Rwenzoris, the Mountains of the Moon."

Adele turned her brass spyglass forward, but any sight of the fabled mountains was hidden in white mist.

"The highest peaks of the Rwenzoris are rarely visible," the Gurkha colonel said. "They are almost always shrouded in clouds and ash plumes. This is a highly volcanic region. It is a mysterious place. In fact, it is said that a secret vampire kingdom is set high in those mountains."

Greyfriar regarded the man. "A kingdom?"

"So they say. I've heard it from Katangan officers, and they believe it to be so. Not just scattered creatures, but a clan. They slink down when the weather allows, to steal babies to raise as food."

The swordsman joined Adele to study the shrouded mountains.

"Is that true?" She intended the question for Greyfriar, who merely shrugged.

Anhalt replied with a smile. "I don't know, Your Highness. It's just what they say. But I do know that the snow on top of the mountains is the origins of the Nile. That is a proven fact."

"Amazing," Adele breathed. "So far away."

Captain Hariri whistled sharply from the quarterdeck. "Your Highness, the tops report a Katangan forty-eight closing."

"Very well, Captain. When possible, signal to the Katangans that we wish to close and speak."

Within twenty minutes, Greyfriar joined Adele at the rail to watch the forty-eight-gun *Ituri* draw alongside, and said, "They may try to sequester you away from us—from me. Don't let them. It is in their interest to control this situation. Despite what you need from them, they also need something from you. That will make them stay their hand. But you are in charge. Never forget that."

His words filled her with confidence. Even with only a single company at her side, she felt as if she commanded an army.

Due to the span of the airships' horizontal masts, the two ships had to stand off over 150 feet. Since it was far too windy to speak with megaphones, *Edinburgh* fired a line with a telegraph cable. The telegrapher waited at the binnacle, finger poised on the key, with Adele, Anhalt, and Captain Hariri at his shoulder. Greyfriar stood at a distance.

Adele dictated, "Lieutenant, if you would, identify us as an Equatorian ship. Tell them that we carry Princess Adele, who wishes an audience with King Msiri." As the telegrapher tapped the key, Adele smiled. "This should be interesting. Surely they're aware that I'm on the run and looking for a place to land."

Distant figures on *Ituri* began to scurry about, followed by telltale flashes from spyglasses on their deck. Adele stepped to the side so she could be seen. She even waved, prompting a laugh from Colonel Anhalt.

The reply ticked in and the young telegrapher said, "It's in Swahili. Shall I read it for you?"

"My Swahili is adequate, thank you." Adele took the sheet of paper. When she could make out the telegrapher's scribblings, she said, "Ah. They want me to come aboard."

Adele glanced at Greyfriar, who nodded knowingly. She wrote a reply and handed it to the telegrapher. "Lieutenant, tell *Ituri*, with respect, that I shall not come aboard. We are pleased to follow them to port, where they may contact their government."

Tapping followed. And another long silence.

Adele waited patiently. Anhalt watched her step to Greyfriar's side, and the two chatted as tendrils of cloud slipped past them along the deck. They were quite natural together, with a complete ease and rapport born of many adventures. Adele had taken firm control of this expedition with natural authority. Despite the Greyfriar's reputation as a man of action, he had ceded command to her with unconcern. There was no traditional masculine jealousy or resistance to a woman giving orders—such as in Senator Clark. Anhalt was impressed by the man's respect and trust in the princess.

Finally the Katangan response came in a short series of ticks. Adele came forward and studied the telegrapher's notations.

"Captain Hariri, please make ready to follow *Ituri*. We are bound for Bunia and an audience with King Msiri."

CHAPTER

I T HAD BEEN nearly twenty minutes without screams in the halls of the Commons, so Lord Kelvin removed the brace from the door and peered out of the cloak room. The tiled corridor was littered with dead and wounded. He recognized several members. Rahim Sonheim, member for Aqaba; Sir Induri Randoor, member for Delhi; and Chief Yenzi Kyerere, member for Tabora. All former colleagues, but now just figures in a vast, tragic tableau.

Lord Kelvin retreated to his nearby office and locked the door so his very important business wouldn't be disturbed. He noted with anger the broken windows and wrecked files. Within minutes, he sent several messages to the palace via the pneumatic tubes and then did his best to organize his world. The clock ticked loudly as he waited for the sound of pneumo tubes dropping into his inbox, but there were no responses. Instead, Kelvin heard noise from the halls as recovery began and the wounded were tended. There were several knocks at his door and his name was called. He didn't answer; he was too busy. His only concern was the situation at the palace.

It had been regrettable but necessary to use Flay and her creatures. They were useful weapons, powerful and sure. Best of all, ultimately they would retreat from Alexandria due to the summer heat. There was no fear of their constant interference. Kelvin could use and dispose of them. Perfect allies.

It rankled the prime minister that the vampire warrior had upbraided him for carelessness, as if he had failed in something. It was Kelvin who had arranged for Princess Adele to make her ill-fated tour of the frontier in the early spring. And it was Kelvin who had alerted Prince Cesare to the fact, so that Adele could be seized and disappear forever in vampire territory, writing finis to the Equatorian-American alliance and, hopefully, the entire War of Reconquest in the north. And it was Cesare who failed; it was the vampire prince who had allowed Adele to survive and then to escape. It was Cesare whose fumblings had brought about the necessity for these desperate measures by Kelvin. The nerve of that creature Flay to imply that Kelvin was less than completely in control of the situation.

Finally, Lord Kelvin unlocked the door, summoned several armed guards, and started for the palace. The city was in unbelievable chaos. Police whistles sounded from nearly every corner. People had begun to emerge from hiding. Many raced for home to check on family. Most knelt beside the injured trying to help, or beside the dead trying to identify loved ones. A few airships rose in the night sky as the Imperial Navy hastily launched patrols. The sight of the military gave some comfort to the distraught people.

The prime minister bemoaned the lack of available carriages as he and his bodyguards made their way north on foot. After a harrowing half hour, they reached the main gate of Victoria Palace to find it open and a group of Home Guard gathered out front. They saluted.

"Who's in command at the palace?" Kelvin asked.

One of the guardsmen shook his head, his eyes wide with shock. "Senator Clark, I think. Isn't he?"

"No," Kelvin retorted crisply. "Who is the ranking Equatorian officer on the grounds?"

"No idea who's still alive, sir. I saw Captain Eskandari and his marines."

"Good. I want you to find the captain and send him to the Privy Council chamber. Do you understand? You, personally. Find him."

"Yes sir. Is the emperor alive, sir?"

"I'm sure he is. Go about your duty." As the soldier padded off, the prime minister turned to another soldier. "Find Lord Aden, if you please." He wrote an address on a slip of paper. "Tell him that Lord Kelvin requests his presence at the palace with all due haste."

Kelvin then proceeded into the royal residence and nearly winced at the sight of blood shining wet on the mosaic floor. Still, he maintained his professional demeanor. A soldier loped down the main staircase, dragging his rifle, his tunic unbuttoned and his undershirt stained red. Kelvin noticed the man's appearance with instant alarm and raised a disapproving eyebrow.

"Prime Minister!" the soldier shouted at his better like a common street vendor. "Everybody is looking for you. Emperor Constantine's been murdered and the General Staff is dead. They're laying up there like slaughtered beef." The soldier appeared overcome by emotion. His mouth clamped shut, and his throat clenched trying to subdue sobs. He lowered his head. "We're lost."

"Do lower your voice. Difficulty is no excuse for vulgar behavior. And button your shirt. You are on duty."

The soldier began to tidy his uniform. "Yes, sir. Sorry, sir."

"I can assure you that we are not lost." Kelvin held up his hand when the soldier started to argue. "We aren't some nomadic tribe. We are a modern state with laws and proprieties." He paused to gather himself from what he felt had been a tirade, even though he had not raised his voice. "What of Prince Simon?"

The soldier nodded with excitement. "He's well, sir. Alive and well, thank God."

"Mind yourself, Private. You would do well to recall where you are and do not spread rumors to anyone that the emperor is dead." Kelvin mounted the main stairs and made for the east wing, where the emperor's business was conducted.

The Privy Council chamber was wrecked, but empty. Kelvin placed his bodyguards in the hall while he picked up overturned chairs and returned them to their proper places around the large center table. He gathered papers from the agenda he had prepared earlier for the emperor's meeting with the General Staff. Absently, Kelvin began to put pages in order, even though sheets were spattered with blood.

Something caught Kelvin's eye. Against the far wall there was a long table typically used by clerks to sort materials for council meetings. But now there was an Equatorian flag draped over the table. Under the flag was a bulky object, and the flag was stained with blood.

The prime minister stepped to the table and lifted the corner of the heavy flag to uncover the face of Constantine II. Lord Kelvin felt his pulse jump as he stared at his sovereign's waxy skin, sunken cheeks, and lifeless mouth. The emperor had been a good man, and it was unfortunate events had to develop as they did. Kelvin was comforted by the thought that it was likely proper for the emperor to be lying near where he died because the appropriate authorities were not available to declare him officially dead. Only then could he be moved. Once the emperor was made official-ly dead, events would have to move quickly to preserve the state. Kelvin wasn't ready to begin that process yet. Not all the pieces were in place.

Political and military personalities whom Kelvin did not trust had to be located should action become necessary. Some would be deprived of their posts for the good of the Empire, and other quarrelsome politi-cians and soldiers needed to be carefully monitored. This included Colonel Anhalt, the commander of Princess Adele's White Guard, a man whose loyalty was to the princess, not to Equatoria. However, the man had left Alexandria a few days before to pursue one of the many Adele sightings. It was believed he had gone to Damascus, but that could not be confirmed. Kelvin would have to make sure to intercept Anhalt upon his return, with or without the princess in tow.

The shuffle of boots alerted the prime minister to the arrival of Cap-tain Eskandari. The Persian officer swept his cap from his head and locked his eyes on the cadaver. Kelvin hastily lowered the flag over Con-stantine's face because it was improper for a low-ranking officer to view the body of the sovereign before it was lying in state.

"Ah, Captain, thank you for coming."

"Yes, Your Lordship. I have dire reports from around the city."

"In due time, Captain. For now, I have two tasks of great importance and delicacy for you."

Eskandari scowled, but remained still. "Yes, Your Lordship."

"I want you to find Her Highness's former tutor, Mamoru, and place him under arrest."

"On what charge, my lord?"

Kelvin took a sheet of paper and scribbled briefly before handing it to the captain. "This should do for now. He is a dangerous fanatic. Do not allow him to escape."

"Yes, sir. And the other task?"

"Where are Senator Clark and his Rangers?"

"I'm not sure of the senator's exact location. I believe he's in the palace somewhere. His men are in the city assisting with the recovery."

"I need you to round up the Americans and confine them to barracks. Nothing overly dramatic, you see. Just keep them sequestered."

"Begging your pardon, sir, but we could use every man available to—"

"And locate the senator and bring him here."

"I'm confused, sir. Are you authorizing me to arrest the Americans too?"

"No, no. Not at all. They are guests and we are concerned for their welfare. It would hardly do for them to be injured while in our care."

"And if they refuse?"

"Well, then I am authorizing you to arrest them." Kelvin reached out and touched a corner of the shroud flag. "This is an important time in our nation's history. The homeland must be protected from foreign threats. We need our sons to stand up and defend us. And also, you are not to say anything that would imply wrongly that the emperor is dead. Equatoria expects that you will do your duty, Captain."

The Persian marine hesitated briefly, then saluted and withdrew.

⌘

It took several hours for Lord Kelvin to get a basic government up and running. He collected clerks and began to dictate dispatches and promulgations. The city's pneumatic system slowly but incompletely came back to life. The telegraph lines had been destroyed by the vampires, cutting off Alexandria from the rest of the Empire. Communication would be restored at some point, and Kelvin could then begin putting affairs in order on a wide scale.

"Dammit, Prime Minister!" came a thundering shout from the door. "Why are you just sitting here?"

Lord Kelvin glanced up from where he was making notations in the margin of a dispatch as Senator Clark burst into the Privy Council chamber with a squad of Persian marines following at a respectful distance. The American leaned heavily on the table and sent the carefully piled paperwork airborne. Kelvin risked a reproachful glance, then began to gather up the government's business again.

"We need to talk," Clark announced loudly. "This place is tearing apart at the seams. It's time for action. We need to get the government back on its feet."

"Precisely what I am doing, Senator. Just not with as much flair and weaponry as some." Kelvin tapped a sheaf of papers into place. He indicated yellow sheets tacked to a wall, where an army of clerks swarmed like bees around a blossoming fruit tree. The emotionless young men pulled notes, cleared their actions, and returned to pull others as quickly as possible. "The government is functioning—slowly, I grant you—but functioning nonetheless."

"There's no time for slow. I've been out on the streets. Your people are shell-shocked. They're afraid of more attacks. They thought they were safe and now they're not. This is a harbinger of a larger offensive! This is war!" Clark grabbed one of the yellow dispatch sheets and crumpled it. "You can't save your nation with memoranda."

"To the contrary." Kelvin plucked the sheet back and smoothed it out. "The Empire is not under general assault. This was not an offensive. It was an attempted assassination."

"Attempted? I'd say it worked! Lucky they didn't get me too."

"Yes," Kelvin countered dryly. "Lucky."

"We have to do something right now. Half the people out there are in tears and the other half are furious. They could storm the palace because you didn't protect them. Vampires came right out of the damned ground! We need to make sure they're all rooted out!"

"I have already addressed that point. The catacombs beneath the city are being searched and sealed. That should leave us well protected." Kelvin exhaled slowly. "Some emotional distress is to be expected, but it is rather irresponsible to predict violent insurrection. And as to your traveling the streets, I would prefer you stop that. I would hate for you to be injured. It would put us in a difficult position with your president and your senate. You are not an Equatorian official."

"What do you mean I'm not an Equatorian official? I'm the next emperor." The American pursed his lips behind his black beard and gave Lord Kelvin a suspicious squint. Then he jerked his chin at the body of Constantine across the room. "Maybe you've had a bit of a shock yourself. He's not sleeping; he's dead."

The prime minister remained stoic and refused to acknowledge Clark's disrespectful comments about the emperor. "At best, you were in line to be prince regent. That aside, the emperor has a unique legal status that transcends the mortal man who holds that position. That status cannot be diminished until certain procedures have been undertaken. In short, despite what may lie under that flag, Emperor Constantine the Second is indeed still alive."

"Are you insane? Look, you've got a city about to explode and you're sitting here scribbling. You need a man who can hold this town together. You need me! Now, when do we stage my coronation?"

"There will be a coronation." Kelvin paused to inspect a memo thrust in front of his face by a clerk blandly unaware of the crackling situation over the table. He made a few notes in silence and handed the paper back. "Where was I? Oh yes, there will be a coronation at some point in the future, although it may take a while because some of the imperial regalia appear to be missing. Perhaps the vampires took it. Such scavengers. Most inconvenient. But the object of that coronation will be His Imperial Highness, Prince Simon. He will be named Emperor Presumptive."

"Simon?" Clark was red-faced and aghast. "That boy!"

"He is young, I grant you. However, I will be named regent. And I believe we can convince Lord Aden to assume the role of prime minister. That will invest Prince Simon's government with a comforting continuity and solidity."

"Simon is second in line! I'm married to the heir!"

"Yes? Perhaps you've noticed the heir isn't about. She has fled the Empire, and even as we speak, Commons is in the process of officially removing her from succession." Kelvin took a moment to consult his pocket watch. "It took some effort to gather a quorum, a breathing quorum anyway. The vote may well have taken place, but communications being what they are, it's difficult to know. But I assure you, the outcome is not in doubt."

"No, sir. I won't have it, you insane bastard." Clark drew closer and the Persian marines inched forward. "Constantine is dead and gone. Princess Adele is the heir to the throne. And I am her husband. Perhaps you recall? You were at the ceremony. You pronounced us man and wife."

"I did indeed. But even my pronouncement isn't sufficient. You see, for a marriage to be legal, the banns must be signed and notarized by the proper authorities. Since the princess, let us say, departed the altar prior to signing the paperwork, your union never occurred. In the eyes of the law, you are not the husband of Princess Adele."

"You miserable mule!" Clark slammed his fist on the table. "Do you think I'm going to stand here and let you pull my throne out from under me? Do you imagine in your wildest dream I'll let some glorified librarian stand in my way?"

"My dear Senator Clark, you have nowhere to stand. You have no voice in our government."

"We're at war and only one thing counts in war! Let's see if your papers can stop a bullet." Clark's hand flashed to the flap of his holster.

Captain Eskandari lunged for him, and his firm hand gripped Clark's wrist as the pistol cleared. The Persian commander's service revolver pressed into the senator's midsection.

Out of the corner of his eye, Clark saw the marines with their rifle muzzles less than a foot away from him. The American's brow knit in confusion. "What in the hell are you doing, Captain?"

Eskandari said, "Your weapon, if you please, sir."

"I don't believe I heard right."

"Surrender your weapon, Senator. Now."

"You cannot possibly be supporting this pathetic worm. You're a soldier." Then Clark locked eyes with the Persian and read the man's earnest gaze. He let the pistol drop noisily to the table.

Eskandari gave a polite nod, released his grip on the senator, and picked up the gun as he stepped back. "Thank you, sir."

Clark smoothed his tunic and tugged his sleeves. He regarded the Persian with his best man-to-man stare. His voice was slow, measured, and reasonable. "Captain, there are times in history when mighty forces turn on the actions of a single man. Today, my friend, you are that man. The future of your empire is being decided here in this room, now in this moment. Look at us, Captain. Who do you trust to guide the future of your nation, to lead your armies into war, and to ensure the safety of your children? Me? Or that man sitting there?"

Lord Kelvin didn't allow for any dramatic, thoughtful pauses. "Captain Eskandari, please escort the senator to his quarters."

The marine immediately extended his hand toward the door, inviting Clark to go ahead of him.

The American displayed a lopsided grin. "Okay. If that's your decision, so be it. But I'll warn you, son, once I know where a man stands, I never forget it." He turned to Kelvin. "So let's get this straight. I'm your prisoner?"

"Oh, by no means. You are a guest."

"So I can come and go as I please?"

"Oh, by no means. You have the freedom of the palace, as long as you have an escort to ensure your safety . . . in case we experience violent insurrection."

Clark barked a cynical guffaw. "You know the worst thing about you, Prime Minister? I can't tell if you're joking or if you're dead serious."

"I'm afraid I haven't time for making jokes, Senator."

"That's what I figured. All right, Captain, let's go." The American spun on his heel and strode from the room so quickly his Persian guards had to sprint to keep up.

Eskandari gave Lord Kelvin a curt bow, then came to attention and saluted the flag-draped corpse of the emperor before he followed his men and his guest.

CHAPTER 23

Bunia, the northern capital of Katanga, was a booming metropolis set among retreating forests. Only a decade ago, it had been a small town with a few stone buildings and great swathes of brick and thatch structures. Now the city core was indistinguishable from any great city of Africa. The center hosted a fine palace structure with grounds and parks with numerous surrounding buildings, many still under construction. Multiple shining copper domes added to the grandeur of the city.

The once fractious and rebellious region now ranked as the most important in Katanga. The vast copper deposits of the Zambesi homeland were still important, but the Great Lakes were a treasure trove of gold and other ores, and provided access to the magnificent Congo River Basin with its rain forests full of lucrative timber. But even more important was the raw power of the region. The Virunga Mountain Range that ran the length of the Great Lakes district was one of the most active volcanic regions on earth, and the technicians of Katanga were masters at harnessing the limitless geothermal power beneath their feet—the Forges of Virunga. Thousands of factories and foundries were folded into the jagged mountains from Luta Nzige to Lake Nyasa. Tapping into the fiery power source, the workhouses ran nonstop with countless lines of workers filing in and out. Cast iron. Steel. Airship yards. Steam locomotives. Finely machined tools. Textiles. In any drawing room or factory or dockyard across Equatoria or Africa, or the civilized world for that matter, a goodly percentage of the objects owed some part of their existence to the Forges of Virunga. So cheap was the power source that it was more economical to ship in raw materials, and ship out finished products. This fact made King Msiri and his monopolistic Guild of Smiths very rich and powerful men.

Princess Adele stood on a balcony overlooking a garden of colorful flowers and palm trees. The spacious guest quarters were adjacent to the royal palace, or boma. The ceilings were high and the windows wide. Breezes cooled somewhat, though the air had grown ever more damp. A storm was coming with the purple clouds that reflected the rising sun.

An elderly woman approached with a tray of fruit, bread, and tea. She was short and round with a colorful dress and head wrap. She smiled at Adele. "Would you care to eat, Your Highness? You must be hungry."

"No, thank you."

"The king could be hours more. He is notoriously slow."

Adele smiled. "Thank you, but I'm not hungry."

"Here." The woman set the tray on a low table. "For when you are hungry. Shall I brush your hair?" The old woman was so kind and unthreatening that Adele didn't react when she touched her hair. "It will make you feel better."

"I believe I'll wait." Adele actually found the fingers of the woman comforting. She didn't resist as hands slid through the tangles and touched her scalp. She had always enjoyed traveling in Africa because of the people's unpretentious warmth. Then the woman drew strong fingers down her neck and along Adele's shoulders.

"You are exhausted. You need a massage. I can summon someone for you."

Adele closed her eyes briefly at the soothing touch and, against her will, said, "No. I will wait."

The woman then took Adele's hands and stared at her while slowly kneading her knuckles. There was something so relaxing in the old woman's strength. Adele felt the tension leave her as she momentarily forgot her many obligations.

The woman said, "You have come far to reach us."

"I have."

"You have far to go yet."

Adele exhaled sadly. "I do, I'm afraid."

The woman kissed one of Adele's hands. "Bless you, my child. It is hard for you, I know."

The princess looked curiously into the dark eyes of the old woman whose soft gaze was warm and reassuring.

A sharp sound from the hallway knocked her back to the present. The old woman released Adele and gave the princess a quick reassuring squeeze on the shoulder.

"If you need anything, daughter," she said, "I'll get it for you."

Before Adele could reply, the old woman trundled through a side door and disappeared. Greyfriar entered and crossed to the balcony. He lifted a hand to mop his brow, but quickly dropped it.

"How are you?" Adele asked suspiciously.

"Perfectly well." He tapped the helmet. "In fact, I'm fearful of catching a chill."

"Shut up," she retorted softly. "Do you need to feed?"

"No. With no activity, I require no sustenance. However, you should eat. And sleep."

Adele leaned against the stone balustrade. Seconds later, she began pacing, tapping her thigh with her fingers.

Greyfriar crossed his arms calmly. "Impatient?"

"I want to get things settled and make contact with Alexandria. I wish King Msiri would just speak with me."

"He is a king. And this is his country." He laughed. "I'd have thought you would be better at being a prisoner."

"It's boring." She folded her arms across her chest in mock exasperation. "So what else can we do while we wait, besides stare at trees? And wait for rain."

"We focus on what we can do. We can plan. Prepare contingencies. If Msiri grants us asylum, what next?"

Adele tapped her bottom lip, contemplating. "I'll need to arrange a meeting with my father. Without Senator Clark around. What do you think? You're a prince. I need your perspective." She wrapped her arms around him languidly. Immediately his arms encircled her.

"I'm rather a bad prince. You need Cesare's perspective. He's quite proficient at manipulative politics."

"Well, using Cesare's methods would be a bad idea. Slaughtering Senator Clark is not an option."

There was a long silence. Adele pushed away and looked up at Greyfriar's covered face.

He glanced down. "What? Oh, I agree. We shouldn't slaughter him." He tilted his head as if in thought, then said, "No. No. You're right."

She patted his chest with a sarcastic grin. "You're wicked. I love that." Then her expression became contemplative. "Time is slipping away. It's already summer."

"Will the war begin without your wedding?"

"I don't know." Adele turned back to gaze wistfully at the lush gardens. "And if it didn't begin, would that be a bad thing?"

"Not to me." Then Greyfriar asked, "But are you willing to be the woman who spoiled your people's best chance to defeat the vampires?"

"Is that what you think?"

"I'm asking you. What will your history say of you? Will they build a monument to your honor or to your failure?"

"I don't care," Adele said in frustration, placing her hands on the railing with a deep sigh. "Even if I never go back, Simon will grow up to be emperor under my father's tutelage. History will probably say how fortunate Equatoria was to avoid the reign of Adele the First. Vampires captured her and the experience drove her mad. She fled the altar and vanished into the desert with a masked man, never to be seen again. Next page."

"Does that epitaph satisfy you?"

She shook her head. "Perhaps there are greater things for me than being empress. Mamoru seemed to think so."

"Perhaps."

Adele grew excited by a sudden thought. "I should find a way to bring Mamoru from Alexandria to teach me here. I could learn more about geomancy. He believes I will change the world. Perhaps I can find a way for our people to coexist."

Greyfriar remained silent, but his lack of response shouted his doubts. The young woman turned. "You don't believe me?"

"I do, of course. My only question is whether there are any humans other than you who would not prefer to wipe out all of my kind if they had the power. Including your Mamoru and your Colonel Anhalt. You and I are unique. I am a vampire fascinated by humans. You are a human intrigued by vampires."

"Maybe I can change others. Perhaps I can change everyone."

"Perhaps."

"I understand your skepticism. Even I don't grasp the knowledge I might command, but I've felt it and used it. It's immense. It's inexplicable. I don't know where it could lead."

"No, you don't." Gareth gathered her again in his arms, trying to forget the taste of death in her. He regarded her softly. "Perhaps you will work miracles."

She put her head against his chest.

There was a sharp rap at the door. Anhalt peered in and then glanced down at the floor. "Pardon, Your Highness, but we are summoned to King Msiri."

—⁕—

King Msiri rose to greet Adele. He was a remarkable figure, tall and strong and of an indeterminable age, likely a vigorous midforties. His face was lined with concern, but not burdened. His eyes were sharp, but not wary. He wore a loose white shirt and linen trousers with sandals, along with a leopard-skin band around his head. His smile was comfortable. He threw out his muscled arms as if family had just arrived.

"Your Highness, what a delight to see you again!" He loped around a long table piled with fruit, porridges, and sweets on copper trays with gold pitchers full of steaming, fine-scented coffees. The king took Adele's hand and kissed it.

"Your Majesty," she replied with an enchanted grin. "It's been years since we last met in Alexandria. Thank you for granting us an audience. Please forgive my poor Swahili."

"Nonsense. You speak like a Katangan. Come. Sit. Eat. Have you breakfasted yet? Of course not. Then, please!" Msiri virtually pulled Adele to the table and held a chair for her. The seat was magnificent teak with a creamy hide upholstery. Then he extended an arm to her companions. "Don't wait. There is no formality at breakfast. This is my private chamber, so I beg you to relax. Colonel Anhalt, please. I am well versed of you from your old friend General Ngongo, commander of my Mountaineer Brigade. He is on a scouting mission in the Rwenzoris, but will come as soon as possible to greet you himself."

The Gurkha was taken aback by the king's attention. "Thank you, Your Majesty. General Ngongo is a fine officer, and I am grateful for his kind words."

"Here, have a mango." Msiri tossed a fruit to Anhalt and then eyed Greyfriar. "And you, sir, are the Greyfriar? Of course you are. Why else would you be dressed so."

"I am, Your Majesty."

"I have heard many stories." The king leaned back in judgment. He glanced at Adele, who was already ladling thick soup into a bowl. "That's cassava porridge, you know."

"I know," she replied. "It's one of my favorites." She knew a few of the customs of Katanga. First and foremost, it was poor etiquette not to eat in front of your host.

"Good for you. You could use a few pounds, poor girl. So, Greyfriar, what will you have to eat?"

Adele dropped her spoon with a jarring clatter. Msiri glanced at her momentarily and then back at Greyfriar.

Greyfriar stated, "I prefer not to eat."

"What?" Msiri asked in confusion.

Adele came to his rescue. "He has a tropical malady. Being from the north, the climate has been debilitating for him." She winced at her own poor attempt at a lie, but the king didn't seem to notice.

"Ah, yes. I understand." The king smiled. "Our doctors will see him. We've done remarkable things with fevers."

"No, no," Adele replied casually. "We couldn't possibly encroach further on your kindness. He's recovering well. It's not a serious tropical malady."

Msiri shrugged, and as he went to resume his seat, he saw Anhalt still standing formally next to the banquet. "Are you plagued by fever too, Colonel?"

"No, Sire."

"Then eat!" The king grabbed a plate and piled it with fruit, bread, and strips of meat. He put it down forcefully and lifted a chair an inch or two and dropped it. "I find it difficult to trust people who don't like to eat. The infirm excepted."

Greyfriar inclined his head graciously.

Adele wiped juice from her fingers, exclaiming without pretense, "Oh my God these papayas are good!"

Msiri laughed appreciatively with a voice that rolled around the chamber. Huge overhead beams were carved intricately from single trunks of forest giants. There were exquisite sculptures of wood and feather as well as metal, and the walls were made vibrant with bright wall hangings. The king alone occupied this large second-floor chamber, where the sounds of government and the surrounding city were drowned out by the roar of rain through the open window.

He kicked off a sandal and dropped into a chair of leopard skin and ivory with his bare foot under him. "What may I do for you, Your Highness? Ask it and it's done."

Adele sat back from the table. "How familiar are you with my situation?"

"One hears things."

"Have you heard anything from the Equatorian government?"

"I have not. Alexandria has been unusually silent of late. Perhaps they are embarrassed about your situation. Or perhaps the telegraph lines have failed again."

"Well, here is the truth. Basically, I decided not to marry one man and ran off with another."

"That's an old story, but always a good one. Although rarely does it involve the daughter of an emperor and a legendary hero. Does Constantine know where you are?"

"No, sir. I would like to tell him, but first I need to know that we are welcome here."

Msiri looked insulted. "Do you feel unwelcome?"

"May I speak plainly?" She paused a moment with her fork.

"Have you not been?"

"I need a place to stay from which I can negotiate my future, whether it is returning to Alexandria or something else. I need a place that is strong enough to stand firm should my father decide to threaten: *give up my daughter or else.*"

"Or else what?"

"Or else anything."

Msiri bit into a lemon and pondered while Adele and Anhalt watched him chew with sour faces. Finally he said, "As you know, Katanga is surrounded by imperial territories and imperial toadies. That is why, no doubt, you have arrived on my doorstep seeking protection. I have no neighbors who would stand with me against Equatoria. In fact, they would all help your father to punish me. So I ask you, would Constantine send troops to retrieve you?"

"In truth, he may. Senator Clark might insist upon it, and he has great influence at court. Do you know him?"

"I do not. I am advised of his exploits in the Americas. If I may be so bold, is Clark such an unsuitable husband? Is he not brave and rich and strong? Does he not bind your great houses together?"

"He is and does all those things. But he is arrogant and crude. His plans for Equatoria are anathema to me. I loathe him. In addition, I prefer someone else."

Msiri gave a swift glance at Greyfriar, trying to puzzle out the man behind the mask. "So you want to know if I will fight Equatoria to protect you?"

"In so many words, yes."

Msiri waved the half lemon in the air with an earnest stare. "I welcome you to Katanga, and I will do whatever I can to bring about the reconciliation of a princess and her country, and more, of a daughter and her father. I myself have five beautiful daughters, and it hurts my heart to think I could part as enemies with any of them."

"Thank you, Your Majesty." Adele took a deep breath and paused while spooning out another helping of porridge. "May I ask you something?"

"Of course."

"What if one of your daughters did what I have done? What if she refused a marriage that was politically valuable to you?"

The king laughed loudly. "Oh, that wouldn't happen. My five daughters are all married to men of influence both within Katanga and without. I have marriage connections to my Guild of Smiths. One daughter is the queen of Matabeleland. And another is married to a prince of Bornu. They are fine girls."

"But what if they did? What if one had refused to marry her husband?"

"Hmm. I have never considered it." The smile vanished from Msiri's face as he thought about her question. His genial expression fell under a heavy slate, and his eyes turned to iron. There was no anger in him, simply the truth. "I fear she would have to leave, and we would never speak again. And I would rather die than have that happen."

Adele watched the king with a sense of sadness, but then he gave her a renewed smile. He jabbed his chin at her hand frozen on the porridge spoon, indicating for her to continue eating.

The princess said, "I am deeply grateful for your assistance in my delicate matter."

"It is my pleasure."

"Thank you. Is there something I may do for you in return?"

The king shook his head as he searched for something else to eat. "What I do is for you. There is no payment. It is to commemorate the great friendship between Katanga and Equatoria. I want you to think of me as your father too. Or perhaps as a slightly older uncle. Your gratitude is enough for me."

"Thank you, Your Majesty," Adele said, though she still did not quite believe that was the end of the matter.

"Of course." The king ripped open an orange and sprayed juice in the air. "In the future, when you are empress and you wish to show your gratitude by ceding me the west bank of the Luta Nzige, so be it."

Adele nodded thoughtfully and began to stir honey into her porridge. She was careful not to make any reply beyond the sound of enjoying the king's meal.

Msiri said, "There is one more thing."

"Yes?" Adele's voice was suspicious.

"I am soon to embark on a campaign to the south in the Rwenzori Mountains. These mountains are the domain of *ndoki*, witches. What you call vampires. These *ndoki* are ruled by a terrible warrior named Jaga. He strikes with impunity and retreats back to his capital through crevices of the mountains. He kills men and carries off women and children. And more, he injures my trade and sows nervousness among my people. I would kill Jaga and clear his *ndoki* from his mountain stronghold."

"Yes?"

"You are skilled in fighting *ndoki*. As is your companion. I would value your counsel on this campaign."

Adele glanced back at Greyfriar. "We will tell you whatever we can, of course."

"Let me be clear," Msiri said. "I would value your presence on the campaign."

Colonel Anhalt stiffened in his seat. "That is highly unprecedented. Highness, I cannot recommend this. These mountains are quite harsh. The enemy is unknown. I will happily join our forces with His Majesty's, but there is no rationale for you to venture into the Mountains of the Moon."

"Thank you, Colonel, I appreciate your perspective," Adele said. It was a curious request the king made, and one that caused Adele to wonder at the reason behind it. She wasn't afraid of fighting vampires, but it surprised her that she had already garnered such a reputation. The Mountains of the Moon were mysterious and legendary, and they greatly intrigued her. Plus, any gesture on her part to strengthen her position with Msiri would be a good tactic. "However, I have every reason to go. Our host requests it. Whatever good I can do, I will do."

Msiri clapped his hands and regained his old cheerfulness. "Excellent! Well done. But it shames me to say I have one further request."

Adele sighed against her will and then forced a smile. "Yes, Your Majesty?"

The king rang a clutch of copper bells, and a door opened far across the chamber. Adele was surprised to see the old woman from the guest quarters enter. She carried what appeared to be a small stack of papers, but soon Adele realized it was a magazine. Passing close by, the woman smiled cheerfully at Adele and handed the publication to Msiri. It was one of the penny dreadfuls from Alexandria entitled *The Greyfriar: Bloody Swords Against England*. On the cover was an exciting scene of a dashing swordsman looking nothing like Greyfriar battling a horrible horde of ravenous vampires.

Msiri gestured to the elderly woman. "No Katangan is allowed to see the king eat, with the exception of the queen mother."

"She's your mother!" Adele exclaimed.

"I'm happy to see you eating, daughter," the queen mother said; then she patted Colonel Anhalt on the shoulder. "If you need anything, you tell me. I'll see to it." She went for the door, but stopped to lay a gentle hand on Greyfriar's arm. The old woman snatched her hand back and took a step away from the swordsman. She whirled to face Adele, who was still watching her.

She knows, Adele thought in horror. Somehow the woman could tell that Greyfriar was a vampire. Adele froze, staring at the queen mother, pleading for silence with her gaze. If there was any form of connection from one woman to another about a man, Adele used it. The queen mother searched the princess's face with her own terrified eyes until slowly a look of confusion, but acceptance, seeped in. Only then did Adele realize the smile had never left the queen mother's face. Msiri and Anhalt were unaware of the volumes that had passed between the two women, solely through their eyes.

Greyfriar understood too, but had not moved. He studied the old woman carefully, and when she turned back to him briefly, he stepped back with deference and gave a slight bow. She paused with a killer's glare that only he could see. Then she bustled out the door as if the heart-stopping moment hadn't occurred.

King Msiri rose and stood over the magazine on the table. "I wonder, sir, if I might trouble you to sign this for me." He held a pen out toward Greyfriar. The swordsman didn't react, as if he hadn't heard, perhaps because his attention was still focused on the departure of the intuitive queen mother.

Msiri looked at Adele and back at Greyfriar. Colonel Anhalt cleared his throat and Adele reacted. She saw the king lift the pen again in the swordsman's direction.

"Would you sign?" Msiri asked a bit more forcefully. "I know it's silly, but I would value it."

"Sign?" Greyfriar now looked at the king.

"Yes," Msiri replied with an embarrassed chuckle. "I have read many of your adventures. And now here you are. It would be a delightful souvenir for me."

"Sign?"

Adele rose from her chair, trying to cover her mild concern at Greyfriar's complete confusion. "Yes. Just sign your name."

"My name?"

"Greyfriar," Adele said pointedly, directing him to the table. "Just sign *Greyfriar* on the cover of this book."

The swordsman stepped forward and took the pen awkwardly. He glanced at Adele for approval, then leaned over the magazine and became engulfed in the picture on the cover. After a few minutes of stillness, Msiri began to look worried and Adele touched Greyfriar on the arm.

She pointed to the cover, purposefully laying her finger next to the printed word *Greyfriar*. "The king is waiting. Just sign your name, please."

Greyfriar took a deep breath and set the point of the pen against the paper as lightly as he could. He began to write, replicating the word *Greyfriar* exactly as it was printed, in a bold typeface.

Adele drew close to his ear and whispered softly, "Just scribble. Don't copy the word. Scribble!"

He shook his head distractedly and continued duplicating. She turned to block the king's view, then jarred Greyfriar's elbow so that the pen scratched across the cover.

"Ah! There we go." Adele snatched the magazine from under his hand and yanked the pen out of his steel grip.

Msiri gave an odd half-smile as he surveyed the autograph, a perfectly iconographic GREYF followed by a peculiar long, inky blot. "Interesting. I've never seen a signature quite like it."

"Yes. It's odd, isn't it?" Adele took Greyfriar by the arm with a too-charming laugh. "But we all have our peculiarities. So, let's talk about this Jaga, shall we?"

CHAPTER 24

BUNIA WAS ABLAZE with activity. Fireworks burst overhead. Music blared from every street. War drums pounded along the avenues. King Msiri was departing in the morning to campaign against Jaga, the *ndoki* chief of the Rwenzori Mountains. A massive parade was planned tomorrow to see off the elite of Katanga's army.

Days had passed and Adele had expected to be confronted at every turn, assuming the queen mother had confessed Greyfriar's secret to her son. But nothing had changed. Adele couldn't help but wonder why. Perhaps it had something to do with the coming conflict with the vampires.

The martial drumbeats surrounded Adele; the deep booming filled her with a confidence, even eagerness for battle. The warm, humid evening had sent Gareth to his quarters and the relief of a cooling kit. Adele sought a calm moment in the dark tropical garden beneath her balcony. Birds flew overhead in slashes of color with strange cries and long plumage trailing. Insect droning was audible even above the drums, but a turgid breeze kept her from being swarmed. The air seemed too thick to draw fully into her lungs.

The bushes nearby shuddered, and the queen mother appeared through dark green fronds. The old woman smiled and waved. The young woman shrank back slightly.

"Bless you, daughter. Are you well?" The old woman settled on the stone bench next to Adele, acting as if she didn't carry a volatile secret on the eve of battle. She noted the colorful cloth Adele wore wrapped from shoulder to ankle in the local fashion, reds and greens and bold patterns. It was certainly more lively than the princess's usual somber tones. "You look beautiful. This suits your brightness."

"Thank you," Adele murmured, a bit hesitant.

"Don't fear." The queen mother squeezed Adele's hands. "I'm not the one to tell the secret of your . . . man."

"Thank you." The princess breathed out heavily and surrendered to the woman's gentle touch. "It's very complicated."

"There is no man who isn't complicated. Yours perhaps a bit more than most."

Adele nodded, a weary smile emerging.

The queen mother asked, "Is he truly the Greyfriar too?"

"Yes. He saved my life, and he wants to help the humans of the north. He's not like others of his kind."

The queen mother stared long into the face of the young princess. "Do you trust him?"

"Yes. More than any human being I know. He is brave and kind and generous. There is nothing false about him."

The old woman smiled. "Even with the mask?"

"The mask is more him than he is," Adele replied quickly. "It's hard to explain."

"No need. I understand masks. Although few follow the old ways now, once we wore masks to show our true selves and to become something better than we are." The queen mother shook her head a bit sadly. She reached up and pulled the bright fabric of her own dress away from her shoulder. "Some of us still wear masks."

On the old woman's shoulder was a tattoo of a dragon. It was identical to the one on Mamoru's hand, and on Selkirk's too. Adele gasped and reached up to touch the sinuous beast scarred into wrinkled skin.

"You know my teacher?" Adele said.

"Yes, daughter. I know Mamoru. He was my teacher once also."

"You're a geomancer?"

"I am. I shouldn't be telling you this. I am sworn to secrecy." The queen mother laughed loudly. "But we all know you are his current favorite. And I know your secret, so now we are even."

Adele reached into her pocket and removed one of the gems ripped from her wedding gown. At the touch, she felt a freezing blast of lonely mountain wind and had a vision of jagged peaks. The Himalayas of far-off Tibet. Adele held out the stone.

The queen mother smiled slightly and took the gem. "Well, I haven't had this test in quite some time. But if you wish." Then she closed her eyes and clutched the stone tightly in her fist.

The princess waited and watched the twitching face of the old woman. Seconds passed. Then minutes. Adele started to grow suspicious.

Finally the queen mother exhaled and said, "Mountains. High mountains. But far away. So far I'd say India, if pressed to it. Yes?" She gave the gemstone back to the young woman.

"Yes." Adele laughed with relief at the seemingly endless reach of Mamoru. There was something comforting, but also disturbing in his shadow network that existed under the normal world. There was so much Adele didn't know about her teacher. But still, she embraced the queen mother. The woman was like a piece of home, an improbable message of comfort in the chaos of exile. She breathed in the queen mother's perfumed scent.

"Can you get a message to Mamoru?" Adele asked. "I want him here with me, but I was told that communication with Alexandria has been interrupted."

"I can try. I have little contact with Mamoru himself, but I know one of his closest confederates. If she is in Alexandria, I can contact her. They use a circuitous route for secrecy's sake. However, once you are in the Rwenzoris, there will be precious few messages coming to you, if any. You will likely hear nothing from the outside world until you return."

"I understand, but I appreciate anything you can do. We leave for the mountains tomorrow. It will be weeks at least before we return to Bunia."

"Yes." The queen mother frowned. "You must be careful. And you must protect my son."

"Protect him? I'm hoping he'll protect me. I'm along as a consultant, to tell him what I know about vampires, but—"

"More. You must do more."

"I don't understand."

"Daughter, it was I who suggested my son take you on this campaign. You will be his salvation. You see, I'm not just a geomancer; I'm also a seer."

"A seer?" Adele couldn't help sounding dubious.

"Yes, daughter." The queen mother smiled. "I know what you're thinking, that Mamoru is a man of strict intellectual pursuit, not some sort of wizard. But you will learn, Mamoru casts a wide net in pursuit of his theories of life. He prejudges nothing, and he knows well my abilities. Before you even came to Katanga, I dreamed you. I know things about you that perhaps you do not know yourself."

"Such as?"

"Here is my dream. Many years ago, Leopard was tawny. He had no spots. He was so proud of his yellow coat. He spent hours every day preening. And he lived in a great palace from which he ruled his people with wisdom. But over the years, Leopard grew lazy. He didn't take care of his palace. One night, hyenas came in. They surrounded Leopard, snapping at him. Every bite that the hyenas gave him turned into a black spot. Although Leopard fought bravely, he was driven from his palace and the hyenas came to live there. And so Leopard lived out in the world. His black spots helped him to hide from the hyenas when they came to kill him, for the hyenas always fear Leopard. They know one day Leopard will come back to his palace. Then Leopard will roar and he will drive the hyenas back into the cold."

Adele waited for her to continue, but the old woman sat back with mouth closed, complacently stroking the princess's hand. Finally, Adele urged, "And? What happened?"

The queen mother shrugged. "That was my dream."

"But . . . how do you know it was about me?"

"It was."

"But . . . am I Leopard? Is your son Leopard?"

"It's not that simple, daughter."

"The hyenas are vampires, though. That much I got."

The old woman breathed out patiently. "In a dream, nothing is anything. It may mean one thing to me and another to you. I am telling you this to prepare you."

"For what?" Adele sounded flustered.

"I don't know. You are the one being prepared." The queen mother stood. "You should sleep now. They will call you early tomorrow, and you will not rest well for many weeks. Please let my son return home. He's all I have." She slipped into the palm fronds and disappeared in a flutter of green.

Adele sat in the din of war drums, the pounding noise echoing in the uneasy emptiness of her chest. She wanted simple words of comfort. What she got was vague dreamspeak about leopards and hyenas. Adele felt alone, and she wished Greyfriar were there with her.

⁂

Lord Kelvin studied papers from a thick portfolio as he walked the dank corridor. He rarely ventured below Victoria Palace, for good reason. It was unpleasant down here, damp and chilled, and it reeked of decades of unspeakable acts carried out at the behest of the old sultans and Equatorian emperors. He disliked these actions, although he knew they were necessary to statecraft. If everyone would just see reason, violence would be forgotten. It seemed so simple.

He nodded to two Persian marines outside a cell door. It occurred to Kelvin how much he depended on Persian soldiers now, which was ironic since the half-Persian Princess Adele was gone. He stopped and made a note in his calendar book: "Diversify soldiery in capital. Turks?"

One marine accompanied the prime minister inside and the door was closed behind them. The smell was atrocious, but Lord Kelvin wouldn't react. He couldn't show that any appropriate government function was distasteful. He finished reading the memo and inserted it inside a folder. Then he closed the portfolio and looked up toward his next bit of business.

"Mamoru," he said.

A short but powerfully built figure slumped in a chair in the center of the grey room. The samurai was stripped to the waist and showed raw welts across his shoulders and chest. His ankles and wrists were shackled together on a length of chain embedded in the wooden limbs of his meager throne.

Kelvin said, "I've just read the report of your interrogation, and you continue to resist reason."

Mamoru's head slowly lifted to reveal a swollen face with an eye bruised purple and shut tight. He actually smiled through lips stained black with old blood.

The prime minister was angered that the Japanese priest didn't even have the decency to act cowed, and he grimaced with obvious distaste. "I don't understand your childish grin. This is not a game, sir. At least not one that you can win. You understand, of course, that I will need to know about your intelligence network? His Imperial Majesty Emperor Constantine the Second seemed content to let you operate as you pleased, but I fear those halcyon days are at an end. It would go better with you if you talked. It's quite simple."

"Simple?" Mamoru slurred.

"Yes. It's irrational to expect that I will allow you to operate a shadow network out of the palace. Just give us all the particulars, and this unpleasantness can end."

"Will it? Would you let me go?"

"Oh, no. I will never let you go. But I will stop this treatment you have brought on yourself. You are far too dangerous and unstable to be free."

"Whatever will you tell the Japanese emperor in Malaya about where I've gone?"

"I know you claim some connection there, but I can come up with something that will satisfy His Serene Majesty. You are a fanatic who has caused untold harm to Equatoria by corrupting Princess Adele. Granted, that was likely simple enough; the girl was always unstable. And it's unfortunate for you that your patrons here are no more. Her Imperial Majesty Empress Pareesa. His Imperial Majesty Emperor Constantine the Second. And Princess Adele. All gone. You are quite alone now."

Mamoru stared evenly at the politician. "You have no idea what you are doing."

"I believe I do. I am protecting humanity from lunatic religionists and occultists such as yourself who prey on the feeble-minded. Your type makes me ill, if I may speak freely. And now that I have full rein here, I will deal with you appropriately. After you tell me about your intelligence network."

Mamoru shook his head and stayed silent.

Lord Kelvin sighed again, reiterating his dismay. "You don't seem to understand that I will do anything to preserve the Empire. Anything."

"You're an idiot!" Mamoru spat. "You're going to doom all of humanity with your slavery to steam and steel, you narrow-minded technocrat!"

"There's hardly need for name-calling, Mamoru. We can have a civil conversation. I must say, I pity you. You've become so mired in your own childish beliefs. I've no quarrel with religion, within reason. I'm told it can provide a diverting hour or so out of the house. But you lunatics who take it too far, and try to bend others to it, deserve nothing more than death. I'd be doing the world a service to execute you. But I have a duty to the Empire."

Mamoru lowered his head, slumping in his chains.

"Have you anything to say, Mamoru?" Kelvin asked and waited, watching the immobile priest. "Very well. You reap what you sow, old boy."

"As do we all," the samurai said in a low voice.

Kelvin indicated for the marine to open the cell, and they stepped outside. The prime minister turned back. "I fear you are in no position to have the last word any longer."

The door slammed closed.

CHAPTER 25

"**J**AGA AND HIS *ndoki* will fight because he has nowhere to live except the Rwenzori. If he is expelled, he will die. His kind cannot live among us in the lowlands." King Msiri's firm hand anchored a map of the Rwenzori section of the Virunga Mountain chain. Unfortunately, much of the map was blank, particularly the central spine of the mountains labeled with the legend *Jaga Grand Boma*.

The king's field camp lay beside a lake in a wide mountain valley. A jagged cleft to the east beckoned with glacial slopes. The landscape had turned strange and otherworldly. The deep green foliage and red soil around Bunia had turned to pale green with black volcanic soil. The stunted forest was composed of black mahogany so overwhelmed by luxurious hanging moss that the trees seemed to be sinister old men with long beards and grasping fingers. The open ground was covered with grey lichen, and there were huge prehistoric lobelia with vast, hard, spiked petals. The ground was sodden and given to stretches of moor and mire with hummocks of high elephant grass.

A flimsy camp table wobbled in the center of the group consisting of the king, Princess Adele, Greyfriar, Colonel Anhalt, and General Ngongo. The general was a sturdy type, all business, without much expression in his voice or face. He was on an even keel at all times, much like his Equatorian comrade, Anhalt. He seemed quite at home in the foul weather in a heavy cloak covering his camouflage tunic and long kilt. Even in the mountain chill, he wore only sandals of heavy hide.

The conferencing party stood under a canvas shelter, barely protected from wind-driven sleet. This was a true military camp, not a royal jaunt. The king and his guests may have been somewhat warmer and drier than the rank and file, but Msiri's accommodations were lavish only to the extent that he felt it necessary to comport himself as the king and elevate himself over his men. His shirt and trousers were a heavy canvas, and he wore a leopard-skin blanket around his shoulders.

For her part, Adele had never been so cold. She wore a Katangan officer's uniform with a heavy fur wrap, but the ice-peppered air passed through as if it were chiffon. She tried to concentrate on the tactics with her jaw clenched tight to keep her teeth from chattering. None of the men seemed so miserable. Greyfriar especially was at home in the elements. His cloak fluttered like wings and he shifted his head subtly, which Adele knew was him scenting the air. Likewise Colonel Anhalt appeared unfazed by the weather; his topcoat was unbuttoned. She cursed at them all silently and began to wonder about the wisdom of her long-held dream to walk in snow. The baking sun of Egypt seemed a wonderful memory in this frigid place.

Anhalt laid a finger on the blank space on the map. "What do we know about Jaga's capital?"

"Little, as you see," King Msiri replied. "Our mapping expeditions have been slaughtered and our airships have been shattered on the mountains. Their capital has never been seen by human eyes, as it is lost in the high mists. But we know it lies through that pass above us."

Greyfriar said, "I will scout the area first to fill in your map."

King Msiri regarded the swordsman. "Our finest hunters have tried, sir. They have failed. How can you, without knowing the land, do better?"

"I am better," he replied without pretense.

Adele added, "He has survived in occupied Europe for years. And no one knows vampires as well."

"My pardon, Your Highness," General Ngongo said, his hands open before him, "but the Rwenzoris are a wild place whose inhabitants will kill a single man, even your man, quite easily. To go forward into the *ndoki*'s domain in less than full force is madness, and death for whomever tries it."

Msiri added, "We have two brigades of riflemen and three companies of heavy machine gunners. Granted, the mountain terrain precludes our using heavy artillery and armor, which conquered the savannah for us. But still, we have the general's Mountaineers to lead the way. They will scout and skirmish ahead. I have no intention of committing my main force without knowing what I am facing. On the other hand, I do not intend to return to Bunia without Jaga's head."

Greyfriar retorted, "You realize that this place is completely favorable to them? They are light. They can attack without touching the ground. Their feet won't be sucked into the mud or leave tracks in the snow. Your men and your machines will be bogged-down cattle to them. Rather than going forward, an even better option, a safer option, would be for you to remove your population from around the mountains and starve them out."

The king laughed without humor and shook his head at the swordsman. "We well know the terrain favors the enemy. But they don't have the decency to come down to face us. Your escapades in Europe are remarkable, but this is central Africa. Unlike you, a mysterious frontiersman who can come and go as you please, I am the king of a nation and of a people, and the commander of a great army. Do you imagine I can uproot hundreds of thousands of them from their homes without great repercussions? I should like to remain king, thank you."

"Then let me scout," Greyfriar argued. "I will determine the enemy positions and their strength. Why would you risk a blind fight?" Adele's silencing hand gripped his forearm, but he continued even more forcefully, afraid for her safety among these foolish warriors. "You are making a terrible mistake. If they number even a quarter of your forces, they will rip you to pieces."

Msiri's tone hardened. "You gravely underestimate our fighting force. They are fully capable of destroying vampires."

"Obviously not, or you would have accomplished that long before now."

Adele exclaimed, "Greyfriar, please!"

"You know I'm right," he said to her. "They are playing with your life!"

The tension in the tent was palpable. Adele dared not tempt the king's anger. Without his backing, they would have nowhere else to turn and would be forced back into wandering the terrible heat of the tropics. Too much was at stake. The cordon around Katanga was tight; the lost Equatorian ship and the privateer had shown them that.

"I must follow this path," she said quietly. "There is no other recourse left to me."

She had referenced only herself, meaning her hands were tied. He straightened stiffly and then gave a scant nod. "May I go, Princess?"

He wasn't asking for permission to leave the war council. He knew the situation they were both placed in. There was nothing he could do for her, hobbled as he was by the humans around him. He was asking her if he had leave to do as he needed. These men could not understand what he could do away from prying human eyes, but she did.

Adele stared at him, a little afraid to let him go. But she knew he was right. Finally, she nodded, her teeth capturing her lower lip nervously. She dropped her hand away from his arm and said softly, "Yes, you may go." She mouthed the words, *Be careful*.

Adele watched him stride away from the table. Outwardly calm, she turned back to the others. "Gentlemen, your forgiveness. His war has been a lonely one; he is not used to collaboration."

To her relief, King Msiri smiled to dispel the awkward moment. "We certainly understand. I wish he could do what he proposed. How much simpler to send one man rather than an expensive army of sons and fathers and husbands. Now, General Ngongo, we will hear your plans for proceeding."

Adele glanced back, but did not see Greyfriar's tall form in the gathering dark.

—⟋∿⟍—

No one saw Gareth leave the camp. It was simple enough for him to deposit Greyfriar's garb and weapons in Adele's baggage with a note that read

"Greyfriar cannot protect you. But I can." Then, clad in a dark shirt and trousers, barefoot in the clammy mud, he slipped past the better part of the Katangan army into the bush. Soon he rose into the battering wind, reveling again in the wildness. He could smell the army, so he knew any vampire within miles could as well. This war was a poorly conceived campaign, born of pride rather than need. King Msiri wanted to show strength to his people, but marching into the vampires' stronghold was a mistake. It was a massacre waiting to happen, with Adele at the heart of it.

Gareth wouldn't allow it. He was no longer interested in scouting the terrain for Msiri. Rather, he intended to find Jaga's people, as Gareth, so they could lead him to the Grand Boma, where he would kill the chief. This would cripple the *ndoki*'s ability to resist the Katangans.

The ghoulish landscape of the Rwenzori passed below him as cottony tendrils of cloud wended their way between scabrous trees and insane groves of giant lobelia. The sleet drove sideways, and the wind was nearly too strong to fly in. Gareth had to guard against being smashed against the serrated rock faces around him, shifting his density constantly to remain steady.

He was a bit unnerved by his surroundings. He had never been so far south before. The scents of the plants were unfamiliar and the sounds of the animals were strange. The staggering scope of the mountains was on a scale with the Alps. This was a daunting task, but he was confident his skills would serve him here as in Europe.

Gareth caught the faint scent of blood, just a distant tang in his nostrils, before the ice drove it away. Humans. But not the Katangan soldiers. It came from higher in the mist. He had been told no humans lived this high, except for vampire herds, so the smell of blood meant the *ndoki* were near. Gareth wondered how to approach the strangers. He wanted to avoid combat if possible. Despite the cold weather, he was still not at his best due to lack of food.

He drifted up, propelling himself from crag to cliff. He caught more sporadic hints of blood and then some thin vampire scents. Gareth came to rest on a pinnacle above a pool of mist. Far below him, out of sight, were vampires and humans.

The prince crawled down the cliff into the cloud bank. He moved with decisive silence, listening intently, and heard voices. Vampires. The language was familiar, but still dissimilar from his own northern dialect. From what he could grasp, the local clan chief, the one Msiri called Jaga, had summoned all his subjects, no doubt in response to the invading army. Two as yet unseen vampires were complaining because bringing human meals to the clan gathering required their traveling by foot.

Gareth drew closer, and the smell of blood prodded his hunger. He had to silence a growl from deep in his throat. He felt as if he were hunting again, waiting to pounce on unsuspecting prey. Through the thinning fog, he finally saw two vampires beneath him. Tall and thin, one was dressed in simple loincloth, while the other wore a knee-length kilt. Even here, the vampires copied human dress. The two stood together near a wretched herd of five humans; three old men and two ancient women wrapped in filthy blankets. The humans squatted, sharing some dry food from a bag. They showed signs of having been fed from multiple times, which was rare in the north, were food was killed and wasted. If these thin-blooded, weak humans were representative of Jaga's herds, then perhaps the *ndoki* were indeed primed for destruction.

It wouldn't do to surprise the two, so Gareth called out. As they spun around, the tall prince dropped lightly to the frosty ground with hands up and no claws displayed. The two *ndoki* eyed him with curiosity.

One barked, "Name yourself!"

"I am Prince Gareth of Scotland, of the clan of Dmitri."

"I don't know this Dmitri."

"Nevertheless, he is a great king in the far north in a land where humans are slaves to vampires."

The vampires exchanged confused glances and one sneered, "As here. In what useful land are humans not slaves?" They chuckled at Gareth's pointless boasting.

Gareth nodded. The *ndoki* never ventured out of their mountains except to raid. They had no memory of living side by side with humans, so any land they occupied, they dominated. By definition, human territory was as uninhabitable as the sea. Gareth's comment was ridiculous from their point of view.

Gareth said, "I would speak with King Jaga."

"Why?"

"Who are you to ask? I am a prince." He took a menacing step. "Take me to your king."

The two travelers continued to observe him with slight smirks as they muttered to each other. It was quite insubordinate and disrespectful, and it rankled Gareth. He slowly extended his claws.

"No matter," Gareth said, raising a clawed hand. "I'm content to kill you and find your king myself."

They laughed with relaxed scorn. It wasn't out of ignorance. In fact, Gareth could see their cool demeanor was born from the confidence that they knew something he did not. Then he heard a sound from behind.

He glanced over his shoulder to see ten *ndoki* emerging from the mist. The sleet and chaotic winds had made it impossible to sense them. He lowered his claws. He had been trapped.

Gareth gave the first two *ndoki* a raised eyebrow of admiration and humility. "How long was I followed?"

They laughed even harder. "A long time, Prince. Perhaps years. Now you may see Jaga."

—◦◦◦—

The Grand Boma of Jaga was a group of caves set on an isolated plateau high in the mountains. Hundreds of vampires circled in the air and crouched on ledges. Humans milled about in the clearing between the caves. There were some signs of paltry agriculture in the thin soil leading up to the boma, proof that the *ndoki* kept permanent herds that labored to feed themselves. Jaga's herds were thin and starved. Even the most miserable stocks Gareth had seen shuffling through London appeared vigorous by comparison. The *ndoki* also seemed malnourished and hollow. Many wore remnants of clothing or fur, but a large number were naked, a sight that was rare in the north since the Great Killing.

Still, Gareth reminded himself, they were smart enough to trap him. He'd do well to fight his sense of superiority, as well as his disdain for his own kind that led him to think he was more clever than other vampires. He couldn't afford to fail by becoming smug.

When he landed with his escort, one of them screeched a loud greeting. *Ndoki* began to gather, fluttering down to clutch onto the rock faces and stare at the robust newcomer. The air filled with soft whispering.

A figure emerged from a large cave, no doubt the great Jaga. The vampire was tall, dark, and strong. He wore long strips of fur—leopard, gorilla, and various other animals—as well as a necklace of bones. His hair was long and tangled, and his beard was turning grey. He moved close to Gareth and smelled him. Behind Jaga came three women, much more vigorous than the typical *ndoki*. They wore strange cuirasses of human rib bones on their otherwise naked flesh, creating a startling effect, a grim style that Gareth thought Flay might have adopted to great advantage and set the whole of London fashion on its ear. He smiled slightly despite himself.

Jaga regarded the newcomer with surprise. "You seem cheerful so far from home."

Gareth bowed and spoke in some semblance of the *ndoki* dialect, which he had begun to pick up from the conversations he had heard. "Are you Jaga?"

"You speak like an imbecile. Name yourself."

"Gareth of Scotland. Clan of Dmitri."

Jaga turned around as he shouted to his surrounding clansmen, "Behold! An ambassador from the great clan of Dmitri come to join me in my impending triumph! The name of Jaga travels far!" The king cut a glance at Gareth. "I have never heard of your clan, but you're welcome anyway. Come. Eat." He strode back into his cave.

"Ladies." Gareth gave the females a charming nod. They laughed as if at the antics of a child or a fool and then fell in behind him.

Once inside the cave, Jaga settled on the hard ground and Gareth followed suit. A young vampire boy came over and looped a thin arm around Jaga's shoulder. The *ndoki* king gave the boy a playful nudge and patted him on the leg. The amazon trio stood nearby while commenting among themselves on Gareth's odd appearance.

"So," Jaga said, "tell me about your herds."

Gareth hesitated. That was a rare topic in the north where food was plentiful. "What do you want to know?"

"Are they large? And fat?"

"Yes."

"Larger than mine?"

"I cannot say. I have not seen all your herds." Gareth noticed a huge pile of human bones deeper in the cave, cast aside with the remnants of human possessions.

"True. My herds are vast. I claim all of the mountains." Jaga looked sharply at the trio of females. "Where is the food? Can't you smell how hungry he is? Go!" The amazons departed, and the king said, "I hope you will find the meal satisfactory. I welcome the friendship of the family of Dmitri, wherever they are."

"My clan is far."

"You must be far; I've never seen your kind here. Why have you appeared to me now?"

"I was captive of Katanga, but I escaped."

Jaga sat up. "What? The Katangans who come against me?"

"Yes, my lord. I am here to help you."

"How can you help me? You are one, and you are clumsy. My men took you prisoner without effort. I have my family around me, or soon will. I will destroy the Katangans and feast. There will be so much blood, it will spill on the ground." The king grinned and rubbed his stomach. "My herds will grow so that I never hunger again. This is what I will do for my people. And I will leave a strong family for my son." He squeezed the boy by the waist and the child giggled.

"All well and good, but—" Gareth was interrupted by bustling at the cave entrance. The females returned leading three relatively young humans.

The king rose and intercepted them. He inspected the humans, noting that two had been fed from before. So he chose the third, a young man, and pushed him toward Gareth.

"Please, eat. None hunger in the house of Jaga."

Gareth was starving, in fact. The scent of blood had roused a fierce ache he struggled to repress, but he couldn't much longer. Here was a meal content with its fate. He whispered to the young man that he would be fine, which made no impact in the food's dull eyes. Gareth made his usual bite on the wrist and began to drink the blood that was thin and weak, not unlike some of the more decrepit herds in Europe, or similar to that of the lean times prior to the Great Killing when he had fed from the dying. The memory of it brought a scowl. There was no emotion to be read in this blood, no spice of fear or bitterness or hatred. The blood was bland, but at least it was plentiful. Gareth drank until he felt the boy's heart racing.

As he pulled his head away and stanched the flow, he saw Jaga feeding from one of the others on a spot above the shoulder. The king released his food and said, "Please, finish him."

Gareth shook his head. "I am full. Thank you."

Jaga sighed with relief that he wouldn't lose part of his herd to a greedy guest and sent the humans staggering out. "Very well, now tell me how you think you can help me defeat the Katangan army."

"It will be difficult. They have many guns."

"Guns? What are guns to me? Unless the Katangans have learned to fly, I'm not concerned."

"These new guns do great damage and fire rapidly. Have you faced a modern human army?"

"I have seen guns in the lowlands. It is no matter. Humans are slow and clumsy. Just as I knew you were about, I know every move the Katangans make. Soon I will guide them where I wish because humans are impatient and easily led. I will let them think their magnificent guns can turn us. They will be delighted by their power and come for me." Jaga chuckled at his cleverness. "I will draw them up into the mountains and then I will fall on them, and that will be the end."

Gareth nodded, feeling sickened by Jaga's plan. It played precisely on King Msiri's eagerness to close with the enemy, as well as on the king's overconfidence in his numbers and weapons. By their own admission, the humans had no idea of the terrain between their foothill camp and the Grand Boma. Their ranks could easily become bogged down and separated. A well-led and motivated vampire force, even as lean as these *ndoki*, could inflict terrible damage on the Katangans.

And Adele would be stuck there with the prey.

General Ngongo's Mountaineers lurked in the moss forest above an outlying *ndoki* camp. The wind whispered through the dripping glade below, creating weird wavering tapestries from the dangling moss. At least ten vampires had been seen coming and going over the course of the night, although there was also an open cave on the far edge of the glade. There was no clear sense of how many creatures might be inside. Now, as the sun sent weak light through the dampness, the vampires began to settle down to rest.

Adele lay on a thick pad of sodden lichen, peering over a ridgeline into the forest clearing. She could barely see the Katangan scouts hidden in the dense foliage, though she knew where they were. It had been a long, tense night as the Katangans crept into position around the enemy camp. She was exhausted and soaked, but the exhilaration from impending action kept her sharp.

Anhalt was on the damp ground next to her, continually shifting his gaze from the vampires to her. He was angry that she was with the Mountaineers on this reconnoitering mission, sure that she had come in hopes of finding Greyfriar, who had stomped off in a huff three days before.

In fact, Adele knew where Greyfriar was, and that was safely in her baggage. It was Gareth who was loose. The princess did not fear for his welfare at the hands of the local *ndoki*, but she was worried that he might fall under the Katangan guns while in the company of the vampires. She doubted he was here at this small encampment, though. He most likely was aiming for Jaga's boma.

Adele glanced at her colonel, whose face was covered with streaks of red, as was her own. Gorilla blood. The entire Mountaineer company of one hundred was coated in ape blood because they felt it hid their scent from the vampires. It was something she should verify with Gareth when she saw him. She smiled at Anhalt and he dourly acknowledged her. She felt something touch her hair. Then her arm. Raindrops. Before she could even think about it, she was in a downpour so thick she could see scant inches ahead.

General Ngongo rose to one knee and put his hands to his mouth. He emitted a weird, high-pitched scream that cut through the heavy thudding of the rain. It was the cry of a leopard. Then he whoofed several times, also a leopard sound. Moss piles detached themselves from the forest and began to move. Mountaineers. The calls were picked up down the line and soldiers rushed suddenly, rifles popping, toward the vampire camp.

Adele strained to see the forest glade with her spyglass through the slacking downpour. She could make out the creatures leaping to their feet. Several tried to rise into the air, but the hard rain pressed them down. Rifle fire peppered the drifting creatures and sent them flying. Some of the *ndoki* streaked at the troopers, who shouldered through the heavy moss curtain into the clearing. Rifles flashed. Vampires dropped, but sprang up and kept coming. In an instant, hand-to-hand combat began with claws, bayonets, and swords. Soldiers screamed and fell dead.

Then a second wave of vampires tumbled from the cave. Adele gasped; there must have been nearly twenty of them. High above the glade, Ngongo screeched again and a line of Mountaineers stood on a ridgeline fifty yards above the battle. They shouldered heavy double-barreled rifles and unleashed a thunderous volley at the new vampire wave. The boom echoed through the valley, and a curtain of smoke obscured the ridgeline despite the heavy rain. The shells tore horrific wounds in the creatures and slammed them into the mud.

"High-explosive elephant loads." Ngongo laughed, an unfamiliar sound, at least to Adele's ears. The Mountaineers were already slapping the breeches closed on their reloaded guns and raising them for another barrage.

The *ndoki* struggled. Those in front fell and writhed in the muck with gaping chests or spilling guts. Those in the rear hesitated, only to be pounded to the earth by the second assault of destructive steel. Unleashing shrill cries, they fell back. Vampires scrambled from the clearing, tearing through the moss in an attempt to flee. The Mountaineers let loose a third volley, and the explosive shells shredded moss, blasting trees and bamboo into shrapnel and sweeping several vampires off their feet.

The vampires who were battling the first wave of soldiers realized they had been abandoned by their fellows, so they too fled the field. The Katangans rallied at the sight of the *ndoki*'s backs, and gave pursuit. The pounding rain kept the vampires afoot. Several even stopped to feed desperately from fallen soldiers in an attempt to heal their vicious wounds. Their reward was a bayonet or sword either plunging into their rib cage or shattering their skull.

General Ngongo gave another strange call, and it too was carried down the line. Fire ceased along the ridgeline. The troopers in the glade began to pull back, grabbing their combat-inflamed comrades to keep them from racing headlong in pursuit, then being trapped far from support. As gunfire in the glade dwindled into silence, the soldiers broke into teams, some attending their own wounded while others executed injured vampires.

"Well done, General," Colonel Anhalt said.

"Thank you." Ngongo gave Princess Adele a helping hand off the wet ground. "These *ndoki* haven't seen such weapons in concentration. We gave them quite a start. I doubt they'll stop running till they reach old Jaga's boma."

Adele said, "They turned awfully quickly."

"Quite. There's no real fight in these things. Shall we inspect their camp, Your Highness?"

Adele made her way down the long, slippery path with the general, the colonel, and a bodyguard of Mountaineers and White Guard. She still felt uneasy about the fight. The Katangan firepower was undeniable, but vampires typically fought until they were in pieces. Perhaps Adele gave the *ndoki* too much credit and they simply weren't the fearsome killing machines humans had nightmares about in the north.

Once in the glade, she studied the cadavers of the *ndoki*, which were much scrawnier than vampires she saw in Europe. She stopped to offer words of thanks and encouragement to the Mountaineers. After she had spoken with every wounded man, she started toward the cave.

Anhalt appeared from the dark and held up a warning hand. "Your Highness, it's not for your eyes."

"My eyes have seen much, Colonel." She wondered if he would always be so protective of her. She hoped so.

Adele proceeded into the cave, where the stench was atrocious. Ngongo, along with several of his men and a few White Guard, stood looking at a group of twenty or so emaciated humans streaked with dried blood from festering wounds on their throats. There were some men, but mainly old women and several wide-eyed, stunted children. In the rear of the cave was a pile of bones and a few decaying corpses.

General Ngongo was tight-lipped and ashen. The soldiers all looked shaken by the scene of death and cruelty. Clearly most of them had never seen a vampire camp such as this. The general walked to the mound of bones and pronounced, "Remember this scene, gentlemen. This is our enemy. This is what we must wipe from the earth. This is why we will pay whatever price we must. Nothing we can do is too much to destroy this evil."

Adele stared into the vacant eyes of an emaciated little girl in the herd. In the girl's face there was no life and no future. Adele would speak to Msiri about arranging some help for her and the others regardless.

"Colonel Anhalt, if you will." Ngongo walked briskly from the cave, eager to be back to straightforward military work and away from the nastiness of clean-up. "We will send word to King Msiri. We have engaged the enemy and secured the pass. The way to the Grand Boma is clear and the army may advance."

CHAPTER 26

JAGA AND HIS skinny son perched on a ledge along with Gareth, studying the Katangan army far below, still days away.

"Have you been treated well?" the chief asked his guest.

Gareth nodded slowly.

"Good. Everyone is well fed. We will remember these days. We will never be hungry again." Jaga began to pace, nearly giddy with anticipation.

The long, meandering line of Katangan soldiers looked like a faltering stream flowing in and out of channels, breaking into pools and eddies, losing momentum, gathering itself and again surging forward. The vampire chief pointed down at the humans, instructing his son in their mysterious ways and giving the boy a sense of how terrain would be the enemy's undoing. The marshy valley, the sheer rock cliffs, and the obscuring mists would contribute to their downfall. All was as Jaga predicted. Victory and future security would soon follow.

Gareth watched the pair. He admired the solicitous nature of Jaga and his delight at his son's questions, which revealed a growing understanding of the hunt and the kill. King Dmitri had been much like that when Gareth was a boy and Dmitri was tall and broad, a powerful figure of wisdom and decision instead of the dribbling simpleton he had become. In his prime, Dmitri had been everything: ruler, hunter, and father. Gareth could recall the feeling of his father's rough hands on his shoulders, pointing at prey, explaining their actions, describing the dangers. They were watching a woman carrying wood not far from Inverness in Scotland. Gareth had expected Dmitri to strike the woman and then allow Gareth to feed, as usual.

"She'll stop long enough to adjust her bundle," his father had said. "Take her when she does."

Gareth had been a thin, gangly thing in rags. He had looked at his father. "Me?"

"You will no longer feed if you don't hunt." The powerful vampire had slid lower into the brush alongside the path. He'd lain a silencing hand on a wriggling young Cesare, who was bored and distracted by discomfort, but knew better than to disobey his father. Dmitri was scarred and leathery from hundreds of years of struggle, but his blue eyes had been quiet and expectant. His gaze had had a hopeful gleam that gave Gareth spirit.

He had studied the approaching woman with new eyes, the eyes of a hungry predator. He had watched Dmitri attack humans countless times. For all his bulk, his father was an elegant hunter, sly and economical in his motions. Many vampires preferred to slaughter their victims and then drink the cooling blood from the dead. Dmitri was not that type. He overwhelmed his targets with surprise and strength, terrifying them into shock. Often humans simply went limp when seized and bitten.

The young woman, a girl really, strolled the forest path. Her long skirt was wet along the hem from the dripping heather. The sun was nearly gone, yet she didn't hurry; there was no hint of fear in her. She hummed to herself as she swayed down the trail. The sweet smell of the day surrounded her.

Gareth sprang out suddenly and loped for her. The girl saw him; she didn't scream, although she did jump with surprise and drop her bundle of sticks. Gareth opened his mouth wide and protruded his claws as he made a long leap for his victim, far too long, as it turned out, because he landed short at her feet. He felt a solid thump against his head. He got up on his hands and knees as the girl raised a heavy stick over her head and brought it down with both hands onto Gareth's back, who splayed flat on the ground. She grunted with curses and unintelligible words as she clouted him again and again.

Gareth wasn't hurt; he was confused. She should have cowered before his terrifying visage. He scrambled back, hissing. Another blow cracked him across the face. He wanted to yell for her to stop, but his father was watching, unless he had already slipped away in shame. No, Dmitri was still nearby, because Gareth could hear him laughing.

Gareth managed to rise to his feet while easily blocking the girl's angry blows. He watched her in fascination now. She was fighting back. He could kill her easily, but she didn't give up.

Suddenly a dark shape appeared behind the girl. Her eyes grew wide, then blank. Gareth heard her last breath as her heart fluttered to a stop and she slumped to the wet ground. His eyes rose from the perpetually startled face of the dead girl to the derisive snarl of his brother, Cesare.

"Why did you kill her?" Gareth snapped.

"Because you couldn't." Cesare knelt and tore her throat with his teeth. He began to suck blood from the gaping wound.

Gareth charged and bowled his smaller brother into the mud. Shouting, he raked his claws deep across Cesare's face, trying to gouge that smug smile from his skull. Gareth fought with a fury that shame gave him, and with rage at his brother for making him look ineffectual in front of their father. Cesare was far smaller, and he cried and thrashed, trying to escape. Gareth felt a vise seize his neck, and Cesare's snarling form dropped away from him. He realized he was suspended in the air with feet dangling.

"Gareth!" Dmitri shook his son.

"She was mine!" Gareth shouted. "She wasn't hurting me. I could've taken her! He killed her!"

Cesare yelled, "You failed, Gareth! I saved you from her!"

"Quiet!" Dmitri slammed a foot against Cesare's chest and pressed him back into the dirt. "I told you to kill only if necessary."

"It was necessary," Cesare argued angrily. "Gareth was being beaten."

"I'll kill you!" Gareth tried to pull free from his father's grasp.

Dmitri tossed Gareth aside, who tumbled, then came to his feet. The king pointed at the boy. "You did fail."

Shocked, Gareth stood with open mouth. "But . . . I didn't want to kill her. Like you said."

"She saw you coming. Clumsy and pathetic."

Cesare started to speak again, but Dmitri squashed the air from him with his boot. Then the king glanced at the dead girl and back at Gareth. "Feed. Before it's wasted."

"No." Gareth surprised himself. He took an involuntary step back, expecting his father to lash out at him. "I won't. Let Cesare feed. It's his kill."

The king hesitated, then with his eyes still locked on Gareth, lifted his foot off Cesare. The younger prince laughed and scuttled for the body. The blood was now pooling, and he began to lap at it.

"Waste." Dmitri turned his back and walked away. "That is what will destroy us all."

Gareth had refused to look at his brother when he fell into step behind the mountainous Dmitri. He never wanted to disappoint his father again. Now another gangly son stared at his father with the same rapturous attention as Jaga talked about the wind, the scents, the reactions of humans. Jaga fixed his claws and demonstrated a killing strike. His son replicated it. Gareth knew how the boy felt. His father knew everything. The boy would never feel so secure in his world as he did at this moment.

Jaga patted the boy on the shoulder and sent him back toward the boma. The child scampered lightly over the rocks and disappeared. Now Gareth and Jaga were alone. Save for the moaning wind, the cliff was empty. It was time.

Gareth straightened and moved soundlessly across the barren rocks toward Jaga. The chief of the Rwenzori turned and beamed at him. He seized Jaga by the throat. The chief looked surprised, as if this were some peculiar greeting of the British clan he wasn't familiar with. He started to speak, but Gareth pushed his claws into Jaga's neck and cut off his air. Jaga struck out desperately, raking him across the chest, but not deep enough. Gareth twisted the chief's head and reached up to strike.

A heavy weight locked Gareth's upraised arm into place.

Jaga's son clung to his forearm with needle-sharp claws. The boy had returned. With a snarl, he sank his teeth deep and tried to tear Gareth's arm loose from his father's throat. Gareth flung the boy down and instinctively drew back a clawed hand to finish him.

But he froze.

Jaga surged forward, snapping at Gareth's throat. The prince felt another thud on his shoulder and prepared to sling the boy away again. This time, he glimpsed the ferocious face of one of Jaga's warrior wives. She yanked Gareth around and smashed a blow into his nose. He grunted as a clawed hand raked his back. He tried to keep his hold on Jaga, but more hands clutched and tore at him. His vision blurred with a rain of blows, claws, and gnashing teeth. Red blood. Dark hands.

Gareth fought back, driving a fist into an amazon's chest. He grabbed an arm and broke it, then gouged a face, barely missing a vicious claw to his own eyes. Gareth sought Jaga amid all the flashing bodies. The chief had to die. That would make Adele safe, and only then could Gareth worry about escape.

He caught sight of the rangy Rwenzori king outside the ring of warrior women. Gareth flew for him, but an amazon appeared. He blocked her strike, dug his claws beneath her windpipe, and ripped. She gurgled, spinning to the ground, never to rise again, as blood sprayed.

Gareth readied a leap for Jaga, but instead found himself toppling to the ground as if his legs had vanished. A quick glance back showed his right leg in shreds. He felt no pain, but he couldn't raise his leg up to take his weight. One of the wives had cut his tendon. He tried to rise on the other leg, but a heavy pressure dropped onto his back, and the two remaining females pushed him into the dirt.

No, no, no! he thought in terror. He couldn't fail. Not now.

"Hold him!" Jaga shouted.

Strong hands slammed Gareth's face against the rocks and pressed him down flat. Then his head was yanked up by the hair so he could see Jaga kneel before him.

"Why?" Jaga asked with genuine confusion. "Why did you do this?"

Gareth futilely tested the strength of his captors rather than responding.

One of the amazons said through clenched teeth while holding her captive steady, "Kill him. He is dangerous."

"No," Jaga replied quietly. "He is an ally from the clan of Dmitri. I can't kill him. I must have allies. To kill him would make me look poor and weak on the eve of battle. I will hold him captive until after the battle. Perhaps the clan of Dmitri will pay for him."

The amazons growled between themselves and smashed Gareth's head against the ground again before lifting him up. Jaga touched the grievously wounded third wife, who was breathing her last. He shook his head in dismay as his son joined him and placed a tentative hand on his father's shoulder.

"You ate my food!" Jaga glared at Gareth. "And you try to kill me in front of my son! What sort of monster are you?"

CHAPTER 27

Flay paced nervously, her boot heels cracking off the floor of Buckingham Palace. She was donned now in a European frock coat and riding pants. She had given her report on the attack in Alexandria to Stryon, who would repeat it verbatim to Prince Cesare. She now waited for the prince to arrive; his reaction would tell her everything about her future. She had rarely felt such uncertainty in her nearly four hundred years of life, because she had never been out of favor before.

Flay hadn't given the truest account of events in Victoria Palace, and the mere fact that Senator Clark still lived was an indictment. The vile man had been in her reach, but she hadn't been able to end his life. She was content with the fact that she may have returned to London only to be killed. She could have fled to another clan and begged for service, but life as an exile wasn't honorable. Not for she who once had been the most powerful war chief in Europe.

A massive door swung open, and she caught a glimpse of Stryon before Prince Cesare appeared with a smile. "Flay. Come. We have much to plan."

Without evident emotion, she began to fall into her familiar place beside the prince. As he turned, Flay saw with alarm that the ghostly Lady Hallow walked alongside Cesare. The pale creature gave a haughty smile and refused to give way, forcing Flay to follow a few steps behind.

Flay glared at Lady Hallow's well-shaped back. That spot beside Cesare was Flay's by right. This highborn female had hovered around the clan royal family for centuries and had been discussed as a likely candidate for queen. Everyone knew Prince Gareth had fancied her once. They had appeared to be the future of the clan, the great king and his brilliant queen. But it ended for reasons no one in the clan seemed to know. Flay had always wondered what Gareth could see in this willowy thing. Hallow's smug reserve infuriated her. This creature showed no emotion or desire, yet had men fawning over her. Flay still felt the humiliation of throwing herself at Gareth several months ago, offering to give him Cesare's head on a tray, before being rebuffed. No doubt, however, if Gareth knew Hallow had returned to London, he would rush here to see her.

Cesare spoke as if his former war chief had never been sent away in shame. "There's a great deal to tell you, Flay, but the most important is that the Undead are battle ready. It's fortuitous you've returned, because I want you to go immediately to oversee their attack."

"Of course, my lord."

"I'm assured we have a squadron of flyable airships, somewhere near fifty. You will have half of them for this mission. There are a few in Portsmouth, and more on the French coast. I have moved Undead in preparation for your return. You will coordinate with General Montrose."

Flay tried not to sneer.

Cesare continued smoothly, "You have no qualms working with these humans, do you?"

"No, my lord."

"Excellent. I would prefer General Montrose survive the attack—he has been useful—but if it doesn't work out, I can find another like him."

"As you will, my lord."

Cesare paused before an open balcony, taking in the smells of London, letting the cool night breeze ruffle his clothes, as Lady Hallow waited patiently like a favorite pup. Flay studied Cesare for signs of anger due to her lack of total success in Alexandria; the young prince was a creature of vengeance, but he seemed completely satisfied. He would certainly never praise her—that wasn't his way—but there was no recrimination in his tone. She didn't sense he was waiting to attack her. Flay began to shed her nervousness and felt like the clan war chief again.

"About Senator Clark," Cesare said quietly, and Flay's heart sank. He didn't face her, preferring to stare over the dark cityscape. "Your inability to kill him is troubling; however, as it turns out, it is now a boon for me. With Princess Adele run off with Greyfriar"—Cesare laughed at the thought—"and Emperor Constantine dead, Clark is a nonentity in Equatoria. It's better that the vicious brute is alive to poison the relationship between Equatoria and America rather than dying a martyr. So events couldn't be better."

Flay stayed silent.

Cesare turned his sharp eyes on her. "And it also turns out very fortunate you never managed to kill Greyfriar. Because if he were dead, who would have carried the princess into oblivion then? It's gratifying when humans do my work for me. Tell me, what did you think of Lord Kelvin?"

"Not much," Flay replied. "Kelvin stinks of weakness."

"Hm. He is a valuable source of information to me. And as one of the great men of Equatoria, he can guide the actions of that government however I see fit."

"Why does he serve you? He seems to have all the power he could desire in his homeland."

"Funny story." Cesare smiled at Hallow. "He fears the ruin of Equatoria. He believes a war with the clans will break his empire once and for all and end his own grasp on power. And he thinks he can use me. But once I've used him to break the human states into pieces, I'll kill him."

Flay said, "I would be happy to do that. I despise traitors."

"Yes?" Cesare raised a curious eyebrow. "Noted. However, for the moment let's discuss the coming attack. Success will go well with you, Flay. I'm inclined to appoint you war chief again, but I want to see you use my Undead as a weapon."

"It shall be done, my lord." Flay bowed and flicked her gaze at Lady Hallow, wondering with suppressed rage if this was just the next in a long list of miracles she would have to accomplish before she was accepted once more.

Days later, Flay stood at the rail of the creaking airship. The sails over her head were poorly unfurled and flapped themselves ragged in the thunderous wind. Other ships in the sky around her were in a similar slovenly condition, although they were visible in the dark only by a few faint lights that blinked like eyes as the fleet wallowed through dense piles of clouds. Flay would be lucky if these dismal airmen didn't slam the ships together and plunge the splintered fleet into the ocean below, sending all these ridiculous Undead to watery graves.

General Montrose stood with his human officers on the quarterdeck, listening to a report from one of his men. The general gave a perfunctory salute and moved toward Flay. As he crossed the deck, he actually put his foot through a rotten plank and fell in up to the knee. He pulled his leg free and brushed off the dust. Flay shook her head.

Montrose said, "Madam War Chief, I am ready to signal the fleet to attack. I believe the weather is favorable."

"Shut your mouth," Flay said. "I'll tell you when the weather is favorable. Go back over there, and if you speak to me again unbidden, you will die."

The general looked as if he were contemplating a retort, which would have ended in his bloody slaughter at Flay's hand. Instead, he saluted and withdrew. The officer hardly seemed chagrined by the vampire's hatred. Instead he appeared excited and rejuvenated by her scorn, assuming he would soon be like her. The Undead all wore their feeding wounds like badges of honor.

Airborne figures appeared in the clouds. Vampires circled the small airship and caught onto the rigging, scrambling down to Flay. She stared up expectantly at these members of her revived special command, the Pale, Cesare's private militia.

"It's good," one said. "The temperature is dropping. Winds are heavy inshore. No rain. There are no vessels aloft and their fleet is tethered."

Flay nodded and snapped her fingers in the direction of General Montrose. His head swiveled quickly as the war chief gave him an affirmative gesture. The general saluted her again and began to shout orders. In a moment, two guns fired and then two more. A nearby ship also fired four guns, and the signal was taken up and carried throughout the shadowy squadron. The wretched ships did their best to maneuver with ripped sails, rotten yards, and poorly trained crews. The vessels struggled in the wind as they vented gas to begin their descents. Montrose and his officers moved to the foredeck to watch the other ships drop lower. They all gave brisk salutes to their departing comrades in the surrounding vessels. Their ship dropped from the slate clouds to find itself barely a mile and a half above the choppy Atlantic. Far ahead, the fleet drove toward distant lights on a speck of land.

Flay turned to watch. She could see the cliffs of Gibraltar in the distance and the glow of the imperial airbase crowded with ships. Mooring towers sprouted like a new forest from the rocky soil, with ships of all sizes tethered tight to them against the coming storm. Masts were shipped, and the vessels were packed dirigible to dirigible.

Flay smiled. Just as in Alexandria, Equatorians simply couldn't conceive of the idea that they weren't safe inside their own territory. Here they were basking in the Mediterranean warmth of Gibraltar, preparing for war, content that the clans could never reach out to them this far south. She had to admit, Cesare was often brilliant. He had bungled Princess Adele's capture because he'd been more afraid of his brother, Gareth, than anything else. However, since that failure, he had set in motion the pieces to successfully outmaneuver Gareth, decapitate Equatoria, and spread terror in Alexandria. Now he was launching a completely unexpected blow against the enemy's greatest weapon—their magnificent air fleet.

The Undead's decrepit airships foundered and listed, but continued gamely on. Inevitably, two ships flew too close to each other and masts shattered. Over the cracking of wooden yards, Flay's sensitive ears picked up a deep thumping sound, and flashes appeared on distant Gibraltar. The enemy had spotted the approaching fleet and opened fire with shore batteries. But it was too late.

Flay said, "General, you may welcome the fleet as our brethren." And she laughed.

Montrose laughed too, mistaking her sentiment for sincerity. New signal guns boomed from Flay's airship. She arched her neck to watch her ships close in on the Equatorian base. Minutes dragged on, and she tightened her grip on a ratline with growing anger at the delay.

Then the first Undead airship exploded in greenish flame. Flay exhaled in relief because she knew the blast was not the result of enemy cannon fire, but the crew's own hands. A second airship blossomed in a mushroom of fire, and then a third and fourth. One clan ship after another flamed bright green and red as the Undead set their ships' buoyancy gases alight. The Undead continued piloting the burning vessels to their targets even as they were consumed by fire. Soon, a swarm of twenty giant, blistering pyres descended on Gibraltar.

The first fireship crashed against the trapped Equatorian fleet, throwing up a plume of roaring flame. The others followed, unleashing a fresh wave of explosions across the crowded airfield, tinting the dark sky red. Airships blew apart, spewing fountains of fire and flaming debris. Gibraltar was soon shrouded in flame and oily vapors.

Flay scanned the burning disaster zone from the deck of her ship. She saw very few Equatorian ships that had escaped damage; most were burning or blasted to pieces. Bodies littered the ground in a hellish scene of flame and wreckage. People ran to escape or to help.

"Kill anyone you see!" she screeched to her Pale, who clung in the rigging like crows. "Do not destroy their telegraph lines. We want news of this to spread quickly." Then she said to General Montrose, "We will kill the survivors on the ground. Make your way back to England, if you are able."

Montrose looked crestfallen. "Yes, Madam War Chief. Soon our brave men will rise to be with you. I only wish I had been among them."

"I wish you had too, General." Flay lifted into the wind and followed her pack for what promised to be a delicious slaughter. She'd like to see the precious Lady Hallow perform this duty for Cesare. There was a war coming and the prince needed warriors. He would soon realize that demure porcelain keepsake could never serve him as Flay could. It would be like the old days again.

"The Western Squadron is gone." The newly promoted Colonel Eskandari's face was pale and drawn.

"Define *gone*," Lord Kelvin said, setting down his teacup.

"Our base on Gibraltar has been attacked and the air fleet destroyed, or virtually so. Ten ships of the line were based there. Twenty-five destroyers. Nearly fifty frigates and sloops of war. Most are destroyed utterly. Fewer than ten ships are fit to sail. The squadron is left with only HMS *Damascus* as a main battleship. Over half the garrison was killed."

Lord Aden sat forward with a stunned look. "But . . . how is that possible?"

"Fireships, my lord. A group of derelict airships were flown to Gibraltar, set alight, and driven into the fleet, which had been locked down for expected hard weather."

"Fireships? Is this the sixteenth century? Was it the Legionnaires?"

"No, sir. Vampires. A pack struck the base during rescue and relief operations. It was a massacre."

Aden turned to Kelvin with mouth agape. "But . . . vampires don't fly airships."

"Bloodmen," Eskandari replied bitterly. "The fireships had human crews. Apparently, they set their own vessels on fire and flew them until they were consumed alive by flame. None survived to question."

"How extraordinary," Lord Kelvin said with an impressed purse of his lips. His bland tone belied his true shock at the import of the event. He'd had no hint from his northern associates that such an attack was planned, nor had they sought his approval for such an action. That was completely unacceptable.

The colonel shook his head. "We've never seen bloodmen perform such complex or devoted duties in service to their masters. The base was taken completely by surprise."

Kelvin paused to consider. "I should think the base commander, General Von Holst, is in line for a severe reprimand."

"General Von Holst is dead, my lord," Eskandari said.

"Is he? In that case, I shall submit the paperwork for him to receive the Equatorian Cross and the Order of Imperial Honor, posthumously."

"My companies built most of those ships," Lord Aden said, drumming his fingers on the mahogany chair arm while crossing and uncrossing his long legs. "I don't mind telling you, I'm in shock. Our Western Squadron shattered. And here we are just recovering from a murderous assault by vampires in the streets of Alexandria, and the assassination of Emperor Constantine by their hand. Had anyone any idea that the clans were capable of mounting such attacks?"

"We were sadly complacent, I fear," Kelvin said.

Aden said anxiously, "The War Committee in Commons should meet and hear a full report. All these new wrinkles in clan tactics are terrifying. And our factories must go on a war footing to replace what was lost, Mr. Prime Minister."

Kelvin stiffened slightly and cleared his throat. "I have revived the old title of khedive, Lord Aden. I am properly addressed as such, or Kelvin Pasha."

"My apologies." Aden rolled his eyes with an exasperated sigh.

"No matter. I agree with you that we must address these new developments. I feel certain the War Committee will recommend that we shelve any plans for a northern offensive this year. I believe the new General Staff will concur, once I appoint them." Kelvin took a thoughtful pause, then said, "War is inadvisable at this time. The Empire is conflicted at present and the people are agitated. Our alliance with the Americans is in some question. I warned the emperor last year that war in the north was not in the best interest of Equatoria. I believe we would be better served to attend to our own affairs and leave the vampires to their frozen kingdom and their mindless herds of once-men."

"If I may," Colonel Eskandari said in a voice unable to conceal his anger at both the massacre and the politics that greeted it, "I believe that Senator Clark made several valid points warning against postponing an offensive and allowing the clans time to bolster their defenses."

Kelvin gave the marine a long, cold stare. "Thank you, Colonel. As my chief military liaison, I will send for you to report to the War Committee later today. I will also expect you to confine your comments to the events on Gibraltar. You may go."

"Yes, Kelvin Pasha." Eskandari saluted brusquely and left the room.

The two great men of the Empire sat in silence as the ever-present army of clerks streamed in and out. Kelvin set about making notes in excellent penmanship for a dispatch to the new chairman of the War Committee, his good friend Tarik Karami, the member for Beyrut. Lord Aden tapped his foot nervously on the teak tiles.

Finally, Aden reiterated, "Who could have seen this coming?"

"No one, I'm sure. Certainly not the valiant General Von Holst, evidently."

The young magnate watched the clerks shuffling about the room. "It makes you think. About vampire capabilities, I mean. Have we completely underestimated Cesare and his ilk?"

"Collect yourself, my lord." Lord Kelvin finished writing a sentence, then set down his pen precisely and said in a measured tone, "The news is disturbing and your agitation on behalf of our Empire does you credit, but please consider your position." His eyes flicked to the many young professionals who didn't seem to be paying attention to their betters, but no doubt were.

Aden slid a finger along his thin mustache. "Quite right, Mr. Prime . . . Kelvin Pasha. I concur with everything you have said about the war. I'm merely surprised by the attack on Gibraltar. A terrible waste." He drew a cigarette case from his waistcoat and offered one to Kelvin, who for once accepted. "And the people, of course. In Gibraltar and here in Alexandria. So many innocents dead. It seems . . . sinful."

"Dreadful times," the prime minister grunted in agreement and slipped the Turkish cigarette between his lips. Only he noticed the slight tremble in his fingers.

CHAPTER 28

SENATOR CLARK PACED his luxurious prison; even rooms as lavish and spacious as these still stank of confinement and fanned his rage. The Equatorians had created one impediment after another for him since he had come to this city. The whole of the Empire had plotted against him, from that insipid girl to her penny dreadful boyfriend to the insufferable Prime Minister Kelvin. Their audacity made Clark's blood boil to the point that he could contemplate war with Equatoria. His friendship had been spat upon. It seemed the only one who ever had any intention of joining Equatoria with the American Republic was Emperor Constantine, and he was dead, leaving Clark alone to sort through the mess.

Clark abruptly halted and spun toward Stoddard. "You say *Ranger*'s gas bags are being filled?"

"Yes, sir. As we speak." Stoddard replied. "They also allowed the full crew aboard. I can only assume they are readying us for departure."

"Departure! You mean expulsion! Kelvin has held me here for weeks while he shored up his hold on the government. I'll be damned if some political weasel is going to steal my title of emperor." A sudden knock on the door made Clark snarl. "Enter," he shouted, "at your own risk."

The aforementioned weasel stepped in, flanked by six Persian marines. Clark sneered at the cowardly man, approaching Lord Kelvin with no fear of the soldiers. "Come to gloat, have we?"

"No need," Kelvin said calmly. "It is merely a sad state of affairs that has led to this. You will be happy to learn that the Equatorian-American alliance is still strong despite the late unpleasantness. Your presence is requested back in the Americas posthaste. We shan't detain you from your duties."

"Mark me, Prime Minister, my duties have recently expanded. A number of items have been repositioned at the very top of my to-do list." He stared pointedly at Lord Kelvin.

"I have revived the old position of khedive, and surrendered the post of prime minister. That said, we're all busy, I'm sure. I'll keep you no longer. Your baggage has been loaded onto your vessel. What has been overlooked will be shipped to you at a later date." Kelvin turned to the guards behind him. "Escort the senator to USS *Ranger* so they may be on their way."

The marines snapped to attention. "When you are ready, Senator."

"I'm more than ready to leave this godforsaken place." Clark stalked past the Persian soldiers, Major Stoddard at his heels.

Within the hour, the dirigible on *Ranger* was ready to sail and the frigate was held fast only by the tether lines to the Pharos One tower. There was no grand farewell ceremony, and Kelvin was not present to spout some pompous rhetoric, for which Clark was relieved. He might have been forced to open fire on the miserable little eel.

The senator looked down toward the shining Victoria Palace that should have been his by rights. His eyes narrowed, not due to the sun's glare, but at the thought of Princess Adele's betrayal. Even so, the girl seemed to be his only way back to Equatoria. Only Adele could make this disaster right and give him what he deserved.

"Make ready!" Clark shouted. "Release the mooring lines!"

The ship listed as she was freed, and Clark shifted his feet to keep himself steady. The mooring tower slipped away, and as soon as *Ranger* was clear, he moved beside Stoddard.

"Heading, sir?"

Clark grinned malevolently.

The American ship lifted into the azure sky. The warm Mediterranean winds filled the sails of the vessel as it arced out over the water.

Lord Kelvin breathed out slowly so that no one nearby could hear his sigh of relief. He also withheld the satisfied smile now that this final piece of the puzzle was in place.

Kelvin turned to go back to his comforting mountain of paperwork, but Colonel Eskandari beside him coughed and gestured to the north. To the khedive's amazement, *Ranger* was coming about. Eyes narrowed against the glare of the sun, and Kelvin wondered aloud, "What is that lunatic American doing now?"

"I don't like it," Eskandari said. "The man is capable of anything. Should I alert the shore batteries, sir?"

"What does he think he can accomplish?" murmured Kelvin. "Does he really think any rash act could win the day?"

"Should I alert the shore batteries, sir?" Eskandari repeated forcefully, pointing out, "*Ranger* is on course for the palace."

Lord Kelvin shook his head, ignoring the startled words from the colonel. Most likely the American was just grandstanding, as he was wont to do, in hopes of frightening them. If so, the senator was sorely mistaken.

Eskandari stated more succinctly, "If we allow *Ranger* to close and then Clark opens fire, civilians will be in danger, sir."

"I'm well aware of that, Colonel. They would die by Clark's hand, not mine."

"That was not my point, sir." Eskandari fumed, dark eyes staring like granite at the khedive.

Kelvin ignored his military commander. Even if the American did open fire, it would buy him nothing. Whatever love the Equatorians still harbored for the brash and outlandish foreigner would be erased by the death of innocent civilians. And Kelvin would be more than happy to contact the American government to inform them that Clark had gone rogue. It would cement Kelvin's plan to prevent Clark from infringing on his claim as the regent. He waited with interest to witness the American's next move and wondered if the unusual excitement fluttering in his chest was how all generals felt on the glorious battlefield.

—✺—

Ranger moved swiftly like the predator she was. Her speed was well beyond safety protocols for maneuvering within populated airspace, but Clark did not care. They had only precious minutes for what he had in mind before the Equatorians came to their senses. Numerous cannons were ready to blast them from the sky, but not surprisingly, Kelvin didn't have the guts to open fire.

The frigate swooped so low over the Ras el-Tin that Clark could actually see Kelvin's sudden frightened expression before he ducked into an alcove off one of the palace balconies. *Ranger* aimed for the east wing of the palace, which was rushing toward them at alarming speed.

Abruptly, Clark shouted, "Hard alee!"

Tether hooks were fired to starboard as the crew grabbed hold of something solid. Iron claws grappled stone ledges and steam pipes, which groaned from the massive weight they suddenly held. Some structures crumpled or snapped, but many held fast. Sails luffed and the ship heeled hard over, screeching from the strain. Men were thrown to the deck or staggered violently, but none stayed down long and all rushed back to their stations.

"Over the sides!" Clark pulled a chemical mask over his face, grabbed a line, and jumped overboard. Major Stoddard was close behind with a squad of Rangers as they landed on a balcony. Disengaging from the lines, they surged into the palace. Startled civil servants and dignitaries scrambled out of the way, confused and alarmed at the sight of armed commandos. Most likely they thought vampires had been spotted in the city again.

The Americans raced down several flights of stairs and plunged deep into the dungeons without slowing. Two Persian guards at the end of the hall barely had time to look up before flash grenades sailed at them, letting off startling bright explosions and spraying tendrils of chemicals.

Greenish smoke filled the hall. Clark and Stoddard barreled into the Persians, hurling them to the ground with the butts of their rifles.

"Damn, that felt good," Clark exclaimed in a muffled voice as he pulled keys from a marine's belt.

"This looks to be the right place, sir." Stoddard replied. "According to what I heard."

Clark threw open the door. "Schoolteacher!"

The room was dark, and for a moment Clark worried that he had made a mistake. Then he saw the figure in the center of the room, bent and chained. "Damn me. I never thought Kelvin was man enough to do this."

Stoddard spun and signaled for the ship's carpenter. The brawny man entered with a bag of tools.

"Strike those shackles," Clark ordered. "And fast."

The man set to work and in a few minutes tossed the chains aside. Stoddard pulled down his gasmask and knelt before Mamoru, staring into his half-closed eyes. The samurai recognized the American and raised his eyebrows.

"Can you stand?" Stoddard asked. "Or do we need to carry you?"

"Where am I going?" Mamoru asked.

Senator Clark grinned. "I'm leaving and I'm taking you with me."

Mamoru nodded as he flexed his raw hands. "What do you hope to accomplish?"

"What I started out to do. I aim to have a bride." Clark enjoyed the look of astonishment that briefly flitted across the samurai's face. "Did you think I would just give up? That ain't the way I do things."

"It *ain't*?" Mamoru mocked, and painfully stretched his legs. "Well, I expected nothing less from you."

An amused smirk emerged on Clark's face. "Glad you think so, schoolteacher, since my plan hinges on you."

Mamoru's eyes narrowed. "In what way?"

"You found Adele for me in London. You'll find her again, won't you?" It wasn't a question. Clark's stare had turned hard as he waited for the schoolteacher to realize he had no other recourse.

"I see," replied Mamoru quietly. "I assume you have your ship."

"Right outside. Now, can you walk or not?"

"I can." The samurai stood on unsteady legs. His torso was a map of dried blood and ropey scars. He pulled his robe up over his shoulders with a wince. "Shall we? I have an interest in finding my student, as I suspect she has been sorely lacking the proper curriculum of late."

Clark gave Stoddard an unusual glance of admiration for the samurai's pure toughness. It was hard not to respect a man who could withstand the punishment he had obviously taken.

The unlikely allies had departed the cell and ascended to the main floor of the palace when an armed contingent rounded the opposite corner. The Americans fell against the walls, slipping into shallow doorways, and opened fire immediately, sending the Equatorian guards scrambling for cover.

"Dammit!" Clark shouted. "I don't want to kill a bunch of Equatorians, but—"

"Where is your ship?" Mamoru yelled over the staccato gunfire.

"Moored to the southeast corner of the palace."

"Come." Mamoru veered left down a short hallway, moving with amazing speed and surety. Clark and the others followed, still laying down cover fire.

It wasn't long before Clark grabbed Mamoru's arm. "You're going the wrong way, schoolteacher. We want to escape, not visit that pompous ass Kelvin in the royal chambers. My ship is back that way."

"This is the way out. Trust me, Senator."

Clark glowered at the samurai but then laughed abruptly. "You better know where you're going."

Mamoru began to feel around the wall, pressing bricks until finally there was a click. A narrow door slid aside with a quiet rumble of counterweights and pulleys. Mamoru waited for an exclamation of surprise from the senator, but instead found the man grinning from ear to ear while gesturing for the samurai to continue to lead.

"Schoolteacher, my ass," Clark said as the Rangers entered the once-hidden cleft in the wall. "The Equatorians sure love their damned secret passages. It must be their leading industry."

The door rumbled closed and pitched them into darkness. Behind them could be heard the marching feet of a passing patrol. Mamoru's hand fumbled for a switch on the stone wall. A snap and a subsequent hiss accompanied the eerie glow of chemical lights as they slowly illuminated one by one down the empty tunnel. The samurai slipped through the passageway, but Senator Clark had to twist his broad American shoulders to fit, as did some of the Rangers.

There were numerous offshoot tunnels from the main passage, and it wouldn't have taken much effort to lose the men if Mamoru had wanted, a fact that Clark realized as he increased his stride to keep close to the schoolteacher. They passed through a series of ancient tombs piled with mummies so desiccated that withered limbs protruded through crumbling linen. A tunnel soon angled up and the group emerged into the hot sun. *Ranger* was anchored to the nearby palace wall.

The senator checked his watch. It had been barely fifteen minutes since the rescue began. They needed to move; even with Kelvin's inaction, the Equatorians would start to make trouble soon. He didn't particularly want to shoot his way out of Alexandria. The Rangers smoothly covered all angles as they started across the lawn toward drop lines that fell from the frigate.

Clark laughed as they ran. "I'm not sure what to make of you, schoolteacher. I just hope you can find my wife."

"I can. But my methods are not your methods."

"As long as they work." *And*, Clark thought, *As long as I control them.*

CHAPTER 29

NGONGO'S MOUNTAINEERS CREPT toward the top of a rock-strewn ridge. They moved slowly, rustling with heavily scented plants stuffed into their belts and headbands. They were also smeared with gorilla blood again, except for King Msiri, who was daubed with the blood of a leopard as befit his station.

General Ngongo signaled for the men to halt, then pointed back to King Msiri and Adele and motioned them forward. She scrambled up as quickly as she could, with Anhalt in tow, and the king breathing heavily with expectation beside her. Cresting the rise, they peered down the other side. The ground sloped away for fifty yards, then suddenly disappeared into a crevasse of misty nothingness. The edge was connected to a distant plateau by a simple rope bridge, a single foot line and two hand lines.

Adele had expected to find an ancient fortress or walled city. She had assumed the Katangans would have to lay siege to their target. However, Jaga's Grand Boma was just an empty plateau, several hundred yards across, surrounded on three sides by sheer cliffs pockmarked with caves and crevices. All of it was empty. No vampires. No humans. The caves stood silent, like blank eyes in a monster's head.

"Where are they?" Msiri looked expectantly at Adele as if she could discern some intelligence from the scene. "They must be here. We must bring this campaign to an end. We are badly undersupplied now. We cannot sustain ourselves in these mountains."

"I don't know." Adele wondered what the queen mother had told Msiri about her abilities. Adele's limited geomantic training was not enough to determine their enemy's location. Flicking down her chemical goggles, she scanned the boma. "They could be hiding in the caves. I don't even see any sign of humans. I don't smell fires. The vampires are either hiding or they fled. Surely we haven't taken them by surprise. They certainly knew we were coming."

Msiri said, "I will have the boma. If Jaga is there, I will kill him. If he is not, I will find him. I will build a permanent base here. Jaga's mountains are mine now."

Without taking his eyes off the empty plateau, General Ngongo said, "We'll cross to the boma and clear it." He slid back down toward the gathering army.

Soon, Mountaineers with rifles strapped to their backs began to struggle up the hill carrying heavy coils of rope with grappling hooks and what looked like mortars. They topped the rise and slid down the far side, gathering at the edge of the crevasse. The men fixed ropes to the hooks and then loaded the grapples into the mortars. They fired the hooks in a barrage of booming puffs of smoke and the lines slithered across the chasm, slamming down on the other side. The Mountaineers took up their ends of the ropes and pulled them taut, if they could. Most of the grapples slid over the rocky ground and plummeted into the ravine. Pulled back up, they were fired again while those lines that held fast were fixed to anchors on this side.

Msiri rose to his feet. Adele and Anhalt exchanged glances as the king slid down the hill and went toward the swaying rope bridge.

"Is he crossing first?" Adele breathed, lifting her goggles.

"It appears so," the colonel said with alarm and respect. "At least in the first wave."

At the same time, other Mountaineers took up positions on the ridgeline with their murderous heavy, double-barreled rifles. As the troopers raised guns to their shoulders, their sights on the plateau, Msiri stood at the place where the rope bridge was tenuously tied off to a gnarled tree, as well as two rusty spikes driven, perhaps decades ago, into the fractured rock. He waited as soldiers repaired and strengthened the anchor points. General Ngongo pulled on each rope with all his strength and then nodded to his king.

Adele slipped down to the edge of the crevasse next to Msiri. The wind battered everyone, fluttering Msiri's heavy cloak and plume. The gale pushed her with such force she had to lean against the wind as she peered over the side onto cloud tops far below. The king looked calm, even casual, and seemed eager for the adventure. The troops smiled and chatted, obviously proud of their leader. It was an amazing and useful example for Adele, though she still thought it foolhardy.

She said, "Good luck, Your Majesty."

Msiri laughed. "Oh, I don't need luck. My mother assured me you would guarantee success. With you here, I cannot die."

"She said that?"

He waved his hand. "More or less. She can be vague."

The princess said, "Prophecy or not, your bravery is prodigious to walk this bridge first. I can't believe you would take that risk."

Msiri furrowed his brow. "I'm not taking the risk. You are."

"What? Me?"

"No!" Leaping in front of Adele, Colonel Anhalt nearly threw her to the ground. "Absolutely not! This is complete nonsense! You have the Mountaineer Brigade. Let them cross."

"It must be Princess Adele," the king replied calmly. "It is what my mother dreamed. The princess must set foot on Jaga's boma first to ensure victory."

"I just remember something about hyenas," Adele remarked.

Anhalt spun and gazed gravely into Adele's eyes. "You must refuse. This is too much. The vampires are obviously baiting a trap."

The princess looked down again into the abyss, her voice holding only a slight tremor. "I can't refuse if the king requests it. We owe him."

Anhalt's dark visage froze in horror. "I beg you, no."

"It isn't that far across. I reckon twenty, thirty feet."

"Fifty meters, Highness," General Ngongo said flatly.

"Oh really? So far?" Adele laughed nervously. She desperately wanted to refuse, but couldn't. The queen mother's mystic visions had convinced Msiri that Adele was required for success. Although they couldn't physically force her to traverse the chasm first, her refusal could lead to conflict with the overwhelmingly superior Katangans, and certainly to the revocation of her asylum. King Msiri wasn't being duplicitous or cowardly; he simply wanted to do the right thing, as he believed it. On the other hand, the queen mother was one of Mamoru's network; that alone gave her vision far more weight than just a seer's prophecy.

She took a deep breath. "Colonel, if I asked you to do it, you would. I have duties as well."

Anhalt stood tight-lipped, shaking his head at the insanity of it all, while the Mountaineers began to crawl out along their grapple lines into the chasm, pulling themselves hand over hand with their ankles crossed on their ropes. The wind tossed them like laundry, their rifles and swords dangling beneath them.

Adele said, "Your Majesty, I'm ready."

"Excellent!" The king clapped his hands. "You will find it a simple task. There are many such bridges across Katanga. Small children walk them every day. I will be right behind you on the bridge. And, as you see, my Mountaineers will be crossing on their traverses too. But you must set foot on the other side first."

Anhalt said, "I will be with you as well."

"Fine." Adele tugged on one of the ropes. "Let's keep it to three, shall we? Until we see how sturdy it is."

"It is as safe as a stroll in my garden." Msiri kicked off his sandals and patted her back with a powerful hand. "Just don't pull on the guidelines to correct yourself should you begin to tilt. You may well spin yourself out of control."

Without another word, Adele placed a booted foot on the rope just off the side of the cliff. It stretched several frightening inches before coming taut. She took both of the guide ropes in her hands and stepped off into the sky, pausing to get her balance on the vibrating cables. The wind kicked up and the rope swayed from side to side, carrying her feet wildly with it. She wanted to yank hard on the ropes in her hands, but

Msiri had warned her about that. She heard the collective gasps of the troops as she struggled for balance, fighting her fear of being tossed into open sky. Finally, she got her feet under her again and steadied the ropes.

Not bad for a first step.

She started with controlled, measured steps, unable to deny there was something exciting about how the rope beneath her bounced wildly. Sliding her hands along the fibrous guidelines, she watched the far cliff draw closer.

Adele risked a quick glance to her left at the numerous rope lines spun like a spider's strands across the chasm. The Mountaineers maneuvered them expertly, unlike her own halting steps on the thin rope that flexed as if it were alive. But still none of the men, however skilled, passed her. Instead they stood ready on the lines, watching the air, watching the boma—watching her.

The weight of these lives rested with her. They were all operating under Msiri's odd belief. She quickened her pace, wanting to be across. As Adele walked the rope with more confidence, the air grew suddenly misty. Clumps of grey-white clouds rose around her and the world vanished in a cottony haze. She felt the guidelines in her fists, but could barely make them out a few feet from her face. Her boots were lost in the fog, and she could see nothing of the rope beneath her. She was stepping from nothing to nothing.

Suddenly a black shape darted in the mist right below her, like a shark cutting the surface of the ocean. Adele stiffened. At first, she hoped it was just a bird, but then she saw another and then another pass so close she could touch them.

"Vampires!" she shouted.

Screams erupted around her in the fog. Behind her, sniper fire started up, but the riflemen must've been firing nearly blind because of the mist. Now there was as much danger from being struck by a wild bullet as from an attacking vampire. They had to cross quickly and get to solid ground. Adele stepped up her pace. The ropes jerked and shivered beneath her palms as the men behind her repositioned or fought off attackers. The gusts of wind grew stronger.

"Carry on!" Msiri called out.

There were breaks in the fog, and through it Adele saw vampires speeding like bullets, careening into the Katangans, ripping them from their tenuous holds on their cables. Flailing, the men tumbled over and over down into the chasm, in comparison to the vampires, who despite the dangerous air currents, maneuvered with daring grace.

All over, men were shouting and screaming. Msiri's voice boomed his command. "The Equatorian must land first!"

Adele was about to shout that he couldn't keep his men hanging helplessly on their lines, that they needed to cross and form a perimeter. Then a dark shape slammed into her. A strangled scream escaped. One hand came loose and her arm waved wildly, seeking anything to hold onto, as her fingers swept through fog. A rope hit the crook of her elbow, and she quickly clenched her arm around it. She managed to keep her balance as her hand found a line again.

"Highness!" Anhalt's voice sliced the clouds.

She managed to croak, "I'm here."

The ropes quivered from wind or other footfalls, and her arm was beginning to strain. A vampire erupted out of the fog and grabbed her by the waist. With her right hand, she reached for the Fahrenheit khukri in her belt, relieved it was still there. It flashed a green hue as she yanked it out and curved it downward. The blade sank deep into the flesh of the vampire, who howled and released her. She scrabbled for the other guideline.

The king said, "Quickly now, move forward."

Adele probed with her right foot. Her toe touched something hard and she lowered the rest of her foot. It fell on a broad and ungiving surface. The ground. The princess pressed harder and heard crunching soil. Through the mist she saw rocks.

"I'm across!" Adele stepped onto solid ground with a rush of triumph and relief. So close to falling, so close to death. She would live to see Gareth again. As she pushed up through a small gap onto the broad surface of the plateau, she noticed that the earth felt warm.

"Go! Go!" Msiri shouted to his men. "She is across!"

The king and Anhalt appeared at her side. The colonel yanked up his goggles to inspect her with worried eyes, and Adele noticed the glow of his Fahrenheit saber in his gloved hand. Msiri was brandishing an intricate Katangan axe and an automatic pistol.

Anhalt lowered his goggles into place once more, prompting Adele to do the same. They both clicked their shroud filters into place to sweep the area for the telltale blue glows of vampires. The Gurkha noted Msiri's red glow and then was startled by Adele's white signature. His first thought was that the fragile chemistry of the goggles was failing, but his own arm was bright red too. The princess was simply brilliant white.

Msiri proclaimed, "Victory is mine."

"Is that so?" Anhalt answered a trifle brusquely, shooting another vampire as it rushed them. "Because we seem outnumbered."

"No matter, Colonel. The princess entered Jaga's boma first. The *ndoki* chief is finished."

The Gurkha grunted in fatalistic acceptance. "Well, every man should have faith in his mother."

Adele's pistol flamed and fired rhythmically at dozens of blue shapes around her. Anhalt stood shoulder-to-shoulder with her. The air and ground were thick with darting vampires, veering this way and that. She almost missed as two dove toward her. She lifted her gun and fired, sending one tumbling into the other. They both landed at her feet.

Adele stabbed deep with her Fahrenheit dagger. She twisted the knife and pulled it out, slashing at the second. A brief resistance told her she'd connected. It staggered away from her, and to her surprise, it attacked the other one, perhaps jealous of the imminent kill.

Heedless, Anhalt stepped in to protect her, his own Fahrenheit blade slashing at the two vampires fighting in front of her. One reacted with a howl of pain before they both fled. Adele turned her attention to new attackers, always moving forward, making room for the Mountaineers who struggled across the chasm onto the boma plateau.

And then suddenly everything changed. Adele's head snapped up at the familiar sensation of power.

In the cold moments before the battle began, Gareth sat on the rock floor of Jaga's cave, where he had been for days. His clothes were in tatters and his hair matted with blood. His eyes darted between the two amazons who glared at him, daring him, practically begging him to try to escape. Their faces were etched with hatred for his killing of their sister. Only Jaga's command kept them from attacking.

Gareth had eaten every day and felt quite fit, aside from the fading results of the brutal beating he'd suffered a few days before at the hands of Jaga's wives. His shredded leg was whole once more, though he had yet to test the strength of it.

For several days, Gareth had listened to the sounds of slaughter outside. He wished he could have stanched the noise, but it was futile. The screams and sobs were similar to the sounds of a clan gathering in England. Jaga's people had fed heartily until their entire herd was killed and drained and shoved off the side of the plateau. Jaga had commanded the massacre for two reasons: one, so that his people would be fit for battle, and two, so that they would have no choice but victory. If they did not triumph, they would starve.

Now the females were distracted by the distant sounds of the approaching Katangan army. Faint whiffs of nonhuman blood couldn't hide the sounds of a human army. Since sunrise, the vampires had been restive as the clashing weapons and boots slapping against rock grew louder. Gareth strained for Adele's voice and waited for her distinctive scent to waft over him, proof that she came with the men who were stumbling into Jaga's trap. If so, he had to escape and find her; he had to be sure she was safe.

Gareth crawled to the edge of the pile of detritus taken from human victims over the years and crouched there, pretending to be cowed by his captors. He eyed the trophy mound and began to shove bones and rusted metal idly with his hands. Then he saw what he was looking for. The steel blade of a long-handled axe was beginning to rust, but its edge was still keen, even though it bore several notches from shattering bone. Gareth pulled it from the skeletal refuse.

The two amazons watched him. So foreign was the use of tools to vampires, they couldn't conceive that Gareth could perform any useful action with the axe. They stared as if he was no more than an animal pushing an object with his snout. He stood, but without aggression, holding the axe hilt loosely in one hand, leaving a trail in the dirt with the blade as he strolled closer. The females growled and showed their claws. Gareth lowered his eyes in submission. His claws were retracted; he was no threat to them.

The chilling war cry of Jaga's people rose from the mist outside, and soon it was accompanied by human shouts and the popping of gunfire. In the chaotic noise, Gareth heard a terrifyingly familiar sound—Adele's scream. The wives glanced outside anxiously, then quickly back at Gareth, who swung the axe with all his considerable strength. The blade impacted one female in the neck, nearly severing her head.

The second wife stared with utter surprise at her thrashing sister, unable to credit what had just happened. She looked up at Gareth, but he was already ripping her throat and cracking both her rib-bone cuirass and her own rib cage as well.

As Jaga's wives twitched on the ground, Gareth flew from the cave and was instantly among vampires rising and diving in the air. The wind had picked up and was beginning to shred the heavy clouds. He fell in with the shrieking flock and among the blood and gunpowder, detected the faint scent of Adele. He rolled and streaked toward her, slamming *ndoki* out of his way.

The mist was patchy and thick, cutting his visibility, but the touch of the wind allowed Gareth to pinpoint Jaga above several humans, positioning himself for a kill strike. With a jolt, he recognized one of the humans as Adele.

Jaga dropped toward the small human beachhead where Adele fought alongside Anhalt and King Msiri. It was a foolhardy attack, but it reeked of nobility and the quest for an honorable kill. Gareth flattened out and dove to intercept the vampire king. The smell of humans grew strong, and he could hear Adele's heavy breathing and smell the acrid burn of her Fahrenheit blade as it sliced the mist as well as the wraith-like *ndoki* around her.

Then, through a fissure in the clouds, Gareth finally saw Adele, her face glowing with perspiration and auburn hair flying. She had a pistol in one hand and a glowing dagger in the other. The woman fought like a machine, an intricate, beautiful machine crafted especially for this bloody production.

As Gareth prepared to slam Jaga aside, he saw Adele turn her goggles toward him. Her pistol came up and flamed. The bullet crashed into Gareth's shoulder, flipping him over. Jaga careened onto his back and together they crashed hard to the ground. He dug his claws into Jaga, who stared in fervent amazement. He felt the heat of a Fahrenheit blade pass close by, and the Rwenzori vampire king howled as it plunged deep into his chest. Gareth threw out his arm instinctively as Adele struck again. The knife sliced his forearm.

Jaga came for Gareth with his teeth. Several bullets thudded into the dirt around them. The prince sensed the wind welling up from the chasm only a few yards away, and he locked Jaga into an embrace, scrambling to his feet. A hellish hot blade cut him across the back, but he bulled toward the edge of the precipice, while Jaga screeched with fury and clawed his shoulders. Then they were airborne.

"What's wrong with you?" Jaga screamed. "I had Msiri!"

Gareth didn't bother to respond. The gaping wound in Jaga's chest still glowed from the Fahrenheit blade, so he dug his claws into the gash, tearing flesh and muscle.

"Stop!" Jaga cried. "You're one of us!"

Gareth forced his claws deeper into the gash, grimacing with the effort, until he felt Jaga's heart. He punctured it. Wide-eyed in disbelief, Jaga stiffened. Gareth released his hold and watched the Rwenzori king's quivering form drift away like a dead leaf.

A sudden blast of wind sent the prince slamming against the side of the chasm, where he clutched an outcrop and gathered his breath. The sound of weapons fire reached him and he climbed, hurling himself upward from rock to rock, ignoring the sting of his fierce wounds, fighting the violent winds.

When Gareth crawled over the top of the cliff, he was slapped by the smell of death. It was not the mundane metallic sting of blood or musk of human fear. This was different. He could taste it, and the fear he smelled was his own.

It was Adele.

Through the wind-ripped fog, Gareth spotted the trapped humans in the distance. Msiri, Anhalt, and numerous Mountaineers were surrounded by dead and wounded, both human and vampire. The Katangans were vastly outnumbered. The ropes the troopers had used to traverse had snapped and the treacherous rope bridge was shredded. Soon the murderous *ndoki* would winnow the humans to nothing.

In the midst of the chaotic battle, Adele was no longer fighting. She knelt with her hand on the ground. Gareth smelled the heat pouring off her and felt it in the earth under his knees and hands. His skin tingled with flame, just like it had when Adele prayed in Edinburgh and dreamed over Nabta Playa.

But this was more.

Much more.

Tendrils of rolling smoke and heat coiled around her limbs like living things seeping up from the ground. She was the nexus of a silver flame that flared around her brighter than the sun.

Gareth started backing up. He had to get away. The Rwenzori vampires were trapped by bloodlust and didn't realize what they were feeling. But he knew.

Adele was going to kill them all.

Suddenly, Adele turned her head in his direction. One hand, wrapped in argent smoke, reached up and slowly lifted her goggles. Her dark eyes locked with his as they shared the unbelievable realization that she was going to kill him. Her eyes betrayed a surging terror, of what she was becoming, and of the fact that she couldn't stop it. Her form blurred within the smoldering fire.

"No!" She tried to rise, but the air rippled around her with unbridled white heat. It flashed a brilliant hue and then surged outward in every direction, racing along the ground like a lit fuse.

Gareth tried to run, but felt a wave of fire wash over him and heard the distant cry of his name.

He felt nothing more.

CHAPTER 30

THE DESERT HEAT blazed across the men on the deck of USS *Ranger*. Senator Clark's collar chafed against his sweating skin and he tugged it loose, but it didn't relieve his irritation. They had been sitting in the desert for two days now, doing absolutely nothing. He had just spent weeks trapped in Alexandria. His men were restless and miserable from the days in the extreme heat. Sails had been rigged for shade from the brutal sun, and the crew had to fight to keep the ship moored in the face of sudden desert winds.

Clark's bloodshot eyes strayed into the distance off to starboard, where Stoddard watched over the schoolteacher. The senator failed to see how crouching in the middle of a sea of sand, surrounded by strange ruins, would give them a lead to the whereabouts of his wife. He snorted. What a fool! And what a fool he was for listening to the crazy schoolteacher.

Clark stomped down the gangplank and made for the ruins. His boots hissed as they sank into the soft sands. Soon he was among the tall, spindly rock columns. It wasn't the ruins of a city or a temple, as far as he could tell. Nabta Playa, Mamoru had called it. The place was just a circle of weird stones in the middle of the empty desert. Yet there was a sense about it that unnerved him.

"Major!" Clark called out gruffly.

His adjutant appeared from behind a stone pillar, signaling for silence, which only aggravated the senator more. He huffed his way over as Stoddard approached.

"Well?" the senator asked.

Stoddard saluted and then shook his head. "Nothing yet, sir."

"Then what the hell are we staying here for? This is damned nonsense. That priest has gone crazy. We can get some intelligence elsewhere. Someone must have seen her and that masked popinjay she ran off with."

"Mamoru is confident in his method."

"His *method* is getting us nothing but sunstroke."

"I recommend sticking with it. I've seen some strange things out in the desert. When Colonel Anhalt and I fought—"

"Don't let these people buffalo you, Major. Their hocus-pocus is crap. Mamoru is waiting for a contact of some kind and playing at swami while he does it. He must be having a good laugh at our expense." Clark lifted his hat and wiped his brow. "Who would meet him out here in the middle of hell?"

"Begging your pardon, sir, but I think it's more than that."

"I knew I shouldn't have let you run around with that Gurkha. He's filled your brain with useless foolishness. How did the Equatorians even build an empire with all these fanatics at the top?"

"Any new tactic is worth looking into. Methods may differ, but some are no less effective."

Clark tried to spit, but couldn't. "Whatever rapport you have with the old fakir, you tell him that he has one more day to stare into his crystal ball or read bird guts or whatever the hell he's doing, because after that, we are out of here and trying an alternate method. It will be much more direct, I promise you that."

The senator stepped past his subordinate to take a look at Mamoru. The samurai knelt in the center of the ruins with an intricate pattern of crystals set around him in the sand. The flat of his hands were pressed against several crystals on the ground, and he was couched in deep concentration. With a well-placed foot, Clark kicked a crumbling standing stone, which clattered to the ground. The schoolteacher paid him no heed; he just sat there daydreaming or whatever he was doing.

Finally, the senator cleared his throat and said out loud, "You have one more day; then we're leaving."

Mamoru was silent and still, but as Clark turned to leave the samurai spoke. "As you will, but I haven't gained any useful information yet."

Clark spun back, eager to argue. "Little wonder! If you're just going to sit and meditate at least do it on the ship where we're up in the cooler air!"

"I have told you. My methods are my own. This place is where I need to be."

"A ruination of sand and rocks isn't going to tell you squat!"

"You do not understand."

"I damn well don't!"

"You asked for my help. I am endeavoring to give it. With enough time I will find her."

"So could my Aunt Tess, but she wouldn't do it sitting on her ass."

"Obviously not."

Clark was tempted to call this whole thing off. However, that would mean formulating a new scheme, and the blistering Sahara was sapping even the senator's prodigious energies. So he would let this foolishness go on, for now.

"One more day!" Clark growled before stomping away past Major Stoddard.

Mamoru stretched out stiff muscles but didn't stand. "To be honest, I am surprised he has gone along with it this far."

"What exactly are you hoping for?" Stoddard squatted in the precious shade of a withered monolith. He eyed the priest, amazed by the man's stamina.

"You wouldn't understand either."

"Is this how you found her last time? In the Tower of London?"

"No, this is different. This time I am waiting for a signal from her, though we both know how stubborn and unpredictable she can be."

"It's been hours since you drank or ate. This wretched heat can kill a man fast." Stoddard offered Mamoru his canteen, which was taken gratefully. "I can arrange some food for you."

"Thank you, yes. I will eat here, just in case." The samurai closed his eyes and sank into meditation once more.

After a few moments of watching, Stoddard gained his feet to head for the ship. Suddenly Mamoru stiffened with a sharp gasp. His muscles clenched and his jaw clamped shut with an audible snap. A painful hiss strained through the man's lips.

"Mamoru?" Stoddard took a step toward the man just as the school-teacher arched violently and collapsed to the hard stone ground, limbs splayed wide and eyes rolling back in his head. Stoddard grabbed hold of him and doused him with the precious water from the canteen in an attempt to revive him.

Mamoru was having some sort of seizure, Stoddard thought. He should have insisted the man drink more. If he took ill, Clark would leave him in the desert. The major swore that wouldn't happen, but even his resolve might not be enough and would only wind up angering Clark more, so much so that he might leave them both stranded.

He called Mamoru's name, and thankfully the man's eyes opened. They blinked slowly a few times and then flew wide as he sat straight up.

"Easy, man." Stoddard held his shoulders.

Mamoru struggled to stand. "It was *her*."

"What was?"

He grabbed Stoddard's arm tightly. "I know where she is!"

The major studied the wide-eyed face. Mamoru was yellow from caked sand, and his lips were cracked and white. He looked as if he'd had some kind of psychotic episode. "Are you sure? You lost consciousness."

"She is in the Mountains of the Moon. To the south." Mamoru wiped his face, lost in his own stunned thoughts. "My God, it was incredible. I felt it! What did she do?"

He wasn't talking to Stoddard; he was babbling and grinning like a madman. Sweat poured down his face.

Stoddard couldn't take him to Clark in this state. "Just settle down a minute. What makes you think she's there? Did you remember something critical? Does she have friends there?"

Mamoru paid him no heed. His voice was low and full of astonishment. "I was right. She is the one."

Stoddard shook him. "Answer me, or I'll take you to the surgeon for heat exhaustion."

"I'm fine." Mamoru scowled at the American and shrugged off the man's grip. "Inform the senator to make for Katanga and the Mountains of the Moon."

Stoddard stood. "You had better have a damn good rationalization for the senator."

"The earth told me where she is."

"Oh? Well, that's brilliant." Stoddard paused, then said, "I'll come up with something. I don't want him thinking he's banking on a crazy man."

"Do you think that?"

"Maybe, but I'm still open-minded, which is more than Senator Clark is." Stoddard helped the samurai to stand on his bare feet. "I'm not a hundred percent sure what just happened, but if she's where you say she is there'll be no denying you're a hell of a drama teacher."

"She's there. But we must hurry."

"Why?" The men waded through sand toward the beached airship.

"The Mountains of the Moon are a dangerous place, it seems."

<hr />

The grass under Adele's feet was scrubby and matted. The field of the boma was as ordinary as ever she had seen. It did not tell her anything until her foot took one last step. Suddenly her body was flooded with a familiar surge and memories that were not hers, of things she could not possibly know.

Instinctively she sank to one knee, gripping the damp soil, deepening her connection to a distant rift. It sang of salvation. What she had experienced before seemed pale by comparison. It was as if her life had been hollow before this moment, and now there was energy filling a void she had never known existed within her. The fiery voice rose eagerly within her, and she welcomed what it wanted her to do. A vast storehouse slept beneath her, and she was only dipping a finger into the rich resource. Shimmering smoke seeped up from the ground, coiling about her, the power in the earth consuming her.

Adele looked up. To her shock, Gareth stood there on the torn field, watching as she crouched on the ground with her hand pulling the very energy from the earth. The look in his eyes told her that he knew what was happening.

She tried to stop it, but the power would not be denied. It swelled, monstrous and furious, disregarding how she screamed for it to remain in the earth. With her concentration gone, the silver fire around her took control. She was aware that she was being overwhelmed as her vision blurred and her entire body writhed with snakelike smoke. She knew in that instant that Gareth would die—by her hand.

His name poured out of her lungs as searing and painful as the heat that rose through her. Her last memory was seeing the scorching wave in the air as it flung itself out and over the battlefield, over the vampires.

Over Gareth.

And then he was gone.

After that, darkness swallowed her. It seemed like she had struggled for years to lift herself from the mire, and when she did, she had only one thought.

Adele's eyes snapped open and she sat up.

"Gareth." His name was a hoarse whisper escaping her dry lips.

Everything hurt as snatches of sound and light rushed back in quick glimpses of a time still separate from her. Her eyes were blurry, and it took a few minutes of trying to focus before the indistinct image before her cleared. Finally, the hide wall of a tent undulating in the wind came into view. Her skin felt hot, as though she had a fever, but she was clear-headed and could see her breath misting in the air with every exhale.

Exhaustion wrapped its arms around her, wanting to drag her back into its embrace, but she adamantly refused. She remembered everything now. The bloody battle and the sacrifices made. The last look on Gareth's face. She reached into her pocket and pulled out the note he had left for her. "Greyfriar cannot protect you. But I can." A chill coursed through her like quicksilver.

All because she had found a rift, tapped it, and the power had taken control. It had risen in her like a wild thing eager to be unleashed.

Turning her aching head, Adele saw that she was alone in the small tent. A pallet on the ground served as a bed, and she was covered by a heavy fur blanket. She shoved it aside to let the air cool her flushed skin. The pain she felt was not sharp, but more like muscles overused and abused. A groan fell from her lips as she shoved herself to her feet.

Other sounds were now making themselves heard, such as snatches of indistinct voices and intermittent shouting. The horrible smell of smoke filling her small tent made her stomach roll. Fighting down the nausea, she stepped outside her thin shelter. Steadying herself against the tent frame she got her first glimpse of the killing field. She saw shimmering waves of heat still emanating from the rift she had tapped. Scores of vampire bodies littered the area, most burned and blackened.

Gareth.

She fell to her knees and dry-heaved, retching up her dread and anguish. She tried to ignore the shouts and shrieks reverberating around her, and the undercurrent of distant hissing that she understood. Vampires. Fearful whispers, angry but empty threats, and screams of outrage abruptly silenced.

"Your Highness!" Colonel Anhalt rushed to pick her up from the ground.

"I'm fine, Colonel," she told him as she steadied her feet, grateful he was there. "Have you seen Greyfriar?" She couldn't help the high pitch of her voice. Fear welled up inside her like the floodwaters of the Nile, and there was no holding it back.

He shook his head. "No, Highness, he wasn't here. We are at Jaga's boma. Do you remember? You should return to your tent."

"No! He was here. I saw him!"

"You have been delirious for more than a day."

"I saw him! During the battle. He was here."

"Very well." Anhalt nodded to assuage her. "Then we will find him. We are just finishing off the last of the vampire survivors."

Adele turned toward the terrified hissing in the mist where Katangan soldiers manhandled a group of bound and near-naked vampires. Soldiers impaled the struggling creatures with iron-tipped spears while other troopers cheered the sight. The humans hefted the dead vampires like cordwood, throwing them onto a pile of cadavers.

"Vampire survivors?" Adele staggered toward the soldiers. "Stop the executions!"

A Katangan private stared at her. "That was the last. All of Jaga's horde are destroyed."

Her chest seized in a fist, and she gasped as she ran for a pile of burnt *ndoki* corpses. Anhalt rushed after the princess, attempting to draw her away from the horror.

"He would not be here with these things," he cried. "Come, let's search the wounded in the surgeon's tent."

Adele would not budge. Soldiers, both Katangan and her own White Guard, stood by in shocked horror as she began to reach deep into the mound of twitching bodies. She stared at the face of each vampire corpse, dragging the freshly dead away so she could inspect the bloated bodies beneath. She yelled back with cold venom. "We will search for him everywhere! Do you hear me?" Her tone brooked no argument on the matter, and her eyes were wide, fierce, and laced with the shine of tears barely held in check.

Anhalt's voice was a quiet plea. "Then shouldn't we inspect the casualties at the surgeon's tent?"

Adele paused with her hands on the blackened corpses. "Yes. Do that. You do that. I'll check here."

"Your Highness, I do not even know what the man looks like."

Adele snapped at him. "His hair is dark . . . black; his eyes are . . . his eyes are blue." Her voice faltered with the futility of the undertaking.

"This is no task for you." Anhalt knelt and again urged her back toward the tent.

Adele stood fast. "I seem to be the only one willing!"

"Not so, Your Highness." His head bowed low.

"Then help me, Colonel. *Please.*"

"I will search with you."

Adele desperately grabbed his hand, squeezing it with dread relief. "We'll search together. We'll find him."

For hours, Colonel Anhalt had to watch his beloved princess do what no human should ever have to do. The White Guard joined in the macabre inspection of bodies, both human and vampire, across the plateau, as did some of Msiri's soldiers. It was horrifying for Adele to be given hope by a call of a man who'd discovered a wounded man or corpse vaguely resembling her companion, only to be dashed again and again when none were the swordsman.

The mists were rising, and soon visibility would be lost as night descended. The imposing King Msiri approached Anhalt, but the king's horrified attention was on the distant Adele as she moved tirelessly through the mounds of vampire corpses.

"Why does she look for her love among the fallen enemy, even if she imagined she saw the Greyfriar here?" Msiri shook his head. "Such a great love could topple a soul over a precipice and into an unholy maw."

"Are you implying she's gone mad? No, sir! She has not!" Despite his protest, Anhalt had asked himself the same disturbing question as Msiri. He offered up the only rationalization he could to the king. "Her Highness says he was here. The scene was chaos. No stone left unturned, Majesty. She will not give up until he is found. Neither should we."

"Yes, I owe her much," Msiri admitted. "She won the day. The queen mother was not wrong about her."

"What did she do during the battle? What did you see?" Anhalt rubbed his face in exhaustion. "What happened? Can you tell me?"

"I saw the *ndoki* fall dead before her. Burned like grass in a fire. I saw nothing else. How did your princess do what she did?" Msiri shrugged. "It is impossible to know everything. Sometimes it's better not to know, eh? It is best to accept what fortune brings us."

"I don't know. I saw her kneel, and then it seemed as if the vampires died." Anhalt shook his head. "Excuse me, Your Majesty. I must help her."

"You believe she's strong enough to recover from this?" It was a blunt question.

Anhalt had a blunt answer. "Yes."

"Then I leave you to what you must do. If you find Jaga's body in your search, be sure to inform me."

"You have not yet found him?"

"No. But I know we will."

Such surety, thought Anhalt. *Just like Adele*. If only Anhalt could feel the same, but he supposed that was the difference between royalty and a mere soldier. Doubt was not something a sovereign could have, or all would be lost.

———※———

After making a second inspection of the reeking battlefield and the piles of burned vampire cadavers, Adele wandered toward the edge of the ravine. Thick pockets of clouds filled the great crevasse, moving swiftly like the water of a swollen river pushed along by fierce winds. She couldn't see across it, much less to the bottom. The winds battered her, and she forcefully steadied herself against its savage breath as though it were the enemy.

He was gone.

She had killed him.

Tears burned down her chilled face, but no sob escaped her lips as she stared out across the darkening Mountains of the Moon. Shaking, she sat down to ease the sudden weakness in her legs. She knew that she might never find him, his body unrecognizable even to her.

I'm so sorry, Gareth.

She could hear him comment dryly that she had done what she had to do to save her people. He was always so damn selfless, caring more about her than about his own kind. He would never be angry with her for surviving. Still, none of that eased the howling pain in her heart.

Booted feet appeared beside her and she looked up expectantly, but Colonel Anhalt's gaze held only concern and alarm. He probably thought she might step off the edge into eternity. All the grief in the world would not propel her from her duty, even though such resolve came at a high price.

"Have no fear, Colonel. I will not do something foolish." She brushed the wildly blowing strands of her hair away from her face.

"Of course not, Your Highness. You are far stronger than that."

Fresh tears fell at the hollow compliment. "I don't feel strong."

"No one could do what you did today and be called weak." Anhalt's hand rested on her shoulder. "If your Greyfriar were here, we would have found him. He is most likely safe down the mountain, worrying about you."

Adele couldn't tell him that was not so; that Greyfriar would never be found among the human dead, only among his own kind. Even if he had somehow survived the event she had caused, Msiri's men had dispatched all the surviving vampires with a swift sword. She couldn't suppress a shudder.

"He was here, Colonel," she spoke quietly, her voice thick.

"I only offer you hope, Your Highness. It is all I have." He draped his long greatcoat over her shoulders as Adele's hand fumbled for his.

"Thank you."

"If you believe he was here, we will continue to search until we find him. Gain your strength and then join us when you are ready. Breathe in the cold air and find a moment's peace in the rugged beauty of this hellish place."

He left her alone and Adele listened to the rush of the airstreams as they careened around the rocky slopes. She closed her eyes and tried to center her thoughts as Mamoru had taught her. However, her stomach knotted at the thought of the grotesque duty that lay before her, and her grief returned again. Her resolve faltered, but then she drew in a deep breath, locked her shoulders, and arched her back stiffly. She would do this for Gareth. She would not leave his body here.

A stone shifted to her right and bounced down the cliff wall.

She whirled, her hand falling to the pistol at her belt. It could only be a vampire who clung to the rocks below. She stepped to the edge, prepared to put a bullet in its brain and send it to the bottom of the crevasse.

Carried on the turbulent wind, a faint voice called, "Adele."

The pistol tumbled from nerveless fingers as she fell to her hands and knees. Below her, hanging on to mere scrabble and rock, was a tall figure. Adele dropped flat on the ground and took hold of his outstretched hand. It was scorched and bloodied.

"Gareth!"

CHAPTER 31

GARETH'S GRIP WAS weak. His shirt was shredded and dark with dried blood. Adele shuddered to think of what his skin looked like beneath.

Tightening her grip, she pulled with all her strength, determined not to let him fall. She screamed for help, but the wind ripped away her breath. Gareth's bare face tipped up at her. He was smiling weakly, almost drunkenly.

"I found you," he mouthed softly.

Adele wasted no words as she tried to drag him up over the edge. Clothes and skin ripped against the sharp stones, and rocks crumbled beneath Gareth as he scrambled for footholds. He was slipping out of her grasp.

"Damn it, no!" Adele shouted, only to have her words shoved back against her by the foul driving wind.

"Don't let go," he urged her.

Gareth's fingers tightened about hers. Then he closed his eyes and abruptly he lightened. His body was immediately caught in the maelstrom of the ravine, and only Adele's desperate hold on him prevented him from being driven by the wind with deadly force onto the rocks.

He flew up, and Adele scrambled to her knees, yanking him toward her. He slipped into her arms, his density changing as soon as he was over solid ground. They crashed together onto the scrubby slope. His body was limp as she rolled over, his strength long spent.

"I thought I killed you!" Her head bent to his, tears of grief changing to those of joy.

"You made a good try."

"The others are all dead. We killed every vampire here."

Gareth nodded, feeling no remorse for his Rwenzori brethren. He took solace in wrapping his arms around Adele. Her arms locked around him, and he couldn't help but wince.

"You feel pain? How badly are you hurt?" She pulled back and started to examine him. "You've been shot." Dried blood stained the upper right of his chest. Luckily the wound had stopped bleeding, but the angry hole was black and vivid. "You're lucky the soldiers aren't better shots."

"You shot me." Gareth blinked at her dully and reached a hand to her face.

"What?" That news rocked her back on her heels.

"You didn't know it was me." His hand brushed at the red line at her temples from the coarse caress of the leather goggle strap she had worn during the skirmish.

"Damn stupid things," Adele cursed. "I should have realized you'd be here."

"Then perhaps I shouldn't tell you that you stabbed me as well."

Her hands flew to her mouth, and she cursed in gutter Arabic, so fast that Gareth couldn't follow. Then she calmed and gave a halfhearted hiccupping laugh. "You have the nine lives of all your cats, you know that?"

Gareth stared at her. "I have never seen a cat live more than one life."

Adele didn't waste time explaining the idiom to him, knowing they would soon be noticed by others. Anhalt wouldn't leave her out of his care for long, and Gareth could not be seen as he was. His face and head were lightly scorched, but much of his body was scarred by horrible, black burns. The red sash at her waist would serve as a suitable headdress. She kissed the cloth over his cracked lips and then helped him sit up so she could button Anhalt's coat around him to hide his blackened skin.

Crunching footsteps rushed toward them, with Anhalt in the lead, shouting, "You found him! He was here."

Adele leaned in to whisper in Gareth's ear. "Keep your hands hidden. Keep your eyes closed. Pretend you're half-conscious."

"Pretend?"

"He needs help," Adele called to the approaching soldiers, who required no prompting. Strong arms gently helped the swathed Gareth to his feet. The troopers were enormously caring of the man who had reached Jaga's boma alone and survived who knew what hardships and horrors.

"A bloody miracle," was Anhalt's awed response.

"Yes, it is," Adele replied quietly.

"I will fetch the surgeon."

"No! Take him to my tent, Colonel. I'll care for him myself. Just please get me some supplies if the surgeon can spare them. Suturing needles, bandages."

Gareth stumbled between two men toward a small tent set away from the slaughter. The Katangans eased him down on the pallet inside. Gareth could smell Adele here, and his anxiety eased. He turned away from them, the coat slipping slightly from his shoulders, revealing the jagged torn flesh from Jaga's claws. To his surprise, one of the soldiers patted him gently on the arm.

"You fought bravely against the *ndoki*. You do us great honor. Live for the sake of your princess."

Then they left him alone and he closed his eyes, too weary to remain alert any longer. Soon Adele swept into the tent. She knelt beside him and brushed gentle fingers across his temple and released a long exhale of relief.

"Apparently, you won't be rid of me so easily, Adele."

"Thank heaven for that."

Anhalt coughed lightly at the entrance to the tent, his arms full of supplies courtesy of the camp surgeon. "I can assist, Your Highness. I have some field experience. The surgeon also offered his services."

Adele sat back and nodded at her loyal commander. "Sadly, I've also had experience of late. But thank you, no, Colonel. I want to do this. I owe him that much."

"As you wish. I'll be outside if you need me." Anhalt withdrew.

She started taking stock of the supplies and putting them in the order as she would need them. Then she turned to Gareth and began removing his tattered, filthy clothing. She winced at the sound of cloth tearing away from patches of seared flesh. Gareth maintained a stoic half-stare at the flapping tent ceiling with only sharp snorts from his nostrils giving away the extent of his pain from the burns she'd inflicted on him.

Finally, she tossed the rags into a corner and tried to objectively evaluate the terrible figure reposed before her. He had suffered the worst burns across his upper body, and his sinewy torso was badly ripped from what she recognized as the claw marks of another vampire. There were several bullet wounds and suppurating gashes from a Fahrenheit blade. He rolled his head slowly toward her with a slight, comforting smile.

Adele swallowed her anxiety and said, "Alone at last."

"And I'm incapacitated again. The Greyfriar in that book always has time for romance. He has admirable stamina. This somehow seems like a cruel joke."

"When you don't have me to tell you what to do, bad things happen." She didn't feel the glibness, but wanted to relax him. She opened an irrigation bottle to clear the searing chemical from the wounds inflicted by the Fahrenheit blade. He hissed as the liquid flooded the slash on his back. Adele paused. "I'm sorry."

"I can stand it," he panted. "The wounds must be cleaned of those infernal chemicals. They may not kill, but they still burn as hot as any desert. It is a most effective weapon."

Her hand grew unsteady as she continued to wash his wounds, listening to his painful gasps. Doctoring him had been much easier when he felt no pain. It didn't tear at her heart so. "How did you live when so few others did?"

"I ran."

"How did you know it was going to happen?"

"I've been on the receiving end of your power before, though not nearly at this strength. I knew this would kill."

"I can't believe it happened. I killed a single vampire in Alexandria using this . . . ability, but this is on a scale I couldn't imagine."

"I saw the waves of heat coming off you. It was . . . terrifying. Your powers have definitely increased. The heat burned all the way through. I've never felt such agony. It hurts still."

"I'm sorry. I'd give anything if Mamoru was here to help me. I can't control it." Adele finished flushing both his back and arm and began to sew up the red, inflamed flesh. Then she inspected the burns across his back and chest, and the blackened flash on the left side of his face from his jawline to his temple.

"These injuries are so horrible, Gareth."

"Those cuts are nothing. The burns are worse, but even they will heal eventually. We can't let anyone see how bad they are or they will wonder why I'm perfectly fine in a few days."

Adele was heartened by his optimism that it would take only a few days to heal this devastation. She had her doubts. "I brought the Greyfriar with me."

"You carried him on the march to war?"

"Of course. It was like having you at my side . . . well, in my trunk at least."

He laughed weakly; then his chest hitched as his scorched skin pulled. He barely suppressed an agonized gasp.

"Damn it!" Adele shoved her medical supplies angrily. "I have nothing here for burns."

"Why would your colonel think you needed them, Adele? Only vampires were burned."

Trepidation rose in Adele. "Do you need to feed? Will that help speed the healing process?"

"I've already fed well." At the arch of her eyebrow, he explained, "Jaga was a most generous host." Gareth explained the events of the last week. Though he was far too tired to relate the details, he hid nothing from her, even his attempt to kill Jaga's son and his failure due to hesitation. His tone turned bitter.

Adele brushed his lips with hers. "Of course, you couldn't kill him."

"I'm a vampire." It was an angry declaration.

"You're a good man."

"Vampire."

"With a kind heart."

He sighed. "The boy has no fault of his own. If he survived the battle, I wonder if I should go find him."

"There were so few survivors." Adele hesitated, then said with a haunted voice, "And there were children among the dead."

"What if he's still alive? Someone should help him."

"Who? You?" Adele placed a firm hand on his chest. "There's nothing you can do. You're barely alive. I understand your wishes, and I'd expect no less of you, but you can't go. And what if you found him? What would you do? Bring him back here? He'd be executed."

"I could be sure that he is with his people. What's left of them."

"And if Jaga's people get their hands on you, you won't survive it. It's impossible." Adele smoothed his hair. "Gareth, you can't save everyone. You're just one man. I'm so sorry about the boy. Believe me. It might have been I who killed him. Do you think I want to kill children?"

Gareth took her hand. "Don't blame yourself. Jaga slaughtered his herds before the army arrived, including many children."

She dropped her head. "My God. What kind of war will this be?"

"The worst ever conceived," Gareth replied.

Adele took a deep breath. "Did you manage to kill Jaga?"

"Yes, I did."

"We haven't found his body yet."

"He's deep at the bottom of the ravine."

She continued to work on him as they talked. Gareth had settled now that the worst of his wounds were treated, and soon the horrible rips on his shoulders were sewn closed and bandaged. She again wrapped her sash around his lower face to conceal the most vivid burns, and swathed his hands. She covered him with the blanket, not for shock or cold, but to hide the evidence of his wounds. Unfortunately, most of his gear was across the ravine at the main camp, so she would have to wait to get him properly outfitted as the Greyfriar.

Gareth's eyes closed at her bidding, content in the knowledge that she would watch over him. Slipping quietly from the tent, Adele saw a soldier nearby and ordered him to stand watch to make sure no one disturbed Greyfriar. He pledged that he would fetch her immediately if the swordsman needed anything. Adele made her way to the makeshift medical tent, where Colonel Anhalt found her rummaging through supplies.

"How is he?" Anhalt asked with genuine concern. His relief at seeing the princess again in her right mind was obvious.

"Sorely wounded, but he'll live."

"I'm very glad."

She smiled. "How goes the mop-up? When do you think we can leave?"

"Soon. Msiri wants to see you."

"He's probably curious as hell about what happened. As are you, I imagine."

"It's nothing that can't wait. You are well. Greyfriar is safe. That's enough for now."

Together they walked to the great tent, where the king was holding court. She stumbled slightly as her adrenaline waned and exhaustion finally found her. Anhalt offered his arm to her, which she gratefully accepted. Katangans stared as she passed. A few actually stepped away, though others shouted and raised their rifles in an exuberant salute.

Anhalt explained, "They honor you for the victory."

"I scare them." She regarded the sturdy Gurkha beside her. "And you?"

"You are my princess. You do not frighten me."

"I frighten myself sometimes."

They walked past even more vampire cadavers that the men had dragged into a pile after systematically decapitating them. The dead that littered the plateau reeked. Adele averted her eyes and shuddered. Anhalt tightened his grip on her as they passed the charnel activity. She had no elation or pride at what she had wrought. She did feel relief that she had saved others; without her intervention, the Katangans and Equatorians would have been massacred.

King Msiri lifted a hand in greeting as Adele approached his tent. General Ngongo and other men of his war council surrounded him. They all parted for her, and some took an extra step back. Adele felt very self-conscious until Msiri rose beaming and bowed to her, leading the others to follow suit.

The king clasped her hands. "I am so very pleased you are well! What you did here will be the stuff of songs and legends for generations to come. Already the men are singing of you. My mother was right. You are a most remarkable woman!"

Adele smiled weakly at the king's praise and glanced quickly at the others in the royal tent. To her relief, more of them looked awestruck than frightened. "Majesty, if you would, please don't spread any stories about what you think happened up here. I can't tell you myself what happened. I want no credit. This was a battle won by the brave men of the Katangan army and a handful of Equatorian allies."

"Very well. So it shall be. History is only what we say it is. If conflict comes between the *ndoki* and Equatoria, I know now who the victor will be. You. They teach remarkable things in Alexandria. Great illness requires strong medicine." Msiri exclaimed loudly, "And your Greyfriar lives to fight through the pages of more books! It is a glorious day indeed!"

"On that we agree." Adele smiled.

"We grieve our losses, but the tally of the battle is most favorable, isn't that so, General?"

Ngongo replied, "My men are scouring the area for stragglers, making sure they cannot escape back to their holes. We think very few of the creatures escaped."

Adele nodded with grim lips pressed together.

There was a commotion outside the tent. A group of Katangans paraded past, hefting a burned and blackened head on a spear. Shouts of "Jaga" reverberated and swept across the plateau until it thundered with echoes. As the gruesome group danced past, more and more Katangans joined in the air of jubilation.

Adele scowled. "That's not Jaga."

"Shhh." Msiri shrugged. "It could be."

"No, it can't. Greyfriar told me that he killed Jaga and the body is over the edge of the cliff."

The king brushed his fingers across his chin. "That is most inconvenient. You and I may know it is not Jaga, but you and I do not need a trophy to know we have won. As royalty, we are much wiser. However, those who serve us do need symbols. After all, that is what we are to them. Someday perhaps our enemy may well march our heads through their fields. As always, a symbol."

Adele couldn't think of a response.

Msiri placed a comforting arm around her shoulders. "Your Greyfriar won the final kill. I am most jealous, but I am also impressed. He is a fine soldier and quite the hunter. He got very far all alone in a land he knows nothing about."

"He's been fighting vampires a very long time."

"Hmm, perhaps next time I will listen to him."

At that Adele smiled. "If I may, how soon before we return to Bunia?"

"I was going to wait until my engineers had constructed a new bridge, a week perhaps. But I see you are distressed and anxious to go. So we shall. Tomorrow. There, it is done. There are already traverse lines across the chasm. We can even rig a basket to carry Greyfriar across."

He'll love that, thought Adele. She thanked the king for his consideration and left the men to their planning, eager to return to Gareth's side. Anhalt fell into step beside her.

The triumphant group went past again. The crowd had grown larger and louder, singing in Swahili.

"Fire brought from the Earth by the hands of the Empress.

"Evil is vanquished and our families are safe."

The head of the new Jaga seemed to stare at her from its rude scepter. Adele looked away. "It's horrible, isn't it?"

"The song? They could use a catchier tune," said Anhalt, but his attempt at levity failed. The corners of his mouth fell. "It is the face of war, Your Highness. One we must get used to."

"I'll be happy to leave this dreadful place." Adele was weary to the bone suddenly. "Let me know when we are ready to depart."

Anhalt said awkwardly, "Shall I have a man sit with you and Greyfriar in your tent?"

"Oh, Colonel." Adele took his arm as she laughed at his endearingly uncomfortable attempt to remind her of her place as a lady. "We are far from society. And I am far from caring about propriety. But thank you for attending to my long-worn reputation."

Anhalt nodded without evident emotion. Adele felt the comfort of him watching as she entered her tent. Gareth was still sleeping. She lay beside him, careful not to jostle him, but laid her hand on his chest, taking joy at its gentle rise and fall, and finally closed her eyes with relief.

<hr />

The march down the Mountains of the Moon was quicker than the excruciating slog up. Even days spent marching in the knee-deep mud couldn't dampen the jubilation and high spirits that sustained the weary soldiers.

Greyfriar had refused to be one of the invalids carried on a litter, so he marched with the men. Adele caught him as he stumbled and steadied him yet again, saying nothing. He glanced at her, expecting a comment, but there wasn't even an arched eyebrow. That made him uneasy, so he scowled at her

"What?" she said. "You're a grown-up."

"That's not what you thought when you forced me to be lifted over the ravine like a baby in a crib. It would have been far easier for me to disappear and fly over. I would have met up with you later." His voice was soft and reserved as usual, but there was a hoarseness to it that gave away his fatigue.

"Oh, and I would have loved to hear how you explained your remarkable recovery only a day after we found you with such gruesome wounds!"

"I'm an enigma. Legends do those sorts of things."

Adele snorted very inelegantly. "Stop reading that ridiculous book about you, please. We're lucky no one's questioning why you're even walking on your own two feet now."

"I refuse to let humans carry me around."

Adele gave a mock gasp. "I'm offended." He turned to reassure her, but she lifted a hand, chuckling. "Trust me. I know how you feel. I don't blame you for refusing." Various parts of her body still ached—she doubted solely from the battle. She'd tried to dress her hair in a manner befitting a member of royalty, but numerous indignant tendrils strayed out of their bindings, giving her a tangled halo of sorts. She longed for a hot bath and a soft bed.

After days of marching, the meandering column finally came to the first town nestled at the base of the mountains. It was small and had often been raided by Jaga. Runners had preceded the column to spread the good news and prepare accommodations for the king and his men. Bonfires now burned, and colorful banners streamed over streets. Triumphal chanting could be heard on the breeze. People thronged around the army, throwing flowers and shoving food into their hands. Gareth tried to pass his hunk of cheese to Adele.

She said, "Best hold it or they'll give you another one."

He regarded the joyful humans. "I like the way you celebrate. It's so sedate."

She couldn't tell if he was serious or not, but then she decided the former, knowing firsthand how perverse vampires were when victorious. "The battle we won means safety for these people. No more lost loved ones," she said, entwining her fingers in his.

King Msiri waved them forward, and together they went into a large building, leaving the shouting and singing behind. Town officials appeared to congratulate Msiri and offer everything they had in homage to their king and protector.

A weary Greyfriar found an empty chair off to the side and eased himself down into it. Adele stayed beside him, uninterested in any bestowed honors.

It wasn't until one of the officials handed the king a sheet of paper and pointed at her that she tensed. Msiri read the page, then glanced sharply her way, his smile gone. Adele straightened and watched the proceedings more carefully.

"What's wrong?" asked Greyfriar, sensing her sudden apprehension.

"I'm not sure. Something's happening, though."

Msiri approached with a somber face. "Princess, I have news. Grievous news, I fear."

"What is it?" she asked quickly.

"I mourn to tell you Emperor Constantine is no more. Dead several weeks now, it seems—just around the time we moved into the Rwenzoris."

Adele stared into the face of the king. She considered his words again, wondering if there was some way she had misunderstood. Surely he hadn't said what she thought.

Msiri asked, "Did you hear me, Highness?"

Obviously, she'd understood correctly. Her chest filled with ice. She felt a hand on her arm, saw Greyfriar's glove, and she seized his forearm like a vise, as if it alone would keep her on her feet. She focused on calming her breath and was mindful to maintain a calm appearance. There were so many watching her for the signs of strength that befit royalty.

"Yes, Majesty," Adele said with admirable clarity. "Do you know how my father died?"

"Vampires."

A startled murmur circulated through the room as people covered their mouths in surprise or looked to their neighbor for proof of their own shock. Colonel Anhalt stepped forward to be near his astonished princess.

"My brother, Simon?" Her chest seized tighter.

"He is well. Don't fear."

"Good, good." She exhaled with faint relief. Then Adele responded with quiet confusion. "Vampires? That's impossible. How? Where was my father?"

King Msiri consulted the sheet of paper he had been given. "In the palace in Alexandria. The city was attacked by a pack of unknown origin. Apparently your people were taken completely unaware. The creatures were driven away, but not before wreaking considerable havoc and causing sizable casualties, including, I'm afraid, your father and several of his leading officials. We know little more than that, but be assured, Your Highness, your prime minister survived the assault and is still the head of government. My ambassador in Alexandria assures us that order has been restored in the city. The Empire appears to be intact." He paused and added in a low voice, "Your brother, the prince, has been declared heir."

Adele looked at Greyfriar, pressed against her shoulder, but he seemed equally confounded. "I must go back now. Simon isn't prepared. This burden will crush him."

"As you will," the swordsman said without hesitation.

Colonel Anhalt added, "I will send to Captain Hariri to have *Edinburgh* prepared."

King Msiri rattled the sheet of paper and cleared his throat. "I haven't yet completed my news for you."

Against her will, Adele's shoulders slumped with exhaustion. "Dear God, what more?"

"Your husband."

The princess's face turned to granite. "I have no husband."

"Well, Senator Clark seems to think otherwise. His ship entered Katangan airspace a few days ago searching for you. My troops have been holding him in seclusion until I could be notified."

"He's come on a fool's errand."

"I'm sure of that." A reassuring smile returned to Msiri's face. "I offered you sanctuary, and you held up your end of the bargain brilliantly. What happens now is up to you. Say the word and I shall send him away. At the very least, I can restrain him while you mourn your father."

"No, there's no time for that now." Adele pondered her choices while Anhalt and Msiri exchanged glances of surprise. Perhaps it was what had happened on the mountain, almost losing Gareth, but Adele was undaunted. "Let the senator come to me when we reach Bunia."

Greyfriar started. "Are you sure?"

"I'm not afraid of him."

"No, I shouldn't think you would be." Msiri laughed in complicity and clapped his hands together. He murmured to himself, "This will be an auspicious reunion. There may have to be cake."

CHAPTER 32

BUNIA WAS STILL celebrating weeks after the extraordinary victory in the Mountains of the Moon. The people chanted their king's name as well as Adele's long into every night. Their joy was infectious, but Adele shared none of it. Her mind was crowded with thoughts of Equatoria, her future, and her concern for Gareth, who was recovering slowly. At present, he was sleeping on her sofa. He had fed twice from her in an attempt to speed his healing, which was even more of a priority given the fact that the terrible news from Equatoria and the sudden arrival of Senator Clark meant they had to be prepared for anything.

The princess's troubled gaze lingered on Gareth's sleeping form. He was covered with a cooling blanket and settled under a slowly spinning fan. Most of his deep wounds had sealed, but the vivid burns on his face still looked like a savage sunburn.

Gareth's eyes slipped open. "You make me nervous when you do that."

"Do what?"

"Brood. Your brooding is rather loud."

"Oh please. I was hardly—" His eyebrow rose. "Fine. I was brooding. It's not like you don't."

"Mine is inherent to my romantic nature. Cloaks and castles."

Adele threw up her hands. "That's it. You are forbidden to look at any more cheap books about yourself."

"What are you brooding about?" he asked. "Your father?"

"No. You."

"Well, that's unoriginal."

She sighed. "And Senator Clark."

"Oh, him." He shifted gingerly and sat up.

"He's furious I won't see him."

"Pity," Gareth replied dryly.

"I will have to at some point."

"Do you know what you are going to say to him?"

"Very little. My plans have nothing to do with him now. They're all about my brother. And my people." A knock on the door sent Adele grabbing for Greyfriar's scarf on the table. "Just a moment."

Gareth grinned at her alarm and wound the cloth meticulously around his face. Adele waited until he slipped on his smoked glasses and gloves before answering the door. Colonel Anhalt stood there, and behind him, Mamoru.

Adele shouted his name with delight and impulsively hugged the schoolteacher. Then she pulled back and stared at him. She touched his still-swollen face and noticed a cutlass in the sash of his robe instead of his sacred katana. "What happened to you? Were you injured?"

He smiled modestly. "It is nothing, Highness. A slight disagreement with Lord Kelvin."

"Kelvin? What did he do?" Adele gasped when she spied the healing scars on his wrists. "He imprisoned you? Were you beaten? I'll kill him!"

"No, no. He can hardly be blamed for his limited vision. To dwell on it only gives him a victory. May we come inside?"

"Of course." Adele drew both men in, clutching Mamoru's arm tightly. "I'm so grateful to see you! I couldn't believe you came all this way with Senator Clark. This I have to hear about."

"It was rather dull." Mamoru's dark eyes were bright with intensity. "There is much we need to talk about that is more important."

"Agreed! However did you find me? I thought we had covered our trail well. Were we careless in Cairo or Abu Simbel? Or was it the colonel's pirate ship that gave us away?"

Anhalt coughed. "Really, Your Highness. You shouldn't jest."

Mamoru glanced humorously at the sheepish officer, then shook his head. "None of those things." He whispered, "What you did in the Rwenzoris sent shockwaves through every dragon spine. Apparently there is an unmapped rift there. I felt it in the Sahara. I must know everything about it."

Adele blushed. The unabashed wonder in her teacher's voice was not something she often heard.

Greyfriar was painstakingly rising to his feet to greet them, his hand extended to greet the renowned Japanese mentor. When Mamoru clasped hands, his expression changed radically. Greyfriar hissed in pain and jerked his smoking hand away. In a blur, Mamoru drew the cutlass. Adele screamed a warning but was too slow to stop Mamoru. His sword flashed, and only Gareth's reflexes saved him. He flung himself backward over the couch that was seconds later cleaved fabric to frame.

"Mamoru! Stop!" Adele shouted.

"Vampire!" the samurai cried out, leaping over the eviscerated furniture to pursue the enemy.

"No! No, it's Greyfriar!"

Mamoru chased the backpedaling Greyfriar, who scrambled to reach his weapons. He tore his rapier from its sheath and barely brought it up in time to ward off a decapitating blow, but the force of the strike cascaded through his weakened muscles. The clash of steel rang out through the room as Greyfriar deflected more blows. Each step of his retreat was hampered by clumsy exhaustion. Adele's luxurious quarters became a battlefield as the two combatants maneuvered for room and opportunity. Mamoru held nothing back, and Greyfriar barely stayed ahead of the vicious assault.

"Enough!" Adele grabbed her mentor's arm. Mamoru shoved her roughly aside, and she went down hard on her hands and knees.

This galvanized the shocked Colonel Anhalt into action, and he raced toward the duelists. Clearly, the schoolteacher was mistaken or out of his mind with sunstroke.

Greyfriar ducked the cutlass, but the feint left him unbalanced, with his back wide open. He managed to block the samurai's downward slash, but he couldn't see that Mamoru's other hand grasped something shiny, a crystal. The moment Mamoru's hand touched the vampire, Greyfriar screamed in agony. Colonel Anhalt tackled the samurai to the ground.

"Get off me, you fool!" was the schoolteacher's angry retort.

"Lay down your sword," shouted Anhalt, putting the muzzle of his revolver to Mamoru's head, then cocking the hammer.

Mamoru struggled, glaring at the soldier. "Didn't you hear what I said? Adele is in danger! He's a vampire!"

Adele again grabbed Mamoru's sword arm. "I know!"

Mamoru and Anhalt froze, looking at her with mouths gaping.

Mamoru's eyes were as hard as his steel blade. "You *know?*"

"I beg you to listen to me. I know he's a vampire, but I swear to you he is nothing like his brethren."

"Obviously. He's far more devious!"

"No! He helped us." When Mamoru scoffed bitterly and tried to lift his arm, Adele held it firm. "Please drop your sword."

"You are misguided," the samurai snarled. "Bewitched!"

"In love," Adele clarified.

"Same thing!"

"Drop your sword, I said!" She was dead serious. "You need me. I don't know why, but you do. So do as I say or I'm lost to you forever."

Mamoru fumed. "You are as manipulative as he."

"I wouldn't have to be if you would just let me explain."

"No, Adele, let me explain," Mamoru snapped back coldly. "Your father is dead! Murdered by *his* kind!"

"I know that, but it has nothing to do with him. Greyfriar wasn't there. He was with me."

"How convenient!" Mamoru said. "He must have been part of it. Why would he be here otherwise? He *used* you."

"No! I am telling you as your student and as your empress, he is not our enemy!" Adele tightened her grip on her teacher's wrist.

The samurai shook his head in disbelief, but let the cutlass clatter to the stone floor. "I should have realized that this was a possibility after your capture. I overestimated your ability to resist. They've swayed you somehow."

"What rubbish! You go too far!" Adele briefly exchanged a look with Anhalt, whose pistol remained pointed at Mamoru, much to her relief, although the colonel's expression was equally pained and even more confused. She backed up to Greyfriar's side, helping him stagger farther away from her enraged mentor. "Are you all right?"

"Never better," Greyfriar croaked, rolling his shoulders, clearly favoring the spot where Mamoru had burned him.

Mamoru said, "You've been cruelly duped, Adele."

"I fought vampires by this man's side." She ignored her mentor's scoff at the term *man*. "I've seen him save humans time and again."

"It's just a game of some kind. He's toying with his food, to win your trust."

"The legend of Greyfriar goes back at least thirty years. Long before I was even born."

"He wears a disguise. No one knows who has been the Greyfriar over those years. Anyone could play that role."

"Is his duplicity less trustworthy than yours?" She lifted her chin. "With your secret network of spies and your hidden agendas?"

Mamoru walked toward her, Anhalt's pistol still trained on him. "I do what I must to save humanity. We are at war with his kind! How can you not see his clear manipulations? You are the heir to the greatest empire on Earth. He was involved in your kidnapping in Europe. Then he interfered on the eve of your union with the American. At least question his motives!"

"I have no need to! He's saved my life and protected me from Cesare in Britain. He has done things no other vampire would bother with. He learned to use tools. He's learned to read and write. It's a miracle, not some ridiculous ploy to win my favor."

"You're romanticizing it. My God! Wake up!"

"I see clearly what's ahead of us." Adele decided to try a new tactic, grasping at straws to sway him to the truth. "War. And there is nothing more valuable than intelligence from the enemy territory."

"My geomancers already provide that."

"Even your people can't go inside the vampire courts."

Mamoru glared at her. "What do you mean?"

Biting her lip, Adele regarded Greyfriar. After a moment of deliberation, he sighed and nodded his consent. He slowly unwound his headscarf. "Because I am Gareth of Scotland, the eldest son of King Dmitri of the British clan." He removed his smoked glasses. For the first time his uncovered azure eyes stared at the two men from Equatoria, though he saw nothing but horror and mistrust in both.

Adele added, "Gareth has provided information straight from the court of Dmitri. We know what Prince Cesare is planning."

"It was the British clan that killed your father." The samurai's voice hardened to an even sharper tone.

"How do you know?" Gareth asked quickly.

The samurai could hardly bear to look at the vampire as he replied, "I'm sure you are intimately acquainted with a female called Flay."

"Flay!" Gareth actually growled. "She lives?"

Adele clenched her fists. Her breath fought against the tightness in her chest, her emotions shifting wildly between rage and despair. She had failed to destroy Flay, and now the war chief had killed her father.

"Was Flay alone?" she asked incredulously.

Mamoru answered. "She commanded a force of hundreds. More than enough to cause untold destruction and death. Your home is still reeling from that dark night."

"Did air patrols not see them coming?"

"They welled up out of the ground. Most likely hidden in the catacombs."

"Clever," said Gareth, receiving a glower from the samurai.

"They were well prepared with knowledge of the city and the palace." Bitterness dripped from the samurai's every word.

Gareth regarded Mamoru. "That could well be true, but it was not from me. I would never do anything to harm Adele or anyone she loves."

Now Mamoru ignored him as if he were a swine trying to plead its case before being slaughtered and said to Adele, "Love has been cruel to you."

Colonel Anhalt cleared his throat, weighing in for the first time. "I have witnessed acts of kindness from Greyfr—from him. Unobserved. He does seem to . . . care about humans."

"He cares?" Mamoru snarled in a voice raw with rage and misery. "Did he care when my wife and child were bled dry by his kind?"

"Gareth did not kill them!" Adele argued. "He doesn't kill humans."

"Then how does he feed?" Mamoru paled. "My God . . ."

Adele's shoulders jerked back and her chin lifted. "I allowed it. He has never harmed me."

Mamoru's knees weakened, and he had to steady himself against the wall. He shook his head back and forth, muttering, "No, no, no, no. How could I have failed so miserably?" He looked up, tears in his eyes. "Adele, please."

The princess stepped toward him, touched by his anguish. If only she could make him see the truth, it would soothe his pain. She reached out a placating hand.

"You are a human being," Mamoru urged her softly. "He is a vampire. He must die."

Adele angrily pulled back her hand. "I will do nothing more to convince you."

"What would your mother think?"

Her jaw tightened at his audacity. "I don't know. But at least my mother would have listened to me. I command both of you, do not reveal what you have learned here today."

Gareth leaned close to remind her, "You no longer have that power."

Adele glared at him and his damnable fact. "Fine. Gareth is right. I cannot order you, but I'm asking you as trusted friends, please keep this secret. You both know me. You both raised me. I do not ask for this favor lightly. I am in my right mind, and I swear to you Gareth has no ulterior motive. He wants only to be with me. I stake my life on it."

"And ours," Mamoru replied with exhaustion in his voice. "And your father's. You know where that has led."

Adele's lips quivered with anger. "I will tell you once more, my father was killed by vampires, yes, but not *this* vampire. We will find those responsible, and they will die by my hands, that I can promise you."

"Well," mocked Mamoru, "at least you don't love all of them."

Adele stepped closer to her teacher, her expression like ice. "Go and see how much love I bestowed on them in the Mountains of the Moon."

Anhalt nodded. "That is true. And Greyfriar did nothing to stop it."

Mamoru's gaze flicked toward Gareth. "That makes you even more a monster."

"I have chosen my side," the vampire argued.

"Enough, please." Adele leaned wearily against Gareth. Her eyes softened with sorrow. "Mamoru, Colonel, I need you to trust me."

"You ask much, Your Highness." Mamoru stood rigid.

"I know the truth in my heart and soul. He is as loyal to me as both of you." She held out her hand again to Mamoru. "I can't make sense of this world without you. Please."

Mamoru closed his eyes. Adele had said the only thing that could have calmed his fears and hatreds for the moment. She wanted to be guided by him, which was the most important key to the future. Mamoru knew that despite his furious desire to kill the creature next to her, he had to be cautious or he might drive Adele away or unwittingly encourage the vampire to strike at her out of fear that his ruse had been overturned. He was loath to leave them alone, but they already had been together for many weeks. Adele would be safe enough as long as the vampire thought his scheme was still in play. Mamoru almost admired the stoic vampire's nerve. The samurai straightened, fighting his surging panic, and took Adele's hand, drawing it to his forehead. "I will do as you ask, Highness, for the sake of you alone."

Adele released her pent-up breath. "Thank you. Your loyalty will not be in vain." Then she regarded Colonel Anhalt. The pain in his face was obvious. How many more times could she test the man before he crumbled? She regretted not taking him into her confidence weeks ago to ease this inevitable blow. She smiled in an attempt to show her appreciation for protecting Gareth from Mamoru, but when he did not return it, her heart broke.

The colonel holstered his pistol and bowed stiffly. "I'm grateful I do not have to tell your father about this situation."

She nodded, not trusting her voice as the two men departed.

Gareth said nothing when her head lifted to look into his blue eyes, full of remorse. She fell against him, and he held her up because she didn't know if she had the strength to stand on her own.

CHAPTER 33

ADELE WAS SHAKEN by Colonel Anhalt's ashen pallor when he entered her chamber. He carried a telegram in his hand as if it were a poisonous snake. Giving him an understanding, bemused smile, she took it, then read out loud: "Princess. Regret to confirm the passing of His Imperial Majesty Constantine the Second. By Act of Commons (Succession Act of 2020), His Imperial Highness Prince Simon is declared Emperor Presumptive. Most Sincerely, Kelvin Pasha, Khedive of Equatoria."

Adele laughed bitterly. "Kelvin Pasha? What sort of foolishness is that? This is the extent of his reply to my message?"

"Yes, Highness," Anhalt said.

She mocked Kelvin's terse note. "Thanks for your inquiry, but the position has been filled."

"Apparently so, Highness."

Adele quietly tapped her foot, her narrowed eyes darting about her lush room in the royal palace in Bunia. Options hung in the humid air around her, and she considered all of them. Politics gave her some respite from her father's death and the memories of the leathery feel of his hand on her wedding day, and how that rough hand must have tried vainly to fend off Flay.

This was Cesare's revenge.

On the opposite side of the room a hidden door clicked open and Greyfriar entered slowly. The colonel stiffened noticeably and took a step back. Greyfriar greeted the Gurkha silently. The princess rose quickly and took the swordsman's arm. Anhalt averted his eyes.

"Has your government replied?" Greyfriar asked her.

"They have. It seems I'm not needed."

"Aren't you the heir?"

She laughed. "I am, but that's not always the point. You know that."

"Could your brother rule in your place?"

"Not yet. He needs guidance."

"Someone other than your Lord Kelvin?"

"Yes."

Greyfriar crossed his arms. "After recent events, my preference would be to go away from here. By all pretense and purposes, you are free. We could leave our people to their bloody business, and it need be none of our concern."

"There's a part of me that wants that desperately."

"As do I. But we are cut from different cloth than that." Greyfriar straightened, every inch a prince. "But if you ask it of me, I could leave tonight and find a place for us to live in peace."

"I can't." Adele lowered his smoked glasses and stared into his blue eyes.

"I felt I should ask. You deserve the chance for some happiness."

"We both do." She embraced him and held him tight for a moment.

"But not today," he whispered sadly.

"No, not today."

"By your leave, Highness." Anhalt's voice was hoarse. He bowed stiffly and started to depart, no longer able to watch this impossible scene.

Before Adele could speak, there was a rap at the main mahogany door and it opened yet again. Mamoru entered, surprised to see the company with the princess. Greyfriar's grip tightened, and she heard a low growl coming from deep inside the vampire.

Mamoru approached, his dark eyes locked solely on Adele, as if she were alone. "Senator Clark can be detained no longer, short of the grave. He comes with the king."

Adele rolled her eyes in dismay. She had almost forgotten about the senator, who seemed the least of her concerns. However, clearly the American wasn't content with being the least of anyone's concerns.

The three men staked their ground around the princess. Adele noted with regret that the two who had guided her all these years were bitter enemies of the man she loved. They were all dependent on her, but incapable of sharing her. Gareth's invitation to disappear with him sounded safe and promising. So simple, yet out of the question.

The princess poured wine for everyone, including Greyfriar, and distributed the goblets personally with smiles and reassuring touches. Anhalt nodded with sadness. Mamoru's face was a blank sheet, but his eyes betrayed the terror of a man inside an iron maiden. She could tell Greyfriar was still weak as he angled his body away from Mamoru but didn't otherwise give ground, which pleased Adele.

The chamber filled with uncomfortable silence broken only by the distant sound of the daily thunderstorm rolling in from the rainforests. Adele crossed to the French windows and threw them open, inviting in a gust of freshening wet air that added a green and overripe smell to the always-smoky haze of Bunia.

With billowing curtains surrounding her, Adele turned to the tense room, took a deep breath, and smiled broadly. "Well, this is nice, isn't it?"

The trio remained mute. Anhalt and Mamoru swirled their wine with disinterest while Greyfriar stood unnervingly still.

Adele said with a sigh, "Gentlemen, I know this is disturbing for you, but it's the situation I find myself in. I have no official claim on your loyalties now, so if either of you desire to abandon my service, I hold no umbrage." Anhalt began to speak, but she held up a hand for silence. "Please, let me finish. I can't predict my future. I have no idea what is in store for me. At most, I desire all three of you to be at my side. At least, I ask for discretion. Obviously my personal situation is . . . unique, and it would create great distress for many people should it become public knowledge."

Colonel Anhalt hissed through clenched teeth, "Your Highness, if I may. I have served you without question since you were a girl and never have you done anything unworthy. Until now."

Adele lowered her head in sorrow. The colonel had never spoken to her in such a way. She knew that her connection to Gareth had wounded him deeply, perhaps irrevocably. The Gurkha officer had been as much a father as her true father, perhaps more, but now Adele had crossed an inconceivable line. Though she wouldn't apologize for it, she understood Anhalt's inability to sanction it. Adele had put him in an untenable situation; he had betrayed his nation for her, and she had left him with this terrible scene. He deserved so much better from her. Until now, she had never before considered life without Colonel Anhalt a possibility.

She murmured, "I understand."

The colonel placed a knotted hand on the hilt of his saber, and Adele steeled herself for the sight of his back, perhaps for the last time.

In a strained voice, he said, "The day my sword is not at your service will be my last day on Earth."

Adele choked back a sudden sob with a grateful smile.

Mamoru said quietly, "And I am but your teacher. Your future is my future. If you are willing to learn, I am willing to teach."

"More than ever." Adele raised her wineglass to the two men, and they all sipped with relief. Finally, something had gone right. Perhaps she might get a decent night's sleep for the first time in months.

Then, even in the vast chamber, even with strong mahogany doors, even with the din of a tropical rainstorm pounding outside, the roar of an approaching Senator Clark echoed, smashing Adele's momentary calm. She drained her wine with a weary groan.

The booming American voice preceded the massive door flying open as Clark argued with those who followed unseen, "I don't need a formal introduction to see my own wife!" And there he was, among them in a sharply pressed dress blue uniform with yellow kerchief, brass buttons, and white gaiters. His eyes burned and his white teeth glared from his black beard. He nodded deeply at Adele, a cynical eyebrow raised.

"Well, well, Princess Adele," he said with posed pleasant tones. "Remember me? I'm your husband."

The princess narrowed her eyes in mock concentration. "The voice is familiar."

"It ought to be." Clark smirked. "The last time you heard it, it was saying *I do*."

King Msiri shoved into the room behind the senator with an embarrassed smile and swinging a royal fly whisk. He wore a traditional robe off one shoulder, showing his muscular frame to good purpose. "Your Highness, the senator requested an audience with you. It seemed unlikely he could be refused. You don't mind, do you? No? Good."

"Quite all right, Your Majesty. I want to see him. We have business."

"Business?" Clark approached with outstretched arms. "Is that how you think of our marriage?"

"I try not to think of it at all."

"Maybe not, but it's a fact. A legal fact." He reached out and took her begrudging hand. "I hold no grudges. So let's just put all this rigmarole behind us and get on with it." Greyfriar stirred ominously, and Clark slipped an eye toward him. "You always wear that thing wrapped around your head?"

Adele extracted her crushed fingers from Clark's meaty grip. "Get on with *what* exactly?"

"Wedded bliss. And ruling the world."

"Senator, before you go on—"

"And on," Anhalt added.

Adele crossed to stand a distance from Clark in front of a wall hanging consisting of elephant tusks and spears. "I am informed that we are not legally married due to the failure to sign the banns. An odd technicality, but the law of the land nonetheless."

Clark gave Mamoru a savage glance. "You've heard that, have you? Well, that sort of trivial legality is for small people, and we're not small people, you and I. We stood together before the world and spoke our vows. Where I come from that makes us married."

"Perhaps. But this isn't where you come from."

"You know your father is dead, don't you?"

Adele's demeanor froze. "I do."

"I was there that night. I was there protecting your throne and your family. Must've been a thousand vampires led by that thing called Flay. You know her, I believe, and you know what she's capable of. I couldn't get to your father in time to save him, but I kept her away from your brother. It was pretty damned horrible. Your men fought well." He turned purposefully to regard Anhalt. "Those who stood with their emperor, anyway."

Adele said stiffly, "I know all about that night from Mamoru. I thank you for your efforts to protect Simon."

"Of course. And speaking of Simon, you know that the boy is under Lord Kelvin's thumb, right? He's a prisoner in the palace. Kelvin has taken over Equatoria. He has a cadre of Persian troops in Alexandria to keep order, and he's doing his best to put his own toadies in positions of power. The provinces won't stand for it. There's already talk of secession in Bengal and the Cape. And"—Clark now added King Msiri to the victims of his baleful gaze—"Katanga is ready to drive across Tanganyika and link up with Zanzibari rebels to cut East Africa in half."

"Mere rumors," Msiri replied blandly. He waved the whisk as if to disperse the accusation, which was common knowledge.

Clark continued, "Equatoria will fall to pieces without a strong hand at the tiller."

Adele tilted her head. "Meaning *you*?"

"Meaning *us*." The American sat on the edge of a table, looking quite comfortable and sincere, almost reasonable. "Adele, you're the heir. Your father fought like hell to keep you in succession. He wanted *you* on the throne. Poor Simon is surrounded by snakes up there. He's just a boy, and he has no one to help him. You should be there. You know that." Clark poured a glass of wine. "But let's be honest too; the people won't accept you alone. There was a lot of dissatisfaction about you even before your recent escapades. There's a lot of concern about your ability. Fact is, most folks think you're crazy. You don't have a lot of support in Alexandria right now."

Adele turned to Mamoru. "Is that your reading of the atmosphere?"

The samurai was silent for a moment, then sighed. "To some extent, among the nobles, yes. However, I sense the common people have a certain appreciation for your romantic escapades."

Clark scoffed. "Nobody wants a breathless heroine as their leader. Particularly not in time of war."

Adele snapped at him, "Then how do you imagine I can go back if I'm viewed as some unstable eccentric?"

"With me at your side. Your people want a firm hand. They need a firm hand. Our marriage is a done deal, banns or no. You're the rightful heir, and I can hold the army. If we show up together in Alexandria and kick Kelvin out, the city would never stop cheering our names." Clark held out his hand. "You have to go back. You know it and I know it. And I am the only way you can do it."

"Retract your plan to cull the northern humans."

"I'm not here to debate strategy. We can worry about that later. Your Empire is going to fall to pieces without us."

Adele felt numb. It was true that she had never been popular among the wealthy old Equatorian families, many of whom provided the Empire's military commanders. That was why Clark the vampire-killer had been courted as her husband in the first place. The grandees wanted a military man next to the throne for a future that promised protracted warfare against the vampire clans. Adele had earned some cachet after her return from the north as a figure of mystery, but she could only imagine what ammunition the debacle of her wedding had given her detractors, led by Lord Kelvin. Her chief asset, in fact her only asset, was Senator Clark. He was respected and feared. He brought the power of the American alliance with him, and the threat of Equatoria losing her strongest war ally if he departed.

"You must go back."

Adele looked up angrily at Clark, but then realized the words came from Greyfriar. She felt light-headed with surprise. "What do you mean?"

Greyfriar said, "You must be empress. You can't leave your people helpless."

Adele clenched her fists. All doubt was gone now. All she wanted was to go with Gareth and leave everything behind, to depend on no one but him. Any other choice was prison and an acceptance of the coming slaughter. Surely Gareth didn't want that.

"He's right, Adele." Senator Clark came instantly to his feet. "The time for foolishness and fantasy is past. I understand why you were drawn to it; I really do. But it's over now. There's hard work ahead. I'll have *Ranger* fitted out immediately, and you and I will return to Alexandria."

"Not you." Greyfriar pointed at Clark.

The American leaned forward and growled, "How's that?"

Greyfriar went to Adele's side, and their hands linked instantly. "You don't need him."

Adele shook her head and whispered, "You don't understand. I have never been respected in powerful circles in Equatoria. To them, I'm not a leader, I'm just a topic of gossip."

"I know who you are," Greyfriar said. "You are the most extraordinary human I've ever met. You will return because you are the one. You are the empress of Equatoria. If someone tries to stop you, fight them. Crush them. Your people will see you as you are. As I do. As we all do in this room, save one. You need no one else."

Senator Clark dashed his wineglass to the floor and started across the room. "By God! I've had all of you I intend to take!"

Swords sang from scabbards, and surprised voices rose calling for gentlemanly decorum. Clark charged, saber swinging. The American was fast and strong, but he was no swordsman. Greyfriar parried his whistling slash with his rapier, then blocked a second stroke and a third. Clark shouted with each ringing blow, trying to smash Greyfriar's defenses. Greyfriar was slowed, but his natural endurance kept his parries firm. He wasn't fit enough to mount an effective counterattack. Nor did he wish to; he didn't want to kill Clark.

The blades sang again and again, with Clark growing furious at what he perceived as Greyfriar toying with him. He cursed as he swung the glowing saber at the laconic swordsman. Greyfriar merely deflected the strokes away with his rapier while resting against the tusks on the wall, seeming almost in repose. Finally, a strong hand seized Clark's wrist and King Msiri pulled the American away with brute force.

"Senator!" the king shouted. "Enough, sir!"

"No!" Clark snarled through the spittle in his beard. "I'll have this stinking cur's life now for what he's done to me! And no man can stop me!"

"Then allow me to introduce my friend, the army." Msiri yanked Clark around so the American could see General Ngongo and five soldiers nearby with rifles trained.

The senator stood with chest heaving. His head snapped back to Greyfriar, waiting with sword up, but not breathing heavily or visibly fatigued. Then he saw Adele standing nearby with Fahrenheit dagger drawn. The savage instinct on her face both disturbed and excited him. She had never shown any emotion other than boredom or anger toward him. But for Greyfriar, she was ready to strike him down.

"Were you going to try to kill me, Adele?" he asked.

"I wasn't going to *try*."

"So," Clark hissed, "that's how it is, is it?"

Adele continued to stare icily from under downturned brows as she slowly sheathed her blade. "That's how it is."

Clark grinned and put away his sword. "Hah. Who knew you had that in you? You always seemed such an idiotic little girl."

Both Greyfriar and Anhalt surged forward, but Adele held out a hand to stop them. "It just took the right man to bring it out."

The senator straightened his yellow kerchief. "I'll just say good day, then. I'm sorry I won't be there to see them blast you out of the sky when you try to enter Alexandria without me."

"I doubt I'll be thinking of you as I plummet to my death."

Clark muttered something vile under his breath, then shoved through the Katangan soldiers; his stamping boots receded down the hall into silence.

King Msiri waited the requisite few beats of respectful silence demanded by the high emotion of the moment before he laughed and slapped Greyfriar on the shoulder, nearly knocking the swordsman to the floor.

Msiri exclaimed, "That was marvelous! I thought he was going to break his shoulder trying to strike you. And I thought you were going to nod off." The king bowed to the princess with a look of remorse. "Your Highness, allow me to express my condolences at the unfortunate turn your marriage has taken." Then he grinned. "My mother has arranged cake in the next room."

"Thank you, Majesty." Adele smiled broadly with relief and conviction, then turned to Anhalt and Mamoru. "Gentleman, shall we plan strategy for our return to Alexandria?"

—⁓—

Senator Clark threw a heavy chair across the room, watching it shatter a table and vase in its wake. The wrath created by yet another rebuke from Princess Adele, that skinny brat who deemed herself emperor, couldn't be calmed. Clark had been assured that she was a disconnected, disinterested romantic with no pretense to rule, but somehow that girl had grown a backbone. She should have been easily manipulated, ravaged when desired, and shoved aside when no longer needed. The Equatorian Empire needed a man's guidance, as did that slip of a girl. A firm hand would do Adele a world of good. If he could only be alone with her for five minutes without her simpleton acolytes around, he would teach her the proper place for his wife.

Clark knew the man who had brought this disaster upon him. That swordsman's damnable interference had sparked Adele to think for herself. That masked bastard thought to replace him.

A red haze of hatred filled Clark's vision. All his careful planning wasted. Only weeks ago, he had had an entire empire at his feet. Now he had nothing. Everything had been going well until the Greyfriar had shoved himself in where he wasn't needed and rescued the princess from the British clan. Adele had been smitten with the swashbuckling legend, like any typical starry-eyed female. All that time together on the run in Europe had given Greyfriar the time to plant the seed of dissent, so that when Adele returned to Clark's arms, she had already turned against him.

It had all culminated in that disgusting circus of a wedding. The memory of it still reeked with the humiliation heaped upon Clark in front of thousands of important guests. Some of the idiots had even had the audacity to cheer the Greyfriar and laugh at Clark's outrage. But he would not play the fool a single minute more. Preparations were already under way to leave Bunia—much to the surprise of Major Stoddard.

"We're leaving, sir?" the major responded to Clark's order, a little relieved that the rest of Msiri's furniture would be spared.

"Yes."

"And what of Princess Adele?"

"She can try to rule on her own. I'll read about her public humiliation in the papers back home."

"Aye, sir."

———

Adele tossed and turned. She couldn't sleep, surrounded by the overwhelming odds against her. The lives of all of those who pledged loyalty to her were in danger. She had put the American alliance at risk, on the eve of war. She knew she would have to deal with Senator Clark again at some point, but at least it would be on more even terms. She had to make her own way, especially now. She was alone in the darkness, so she allowed tears to fill her eyes as she remembered how bitter her last days with her father had been. She would give anything to change that fact.

There was a gentle knock on Adele's door. The morning light was still at least an hour from breaking over the distant mountains. Wiping her eyes roughly, Adele rose in her nightgown and opened the door to find Greyfriar standing there.

Quickly she drew him inside. "What's wrong?"

"I felt . . ." He took in her flushed face and reddened eyes. "I couldn't sleep."

"Aren't you nocturnal?" she said, forcing a smile. "Come in. Sit with me a while." Adele was grateful for the company to distract her from her depressing thoughts. She pulled Gareth toward the bed as he pulled the scarf from his face, and together they made themselves comfortable. Adele lay back next to him as he brushed a gentle knuckle over her cheek.

"Remember how nice life was in Edinburgh?" she reminisced forlornly. "No mortal peril or doom. I miss it."

"Yes, I too miss those idle, carefree days of having my veins ripped open by Flay's hunters over the castle and dodging your well-aimed barbs when you thought I was just another vampire."

"It's still one of my happiest memories."

"And mine." Gareth smiled and reached into his tunic, pulling out the well-worn copy of *The Princess and the Swordsman*. "There's a section in this book about Edinburgh."

Adele sensed his eagerness, so she nestled against his shoulder. "Read it to me."

He carefully thumbed the pages until he reached the proper spot. "It seems that Princess Adele and the Greyfriar have made their way to Edinburgh, for reasons I couldn't quite understand. But still, there they are. They have taken refuge in Greyfriar's Kirk because, apparently, the Greyfriar's parents lived there in the past." He shook his head. "I couldn't follow everything. It seems odd that—"

"Just read," Adele urged gently, and his voice sounded in the dark:

"The Highland winds howled like spirits of the damned outside the kirk. They shook the old stones and threatened to rattle windows from their ancient frames. The warming light from the fire flickered over Princess Adele's face and sparkled in the crystal tears that cascaded down her terrified face. Her frozen fingers trembled before the crackling flames in their shadow-haunted sanctuary. The Greyfriar knelt beside her with the warm mantle of his great cloak spreading around the girl's shoulders.

"'Don't cry, my darling,' the master swordsman intoned. 'I will soon have you home to the desert breezes of Equatoria.'

"The princess raised her dark eyes to the hard but inviting gaze of her rugged companion. 'But, Greyfriar, what of you? How can I stand for you to remain alone among these terrible monsters, so far from civilized intercourse?'

"The magnificent hero laughed like the cavalier he was and said, 'I do what I must, my darling. You have your destiny as well. We can only pray they intersect at some sweet moments.'"

Greyfriar stopped reading and glanced at Adele expectantly.

Adele studied his face. "So what happens?"

Gareth's gaze did not leave her face as he flipped to the last page and said softly, "They live."

She rose up and kissed him as he curved his arm around her, drawing her closer. She pressed her face against his chest for several minutes before she gave voice to her emotions.

"It still frightens me how close I came to losing you on that mountain. But you're alive and here with me. That's enough." Her voice grew softer, as if weighed down by the immensity of all that had happened these past few weeks. "Right now these four walls are our haven. I don't care what's beyond them. I'm tired of being manipulated. I'm tired of seeing you pay for trying to protect me."

He shushed her with a gentle finger against her lips. "It's a price I've been willing to pay since the first day I met you."

She shook her head. "I always thought we'd find a way to be free, to live some idyllic life away from all this up in the Highlands. When I'm lying here with you I can almost dream it's possible."

Gareth knew she was occupied with fears of the future. Logic demanded there was little chance for happiness between them, but they both refused to give up. "We have weathered crisis after crisis, and we're still together. If all we have are these brief moments together, I would be content."

Adele embraced him. "I would too."

"We will find a way to make you empress and return you to your home," he said quietly.

She caressed his face with her hand and turned him to look at her, to see her steadfast conviction matched his own. "I am home."

They lay together, while on the other side of the drawn curtains, the sun rose high.

CHAPTER 34

"**C**AN YOU FEEL it?"

Adele heard Mamoru's question as if through a long tunnel; even so, she didn't pay him any mind. She was too occupied with reaching out around her, but not with her hands. She couldn't explain or understand what was happening. Still, it felt perfectly natural for pulses of energy to be slipping all around her and pushing through her outstretched fingers like soft, warm sand. These energies had different textures and smells, and in some cases she actually tasted them. Sour. Bitter. Sweet. Others were vile and poisonous, and Adele was repelled by them.

She had only the vaguest sense of location, but she comprehended near and far, so she pushed away even farther, like an unsure swimmer testing the waters while the beach turned into a distant white line in the dark green of the sea. She wondered how far she could go if she kept swimming.

Suddenly, the energies crackled around her with more aggression. They flashed past, unwilling to be touched, too strong to be caressed. Adele realized with a shock that she could see no beach at all. There was only blackness and startling explosions of power that threatened to overwhelm her. She felt something seize her hard, and there was a blinding light. Noises echoed in her head.

Mamoru's frightened face filled her vision. He was shouting. Her eyes fought to focus on him or the bright flowers that swam in the background. Calming green filtered into her. Her fingers dug into the damp soil beneath her, comforting in its mustiness. Mamoru was speaking, but she couldn't understand his slow and primitive sounds.

A sharp stench filled her head, and Adele jerked up. She shook herself violently. Mamoru reached out to her, a bundle of leaves in his fingers. Adele felt slapped by the stink again.

"Princess?" Mamoru asked clearly. "Do you hear me?"

"Yes." She wiped her nose to drive away the pungent bite that clung to her palate.

The samurai sat back, exhaling in relief and running a hand over his close-cropped hair. Adele briefly wondered why he was sitting on the ground in the garden outside her quarters in Bunia; that seemed unlike him. Then she saw the bench where they had both been sitting. She was on the grass too. Adele reached out to lift herself, but Mamoru merely took her hand without offering to help her up.

"Rest," he said gently.

"I'm fine. Weren't we studying crystallography? Where are my notes?" Adele fumbled around for her notebook on the bench. As she dragged the folio over, Mamoru tried to stop her.

"Please, Highness. Relax for a moment."

"Nonsense. Let's continue." Adele looked at the page. They had been discussing energy absorption and reflectivity in crystals. She saw the drawing Mamoru had made for the exercise, a crystal structure with twenty-five facets identified and labeled for her to assess their function. She realized now how simplistic, even wrong, the drawing was, and took up her pencil to correct it.

Her teacher paused midword as she began to sketch, his mouth open and eyes widening. He glanced between her gaze fixed on the drawing and her sure hand that scratched pencil across paper. Finally, without a pause to consider it, she gave the notebook to him.

"Is that right?" she asked.

"I . . . I have no idea." The labeling system she had scrawled on the drawing was infinitely more nuanced than his had been. "You couldn't possibly know this because it is far more advanced than we have ventured. I grasp aspects of your work, but other things are, frankly, a mystery."

Adele took the drawing back, and some of the elements she had changed were already incomprehensible to her. It was like a dream that burned lucid on waking, but became increasingly distant and nonsensical as the rational day set in.

She hung her head. "What's happening to me?"

Mamoru rose to one knee and squeezed her hand. "I can only imagine. What do you remember?"

"I don't know. Colors. Smells. I felt lost, as if I might never find my way back. But I still wanted to keep going."

Mamoru closed her notebook and tossed it aside. "Petty academic theory, it would seem, is now a moot point for you. I believe you are experiencing what ancients called the Belly of the Dragon. You were among the energies of the earth. One day you will master them, but for now you are not prepared."

"Master them? For what?"

Mamoru helped Adele to her unsteady feet. "That remains to be seen, Highness. There has never been anyone like you in my lifetime. Perhaps we should conclude our lesson for today."

"Must we?" Adele took him by the shoulders. "I want to explore—"

Mamoru held up a stern finger. "No! I know that look on your face. Do not attempt these practices alone. I must be with you. You have no conception of the peril. You will become lost, and there is no one who can bring you back."

The princess raised her chin. "I performed adequately up in the mountains."

"Adele!" Mamoru shouted angrily. "Listen to me! This is no game. This is no masquerade in the alleys of Alexandria. You were very lucky not to have been swept away just now. These energies are terrible things and can easily destroy you. I beg you to believe me that you are not ready to act alone!"

She had rarely heard Mamoru shout. "Yes, fine. I understand."

"Promise me."

"I promise. I won't do anything without you."

Mamoru visibly relaxed. "Thank you, Your Highness. It's only that we are so close, and yet we have so much more work. I shouldn't like to see anything put the future in peril."

Adele took his arm, linking elbows. "Thank you for teaching me. I can just hardly believe any of this is true."

"I understand that, but it is true. Finally."

She laughed from the excitement of it all and danced a few steps, barefoot and dressed in a colorful, flowing dress of local cloth. "I can't believe you and Selkirk have been experiencing these miracles for years. And you didn't tell me."

The samurai nodded with a sad smile. "No one has ever experienced what you are now seeing, certainly not me. If you'll excuse me." He took his leave of her with a warm, familiar bow.

Adele breathed in the morning heat. Gareth would be ensconced in her apartments by now, huddled under a cooling blanket. The ever-present heat of the Katangan day, and his infrequent feedings, wore on him. He was becoming ever more distant and isolated and found excuses to spend less time with her just when she was most excited to share her lessons from Mamoru.

The climate of Alexandria would be less oppressive than Katanga. Once Adele assumed power, Gareth could come and go as he pleased. It would be perfectly logical that the Greyfriar would coordinate his actions with the Equatorian government. She couldn't plan much beyond that, but it was sufficient for now that there was a future together, in some fashion. That alone brought a bright smile.

Adele was waiting for the results of political feelers sent out by Colonel Anhalt to determine the receptivity to her return to Alexandria. She had to go back in any case, but the willingness of the army to accept her would be key. The last thing she wanted was to spark a civil war with Simon as the titular leader of her enemy. Adele had tried through various channels to communicate with Simon, but it was impossible. The young boy was no longer her brother; he was the emperor presumptive and therefore shielded from the outside world with no will of his own, controlled by a puppeteer. The idea of finding some way to assassinate Lord Kelvin had even been floated, but that was out of the question, or so Adele hoped. A reign launched in bloodshed was unacceptable.

Colonel Anhalt pushed through the garden gate and approached. No matter the heat, he was in full uniform with every button done up and every seam sharp, his hair immaculately trimmed. He carried a sheaf of papers under one arm and briskly doffed his helmet under the other.

"Highness, are you at liberty?"

"I am, Colonel. What news?"

Without a flutter of hesitation, Anhalt reached into his jacket and proffered a handkerchief. He pointed to his own face, indicating that Adele needed to clean up.

"Studies can be vigorous at times." Adele wiped at her cheek, coming away with dirt. She grinned at the meticulous Gurkha and patted her skirt without finding a mirror, which wasn't surprising since she was a young woman who rarely carried a makeup compact.

Anhalt reached to his boot and withdrew a dagger with a bright, flat blade. She took it gratefully and studied her distorted face in the weapon. Her cheeks were streaked with black volcanic dirt that she now noticed covered her hands too.

Chuckling, she wiped her face. "Quite the horror. I look like Simon on a good day. Pray continue, Colonel."

"I am reliably informed that the Fifth Nile at Khartoum would support your claim. In addition, the provincial governments at the Cape and in Ceylon, and perhaps in Bengal, would need little prodding to proclaim Kelvin's regency illegal."

"As a precursor to secession, I imagine." Adele's expression sobered. "No, Colonel, I won't assist the Empire to dismember itself. And I will not use the Fifth Nile to storm Alexandria. I won't be remembered as the one who destroyed Equatoria. What of the garrison in Alexandria?"

"I have little hard information, I fear. Former members of the White Guard have been cashiered or reassigned far from the capital. Many old officers of your father's army have been forcibly retired. Lord Kelvin has done a thorough job in putting his loyalists in command."

The scowl on her face matched her colonel's. "There's no one in Alexandria you trust?"

"Perhaps. Captain Eskandari, now a general, is the head of Home Defense."

"I don't know him. Persian?"

"Yes, Highness. A Marine. A thorough soldier. He served with Senator Clark at Bordeaux. Apparently he was also the key to Lord Kelvin consolidating his authority over the senator in the chaos following the vampire attack on Alexandria."

"Kelvinist, then?"

"Perhaps not. It may simply be that he was unwilling to cede power to a foreigner. If Eskandari is a strict imperialist, then he may well support your return as rightful heir. In any case, he is the one who holds the gates of Alexandria in his hands."

Adele nodded knowingly. "I want to know everything you can tell me about him. I see no reason to delay further; let's go home and see what fate awaits us. I'll check with Greyfriar to see if he's just as willing to rescue me from the gallows as from the altar."

———

Adele descended stone steps into a damp cellar. Gareth had moved out of his room near Adele's quarters, which, in truth, had been designed for storage. It had satisfied him perfectly well, until recently, when he relocated to a room deep below the palace complex, claiming it was cooler. She couldn't help but think of her snide comments months ago to Gareth about vampires living in holes in the ground. She pushed open the clammy door and held up a lantern to fill the blackness.

A shape moved in the corner and Gareth hissed.

She stepped in as her chest tightened with concern. "Are you ill?"

"No." He shuffled farther away.

Adele stood in dismay. "What's wrong?"

"Nothing."

"Gareth, this isn't like you. Is it the climate? We're returning north soon, so that should help."

"Fine."

"Are you hungry? Do you need to feed?"

"No." His voice was clipped and strained.

She stared at the hunched outline of the prince. She couldn't make out his face to read his emotions, so she kept her voice calm. "Gareth, don't do this. Tell me what's wrong."

He grunted.

"Say something," Adele said. "You can't become this"—she waved her hand toward him—"this thing. I need you. You're all I have. What is it?"

"It's you."

She froze with uncertainty and fear. "What do you mean?"

Gareth inched forward with his head down, as if avoiding her gaze. "You've changed. I can't bear to be near you."

"Changed? I've done nothing but reach out to you, to plead with you to stay with me in Alexandria as much or as little as you can. I've done everything for us. You've crawled into this tomb to live in the dark. How have I changed?"

He looked up, and his blue eyes were bloodshot and exhausted. "Every day you spend learning your secrets, I feel more pain when I'm with you. Adele, you are becoming something I can't be near."

She gasped. It had never occurred to her that all the geomancy practice with Mamoru was altering her. She was turning into a reservoir of pain for Gareth.

In her training, Adele had experienced the sublime and the miraculous, a powerful sense of nurturing unlike anything she had ever known, comparable to vaguely held memories of her mother's arms. Her journeys were sometimes confusing or frightening, but she always returned invigorated, almost vibrating with life, as if her skin didn't just enclose her body, but rather was touched by everything she could imagine.

Now, in one succinct instant, the void between her and Gareth yawned inseparably wide. Again, it hit home that they were different species. There was nothing they shared. What nurtured one, killed the other.

Her heart fell.

Gareth said, "I'm sorry. I didn't want to tell you. It obviously means so much to you. When you go home and become empress, I will return to the north. You will be free to become what you should."

"I don't want to continue if it's driving you away."

"We will stay in contact."

"No!" Adele shouted. "We won't part again like this. I will find a way. If I have to suspend my studies, I will."

"No, Adele. Don't stop—"

"I'll do what I wish. My days of being told what to do are finished. If I want to give up my studies, I will. Or I'll only practice when you are away in the north. But you will not disappear again." She lifted a stern hand, bristling with conviction, cutting off any retort from him. "I don't care what you think. I don't care what anyone thinks. I don't care if I turn into a feeble old woman and you're still young. I will have you with me! Is that clear?"

"Yes." He regarded her. Every day she became more empress than young woman. He drew a haggard smile. She was too magnificent to deny.

"Good." Adele nodded curtly, her anger swiftly subsiding with relief that he agreed. "You know, this noble, anguished hero routine of yours goes only so far. Now, we are departing on *Edinburgh* in two days. I'll suspend my meditation and exercises so hopefully you can bear to be in my presence by then. It may be a moot point because the Equatorian army could destroy us before we enter Alexandrian air."

"Do they know you are coming?"

"They will. I'm cabling the sublime Kelvin Pasha to inform him of our arrival time. We have a few other contacts who will ensure that the city is aware."

"Princess Adele and the Greyfriar return."

"Curtain rises."

CHAPTER

T HE PREVAILING NORTHERLIES off the Mediterranean
forced *Edinburgh* to take valuable time tacking repeatedly as she
approached Alexandria from the south. Captain Hariri crossed the quarterdeck to Adele and Greyfriar. "Three Equatorian frigates moving to
intercept."

"Where?" Adele studied the skies around her with a spyglass. The
air was crowded with vessels of both commerce and war, but she couldn't
discern any immediate threat.

The captain pointed at three ships out of the scores filling the sky,
at varying distances and directions.

"Can we avoid them?" Greyfriar asked, his scarf blowing in the
wind. He moved vigorously with no trace of weakness. All his burns
were healed.

"Not all of them. And even if I could, there will be others. Even
hidebound imperial captains can manage to rule the air over Alexandria
through sheer numbers. They'll have us hemmed in before we can reach
Pharos One."

"Good thing we're not going to Pharos One," Adele said.

Hariri glanced questioningly at the princess. Greyfriar had been
with her too long to show surprise.

She faced the captain. "I should like to put down on the north shore of Lake Mareotis, if you can."

"There are no mooring towers in the Limehouse district, ma'am."

"Yes, I know. I won't need to stay long. We'll be going over the side on drop lines. Can you do it?"

The captain shrugged. "I can."

"Excellent. Thank you. We are ready when you are."

Hariri returned to the binnacle to plot a course and issue orders for a ground-anchored stop in an inhabited area. Adele stood at the rail, watching the yellow desert intermingle with the blue-white sparkling Nile delta and then blur into the grey, sprawling city of Alexandria. Through the haze, she could see the dim silhouette of Victoria Palace on the coast. Her breath sharpened at the sight of so many familiar old places. But they seemed different to her, almost mysterious, as if she were a visitor unsure of her reception in this strange city. This was a different home from the one she had left. No matter what happened today, this city, that palace, would never be what they had been to her as a young girl. Those days were gone forever.

Greyfriar said, "Would you care to share your plans? Why set down so far from your palace?"

"I intend to walk."

"Walk? Across Alexandria?"

"Yes. I should like the people to know that their princess has returned."

"Your Lord Kelvin will find that quite antagonistic."

"Oh, that ship has sailed long ago. I can't trust the army. I don't trust the lords. But I do trust the people."

"The people are a touchy weapon. They're powerful, sure, but likely to go off at the wrong time."

"I've got little else. I spent time among them, and I realize that they love me. Or at least they love the idea of me. Plus, I've brought my secret weapon."

"The Greyfriar?"

"Yes." Adele smiled and patted his chest. "One thing I know is that the people love a happy ending. And we're going to give them one."

Enough time had passed since Adele last trained that her touch no longer caused him pain. That simple fact sang in her heart.

"So dangerous, Adele."

"All hands brace for descent!" the bosun shouted, and a claxon rang across the ship.

Adele assumed a wide stance and grasped the rail. "I'd say in twenty-four hours you will either be the consort of Empress Adele the First, or we'll all be dead."

"Both have their challenges," Greyfriar replied wryly.

She laughed over the roar of venting buoyants overhead as poor, repaired *Edinburgh* fell rapidly. The wooden hull creaked with the strain, and boards shuddered. The dusty air rushed upward, and shining Lake Mareotis appeared. As they plunged, they drifted north, and the buildings of Alexandria rose into view. Captain Hariri grinned with excitement and shouted a command; chemical pumps pushed buoyant back into certain bags, and *Edinburgh* slowed its descent. The yards and deck were full of scrambling men securing sail and sending drop lines and anchors over the side.

"Your Highness," Hariri shouted as chaos flowed around him. "We can moor temporarily to a building if necessary. How long do you need us here?"

"Not long, I should think." Adele already saw Colonel Anhalt leading his men up from the companionway onto the deck. Their tramping feet filled her with excitement, but she beamed at the sight of Anhalt and troopers in their red jackets with blue trousers and white helmets. They were the White Guard once again.

Colonel Anhalt came to attention before Adele and saluted. His cool façade couldn't hide the pride he felt commanding his White Guard. "Ready to proceed, Your Highness."

"Carry on, Colonel. Form ranks below and await my orders."

"As you will." He spun sharply and bellowed, "Over the side! Form square and hold!" The colonel seized a drop lever with a gloved hand and swung over without hesitation.

From the corner of her eye, Adele saw Mamoru crossing the deck. The wind whipped his green silk robe, and he clutched the cutlass thrust inside the obi around his waist. He bowed to her, then glanced over the side with an uncertain tremor.

"Hm," he said. "Quite high."

"You should stay with the ship," Adele said. "If this goes badly, there's no reason for you to be injured by it. You can return to Java and teach."

The samurai shook his head. "There is no one else to teach. I shall stay with you. I know what you hope to do, but I remind you, there are many secret paths into the palace."

"Secrecy doesn't accomplish my goals. The Empire must witness me take power. Have you ever used a drop line from an airship?"

"Of course not. I'm not insane." Mamoru held up his hands, which were wrapped in thick oilcloth. "But I can learn as well as teach. Wish me luck." He took hold of a thick cable and climbed over the rail. With one more furtive gaze at the street far below, he took a deep breath and started down.

Adele held up her hand to the quarterdeck. "Captain! I thank you and your crew. Once I'm away, make for the rendezvous point and await my orders."

Hariri touched head, mouth, and heart, and many of the crew joined his salute with shouts of "Good luck!" or "*Bon chance!*" The grinning young telegrapher called out his well wishes in broken Swahili.

Adele dropped her cloak to reveal her new clothes designed for her return home. The best Katangan tailors had provided her with a long, heavy silk skirt of shimmering pearl, and a short jacket of light violet, all designed to draw the eye whether she was standing near the scarlet-coated White Guard or the grey shades of Greyfriar. Simple and functional, but elegant—the image that Adele wanted to portray.

The princess looked over the side. Mamoru was nearly down, and several guardsmen held his line taut. The redcoats had formed a square on the street, and a crowd was gathering, watching the soldiers, pointing up at the ship. From her vantage point Adele could see lines of people meandering in their direction through the narrow streets.

Alexandria was a small town masquerading as a metropolis. Word still spread rapidly through the districts. Adele and Anhalt had used all their contacts to alert the city that the princess was returning. They had picked this very day, giving themselves time for delay on the route from Katanga. They'd actually made such good time they spent several days circling in the desert so they could meet their prophesied arrival, allowing the news to expand throughout the streets. Hopefully the city was primed for her appearance, and this strange airship disgorging imperial soldiers, which surely some recognized were dressed in the colors of Adele's household guard, would light a wildfire of rumor.

As she placed a foot on the rail, Greyfriar said, "Adele, please. If I may." He took a line in one hand and reached out the other to her. "If you wish to make a real entrance."

The princess eagerly looped her arms around his shoulders. He swung madly over the side into the open air, and she laughed. He lightened his frame so that he was virtually gliding down, one hand holding the cable and one arm tight around Adele's waist. His cloak cracked like a whip in the wind.

"Not too fast," Adele shouted into his ear as she clutched her skirt with her free hand, wondering about the wisdom of a dress on an air drop. "Let them see us."

Greyfriar tightened his grip on the line and slowed their descent. He spun slowly so that all gathered below could witness the glorious appearing. Even the White Guard stared while Anhalt and Mamoru seized her cable and held it firm. Thousands of faces peered up from the street. Hundreds more showed at every window and doorway. Even rooftops swelled with people.

Finally—after a long, wind-blasted, fifty-foot drop—Greyfriar's boots touched firm earth. Adele stepped to the cobblestones as cool and calm as if she were descending from a carriage of state. The crowd exploded in a frenzy of adoration, screaming her name.

Adele glided away from Greyfriar with a long, lingering touch and moved toward the crowd despite Colonel Anhalt's expression of dismay. The Gurkha followed several steps behind, signaling with his hands for the White Guard to stand ready. The princess paused just yards from the tide of exultant people. Resting her hand on the hilt of her dagger, she surveyed the crowd. Then her hand rose, and they began to quiet, even shushing others around them. The hush moved like a wave through the mob until finally the street was eerily silent.

Adele called out boldly, "Will you follow me?"

The crowd erupted again in a blast that shook the buildings. Adele threw up her arms, knowing there would be no silence again. "Then follow me!" she shouted as she started into the body of the mob, carried by her own power. Anhalt rushed his men up to surround her and protect her from rough, loving hands.

Greyfriar vaulted over locals and soldiers to reach her side, but he remained a few feet behind her; this was her moment. She was controlling this herd in a way he couldn't conceive. She exuded authority and power. He had sensed it in her long ago, but here it was played large.

The giant, living wave surged north through the city. Streams of people engorged the dark alleys and streets, and great torrents of them rolled up the tree-lined avenues, flowing around benches, fences, and lampposts. Trams stopped in their tracks along with wagons, cabs, and omnibuses frozen by the flow of humanity.

Adele felt her people around her in a way she never had. Men, women, and children. Brown, black, white. Arab. African. European. Asian. Rich, poor, working class. The Empire was afoot, chanting her name, growing in size and voice with each block. She sensed both their uncertainty and their desire. They so badly wanted to believe that the mere presence of the head of the Royal House would ensure the safety of the city from further vampire attacks. Adele was the force to make it happen. All their hopes and fears were poured into the young princess. Only she had the power to make it real. This was a day when life would change and all their woes would vanish. And they were playing their part, propelling the young princess to her place as their savior. The White Guard maintained a protective square, but the crowd closest to Adele had assumed the role of escorts too. They felt as if they were part of her entourage and worked jealously to keep the princess's path clear.

As the crowd passed the Soma, the crossroads of the city, every window was filled with people. Flags waved high overhead along with handkerchiefs or towels or sheets—anything people could use to express their joy and excitement.

The horde plunged north into the Turkish Quarter, where the wide avenues vanished into the alleys and warrens of Old Alexandria. Then the mob snaked out of the Turkish Quarter and streamed into the Imperial Quarter, where Victoria Palace waited. The crowd began to fill Victoria Square and pile up against the wall that protected the palace grounds.

Finally, Adele approached the palace for the first time since she had fled her home. Her father was no longer there and her brother was likely secluded in some windowless chamber surrounded by soldiers. Surly men patrolled the wall and crouched on the corner posts, where machine guns were now mounted. Warships overhead cast their dreadful shadows. Her beautiful home had become an armed camp.

Adele's guard muscled its way through the mob until the main gate of the palace walls towered above her. Inside that ornate iron barrier, which was closed and locked, waited a line of grim-faced Home Guard, their rifles clutched against their chests. Citizens swarmed to the outside of the gate, screaming at the soldiers to open it for the princess, all the while chanting, "Adele! Adele!"

A thin, lanky Home Guard officer peered out of the iron rails. He was a handsome young man with a stern face, olive skin, and Persian features. He seemed too young to be a general. He gave Adele a curt nod before turning his worried eyes to the earthquake of humanity around her.

"This mob," he said in a low voice, "is a public menace. It must disperse."

"Are you General Eskandari?"

"I am, Your Highne—ma'am."

"May I enter my home?"

"The gates must stay locked." Eskandari's gaze darted to Colonel Anhalt, and his eyes lit up with recognition before settling on the mysterious Greyfriar. "The city is in a state of emergency."

Adele spied a motionless figure on a high palace balcony. Even at this distance, she could recognize the vulturous form. "I demand to speak with Kelvin Pasha."

"That's quite impossible. Please, disband your followers immediately."

"General, Lord Kelvin's government is illegal and I—"

361

"That's not my concern. Now, please, you must comply for public safety." He had to shout over the rising din, "There is no other solution to this that doesn't end in bloodshed!"

Hearing Eskandari threaten bloodshed, overly fervent screaming young men rushed the gates with their hands full of rocks and bottles. They pushed against the ornamental wrought iron, and some started to climb it. Stones and bottles flew at the Home Guard inside. Handguns appeared in the crowd. Rifles snapped up. From somewhere a loud crack broke the humid air and gunfire erupted.

"Get down, Highness!" Anhalt shouted as he shielded her from the palace wall.

Adele felt hands grab her and pull her away from the bodies and shouting, the smoke of guns and the dust of trampling feet. Her White Guard backed away from the gate with rifles flaming. From above came the merciless staccato popping of machine guns spraying bullets into the crowd, which desperately fought to escape into the alleys of Old Town, only to find them choked with surprised new arrivals unsure what the uproar was about. People fell with their faces masks of pain or surprise, bullets tearing through workman's twill, banker's wool, and lady's silk alike.

Greyfriar wrapped Adele in his arms and cloak as her small entourage battered their way back through the terrified madness. The dreadful snapping of gunfire outside her home horrified her. This was Alexandria. This didn't happen here. She was carried behind the substantial marble base of the equestrian statue of the first Equatorian emperor, Simon I, and pressed to the ground. It had been years since she had been small enough to see the mighty monument that dominated Victoria Square from this low angle. Greyfriar hovered over her back with Anhalt beside her, while Mamoru crouched behind. White Guardsmen went to one knee around her, firing back at the gate.

Mamoru shouted, "There is a secret entrance into the palace nearby."

"No!" Adele snapped as bullets ticked off the statue, spraying marble fragments. "I won't sneak into my own home like a thief. My people are dying in the street before me!"

"You must see reason," Mamoru retorted. "We cannot storm the gate with a handful of men under fire."

In that instant she knew what she had to do. Her people were dying because of their faith in her. Her eyes locked with Greyfriar's, and despite the smoked glasses she saw that he knew what she was thinking. Perhaps her scent had changed from frightened to determined. He shook his head, but she was committed.

"I don't intend to storm it," she stated.

Adele stood.

"My God! Get down!" Mamoru shouted as many hands reached up for her.

The princess roughly shrugged off her protectors and stepped into the open. Bullets ticked all around, but by the grace of God none struck her. Greyfriar rose to his feet with her, but Adele's stern glance stayed him. He nodded his unwilling compliance but remained with her in the open, refusing to slip back behind cover. Her raised hand signaled the rest of her entourage to stay where they were. Colonel Anhalt repeated a prayer he vaguely remembered from his childhood as he watched the small young woman traverse the killing field, which still hung with gunsmoke and was puddled with blood.

Adele walked through the hail of gunfire straight toward the nearest wounded, a young man. Dropping to her knees next to the man, who was bleeding profusely, she attempted to stanch the flow with a bandage torn from her dress. Only moments ago he had followed her wildly through the streets chanting her name. Now here he was, dead or dying, far from help.

General Eskandari's voice rang out from inside the grounds, "Cease fire! Cease fire, damn you!" The guns of the palace fell silent and the White Guard likewise halted, but kept rifles to their shoulders. The hot silence of the square was broken by the pitiful moaning of the wounded. At least twenty bodies sprawled on the paving stones.

"I warned you," Eskandari cried with an anguished voice from behind the wrought-iron bars decorated with an intricately worked family crest. "I begged you."

Adele looked straight at him. "General, I am Princess Adele, the heir to my father Emperor Constantine the Second. My father is dead. I am your sovereign. I command you and your men to lay down your arms and bring aid to my people."

The Persian marine studied the firm expression of the woman. She was not playacting. Her aura of command was impressive; her bravery was unquestionable given that she now waited unarmed, far from her men, with nothing more than her character to protect her, kneeling in the blood of her subjects.

"Your Highness," he said, "you are no longer the heir—"

"The decision of Commons is illegal. They have no authority over succession. Lord Kelvin's regency is illegal. You are serving an outlaw regime."

"I don't know about such matters. I am only a soldier."

"And I am your empress," Adele said loudly. "I thank you for your service preventing Senator Clark from usurping power. Your actions were directed toward safeguarding Equatoria. You must now be consistent in that principle. There has been enough blood shed here. I give my word that no revenge will be taken on you or your men. You are bound to defend Equatoria; you have sworn an oath to that. Do so now."

General Eskandari glanced back at the small figure on the balcony, so far from harm's way, before slowly turning to the young woman who faced his guns, and the wounded citizens around her. Unbuttoning his tunic, he reached in and, with a strong tug, produced a sturdy key on a thin chain. He inserted the key into the lock on the gate and turned it with several loud clacks, then swung one side of the iron gate inward.

The general stepped out and handed the key to Adele. "Your Highness, Victoria Palace is yours." He then drew his sword, dropped to one knee, and held the hilt toward her. "I surrender myself into your mercy. All I have done was for Equatoria."

Adele looked up at the balcony. Lord Kelvin was gone. She heard footsteps rushing up behind her, and then Greyfriar, Anhalt, Mamoru, and her men appeared at her side. Some of her White Guard darted to the aid of the wounded while the rest formed a half circle about her.

"General, rise and resume your duties. I want the wounded tended to immediately. Your men on the gate should be confined to barracks for their own protection. Colonel Anhalt, you are now commanding officer in Alexandria with the rank of brevet general. General Eskandari, you will inform imperial troops of this change in command." She relinquished the bloody tourniquet to one of her soldiers. "I would like Lord Kelvin brought to me."

No sooner were the words out of her mouth than Adele saw the long-limbed bureaucrat approaching across the manicured palace courtyard. She almost laughed as he loped toward her in a manner that was both reticent and eager. He seemed remarkably calm and unflustered for a man whose government had just been toppled.

"Your Imperial Highness," he intoned with a deep bow as he reached the gate. "Allow me to join in with a hearty welcome home."

Adele rose. "Welcome home? That's an odd sentiment given the gates were locked against me." She accepted a handkerchief from Anhalt and tried to wipe the blood from her hands.

"Against you?" Kelvin stared like a confused owl. "No, Your Imperial Highness. Not against you. We had word of an unruly mob rioting through Alexandria, and had no firm knowledge of its intent. So we took reasonable precautions. The gunfire was unfortunate, but after your rabble attacked the palace guard, there was little alternative. Naturally, tense young men defended themselves. Sad, but predictable."

"Where is Simon?" Adele had no time to counter his ridiculous summary of events.

"In the palace. Quite safe and no doubt eager to see you. As we all are."

"You didn't seem so eager judging from your cables to Bunia."

Lord Kelvin raised his eyebrows innocently. "It's unseemly to bicker about policy in front of the casualties."

Adele glared at the man angrily. "Indeed. Why aren't doctors out here? Get them now! Then we can go inside to plan my coronation."

"Yes. Delightful. It may take some time to prepare. We can't use your original crown when you were to be wed to Senator Clark."

"I will use my father's crown."

"Oh? I doubt that will fit."

"I think you'll find it will."

CHAPTER 36

ADELE, GREYFRIAR, AND Simon passed among the marble sarcophagi as if they were walking between rows of wheat. Their footfalls echoed in the dim recesses of the crypt. It was cool and quiet, with calming white marble, red quartzite, and black basalt forming the vault. The monuments were lavishly decorated, boasting imposing sculptures of dead men. The crypt was similar to many of the tombs of the north where Gareth had sought rest before the Great Killing. It was pleasant when compared to the balmy air above; he could easily reside here while in Alexandria. But that would likely cause gossip around the court.

Greyfriar walked beside Adele, whose long, crimson cloak flowed behind her. Her stride was sure and steady now, even if her scent was altered by a tinge of fear. He touched her arm to reassure her, and she looked nervously at him. They stopped before a large sarcophagus of black basalt. Compared to many of the others, it was relatively plain, with straight edges and no frivolous accentuations. Great thick letters carved into the base proclaimed the name *Constantine II*.

Adele removed her glove before laying her hand on the hard surface of the tomb. Her head dropped, but no tears fell. Greyfriar waited to comfort her, but she simply stood over her father's resting place without overt reaction. Reaching out with her other hand, she drew her brother, Simon, closer. The lad was resplendent in a blue naval uniform complete with white gloves and dress blue cap. He seemed grim, but not distraught, as if he were playing the part of a mourner. Simon had already had time to come to terms with his father's death. The boy watched his sister with concern. He glanced at Greyfriar, who gave him a supportive nod, appreciating the boy's kindness toward Adele.

"I can't even cry," Adele said.

"Why?" Greyfriar asked.

"I don't know. I thought it would destroy me to come here and see his grave for the first time. But I feel numb."

"Can you tell me what he was like?"

There was a long silence. Adele stared at Greyfriar with a sad smile, unable to see his eyes through his smoked glasses. "I don't know. I never really knew him. I knew my mother much better, at least so I thought. I suppose I never knew either of them. Now they're both gone."

Greyfriar studied the crypt. "Where is your mother's place? I thought it was customary to bury couples together."

Adele shook her head. "This crypt is for emperors. My mother is in another mausoleum. Not far away. I'll be here too. Maybe I could have her moved."

"Didn't you spend time with your father?" Greyfriar asked.

"He was always busy," Simon offered.

"When I was very young," Adele added, "I remember some state events and a couple of family trips. After our mother died, our father stayed close to us for a year or two. But it didn't last. He was the emperor. His time was not his own."

"My father was similar," Greyfriar said.

Adele replied warily, eyeing Simon, who was not privy to Greyfriar's secret, "But you said he taught you to hunt. And taught you lessons about . . . survival."

"Yes. Surely your father taught you similar lessons."

The princess shook her head. "No. My mother, yes, but my father taught me very little."

"Do you think he wanted to?"

"I don't know. At the end, he seemed to want to reach out to me. Maybe he sensed something. Maybe he was sorry about the marriage to Senator Clark. He tried, but I was so angry." Adele took Gareth's hand and leaned against him. For the first time there was a slight hitch in her tone. "They say he fought back against Flay. That he wasn't afraid."

Simon said with pride, "They found him with a sword in his hand."

Greyfriar bobbed his head in admiration. "Good. I hope he hurt her."

"He didn't stand a chance," Adele said.

"I hid." Simon spoke in a low voice, toeing the marble floor. "I hid in a servant's pantry."

Greyfriar said forcefully, "Smart. I would've hidden too."

"No, you wouldn't," the boy argued. "You're the Greyfriar. You would have killed that vampire."

"No, you're wrong." The swordsman regarded Simon like the little prince was a fellow warrior. "I've faced Flay before, but not by choice. I've never defeated her, and only escaped with my life by sheer luck. Simon, there's no victory in being goaded into combat by a stronger enemy. The wise war chief chooses the proper time to strike. That night was Flay's time. Escaping her was the greatest victory you could have scored. In time, we will have her, and you will be a part of that success. If you had played her game on her terms, you would be dead too, and her victory would be complete."

Simon nodded, smiling slightly as though a burden had been lifted. "Now that you're here to help Adele, can we really win this war?"

"She doesn't need me." Greyfriar's voice was assured and confident. "But we will win."

Adele was grateful for him engaging her brother, easing the boy's guilt over the night their father died and softening his fears of the future. She cuffed the back of Simon's neck playfully, and he pulled away with typical boyish annoyance to wander off among the other sarcophagi.

Adele asked Greyfriar in a low voice, "So, is Flay better than you? In a fight?"

He thought about it as Adele studied what little of his face she could see, measuring the question. He said cautiously, "I'm not sure. It would likely depend on who struck first. Surprise would decide it. Flay is fast. Deathly fast."

Adele looked around for Simon, then whispered, "What about your brother? Is he better than you?"

"Cesare?" Greyfriar gave a derisive snort and said quietly, "He's no match for me. I'm much stronger than he."

"Really?" Adele felt a pleasant flush. He wasn't bragging, merely stating a fact. His arm did feel like iron under her fingers.

"I am capable of decapitating and disemboweling with my claws. In my society, that makes me quite desirable."

"No doubt. Though in my society, keep it to yourself." Adele gave him a sly look. "I'm in this relationship for the capes and castles."

"So am I," he said with mock seriousness.

"We can't both be romantics. One of has to be a realist."

"I nominate you."

"Thank you." Adele crossed her arms. "So what about me? Do you think you could beat me?"

His head lifted slowly, and he reached up to remove his glasses, revealing his crystal blue eyes. "In a fight to simply defeat one another, in practice, I would easily best you. My strength and stamina would overwhelm you. In a fight to the death, however, I stand no chance."

"Are you being serious?"

"Of course. In life, I am your master. In death, you have no equal. You would slay me."

Adele stared at him open-mouthed. She couldn't respond. She didn't know how to take what he had just said. His expressions and tones were not always the same as a human. Part of her felt some sliver of pride that he judged her so powerful and competent. But another part felt there was an accusatory undertone to his statement, some unspoken fear, some untapped unease about her. Perhaps it was an inbred resentment about her *power*, her native ability to kill his kind. Still, it was unlike him. Even when they had been at odds early in their stay in Edinburgh, he had never expressed such confidence in her savagery. Maybe in his world, he had just paid her a great compliment.

She asked hesitantly, "Do you think I would kill you?"

Gareth didn't pause. "I think you could. That's all. That's what you asked me. That is what you are training to do. Your . . . what do you call it, geomancy? Your lessons with Mamoru. You are becoming a weapon to destroy vampires."

"That's not what I'm doing! Just because I may have an ability doesn't mean I have to use it. I have control over myself. I think this ability—whatever it is—can lead to better things. It doesn't have to be a weapon. I will learn to control it so what happened in the Mountains of the Moon doesn't have to happen again. Don't you trust me?"

"Of course."

Simon's voice came from the distance, low and conversational. "Who are you? What are you doing here?"

Adele and Greyfriar both bolted toward the boy. Greyfriar leapt over a sarcophagus to find Simon face-to-face with a strange man, his beard unkempt and his long, matted blond hair hanging about his face in clumps. He wore filthy clothes and stank of sweat and dirt.

"Selkirk?" Adele said in confusion as she reached Simon's side. She stepped in front of the boy, but waved Greyfriar off his aggressive stance.

The man was on one knee beside a large tomb. He made no threatening move, but slowly looked up with recognition in his intense eyes. Greyfriar eased his sword back into the scabbard, sensing Adele's alarm shift to curiosity.

Adele asked the disoriented man, "What are you doing here? What happened to you? Does Mamoru know you're here?"

Selkirk rose and took an unsteady step toward her. He seemed weak, perhaps hungry, not quite sure of his surroundings. His hand lifted from the folds of his stained coat holding something. He launched himself the few feet to Adele and plunged a dagger into her chest. The princess gasped and raised her hands.

Greyfriar shouted in alarm, and his rapier tore free. Selkirk pulled the knife out and stabbed her again with a sick, solid sound. The swordsman seized the man by the shoulder and threw him away from Adele. Selkirk grunted as he crashed against a tomb. Greyfriar drove his blade deep into the man's rib cage, and Selkirk collapsed with a whimper.

"Adele!" Greyfriar turned as the princess stumbled and fell to the ground. The swordsman dove to the floor beside Adele and scooped her into his arms.

Wet scarlet spread across her white silk gown. She looked up at Greyfriar, but her eyes were wide and jerking side to side. Her mouth moved soundlessly, and her breath rasped.

"Adele," Greyfriar cried. "Can you speak? Can you hear me?"

Her eyelids fluttered and her eyes rolled up in her head. Adele went limp and heavy in his arms. Her heartbeat faltered.

"No, no!" He looked up at Simon, who stood petrified next to them. "Get someone, anyone. Go! Now! Please!"

———— ∞ ————

Greyfriar huddled in the dark corner of a small room in the Iskandar Hospital. Adele's blood was dried stiff on his clothes, but he could still smell her as if it were fresh. It had been hours since General Anhalt, never far from her side, had responded to Prince Simon's cries for help and fell into action. Military doctors had attended Adele on site, struggling to halt the bleeding, while word was sent for surgeons to assemble at the hospital. Simon was taken under guard in case the attack on Adele was part of a larger scheme. The mysterious assassin was still breathing, so he was bundled unceremoniously onto a gurney and rolled away, with instructions from Anhalt to preserve his life. Then, Adele was rushed, pale and unconscious, from the palace grounds in an ambulance, a shrill blast of steam erupting from the brass whistle as it departed.

Greyfriar had almost been forgotten in the chaos. He pushed into the ambulance with Adele. Only when orderlies at the hospital carried her poor, helpless form through the swinging doors did General Anhalt place a firm arm against his chest.

"You can't follow," the general said. "She is going into surgery."

Greyfriar stood helplessly as the door closed on Adele. He was overwhelmed by the scent of blood and alcohol and death, and by the sounds of fear and sorrow that surrounded him in this place. He turned to the Gurkha. "They will save her, won't they?"

"She will have the best surgeons in the world." Anhalt glanced around. "We have not told the public that the princess has been injured. You must wait out of sight. If the Greyfriar is seen here it will cause talk. Come." As the two men walked the tile hallway with its flickering gas lamps, the general said, "I will have a change of clothes brought for you."

"Why?"

Anhalt left the swordsman in the small, cool room with orders to stay inside until he was summoned. And so he did. Hours passed as figures moved through the hallway beyond the door, but Greyfriar's ears never picked up word of Adele's condition. Finally, he strode to the door, ready to demand information. Then he smelled something harsh and acrid.

The door swung in and Mamoru appeared. The samurai was dressed in a fashionable black suit with a pearl-grey bowler hat. A walking stick was gripped tightly in his fist. Greyfriar withdrew across the room with a deep rumble in his throat.

"What happened to her?" Mamoru snarled at him.

"I've been here for hours with no word. How is she?"

"I don't know." The priest suppressed a smile, savoring the pain he was inflicting on the vampire through his various amulets and crystals, and by withholding information. "I ask you again, what happened to her?"

"She was attacked by a man who was hidden in her family tomb. Stabbed before I could intervene. I was not cautious enough. She seemed to know him." Greyfriar raised a baleful eye at Mamoru. "She said you knew him as well."

"What do you mean? Explain yourself, damn you!"

"She called him *Selkirk*."

Mamoru stiffened, and his eyes darted with confusion as he whispered, "What? That's impossible. You misheard. Where is the assailant's body?"

"They brought him here. He's still alive, to my shame. My first concern was Adele."

The schoolteacher leaned out the door and shouted to an unseen figure, "You! Send for General Anhalt."

The samurai and the vampire stared silently at one another for minute after minute until finally the doorknob rattled. Mamoru moved swiftly and went outside before Anhalt could enter. He closed the door on the vampire and confronted the general in the hallway.

"Where is the assassin?" he asked.

Anhalt replied coldly, "He's recovering. His surgery was successful and he will likely survive long enough to attend his execution."

"I need to see him."

The general looked surprised, but said, "As you will. Follow me."

The two men climbed an echoing stairwell to a vast, dim ward, now deserted but for one lone bed surrounded by White Guardsmen. A pale figure with matted hair and bandages wrapped around his midsection lay in a metal-frame bed. Clicking footfalls halted yards from the patient as Mamoru caught a glimpse and faltered. Anhalt stopped too.

"What's wrong?" the general asked.

Mamoru breathed as if he were injured. "I know him."

"How so?"

"He is a student of mine. I don't understand."

Anhalt grew grim. "I don't either, but I intend to."

Mamoru ignored the potential threat to his affairs. He had outmaneuvered greater dangers to his secret cabal than this simple soldier. The extraordinary thing was that Selkirk, one of his chosen geomancers, was here in Alexandria as the would-be assassin of Princess Adele. He couldn't imagine what could have happened to the lad between here and Britain. He had to find out. The implications for his network were catastrophic. The samurai turned abruptly and left the ward with Anhalt following. "I'll want to see his possessions."

"He had only his clothes and a dagger. They've been searched to no benefit."

"I will want them. I may see value where others do not. General, even in this horrific time, we have been given an ideal opportunity to end the blight on what we both hold dear. We both know this grotesque situation with the princess can't continue."

"What grotesque situation would that be?"

"That monster that has latched onto her. You have no idea of his power. We can't know what happened to her in the north, but we both understand that this cannot be allowed to stand. The princess must be free of that parasite. We can do it now while she is not here to protect it."

The Gurkha general stared at the teacher with no outward emotion. He clasped his hands behind his back. "Prince Gareth is under Her Highness's protection. He is, therefore, under mine as well."

"But he's a vampire. And the princess is not in her right mind. We must do the right thing!"

"Keep your voice down, sir. This is a hospital."

The samurai paused, then smiled with recognition at what he took as Anhalt's cleverness. "Ah, I see. Will you then leave me alone with that creature? You need have no knowledge of events."

General Anhalt pursed his lips and said in an even voice, "I play no games with you, sir. I care nothing for your secret, occult studies with Her Highness. If she enjoys it, teach her; that is not my concern. But if you act against Prince Gareth, I assure you I will fall on you like unholy hell. Do I make myself clear?"

"General, I—"

"Do I make myself clear, sir?"

Mamoru eyed Anhalt with new suspicion. "Yes, General. You are crystal clear."

"Thank you. I will expect a full report on your relationship with the assailant."

"In due time. We have more pressing matters. This man, Selkirk, could not have acted alone. He carried no food. Where is his transport? How did he get into the imperial crypt? The doors are always locked and the keys are held by a loyal few. Clearly, he has confederates here in Alexandria, perhaps in the palace itself. We must move before they flee."

"All traffic—air, sea, rail—has been halted. If he has allies, they can go nowhere." Anhalt paused, then added, "The only contact we know he has here in Alexandria is you."

Mamoru reddened, and his mouth tightened in anger. "How dare you! Damn your implications! If you bring me his possessions as I asked, I may be able to track his recent movements. I saw how efficient your dragnet was in preventing Princess Adele and that monster from escaping the city after the wedding. Your men couldn't even find a vampire and a woman in a wedding gown! Now, every second you delay costs us a chance to apprehend whomever may be party to this conspiracy."

"Do it," came a voice from down the corridor. Greyfriar emerged from the shadows. "The teacher has abilities that may help."

Anhalt nodded and barked an order to a nearby soldier to fetch the assassin's belongings from the hospital director's office.

Mamoru said to Greyfriar, "I see you followed us. How much of our conversation did you hear?"

"My hearing is good and you are loud."

"Then we can stop pretending about where we stand, you and I."

"I stopped pretending when you tried to take my head in Bunia. Adele covets your teaching, and appears to need it. I don't intend to stand in your way as her instructor. Also, I don't intend to turn my back on you."

Mamoru's smile transformed into a savage sneer. "You're wiser than I thought."

CHAPTER 37

MAMORU REMOVED SELKIRK'S filthy clothing from the canvas bag stenciled *Iskandar Hospital*. He laid it out in the empty operating room where the surgeons had recently labored to save the assassin from his wounds. The samurai priest searched the items, checking seams and cuffs particularly. Then he examined a pair of heavy leather boots with rubber soles, now worn thin. These were the same boots Selkirk had when he had departed Alexandria for Britain nearly two years ago. Mamoru studied the soles, picking at the seams and cracks with his fingernails.

"Ah!" He held up a small stone. "This will do."

General Anhalt asked, "What can you learn from that pebble?"

"Something, I hope." Mamoru opened a leather satchel and began to arrange metal instruments on the porcelain tabletop. "Not as much as Selkirk himself could tell me; a finer geolocationist never existed." He popped the blue flame on a small handheld torch. "You may wish to remove our vampire friend, as he could find his senses offended by some of my practices. Return in an hour."

Gareth followed Anhalt into a guarded corridor as he lifted his wrap over his face. The general glanced at the soldiers who stood tensely along the walls, feeding off the stressful mood of the hospital.

"General," Greyfriar said, "may I please see Adele?"

"She is still in surgery."

"I just want to see her. Please, I beg you." His tone held a hint of a man on the brink of losing everything.

The general considered for a moment, then nodded. He ordered nearby troopers not to let the priest out of their sight before departing with Greyfriar. Passing countless soldiers, they turned several corners, striding endless pale-green tiled hallways. Anhalt led the way onto an inconspicuous staircase, and through another door into a theater of sorts. Troopers saluted as the two moved quietly down the steps between the rows of benches until they reached a railing. Both men faltered.

In the arena below lay Adele, bathed in a pool of stark white light. She was naked, but partially covered by a blood-soaked sheet. Her soft body rested on a hard, cold table as men and women in gowns, their heads and faces covered, moved around her. Arms reached quickly across her torso for instruments and gauze. A heavyset man took a long, thin piece of metal and reached over the helpless girl, inserting the tool into a raw gash in her chest. He did it without hesitation or concern, as if it were a normal activity.

Greyfriar gripped the rail as his breath rushed out. The smell of Adele's blood washed over him in a great offensive blast. It had no nuance or spice; instead, it was blunt, sour, and overwhelming. It had no life. He also smelled other blood blended with hers, cold and flat with no sense of person.

"Adele," Greyfriar moaned. He staggered back onto a bench and dropped his head, unable to watch her poor form being abused.

General Anhalt stood rigid, staring at his princess. He studied the doctors and nurses and watched the facile hands of the surgeon. He noted the glass jars of dark red blood as the doctors struggled to pump new life into the girl who had nearly bled to death on the floor of the crypt.

The surgeon lifted the tool out of the young woman while a nurse snipped a thread. The nurse whispered, and the surgeon glanced over his shoulder at Anhalt and Greyfriar. He said to the man beside him, "Doctor Kemal, begin to close, if you please. I will return shortly." Then he stepped from the girl's motionless body and approached Anhalt.

He yanked his bloody mask down to reveal the mustached face of an older man, jowly and ruddy. Sweat beads dribbled along his forehead as he nodded at General Anhalt. "Sir. Surgery is nearly completed."

"Will she live?" Greyfriar asked quickly, surging up to the rail. Instantly, he caught a whiff of the acrid flavor coming off the doctor that he associated with Mamoru and Adele when they were in their practices. The swordsman almost turned his head away in annoyance.

Anhalt extended a hand toward the perspiring doctor. "This is Sir Godfrey Randolph, one of the finest surgeons in the Empire. He was fortunately summoned by Mamoru."

"Doctor Randolph? The vampire anatomist?" Greyfriar asked, but a flurry of activity around Adele took his attention off the surgeon and back to the helpless girl across the room. Another doctor was sliding a long, curved needle into her flesh, closing one of the wounds. Adele had done much the same thing to Gareth in Scotland after his fight with the hunters, but he didn't feel it. She must. He cringed as the needle poked through her pale skin.

"Yes," Sir Godfrey replied with surprise. "I have written studies on vampire anatomy." The old gentleman noticed the swordsman was no longer listening to him, but he continued to stare at the Greyfriar with such intensity that Anhalt wondered if he realized the truth. Then the surgeon regarded the general with a slight smile of embarrassment. "I regret to tell you that Her Highness's wounds are dire. The knife came very close to severing major blood vessels. We've had to give her a great deal of blood." He glanced quickly at Greyfriar and then away.

"If you will speak plainly, Doctor, what are her chances for survival?" Anhalt's voice caught as he asked the question.

Sir Godfrey knitted his eyebrows in confusion. "Oh, she'll survive. Did I lead you to believe otherwise?"

The two men at the rail came forward, eyes wide.

"She will?" Greyfriar cried.

"You were so dour," Anhalt added. "Her wounds. The damage. The blood."

"Gentleman, please, I am a marvelous surgeon." Sir Godfrey laughed. "I don't lose patients. Certainly not the future empress. Her Highness will recover fully with time and care."

"Thank God." Anhalt leaned heavily on the wooden rail with his hands clasped together. "Thank God." Then the general straightened with an ecstatic smile so rare to his face, and wiped his brow. He turned and extended his hand to Greyfriar. The swordsman looked at the offered hand for a second, then grasped it. They clutched each other's arms and the two laughed loudly.

The surgeon said, "We will keep her under very close attention for several days, I assure you. But I have every reason to expect the best. She's a strong young woman."

Greyfriar was silent for a moment, but then he nodded and turned to Anhalt. "Shall we see what the teacher has uncovered? I would welcome the opportunity to find any who were involved in this event."

Anhalt's hand went to his saber. "Quite."

—◦◦◦—

Mamoru crept along the shadowy wall of the imperial crypt. He held a stick of incense that gave off a thin line of smoke. He moved the joss stick slowly up and down close to the marble wall from top to bottom and then stepped aside a few inches to repeat the process. Greyfriar and General Anhalt stood near the door as motionless as possible, just as Mamoru had instructed.

The samurai had told them that the tiny crystal from Selkirk's boot had almost certainly come from Alexandria itself, but from the city's subsurface close to the harbor. He did not detail how he had acquired this information, but he surmised the assassin had spent time in catacombs near the palace. And since there was no possible entry to the imperial crypt from outside without being noticed, due to the locked door and proliferation of soldiers around the palace, there was necessarily a secret entrance into the tomb from those catacombs. Mamoru knew that Alexandria was honeycombed with tunnels and cisterns, although he was unaware of any connected to the crypt. However, it must be there, and he would find the telltale draft that would betray the opening.

Mamoru moved the incense stick with painstaking slowness, watching for a shift in the smoke trail. It took an hour to complete all four walls of the tomb. Then he turned and began to eye the many sarcophagi in the crypt. He decided to begin with the massive tomb of the first Equatorian emperor, Simon I. Dropping to his knees, he held the incense close to where the sarcophagus met the stone floor.

The smoke twisted into a curl.

Mamoru froze and pulled the incense back to let the smoke straighten. When he brought it back, the smoke trail broke again.

"Here. Somewhere around this crypt. There must still be a passage into an underground catacomb. Lord Kelvin's government supposedly sealed them all, but perhaps they missed one. There must be a switch and a counterweight here somewhere. Search for a trigger of some sort."

The imperious statue of Simon I in his marble robes of state glared down at them. The old emperor seemed quite unhappy and unpleasant, as history indicated he was. Indeed, he had been a man willing to spill blood to define his own empire of chaos in the wake of the Great Killing.

"So," General Anhalt said to the samurai as he and Greyfriar prodded the sarcophagus, "there's a secret passage in Alexandria that you don't know?"

"I'm as shocked as you," Mamoru replied. "Built into the imperial crypt. A lovely touch."

"I have an idea." Anhalt climbed on top of the tomb and stood next to the stone emperor. "His Majesty Simon the First supposedly died of a seizure."

"Supposedly?" Mamoru asked as he puzzled over some ornate carving.

"It is said within knowledgeable circles that he was stabbed in the eye by the wife of an Armenian general whom the emperor had put to death. Apparently, he rather fancied this general's wife." Anhalt put his hand on the angry marble face. "His left eye, I believe." His finger poked Emperor Simon in the left eye and there was an audible click. The general laughed as the crypt shifted on its base.

Mamoru and Greyfriar put their shoulders against the tomb and shoved while Anhalt leapt off. The massive structure pivoted easily to reveal a rectangular opening with carved steps going down into the dark earth.

Greyfriar said, "I can go first. I need no light."

Mamoru held up a chemical torch. "We have mastered the dark too."

"You'll give us away."

"I shouldn't care to be at your mercy in the darkness."

"Enough," Anhalt exhaled in exasperation. "Prince Gareth, scout ahead. Do not go too far or you may become lost."

Greyfriar descended quickly before Mamoru could argue. The stone stairs dropped fifteen feet into a tunnel carved out of the rock. It was high enough to stand, but narrow. He moved along the rough passage, stopping at intervals to listen and sniff the air. There were no branch tunnels, so he continued for several minutes without pause. Then a sweet scent reached him; it was strong and artificial like perfume, but there was also a faintly human smell underneath it. He crept forward carefully until he finally reached a blank wall. The cloyingly sweet smell was coming from the other side of the slab, as was the faint sound of music.

Greyfriar returned to the crypt and motioned them forward, explaining what he'd found. Mamoru flicked on the torch, adjusted his beloved katana, which he had retrieved from Kelvin's office after his return to Alexandria, and indicated that Greyfriar should take the lead. The three men moved quickly through the tunnel. Neither human smelled anything but musty rock, and certainly they heard no music.

Mamoru pressed on the stone slab and whispered, "Simple counterweight. A push and we are inside."

They filled their hands with weapons, and Anhalt nodded in the torchlight. Mamoru pushed, and the slab swung open with a flood of light, and they rushed into a spacious chamber. Countless rows of candles burned throughout the room, giving off rich, sweet scents that crowded Greyfriar's senses. The shadowy walls were covered in red-and-white tinted murals, while upright sarcophagi surrounded the perimeter, their round, beige Hellenistic faces staring with blank eyes. In the center sat a man at a large, modern desk next to a lantern that cast a yellow glow over stacks of paperwork. Next to the desk was a small table with a phonograph playing sad music.

"Stand where you are!" General Anhalt pointed his revolver at the figure at the desk.

The man looked up in alarm and jumped to his feet.

"Lord Kelvin?" Anhalt said incredulously.

"Don't shoot." Kelvin raised his hands, staring from the pistol to the blue-robed samurai and Greyfriar on either side. "What is this?" He looked with confusion over his shoulder toward an open doorway on the other side of the chamber.

General Anhalt moved steadily closer to Lord Kelvin. The former prime minister had virtually disappeared since Adele's return several weeks before. "Your Lordship, this is a rather peculiar place for a man such as yourself."

The politician smiled nervously. "Gentlemen, I can surmise why you are here since that passage leads only to the imperial crypt. However, if you allow me to explain, I believe you will understand the overwhelming danger to the Empire that we are facing."

Lord Kelvin reached for a desk drawer, causing pistols to click with thumbed hammers, while Mamoru moved like lightning to the desk, halting only a few feet from the man, his katana raised at throat level.

The wide-eyed politician froze. "Please, I am not drawing a weapon. I'm not an idiot. I fully realize my difficult situation here. I can tell you that I only did what was necessary to protect Equatoria, but I worry that the princess will not look so favorably on my efforts. I am, of course, willing to make you three very rich. All I require in return is for you to turn your backs for a few moments."

"Kill him," Greyfriar said.

Anhalt's eyes narrowed to slits. "Your Lordship, did you have a role in the attempted assassination of Princess Adele?"

Mamoru asked Lord Kelvin, without lowering his sword, "What is your connection to Selkirk?"

"Who?" Kelvin snapped his fingers. "Ah. That rather drab fellow with the knife and the blank stare." The politician tugged on the cuffs of his coat with remarkable placidity, given his predicament. "Selkirk was the choice of my partner."

"Your partner?" Mamoru snapped. "Who is that?"

Kelvin suddenly smiled with raised eyebrows. "Why, here she is."

A blur swept through the chamber, and General Anhalt was slammed off his feet. A slender figure whirled, and Kelvin's massive desk rose into the air and smashed against Mamoru. The samurai yelled in surprise and pain as his katana pirouetted through the air and he crashed into a wooden sarcophagus against the wall.

"Flay!" Greyfriar shouted as the war chief streaked for him. He threw his pistol aside and engaged her with his blade, blocking her claws just inches from his throat.

She hissed in the ecstasy of battle as she dropped and swiped again and again. Greyfriar parried her strikes with his sword and furious kicks to her wrists and forearms. Then Flay sprang, spun, and landed behind him. He barely turned in time to keep his spine from being shredded. Flay darted about, dodging and attacking. She was fresh and well fed; Gareth had not eaten fully in weeks. Her claws hit faster and deeper as he weakened, ripping his tunic and gouging his flesh with bloody slashes. Then she stopped dead and stared at him. She smelled the air. She smelled his blood and her eyes widened.

"Gareth?" she said with disbelief.

Greyfriar found the strength to lunge and send the rapier toward her heart. But even stunned by the most unbelievable of realizations, she twisted slightly so the long blade penetrated just under her arm. Flay ignored the sword and seized Greyfriar by the wrist and elbow and, with a scream of fury, broke his arm. His fingers numbed on the sword's pommel and his arm dropped.

Flay clawed the cloth from Greyfriar's head and gasped at Gareth's exposed face. "What are you doing? What are you playing at?"

"Not playing." Gareth buried his teeth in her throat.

Flay shrieked and reached around his back with both hands to tear viciously across his shoulders, nearly laying bone bare. Gareth still ripped into her throat, using his sound hand to seize her long braid and pull her head back. She dug her claws into his face and pushed him away, losing flesh and tendons from her throat in the process.

Flay staggered back, glaring at the prince's savage face smeared with blood. It was a Gareth she hadn't seen since the Great Killing, when he was one of their people's greatest warriors.

Flay rasped, "Why, Gareth? Why are you pretending to be the Greyfriar?"

"I am Greyfriar." He dropped to one knee as blood dripped from him.

"I don't understand."

"Give me a second and I'll enlighten you."

Lord Kelvin came out of a shadowy alcove where he had taken refuge. "Don't talk to him! Kill him!" He grabbed Flay by the arm, indicating the battered Anhalt and Mamoru, who both struggled to rise to their feet. "Finish them all. They know everything."

Flay shrugged off Kelvin's grip and, with a growl, plunged her clawed hand into his abdomen. He looked at the vampire as she pulled out a chunk of dripping flesh. The former prime minister made a palsied attempt to button his jacket properly over his bleeding, open gut before falling over dead.

She kicked his twitching body. "Prince Cesare has no further need of your services, Mr. Prime Minister." She pulled Greyfriar's sword from her side and tossed it aside.

"Come." Gareth rose unsteadily to his feet, gripping a sarcophagus for support. "Let's finish this."

"I'm already finished here, Gareth." Flay pressed a hand against her bleeding, savaged throat. She wasn't standing as straight as she had before.

"Do you really think Cesare will believe you? That the worthless Prince Gareth is the Greyfriar?"

Flay edged toward the passage. "I've learned much from your brother. I'm playing a different game now. And you've just become part of it. When I call you, Gareth, I advise you to come. Otherwise, I will slaughter your precious herd in Edinburgh."

"You don't dare."

"If Cesare finds out that you are the Greyfriar, I won't be able to stop him. You will be the greatest traitor to our kind in history."

"What would you have of me?" Gareth staggered forward, trying to impress Flay with how brutalized he was and how incapable he was of continuing with combat. Flay was an unpredictable mass of savagery and emotion, and he could not let her leave this chamber.

"In due time." Flay smiled. "When it suits me."

He prepared to strike. Suddenly, a burst of heat pierced him. His immediate thought was that Adele was present, but then he saw the bleeding Mamoru crouched in darkness next to a desiccated mummy. The priest hunched over several crystals in an intricate pattern in the dust, waving his hands over them.

Flay hissed and streaked for the open doorway.

"No!" Gareth yelled. He started to pursue her, but a scorching wave slammed against his raw back and sent him toppling against the wall with a scream of pain. Flay slipped from sight while Gareth burned helplessly. He looked back at Mamoru, furious at the teacher's ill-timed attempt on Flay.

The samurai's intense eyes were locked on him, and Gareth realized it had not been an attempt on Flay.

A booted foot swept in front of Mamoru, sending the crystals flying, and Gareth felt an instant drop in the wave of heat. A battered General Anhalt lowered his Fahrenheit saber in front of Mamoru, its glow deepening the lines and deadly intent on both of their faces.

"I warn you," the general said to the samurai. "Stop what you're doing."

Mamoru glared up at Anhalt, contemplating how fast he could move. Finally, he exhaled and slumped to the floor. "Dear God, General, if only you knew what you've done."

CHAPTER 38

VOICES AWAKENED ADELE from a drowsy slumber. She should have felt terrible, but pain-killing drugs left her pleasantly numb instead. By the time she dragged her eyes fully open, Greyfriar stood inside the door, cowled behind his scarf but clearly agitated. Adele cautiously raised herself up farther on the mountain of pillows behind her head and asked groggily, "Trouble?"

"No," Greyfriar assured her immediately, raising an arm that was encased in a splint. "Everything is fine."

"I know that's impossible." A drug-induced laugh that bubbled up made Adele wince, which bought Greyfriar rushing forward. "I'm fine. Just a twinge. Dr. Randolph said laughter is the best medicine, but he's a lying son of a . . ." She curbed her language with a groan as she thought she noticed something moving under Greyfriar's cloak.

His brow furrowed with concern. "That does seem like foolish advice given your chest is a patchwork of stitches. No wonder everyone believes such an acclaimed anatomist to be a crackpot."

Adele gasped, and that made her cough. Gareth brought a glass of water and lifted her up so that she could drink. After a few swallows she nodded.

"Do you need me to get the crackpot?" Greyfriar asked, easing her back down, using one arm.

"Where on earth did you hear that about Dr. Randolph?"

He shrugged. "Around. People were talking in the hallways." He sat on the edge of her bed. "You do look remarkably better, however."

"Well then, thank heaven for crackpots."

"I am eternally grateful to him." His cloak rippled again, and Adele noticed the flurry.

"Why is that moving?" Adele asked. "Or am I hallucinating?"

"No." Greyfriar threw back his cloak and held out a grey cat.

"Pet!" Adele exclaimed and tried to raise her arms, without success. She hissed as stitches pulled at her.

He set the animal on the bed near her shoulder, and she winced as the cat nudged her arm and sniffed her face. She could feel the tickle of whiskers on her cheek and smiled through the pain. Pet shoved his face against her neck and commenced purring.

"Thank you," Adele slurred, resting her chin against the warm cat. Her eyelids drooped and the call of slumber beckoned, but she rebelled against it. Her hand lifted and tugged weakly at the headgear wound around his face. She asked softly, "Take off your scarf and glasses. I want to talk to Gareth." He complied and she saw his anxious expression beneath. His cheeks held fading scars from Flay's attack.

Adele shifted, vainly attempting to find a position that didn't wake all her aches and pains. Her struggles were not made any easier by the tube attached to her arm that went to a unit of blood hanging from a metal pole. A yank of her arm sent it teetering, so Gareth reached out to steady it.

"Hands off. That's mine," she warned. "Well, for now."

"Are you being funny? I can't tell." They shared a wry smile; then he studied the bottle of blood. "What is this? What is it supposed to do?"

"They're giving me blood. Apparently I lost a lot."

"Giving you blood? They can do that?"

"Yes. It helps me heal." Adele giggled foolishly. "I guess we're not that different after all."

Gareth was sniffing the air, but trying to be subtle about it. "Whose blood is it?"

"I have no idea."

"Will it change you? Does it give you that person's feelings and thoughts?"

Adele closed her eyes. "No. It doesn't work that way. I don't know how it works, actually. But I need it, so they're giving it to me." Suddenly she had a thought. "Could you use this blood? Is it viable for you as a food source while you're here?"

Gareth gingerly took the bottle and smelled it with a wrinkled nose. "No. It has already lost most of its value. It is hours out of the human."

She leaned back, already weary from that small activity.

He hung the bottle again. "Don't worry about my diet. You're lucky to be alive."

"Yes." Adele saw the deep gouges in his skin by his neck. "We really should travel with our own surgeon."

"Perhaps you should just be thinking about yourself."

"You know me." She was too exhausted to fight the yawn that snuck up on her.

"I know you think about everyone else more than you do yourself."

The fear Gareth had held for her these past few days showed plainly in his voice. Adele's hand covered his. She knew all too well how close to death she had come, so she deflected the subject. "I heard Flay was here again." Her expression did not change, but the barest of dark shadows crossed her pale face.

"Yes. And I failed to kill her. Again."

"We'll get her. Together." Adele's teeth ground together as she started formulating battle plans. "We will need to survey the city for every catacomb and cistern and then post guards to ensure vampires can't use them."

"I'll see to it with your Anhalt."

Adele smiled with relief that her two trusted allies were finally on speaking terms. That was one thing, at least, she didn't have to worry about. The list of other worries, however, seemed monumental, including why one of Mamoru's most trusted acolytes had tried to kill her. Her mouth quickly drew into a hard line. "And what about Flay knowing that Gareth and Greyfriar are one and the same?"

"You are amazingly well informed for an invalid."

"I am a future empress, remember? I have other sources of information besides you. Colonel Anhalt . . . General Anhalt tells me everything."

Gareth didn't know if Adele knew anything of what had happened between Mamoru and himself in the catacombs. Perhaps Anhalt had told her; certainly Gareth had not. She needed peace to recover before he informed her that her beloved mentor had tried to murder him.

He continued, "Flay said there was another game to play."

"Do you know what she meant?"

"Not at all."

"What can you do to stop her?" Not that she wanted him going alone into the hands of those who despised him for what his alter ego had done over the years. The idea of Cesare's hatred for his brother being magnified chilled her even more.

"Whatever Flay might have planned is already in motion by now. I'm only thinking of those left behind in Edinburgh."

Adele's stomach fell at the thought, and her chest tightened, wakening the ache of her wound.

"All of my people." There was such pain in his voice.

She took his hand. "Promise me you won't go alone to face this. Wait for me. We'll handle this together." She sat up and gasped at the pain it brought, but she didn't care. Pet mewed plaintively as he tumbled from her shoulder.

Gareth held her and eased her back against the pillows. "I seriously doubt I'll be taking you back into my brother's territory. You are soon to be empress."

"And I'll have a bloody army at my back!"

He shook his head. "I fear we'll both have to wait for Flay to make her next move before we do anything."

"But think of it, Gareth! If I can get a grasp on this power of mine I could defend Edinburgh from her or anyone."

"Your mentor will just love that."

"Protecting the humans of the north has been my intent from the beginning. I don't care what my father or Mamoru or Senator Clark intended with this war or this power. This is what I am, and this is what I intend to do."

"Of that I have no doubt." Then Gareth kissed her, putting an end to further conversation.

—◈—

Prince Cesare stood next to his father's throne in Buckingham Palace. Lady Hallow waited quietly to one side. General Montrose and Goronwy posed before the prince like dutiful servants. A line of Cesare's Pale stretched behind them.

Cesare's quiet voice resonated in the empty chamber. "Witchfinder, I have reports from Flay in Alexandria that your man has failed. Princess Adele is still alive. Plus, I have lost one of my greatest contacts among the Equatorians. This is not pleasant news."

"Interesting." Goronwy considered the information like a scholar. "What happened to Dr. Selkirk?"

"You are not here to ask questions." Vampire eyes narrowed. "You are here to answer them, and likely to die."

"Oh. Well, that would be a shame, my lord. Before you sent Dr. Selkirk back to Alexandria, a bit prematurely I felt, he told me a great deal about the very exciting research being done on geomancy in institutions across the south. Even beyond what he revealed to me about the princess."

"He told you she was some sort of weapon that could destroy us. What could be more important than that?"

The old Welshman casually shoved his hands in his pockets. "Perhaps a way to disarm that weapon, my prince. He left many notes that I've yet to decipher. But I shall, never fear."

Hallow started toward Cesare, but he signaled her to keep her distance. He wasn't about to share the stage in front of his human underlings. All information and decisions must pass through him alone.

The prince drummed his fingers on the back of the throne. "You have a month to tell me more, Witchfinder." He then glanced at General Montrose. "And you? What is the state of your Undead?"

"We are prepared to move immediately, my lord. We do not need a month." Montrose cut a brief glance at Goronwy. "We have airships heading south as we speak. We will take Marseilles unaware, as you command. And I have nearly a battalion of infantry ready for action."

"Good. Marseilles must burn. King Ashkenazy has taken my lead and created his own Undead forces, which he is aiming at Constantinople. We will smash the major port cities within reach of the Equatorians. General, have your numbers rebounded after the attack on Gibraltar?"

Montrose's chest swelled with pride. "Indeed. Recruitment surges. The Undead movement is sweeping the north. There is no shortage of humans who want to die in your service so they may be reborn."

"We welcome them to our ranks." Cesare smiled, then turned. "Anything to add, Lady Hallow?"

The elegant female said, "Will Flay return to assume command . . . of the humans?"

"Flay has further business in the heat of Equatoria. When she returns to London, I will name her clan war chief again."

Hallow stiffened with surprise. "You will?"

"Yes," Cesare hissed to stifle argument. Then he continued pleasantly, "But you will be named seneschal. You will have the considerable responsibility of coordinating all alliance matters, including our clan forces. You will be my right hand during this war."

Now the alabaster face of Lady Hallow softened with satisfaction. "Thank you, Prince Cesare. I welcome the challenge."

"Very well." Cesare nodded and smirked. Hallow had no idea what a challenge it would be, particularly once Flay returned to the north. "I am satisfied, for now. General, let our offensive begin. Witchfinder, one month. I must inform the king of these details."

With that, Cesare turned and strode away.

※

King Dmitri lay on his bed with half-closed eyes, his mouth gaping for ragged breath. He was immobile except for the occasional twitching of his hands clutched together on his chest.

Cesare kept his distance from his father to avoid staining his clothes with filth. He paced, alone in the disgusting room with the horrible spectacle wheezing before him. Anger welled up in the prince at the weak, pathetic thing his father had become.

"If you can even hear me," Cesare said, "I've come to tell you that the clan is thriving under my hand. I have delayed the Equatorians' war. I have scattered their airships and will soon begin to cripple their ability to come for us on the ground."

The young prince stopped walking. "I alone have had the vision to spawn a new theology among the humans based on their old myths about us. Increasingly, they believe they will rise from their grave as vampires. They are desperate to escape their fate as food." He laughed. "And I am gathering knowledge about their magic and religion. Remember the old days when they had power to cause us harm? I will find a way to put an end to it once and for all."

Cesare laid a hand on his chest and towered over Dmitri. "I am doing it. No other clan lord would dare. No other would even consider it. No other clan lord in history has done what I am doing. Not even you! I will save our people. I will do it!"

The king's dewy eyes rolled slowly toward the figure of his son standing over him. His mouth closed slowly, and he tried to lick his cracked lips. "Gareth?"

Cesare screamed and extended his claws through reddening vision, lunging for Dmitri. Claws sank into the king's papery throat and tore flesh with terrible ease. The young prince raised his hands and slashed again and again, ripping the face beneath him until there was no sign of his father left. He continued to rain blows on the unresisting body. The last gurgling breath racked from Dmitri and the old vampire's chest sank in death.

Cesare paused with a dripping hand above his head. He looked at the carnage he had wreaked on his father and struggled to bring his snarling, heaving breath under control. He stared in horror at the flecks of blood and flesh covering his coat and shirt. He tore off his jacket and flung it across the room to the stone floor. His bloody hands left red stains on his once-pristine white shirt.

"No, I'm afraid you're mistaken," the prince said in a strangled voice as he retracted his claws with a mixture of pleasure and shame. He could barely contain a manic laugh as he dared taste the blood of his father on his fingers.

"I am King Cesare."

CHAPTER 39

"**I** AM ADELE the First, Empress of Equatoria; Sultan of Egypt and Arabia; Shah of Persia; Maharana of India, Bengal, and Ceylon; Lord Protector of East Africa and the Cape; Queen of England, Scotland, and Ireland. I do hereby proclaim and foreswear to defend this Empire from all enemies. Done this day in Alexandria, the seventh of September, in the year Two Thousand and Twenty."

Adele took her father's golden crown from her brother's outstretched hands. She broke her immobile ceremonial face to give Simon a wink, and the boy's lips turned up slightly. Then she held out the glittering crown for the throng gathered in the palace square to see.

Normally an imperial investiture would have been held in stately Suez Hall with only Equatorian grandees in attendance; only later would the new sovereign have been paraded onto a public viewing balcony. Adele, however, stood atop the main portico entryway to Victoria Palace, where the grounds had been opened to the public. The dour grandees were still in privileged places in the front, but a shoulder-to-shoulder citizen crowd jostled behind them, cheering at the sight of the old crown of Constantine about to grace the brow of their beloved Adele.

Prince Simon stood on one side of her while General Anhalt took the other. The general was stone-faced and resplendent in his dress uniform covered with medals of valor. The fully reconstituted White Guard lined the wide semicircular steps like statues.

Adele lifted the heavy crown high over her head. A shaft of pain seared through her, but her face remained serene. A light breeze ruffled her crimson-and-white gown. Slowly, she lowered the crown onto her head, and her wild auburn curls were finally captured.

The mob exploded in a frenzy of exultation. The cheering was all the louder because everyone knew how close their empress had come to death at the hands of an assassin, an agent of the late Lord Kelvin, it was said. Explosions came from on high as fireworks erupted into the fading sun of late evening. The sounds and colors of rockets were the signal to all Alexandria that their new empress was crowned. The cheer that rolled across the capital was like an earthquake that had the power to shake the world.

Adele held out her arms to her people, still careful to keep her head high. Her father's crown had been augmented with an inner ring of foam, but it was still unsteady on her brow. On the first step below her, she noted a beaming King Msiri of Katanga, who had taken his fastest airship to make the ceremony. He cheered loudly, to the annoyance of the Equatorian lords clapping politely beside him.

She regarded General Anhalt, who stared stiffly over the crowd. "Thank you, General. This wouldn't have been possible without you."

"You're welcome." The stoic Gurkha turned his head to reveal a tear dripping down his cheek. He could barely find the voice to say, "Your Majesty." He looked forward again to hide his unmanly face from her.

Adele laid a hand on the general's shoulder, which brought even more cheers from the crowd. Then she looked at Simon, who was grinning now, not so reserved as before.

"Congratulations, Adele," her brother said. "Better you than me. Can I have the cat?"

"No."

The vast sea of faces below her began to turn upward in a wave. Hands lifted to point. Adele thought they were reacting to the spectacular fireworks booming overhead, but then she realized the adulation had become louder yet again. Even King Msiri was holding up his hands and applauding something high behind her.

Simon turned. "It's the Greyfriar! He's on a balcony, watching."

Adele could picture him clinging to the shadows, swathed in his cloak with a hood obscuring his wrapped face. She had offered him a place of honor on the dais. Everyone in Alexandria knew the Greyfriar was the imperial consort; it gave Adele an aura of mystery, romance, and power. However, he had refused to join the coronation ceremony; this moment was about her.

Adele smiled, but didn't look back. She need not see him; it was enough to know he was there.

EPILOGUE

LAURENCE RANDOLPH, LORD Aden, had spent a long day with matters of state. Despite his noble title, Randolph was a member of parliament, representing some rotten borough in Aden where he had never actually set foot. In truth, he was a member of parliament by virtue of his empire-tilting wealth. There were few economies of steam and steel that his fingers did not at least graze. It was this power that allowed him to retain his influence at court despite his connections to the government of the disgraced Lord Kelvin. He had willingly resigned his briefly held post as prime minister, but that was not a change he regretted. He wasn't built for a life of politics; it was too limiting for him.

Aden enjoyed his first gin and tonic of the evening and perused dispatches from his vast business concerns. The wind had picked up a storm from the sea and battered the coastal city. The long fingers from the branch of a palm tree outside scraped wildly against the patio door. Aden paid it no heed, pulling his tuxedo jacket tighter about him to ward off the chill. He sat stone still with his hands flat on the desk, letting anarchic thoughts run over him.

The coronation of Empress Adele had sent the capital into a frenzy of delight and celebration. However, not all of the centers of imperial powers were quite so pleased. Many of the old families were mortified that the new empress had betrayed the great Senator Clark, sent him away, and replaced him with some masked brigand she wasn't even married to. The Persian lurkers would begin to seek undue influence on imperial affairs, as if they didn't already have it. The more fractious provinces would push for greater autonomy. Commerce might suffer and the cost of doing business would soar. Equatoria's foreign partners might lose confidence, and Lord Aden might lose money.

These were the very disasters that his old friend, Lord Kelvin, had fought to prevent. How ironic. Kelvin had nothing but the good of the Empire at heart; he distrusted Princess Adele, hated Senator Clark, and feared the impact of a long, exhausting war in the north. To prevent his fears from coming about, he had sought the assistance of humankind's greatest enemies.

However, there were secrets even Lord Kelvin didn't know.

The scratching outside grew more insistent until finally the handle of the ornate French doors turned. Aden looked up but never flinched at the sight of a nearly bare-breasted female walking toward him, her throat covered by a purple silk scarf.

The vampire's lips curved into a wicked smile around her teeth. "We have much to discuss, you and I."

"Quite," replied Aden, lounging back in his chair and sipping his drink. "Everything has changed, Flay. I fear we must prepare for an uncertain future."

ABOUT THE AUTHORS

CLAY AND SUSAN GRIFFITH are married. Coincidentally, they write together and have published books, short stories, and graphic novels. They share a love of adventure stories, sprawling epic romances, pulp-action tales, Victoriana, and dark fantasy. And since they both like those things, they put them all in the Vampire Empire trilogy.

Follow the Vampire Empire trilogy online:

http://clayandsusangriffith.blogspot.com/
www.facebook.com/vampireempire